# PRECIPICE

# PRECIPICE

# COLIN FORBES

MACMILLAN

First published simultaneously in hardback and trade paperback 1996 by Macmillan

an imprint of Macmillan General Books
25 Eccleston Place London SW1W 9NF
and Basingstoke

Associated companies throughout the world

ISBN 0 333 64709 2 (hardback)
0 333 64734 3 (trade paperback)

5 7 9 8 6 4

A CIP catalogue record for this book is available from
the British Library

Photoset by Parker Typesetting Service, Leicester
Printed and bound in Great Britain by
Mackays of Chatham PLC, Chatham, Kent

# Author's Note

All the characters portrayed are creatures of the author's imagination and bear no relationship to any living person.

I have also taken liberties with the geography of Dorset, creating a non-existent ridge, Lyman's Tout. In the same way with Switzerland, I have invented a mountain, the Kellerhorn, and two other areas – the Col du Lemac and the Col de Roc.

# TO JANE –

my late wife, without whose constant and devoted support I would never have become a writer.

# Prologue

'This could be dangerous,' Philip Cardon said as he felt the wheels of the Land Rover sliding in the mud.

'If you're nervous give me the wheel. I like to be in the driver's seat,' suggested Eve.

There was a challenging note in her tone which jarred on Philip. He switched off the engine and Eve, sitting beside him, lit a fresh cigarette from the one she had just smoked. It was night and they were high up in the Purbeck Hills, approaching the cliffs which dropped into the sea.

Philip thought that Dorset in February was hellish. For days it had rained nonstop and the lowland fields they had long ago left behind were lakes, swamps. They were driving along the deep ruts of a track which led up the spine of a high ridge. It was bitterly cold and Eve was buttoning up the collar of her camel-hair coat round her neck.

At this point they were sheltered from the wind. Philip found the silence was eerie, as though issuing a warning. The sky was clear and the moon cast an unsettling glow over the vast landscape to their right. Only a few yards from the track the ridge dropped in a steep slope to a small valley hemmed in by another slope on the far side. They had their first sight of the sea, of the grim coast stretching westward. Jagged capes projected into the sea which was rough. Surf-tipped mountainous waves rolled in endlessly.

'That must be Sterndale Manor down there,' Philip remarked.

At the base of the valley – little more than a wide gorge – stood an Elizabethan house, its chimneys rearing up. As he watched, lights came on and Philip took a monocular glass from his windcheater pocket, focused it.

'General Sterndale must have arrived back from our hotel with his son. Someone is closing all the shutters . . .' He watched as lights came on, vanishing again as more shutters were closed. 'It's like life being extinguished,' he mused.

'Now you're being morbid,' Eve chided him as she jumped to the ground, nearly slipped in the mud, grabbed the side of the vehicle.

'Watch it. The ground's like a marsh.'

He resumed watching the manor. He couldn't rid himself of a premonition that a tragedy was imminent. Must be the weird atmosphere up here, he told himself.

'He certainly locks himself in at night,' he observed.

'Well, you remember in the bar back at the Priory Hotel he said he was so isolated he turned it into a fortress at night,' Eve reminded him. 'Just the two of them inside that great house and the servant. Marchat. Funny name. Wonder what nationality it is.' She flashed the smile which had first attracted him when they'd met by chance at the Priory. 'Move over so I can take the wheel.'

'Get back where you were. I'm driving and that's it.'

'Be stubborn, then. But don't take us down into that gorge.'

She sounded annoyed at not getting her own way. As she settled herself back in the passenger seat her buoyant mood seemed to return.

'Is this Lyman's Tout we're climbing? And what does Tout mean?'

'Cape. Lookout point. Local word. Over to our left is Houns Tout. Don't ask me what Houns means.'

2

Philip started up the engine and continued up the track. To his left stretched a large area of scrubby grass running up to a drystone wall. Earlier he had tried driving over the grass and found it sodden with water. Still disturbed, he glanced down at Sterndale Manor and drove higher and higher.

'They told us back at the hotel the wind would hit us when we cross the crest of that ridge – straight off the sea. Batten down the hatches.'

He had just spoken when they arrived at the highest point of the ridge. The wind hit them like a huge door slamming in their faces. Eve pulled up the hood of her coat, wrapped it round her head. Philip slowed down as the earth became a flat plateau of miserable grass. To his left the drystone wall bent away east, as though shrinking from the onslaught. The roar of the sea was a drumbeat. Philip stopped the vehicle, turned off the engine, leaned over so Eve would hear him.

'I'm going a bit further on foot. I think we're close to the edge.'

'This is close enough for me.'

'I wonder who that weird old pile belongs to?'

Way over to his left, well back from the sea, crouched a bleak mansion, two storeys high, its walls of granite. It had a deserted look and from it the ground sloped downwards steadily towards what he suspected was the cliff rim.

Bending against the force of the gale battering him he walked cautiously forward. He stopped abruptly. With nothing to indicate the danger he found himself at the brink and thanked God the wind was blowing against him.

The precipice sheered three hundred feet down past outcrops of rock to where the sea thundered against its base. Rocks like enormous teeth protruded above the sea. As a giant wave came in and burst like a bomb against the cliff the rocks vanished and Philip felt wet spray on his face. The sea receded briefly exposing the rocks, then again they were inundated as a fresh wave came hurtling in.

That was when he remembered once again his late wife, Jean, who had meant more than life to him. If I took just one step forward the edge would crumble, taking me with it, he thought. Then the loss of being without her would end. And he had a witness who would say it was an accident. Gritting his teeth, he forced the idea out of his mind. Jean would not have wanted him to give up, would have wanted him to go on to see what kind of a new future he could build. If any . . .

He blinked. Out at sea a light had flashed several times. From the corner of his eye he caught a flash inland. As he stared at the ominous-looking granite house he saw several answering flashes. Someone was exchanging signals with something out at sea. Then the hulk on land was just a black hulk. Had he imagined it? He went back to where Eve stood sheltered by the Land Rover, staring to the east. She pulled back her hood to hear him.

'Did you see a light flashing from that big dark house?' he asked.

'No, I didn't.'

'Are you sure?'

'Yes. Did you reach the cliff edge?'

'It drops like a sheer wall. For a moment I felt dizzy.'

'Which is why you're seeing lights.' She jumped up into the driving seat before he could stop her. 'I think I'd better drive back. Come on. Get in.'

He swore under his breath. She *did* like to get her own way. An alarm signal triggered in his brain. She had the engine going when he climbed up into the passenger seat beside her. Then she turned the vehicle in a semicircle and began heading back down the ruts of the track.

Shaken by his experience at the cliff edge Philip kept

quiet for a short time. He soon realized she was a first-rate driver, which was a relief. He gazed westward at the series of savage capes thrusting into the sea like giant spears. He thought it was one of the grimmest coasts he had ever seen. No trees anywhere. Just a series of ridges ending in those huge capes. Then he gripped Eve's arm gently to avoid startling her. They had just crossed the crest of the ridge, dropping behind it, so the gale was turned off as though someone had pulled a switch. The weird silence was back.

'Stop, for God's sake!' he shouted.

He could see Sterndale Manor in the distance way below them. The large house had flared up like a gigantic torch. The entire edifice was enveloped in flames from end to end. Eve had stopped the vehicle as Philip took out his monocular glass again, focused it. A ferocious red glare filled the lens. He scanned the grounds fenced in by a drystone wall. Half inside a large barn standing away from the burning house was an ancient Bentley with running-boards and huge headlamps. General Sterndale's.

'We can't do anything about it,' Eve said, lighting a cigarette.

Recalling the remark later it struck Philip as cold-blooded, indifferent. But she was right. He couldn't reach the mansion by driving down the slope to their left – it was far too steep. He couldn't even scramble down it if they drove closer down the ridge – the wet muddy surface was so treacherous he'd lose his balance and plunge down a lethal distance.

'Pity we couldn't raise the alarm, call the fire brigade,' he worried.

'You haven't a mobile phone, then?'

'No.'

Tweed, his chief and Deputy Director of the SIS at Park Crescent in London, had banned his staff from using the instrument. It was so easy these days to intercept any phone calls and Tweed was wary of a hostile group listening in.

'I can't see how either Sterndale or his son could have escaped such a conflagration,' he remarked.

The flat gorge inside which the house stood ran straight from it to the sea. The gale was screaming down the natural funnel, fanning the flames, blowing them in crazy shapes. Reluctantly Philip put his monocular glass back into his pocket.

'Get moving,' he said. 'We'll report it as soon as we can. Those bloody shutters Sterndale told us he locked every night must have trapped them. Stop! Just a minute . . .'

He had seen movement beyond the doomed house. For the first time clouds crossed the moon, blotting out the landscape. Suddenly it was dark apart from the blazing mansion. He still tried focusing his monocular on the road beyond the mansion, leading to the village of Langton Matravers by a roundabout route. In the darkness he could see nothing.

'What are you looking for?' Eve asked, letting the engine idle. 'It's ruddy cold up here.'

'Thought I saw another four-wheel-drive heading away from the mansion with several men aboard.'

'Could it have been Sterndale and Co?' she asked in a bored tone as she lit another cigarette.

'No. He'd have used the Bentley – and that's still parked half inside a barn. He told me his only other transport, another vintage effort, was in for repairs.'

'You probably imagined it. Still dizzy from looking over that cliff. Can we get moving? It's freezing up here.'

'Yes . . .'

Again Eve could have been right. He had caught only a brief glimpse of a vehicle tearing away from the inferno. Eve handled the Land Rover with great skill, driving faster than he had, frequently slithering almost out of the ruts on to the spongelike ground on either side, but managing to keep to the track.

'I'm enjoying driving your jalopy. It's fun – a test of nerve under these conditions.'

'Is it?'

Again a danger signal flashed at the back of his mind. He dismissed it as they passed the mansion below, which was now assuming the appearance of a blackened funeral pyre in the moonlight, which had reappeared. The bleakness of the Dorset landscape returned – barren-looking ridges marching away to the west one behind the other. They were descending to the point where the track met a road when Philip heard the sirens of a fire engine below, saw it pass with blue lights flashing, then another.

'Turn left for Kingston,' Philip said as they entered a lonely road with a decent tarred surface and left swampland behind.

'OK. But why?'

'Because – it's a long way round – but if we take another left later we'll eventually reach the road which leads to Sterndale Manor. We could report what we saw.'

'What *you* think you saw. Sheer waste of time. We know the fire brigade has arrived in force. Is there a pub in Kingston? I could do with a drink.'

'A good one. All right. We'll keep on for Kingston.'

Philip was puzzled. Even though his brain was muddled – still reeling under the grief of the sudden death of his wife over a year before and now experiencing for the first time a rapidly growing interest in another woman – one part of it was functioning normally. Why was Eve so reluctant to report the tragedy they had witnessed?

*   *   *

7

They had descended a tricky hairpin road to Kingston. Eve swerved several times to avoid water-splashes which were like lakes. The gradient was very steep and Philip had further proof she was a first-rate driver. I don't know a thing about her since that first meeting at dinner at the Priory, he was thinking – only that she's enormously attractive. I must ask a few questions while we're having a drink . . .

The Scott Arms, perched at one end of Kingston, was built of dark ancient stone like the rest of the small village, still high up in the Purbecks. Inside it was a labyrinth of different levels and secluded nooks, some with only a single table in front of a banquette.

'Be careful here,' Philip told her, taking her arm. 'It goes up and down and there are tricky steps everywhere.'

'I'll be all right.'

She took her arm away, again demonstrating her almost aggressive independence. Philip chose a table at the lowest level in a nook which faced a large window looking east. He ordered a glass of French dry white wine while Eve requested a large vodka.

'I'd better drive the rest of the way to the Priory,' he said with a smile.

'Why? You think one drink makes me incapable?' she demanded.

'Let's see how we feel later.'

'Philip, what do you do for a living?'

'I'm in insurance. It's rather specialized, confidential. How about you?'

'I'm in security. And it's rather special too . . .' She paused. 'I've probably said too much already.'

As they sampled their drinks a burly youngster clad from neck to foot in black leather passed them, carrying a helmet. He never gave their table a glance. It seemed to Philip he very deliberately didn't look at them and Philip sensed something odd about him.

'How long are you staying at the Priory?' Eve asked casually.

'About a week. Unless the office calls me back. What about yourself?'

'I'm a free agent. Let's explore the Purbecks together. You need company after what you told me about Jean. Is this your first trip away since she died?'

He swallowed, had trouble controlling his emotions. It was the offhanded way – something in the past – she had recalled his wife's death that disturbed him. Get a hold on yourself, he thought.

'Nice idea,' he said eventually. 'Yes, we'll do that. I welcome the very desirable company.'

Eve Warner had taken off her coat and wore a trim navy-blue suit over a white blouse with a high collar. Her jet-black hair had been coiffured close to her head and her shapely neck. Her face was almost triangular with the apex a pointed chin below a wide mouth suggesting determination. Her nose was Roman but it was the eyes below dark brows which were so arresting. A dark brown, they watched him as though they could see inside his head. A striking woman, in her late thirties Philip guessed, with a forceful personality.

The pub was very quiet and no one else was near them as she flashed her engaging smile.

'Philip, what are you thinking of? You looked miles away.'

'That I could do with some female company.'

'There you are, then. We *will* explore Dorset together . . .'


His mind had gone back to how they had first met a few hours ago at dinner in the large cellar with high old stone walls where the meal was served. Philip had been sitting at a table by himself and nearby another single table had been laid. The only other occupants had been a middle-aged couple at a table at the far end of the room lit by wall lights.

Eve had appeared suddenly as she came down the curving stone steps leading into the cellar. At the foot of the steps she had paused before a waiter approached, scanning the strange room.

Philip had been attracted from the moment he set eyes on her. Bet she's got a boy friend with her, he told himself. No rings on her left hand.

'Is Madame waiting for someone?' the waiter had asked, hurrying towards her.

'No. I'd like that table there. Is it available?'

She had pointed to the table by the end wall next to where Philip was sitting. He waited until she was settled only a few feet away and alongside him. She was slim and about five feet six, wearing golden pumps. As she studied the menu Philip nerved himself to speak to her. He hadn't approached another woman since Jean had died, hadn't felt any inclination to do so. She felt his gaze on her, glanced sideways, gave a half-smile. He plunged in.

'Good evening. You wouldn't be on your own, would you? I am. I can recommend the sole. That is, if you like fish.'

She immediately sensed his awkwardness, gave a roguish smile to put him at his ease.

'Why don't you join me? Then I can complain to you if I think the sole is rotten . . .'

That was how it had started. No, Philip thought as he sat gazing back at her in the quiet of the Scott Arms at Kingston, it had started earlier in London at SIS Headquarters in Park Crescent. In his chief's large first-floor office overlooking Regent's Park in the distance.

\* \* \*

10

Tweed had asked his faithful long-time assistant, Monica, to leave them alone for a few minutes.

'Philip, I think you should take a holiday.'

'I'd sooner not.'

'Philip, I'm ordering you to take a holiday. You have to. I've booked you a suite at an interesting hotel in Dorset. On the outskirts of Wareham. The Priory Hotel. The suite is booked for a week in your name. Oh, and while you're down there you might make a few discreet enquiries about a General Sterndale. He's over eighty and owns Sterndale's, the private bank which has been in the family since it was founded back in the early 1800s.'

'What do you want to find out about him?' Philip asked.

'I'm not sure . . .'

Tweed stood up from behind his desk, removed his spectacles, began cleaning them with his handkerchief as he paced round the office. Of medium height, with dark hair, middle-aged, when he wore the glasses he was the man you passed in the street without noticing him. Which was an advantage for the exceptionally shrewd Deputy Director of the SIS.

'One thing I'd like to know is has he still got all his marbles? He had when I met him at a club, but that was several years ago. He was celebrating his eightieth birthday then. He runs the bank personally with an iron hand. He operates secretively, so if you can contact him you'll have your work cut out to extract any data.'

'What sort of data?' Philip persisted, disliking the whole idea.

He suspected Tweed was anxious to get him out of the house he had occupied alone since Jean's death. But now he had been given a specific job to do it would be useless to argue the point.

'Another thing I'd like to find out – which will probably be impossible to extract if you do get close to him – is the names of his big clients. Take the case you always keep packed here for an emergency trip. And there's a Land Rover outside to get you there. Here are the keys. Philip, do try and relax in Dorset. Talk to people . . .'

'Finished dreaming?' Eve demanded as she started to put on her camel-hair coat inside the Scott Arms. 'I'm still here. Just in case you'd forgotten.'

She likes a lot of attention, Philip thought as he donned his duffel coat. No, that's not fair. I must have been silent for quite awhile. I'm out of practice at dealing with women.

He quickly slipped in front of her and mounted the first flight of flagstone steps. The floors were paved with the same material.

'I know the way out. You could be stuck in this maze for hours,' he joked over his shoulder.

'That was Corfe Castle we could see through that window in the moonlight,' she rapped back.

'I thought you said this was your first trip to Dorset,' he replied.

'Like other people I do study guide books – they have pictures in them, in case you didn't know,' she replied sarcastically.

Outside he hurried to the car park behind the pub and climbed up behind the wheel as she ran behind him. He kicked mud off his boots on the edge of the vehicle. She climbed into the passenger seat.

'Move over,' she demanded. 'I want to drive.'

'So do I. You've had a good run.'

'You think one vodka affects my ability to handle your chariot?'

'My turn.'

Leaving the car park he drove down another steep

winding hill with more hairpin bends, hit a water-splash, and water showered over the vehicle and through an open window.

'My coat is soaked,' she said in an icy tone.

He glanced at her. The camel-hair coat had only the odd sprinkle of water. She was staring straight ahead, in a bad mood because he wouldn't let her drive. In the distance and well below them two ridges of a Purbeck range dipped, enclosing a gap which must have been a strategic pass in the time of Cromwell. Corfe Castle was perched on a high mound in the gap. Its naked rocks and ruined towers reminded Philip of a skeleton, which took him back to the great fire at Sterndale Manor.

Were General Sterndale and his son, Richard, now real skeletons consumed by what must have been incredibly high temperatures? A morbid thought, but earlier that evening he had met General Sterndale having a drink in the bar at the Priory. He had gathered the old boy made a nightly visit. It had been one of those long-shot coincidences you hope for but which rarely happen. At one stage the General had stared hard at Philip and, as they were alone, made a remark.

'I see pain in your eyes. You look like a man who has suffered . . .'

Philip had found himself telling him briefly of the tragedy of Jean's sudden death, something he rarely talked about to anyone. They had talked for a while so Philip had something to report to Tweed when he got back.

Reaching Corfe, a village of old stone cottages which stood on the level, they followed the road back to Wareham, turning in a semicircle below the mound with Corfe Castle rearing above them. It was then a straight run along a good traffic-free road. Eve relapsed into a brooding silence, never once looking at Philip or saying a word. Pique.

A great glaring eye filled his rear-view mirror. A

motorcyclist in black leather, wearing a helmet, was perched on his tail. Philip waited for him to overtake as the macho boys always did. Black Leather remained glued to his tail. Philip recalled the burly youngster who had entered the Scott Arms.

'Pass me, damn you!' he said to himself.

The motorcyclist refused to oblige. Philip began to wish he had brought his Walther automatic. If the rider was armed and hostile . . .

Oddly enough Eve seemed unaware of their follower. She remained quite still, arms folded on her seat belt. Philip slowed down, crossed the bridge over the River Frome at the outskirts to Wareham, signalled, turned right into a small old square and down a short lane leading to the Priory.

He was parking close to a stone wall near the entrance to the hotel when he saw the motorcyclist stop on the far side of the square, switching off the blinding lamp.

'Well, we got back in one piece,' Eve remarked as she jumped down onto the cobbles.

'Nothing to it,' Philip responded, locking the vehicle.

Eve stroked the new red Porsche he had pulled up alongside.

'Now this I love. *My* chariot. Not bad, don't you agree?'

Philip froze where he stood. On the drive down from Park Crescent he'd had the feeling he was being followed by someone in a red Porsche. The flash car had always kept several vehicles behind him and he'd lost it while he was approaching Wareham. The driver had worn a helmet so he'd never decided whether it was a man or a woman behind the wheel. Then he reminded himself there were quite a few red Porsches floating round. He glanced back at the old square and the motorcyclist had gone. No sound of his engine starting up, so he must have wheeled it back to the square before firing the engine. Very odd. He walked round to admire the Porsche – Eve's normal radiant cheerfulness seemed to have returned.

'That's something else again. Must have cost you quite a packet.'

'Company car.'

She unlocked it and the courtesy light came on. Expensive clothes were thrown together on a seat as though they were rags. She rummaged through them, hauled out a pair of blue silk pyjamas. As she did so something beneath the pile of clothing slid out onto the floor. A crash helmet.


They entered the centuries-old building which was the Priory Hotel under a stone arch into an enclosed courtyard unevenly paved with cobbles. Thrusting ahead, Eve pushed open the heavy wooden door leading into reception. Behind a narrow counter the proprietor, a warm able-looking man, greeted Philip.

'Glad to see you back, sir. There was an urgent phone call for you from Monica. She asked you to call her the moment you returned. You can use this phone . . .'

Tactfully the proprietor disappeared as Philip grasped the phone. Behind him Eve enquired: 'And who is Monica?'

'My aunt,' Philip said quickly. 'She's looking after my house,' he continued, lying smoothly.

'I'm going down to my suite. See you in the bar . . .'

Philip would have preferred a less public phone but he was alone when he dialled Park Crescent. Monica, Tweed's assistant, spoke hurriedly.

'I'm putting my boss on the line . . .'

'Tweed here,' the familiar voice said. 'Are you calling from the hotel?'

'Yes . . .'

'Then get to a public phone damned fast and call me back.'

The line went dead.

Philip, still wearing his duffel coat, hurried back into the night which was now dry and still bitterly cold with a star-studded sky above him. Earlier, arriving at Wareham, he had noticed a phone box in South Street, no more than a five-minute walk away at the pace he moved. South Street was deserted as he entered the phone box, carrying a heavy torch he'd retrieved from his car. It had a powerful beam and was heavy, padded with rubber. A useful weapon if he happened to encounter Black Leather.

Tweed himself answered the phone, began speaking rapidly after checking where Philip was speaking from.

'All hell has broken loose down there. General Sterndale's house has gone up in flames. The fire brigade has recovered two bodies – the General's and that of his son, Richard, burnt to a cinder but just recognizable.'

'We saw the mansion burning from a distance . . .'

'We?'

'I'll explain later. I thought I saw a four-wheel-drive leaving with several men aboard . . .'

'Thought?'

'Yes, I couldn't be sure. It all happened so quickly.'

'In that case you saw nothing if you're questioned by the police. I'm referring to the phantom vehicle.'

'Why . . . ?'

'Just listen. The fire brigade chief on the spot called the police chief at Dorchester. Because Sterndale was such a bigwig Dorchester contacted Scotland Yard. As luck – bad luck – would have it he talked to my old sparring partner, Chief Inspector Roy Buchanan. He may be on his way down there now by chopper. You could find yourself being grilled by him, so watch it.'

'But I don't understand. Buchanan is Homicide.'

16

'The fire chief reported the whole of the exterior of the mansion had been sprayed with petrol. This was no accident. It was arson. Cold-blooded murder.'

'Oh, my God . . .'

'I said *listen*. I've just phoned the General's niece – I know her slightly. She told me the bulk of the bank's capital was kept by the General in his study at the mansion. In the form of bearer bonds – negotiable anywhere and no questions asked. He left just enough cash in the branches to keep them turning over.'

'How much money are we talking about?'

'Three hundred million pounds. Plus. I must go now. You stay put down there. Mooch around a bit in the morning, but go carefully. And I've sent you help – back-up.'

'Who?'

'He could be there now. You'll recognize him when you see him . . .'

# 1

Philip walked more slowly back to the hotel. He wanted to get his thoughts into order. Arson? Murder? And he had witnessed it with Eve. He arranged the facts in sequence.

At the cliff edge he was sure he'd seen signal lights out at sea flashing, lights which were answered by what appeared to be an empty old hulk of a house. *If* he had seen them. Eve had denied seeing anything and already he had realized she didn't miss much.

Then the horrific fire. And the vehicle he had seen rushing away inland. *If* he had seen a vehicle. At the Scott Arms the burly motorcyclist who had walked past their booth. Nothing to that. Except later they'd been followed all the way back to the Priory by a motorcyclist – one solid fact which was not the product of an over-heated imagination brought on by the devilishly attractive Eve.

As he pushed open the wooden door into the lobby of the hotel he felt grateful to Tweed for warning him to say very little. Taking off his duffel coat, he walked along the corridor and peered into the bar, which was a separate room at the end. He had another shock.

Eve, seated almost with her back to him, had changed into a dark blue dress, a gold belt encircling her waist, with her long shapely legs crossed, revealed by a deep slit in the skirt. She was talking to Bob Newman, who sat listening to her, poker-faced, with a glass of Scotch in his hand.

So this was the 'help' Tweed had despatched so urgently as back-up. Newman, foreign correspondent, was a trusted and close friend of Tweed's. He had been fully vetted long ago. Now in his forties, he had taken part fully and with great effectiveness in several SIS missions.

Philip decided to leave them alone for a few minutes while he went on collecting his thoughts. He had not been seen as he slipped into the empty comfortable lounge at the rear of the hotel, sat down on a couch. I wonder what they're talking about, Philip mused.

Bob Newman had arrived earlier that evening, in the dark, after a hair-raising drive down to Wareham. Newman liked to put his foot down behind the wheel, but never had a drink before driving. Registering, he had taken his case up to his room, had thrown back the lid, quickly hung up a few jackets, then made his way down to the bar for a much-needed Scotch.

The bar, a long room with the counter on his left as he entered, was empty except for the barman. And an attractive woman wearing a dark blue dress. She had made the first move as he prepared to sit some distance from her.

'I'm on my own. Could we possibly chat together over our drinks? You're Robert Newman, the world-famous correspondent. I recognize you from pictures in the world press.'

'Not world famous. Notorious is the word,' he told her as he sat in an armchair close to her. 'Cheers!'

'I don't see many articles by you these days,' she went on, flashing him a warm smile. 'I suppose that bestselling book you wrote, *Kruger: The Computer Which Failed*, must have netted you a fortune. It went all over the world and is still in print.'

'It made me comfortably off,' he said shortly.

No point in revealing he was a millionaire. You didn't say that to strange women. Newman didn't say it to anyone. She was studying him.

He would be about five feet ten tall, well-built, strong face, clean-shaven with light brown hair and an aura of a man who had been about and seen the world at its best – and its worst. A very tough individual, she was thinking, but pleasant on the rare occasions when he smiled.

'I'm Eve Warner, by the way,' she remarked.

'What do you do to earn a daily crust?' he asked. 'Or are you a lady of leisure?'

'Do I look like one?' She reared up indignantly. 'I've always had to work for my living. Unlike you,' she teased.

She gave him a wide smile which struck him as wolfish. He didn't react to her dig at him. There was a long pause and he waited for her to feel she should say more. She didn't, which he found interesting.

'What sort of a job have you got, then?' he asked eventually.

'I'm with a security outfit.'

'Which one?'

'It's a bit hush-hush.'

'They all are.'

'But the pay is good and I work like a Trojan.'

'You mean you're a Trojan horse?' he shot at her.

The staring brown eyes flickered. He'd caught her off guard. She looked behind him. Philip had entered the bar, waved to her as she turned round.

'I'm buying. What's your poison, Eve? Oh, hello, Bob. Long time no see.'

'I'm staying with vodka. Another double,' Eve replied.

'A Scotch for me, Philip,' said Newman.

'Oh, you two know each other?' Eve asked, the surprise showing in her voice.

'Off and on. Here and there,' Newman replied, raising

his voice slightly so Philip would hear what he'd said. 'Philip's in insurance. I was once investigating a big fraud case and he gave me a few tips . . .'

Philip blessed Newman for guessing so accurately what he had told Eve. He ordered a glass of French dry white wine for himself, brought the drinks over. Eve watched him. In his thirties, Philip was leaner than Newman, more sensitive, she guessed. Less able to cope with life. In this she guesed wrong and badly under-estimated Philip. He hauled up a chair so they formed a close circle. Eve drank her fresh vodka and immediately half-emptied her glass. She lit another cigarette from the one she had been smoking. Newman had fished out a lighter but she shook her head.

'I *can* light my own cigarette.'

'Good for you. You'll learn how to smoke it in time.'

She gave him a cold look, clenched her full lips, then smiled.

'Talking about smoke, you've heard about the terrible fire out near Lyman's Tout?' she asked Newman.

'What fire?'

Eve rattled on about the experience she had had while driving with Philip. She talked about it as though it had been a remote event in the past.

'A bit grisly a topic for such a pleasant evening,' she concluded.

'Grisly if you say Sterndale and his son were locked up inside the place. How do you know they *were* locked up? That detail about the General closing the shutters himself every night sounds as though you know him,' Newman pressed.

'I can see why you were such a success as a foreign correspondent. Actually, Philip told me. Before dinner he'd met General Sterndale in this very bar. The old boy was quite talkative, I gather. I didn't see him. I was in my suite taking a shower.'

22

'I heard he was a very old man,' Newman commented. 'I suppose in a place like you described he'd have great log fires. One could have rolled out onto a rug and there we go. A tragedy.'

'There was a log pile, I think,' Eve ruminated, chin perched in her left hand, the right holding the vodka so it wouldn't disappear. 'Outside a barnlike effort. Stacked up against the end of the building, the one where Sterndale kept his old Bentley. The rear of the car was sticking out in the open.'

Philip stayed quiet, sipping his glass of wine. He had no recollection of the log pile Eve had described. But up there on the cliff-top his mind had been a turmoil of emotions – his growing fascination with Eve, remembrances of his dead wife, Jean. He couldn't swear there had been no log pile at the end of the barn. He couldn't be sure of anything. He wondered whether Tweed was still in his office.


'You sent Philip down to Dorset on the excuse of his needing a holiday but your real purpose was to have him on the spot to watch over General Sterndale. Now look at the mess he's in,' Paula accused.

It was ten o'clock at night in Tweed's office at Park Crescent. He sat behind his desk and studied Paula Grey without replying at once. A very attractive slim brunette, she sat behind her own desk, her eyes blazing. His closest confidante and chief assistant, she never hesitated to speak her mind, something Tweed admired. Paula, unmarried after an unhappy love affair, was in her mid-thirties.

The only other occupant, behind her own desk in a corner, was Monica, also a trusted deputy. A small woman of uncertain age, she wore her greying hair in a bun and now she listened to the duel of words, enjoying herself.

'You're partly right,' Tweed admitted. 'But he's spent too many nights and weekends in that nice house he lived in with Jean. I wanted to get him out of the atmosphere of the place. Somewhere in this country – not abroad until I'm sure he's stabilized emotionally. I certainly had no idea his trip would turn out to be so dramatic. And, as you know, Bob Newman has rushed down there at my request as back-up.'

'That will help,' Paula agreed. 'But what is this all about? How did it start?'

'In Paris.'

He rather enjoyed the look of astonishment on her face. All trace of indignation vanished.

'In Paris?' Paula repeated. 'How?'

There was a tap on the door, Tweed called out, 'Come in,' and Marler entered. The deadliest marksman in Western Europe, the new arrival, a long-time member of Tweed's staff, was of medium height, slim and smartly dressed in a shooting jacket, corduroy trousers, and brown hand-made shoes which gleamed like glass. Clean-shaven, he had a cynical smile and was known not to trust a word anyone said to him until he had triple-checked it.

'Evenin',' he drawled in an upper-crust voice. 'Nice to see you're all having an early night for a change.'

He adopted a typical stance, leaning against a wall while he lit a king-size cigarette.

'Marler,' Tweed began, 'Paula is puzzled about what's going on. Tell her about your Paris trip. You've come here straight off the plane, I imagine?'

'Of course. Paula is puzzled? So am I.'

'Tell her what happened, for Heaven's sake,' Tweed suggested.

'Please do,' Paula urged.

'Started with a phone call from an informant of mine in Paris. Jules Fournier. I can give you his name now the poor sod is dead. We met at five o'clock – after it was dark – outside a bar in the Rue St-Honoré. He told me on the phone something big was soon to break, mentioned a name which shook me up a bit. I boarded a flight this morning to suss out the meeting place. Seemed safe enough. A main street in Paris when there'd be lots of other people about. I didn't realize that could be dangerous. Black mark.'

'What name did he mention?' asked Paula.

'All in good time. It's that quick mind of yours. So bear with me. Fournier was a slip of a man with greasy hair. He'd been a totally reliable informant of mine in the past. I was leaning up against an outside window of the bar, pretending to read *Figaro*. Lots of people about, hurrying home from work, as I'd anticipated. I was carrying a Walther automatic in a hip holster – borrowed from a friend in Paris earlier. You never know on an assignment like that. Fournier turned up out of nowhere.'

'On foot?' asked Paula.

'That was my impression. He seemed unusually nervous, glancing over his shoulder. He spilled out his so-called information in French. Didn't make much sense. He mentioned the same name again, said the chap concerned was engaged on an operation to change the world, that he had contacts everywhere. That was when a group of motorcyclists clad in black leather, wearing crash helmets, came staggering along the pavement. I thought they were drunk. They were shouldering people out of the way, making rude signs if anyone protested. I saw them clearly, but not their faces, of course. As they came up close to Fournier one of them stumbled. I was an idiot.'

He paused, took a deep drag on his cigarette, stubbed it out in the crystal-glass ashtray Monica had pushed close to him on her desk.

'Never heard you say that before,' Paula said quietly.

'I was too intent on what Fournier was trying to tell me. He said he'd sent me a letter. Then it happened. I still curse myself.'

'What happened? I doubt if you could have prevented it. Not in rush hour on the Rue St-Honoré,' Paula commented.

'These drunken roughs, as I thought, almost formed a circle round us. My alarm bells started shrieking then, but it was too late.'

'What was too late?' Tweed enquired.

'It was the chap who had stumbled – appeared to – when he cannoned into Fournier. Said, "Sorry, mate," in English. As they disappeared Fournier gave a gulp and fell forward into my arms. I grabbed him round the waist and my right hand was sticky. Blood. The stumbler had rammed a knife up under Fournier's left shoulder blade. As he sagged I checked his pulse after I'd rested him against the window. Nothing. He was dead. A very professional job.'

'What about the motorcyclist gang?' Paula asked.

'They'd disappeared like the wind. I decided I'd better do likewise. Carrying a Walther without a certificate I didn't fancy an interview with the flics – or the big boys they'd summon. I signalled to Archie and left poor Fournier after telling a woman who'd stopped he'd had a heart attack and could she get a doctor. Not a thing I could do to help my informant.'

'And who is Archie?' Paula enquired. 'Archie who?'

'His second name doesn't matter. He's probably the best informant I have in the world. He's based in Paris but flits all over the place. When I arrived at De Gaulle Airport on the way in I'd phoned Archie, asked him to be close by as back-up. He's quite a character.'

'Where was he at the moment of the murder?' Tweed interjected.

'On the far side of the street in a doorway. I doubt if he saw much, with the traffic being so heavy. But he got my message and disappeared. That's it.'

'No, it isn't,' Paula persisted. 'What was the name Fournier mentioned on the phone which startled you – and then repeated in Paris before he was murdered?'

'I suppose I heard him correctly. He was gabbling on both occasions.' Marler paused to light a fresh king-size. Outwardly calm, Paula sensed he was upset by what he regarded as a lethal failure on his part.

'Leopold Brazil, if you can believe it . . .'

# 2

There was a stunned silence inside Tweed's office. Paula's and Monica's expressions suggested sheer disbelief. It was Paula who broke the silence.

'Leopold Brazil? The international power-broker? The mystery man who it's rumoured has the ear of the American President, our Prime Minister, the President of France, and Lord knows who else?'

'That was the name I'm pretty sure I heard,' Marler said. 'And Fournier mentioned it twice.'

'He must have made a mistake,' Paula insisted.

'Maybe,' intervened Tweed. 'I'll let you into a secret. For the past few weeks I've personally been making discreet enquiries about him. He's like a second Kissinger, but without the publicity. And like Kissinger he conducts shuttles between the world's capitals in his private jet when trouble is looming. He's a very powerful man and rich.' He paused. 'So powerful that earlier today I was summoned to Downing Street. Someone talked. I was told by the PM personally to discontinue making any more enquiries about Mr Brazil.'

'Keep off the grass,' Marler said laconically.

'So what are we going to do?' asked Paula.

She was interrupted by the phone ringing. Monica took the call, spoke briefly, then put her hand over the mouthpiece and looked at Tweed.

'It's René Lasalle, your old friend in the DST.' She was referring to the Direction de la Surveillance du Territoire, French counter-espionage.

Tweed pressed a button on his phone. He lifted the receiver and greeted the Frenchman cordially. Lasalle sounded agitated.

'Are you on scrambler?'

'Yes. You sound bothered.'

'Does your man, Marler, wear a shooting jacket and corduroy trousers?'

Tweed glanced at Marler who was dressed exactly as Lasalle had described.

'What's all this about?' Tweed asked tersely. 'I don't like questions about my staff any more than you would.'

'Has Marler visited Paris today?'

'Same reaction. I repeat, what is this all in aid of, René?'

'Murder.' Lasalle paused as though expecting Tweed to say something, but Tweed remained silent. 'Murder,' the Frenchman repeated. 'Cold-blooded murder in the middle of Paris. A man called Jules Fournier, occupation not known, was stabbed to death a few hours ago during the rush hour. In the Rue St-Honoré, of all places.'

'So?'

'Fournier was with another man who laid the dead body against the window of a bar. He then told a woman – in French – Fournier had had a heart attack and told her to get a doctor.'

'So?' Tweed repeated.

'She gave a good description. A very observant lady. I was reminded of Marler.'

28

'No one else in the world looks like him? Is that what you're getting at?' Tweed demanded.

'What about the clothes description? Very British garb.'

'What about it?'

'Tweed, you're stalling . . .'

'I'm damned annoyed at your absurd assumption. And no, I've never seen the said person wearing such clothes. Also he's been in London all day. I can vouch for that myself.'

Heaven help me, Tweed thought, and that's one place I won't be going to. He changed the subject.

'While we're on the phone – on scrambler as we agreed earlier – have you got any further with your clandestine check on Leopold Brazil?'

'More rumours about him I don't like. That he's planning something global. Oh, I've been warned off checking any further on him. Would you believe it – I was summoned to the Elysée and the President himself told me Brazil was an important man and I would now stop any further investigation.'

'And your decision?'

'Blast the Elysée. They can sack me and I'll continue the investigation on my own time. Something's rotten in the state of Denmark.'

Tweed smiled to himself. Lasalle prided himself on using English colloquialisms and well-known phrases.

'Why not proceed very secretly? Only use a small circle of people you know you can trust with your life.'

'That *is* a small circle in today's world. Let's keep in touch. I'm sorry I went off the deep end when I started this call.'

'Forget it. Look after yourself. And I agree – we'll keep in touch . . .'

Tweed put down the phone. He stared at Marler.

'I went out on a limb there. Did you travel to Paris under your own name?'

'Of course not. I used one of my false passports. The call from Fournier bothered me so I took every precaution.'

'Get rid of those clothes fast. Lasalle has a woman witness – the one you spoke to after Fournier was killed – and she gave a perfect description of you. I'd like to have told Lasalle about the gang in motorcyclists' outfits, but I couldn't.'

'Understood. Agreed,' Marler said.

'You were never in Paris,' Tweed went on emphatically. 'If you were caught up in a murder investigation by the French police you could be kept there for weeks. Lasalle wouldn't be able to help you. Now, lose those clothes.'

'Will do.' Marler paused at the door just before leaving. 'I've remembered something Fournier said when he was gabbling on. He'd just mentioned Leopold Brazil. Said I might get info from a servant working for General Sterndale. I suppose that couldn't be the Sterndale's Bank chap?'

'Anything else?' Tweed asked brusquely, worried about the clothes problem.

'Also said Sterndale trusted his servant who lived in with the General. Chap called Marchat. No idea of his nationality . . .'


'That gives us a link at last between Leopold Brazil and Sterndale,' Paula commented, hiding her excitement.

'I had one already,' Tweed told her. 'Recently I bumped into Sterndale again. I was visiting someone at that boring club where I'd first met him. I met him on his way out. He started talking about Brazil, about what a brilliant man he was. Then he had to rush off.'

'Which is why you sent Philip to Wareham on a so-called holiday – then asked him to check up on Sterndale.'

'You're right.' Tweed shifted in his swivel chair. 'I have an unpleasant feeling something pretty big is being planned. International. I don't like Fournier's reference to "an operation to change the world".'

'Could anyone really do that?' Paula asked sceptically.

'Depends on how clever they are, how powerful. There's nothing standing in their way, which keeps me awake at night. We have a hopeless PM. Washington is a joke. Bonn has a man who just wants to go down in history as creator of the United States of Europe. Barmy idea – the German doesn't recall history. The Austro-Hungarian Empire, controlled from Vienna before the First World War, was a hotch-potch of nationalities, just as Europe would be. So what happens at the end of that horrible conflict? The Empire collapses, breaks up into various individual nations – Hungary, Czechoslovakia, et cetera. Austria is left as a tiny state of no account.'

'What about today?' Paula enquired.

'The situation reminds me of what I've read about the 1930s. A man called Adolf Hitler, evil but a brilliant psychologist, manipulates the Western leaders like pulling the strings of puppets.'

'You mean Brazil could be a new Hitler?'

'No! But you queried that phrase "engaged in an operation to change the world" – the West is leaderless, ripe for a genius to manipulate it.'

'You think Brazil is a genius?'

'I met him not so long ago at a party. *He* came over to talk to me briefly. I had the uncomfortable feeling he knew who I was, about the SIS. He has contacts all over the place. Like an octopus. A very clever man – and a great charmer. He wants to meet me again but I'm dodging him. For the moment.'

'So we have a murder in Paris, which could link up with two more murders in Dorset. That's pretty widespread,' Paula mused. 'And I wonder what happened to the missing servant, Marchat.'

'You noticed that, then?' Tweed smiled drily. 'Over the phone, as I told you earlier, Chief Inspector Buchanan told me quite specifically the fire brigade had searched what remains of the manor and brought out *two* bodies – identified as Sterndale and his son, Richard. So what happened to this shadowy figure Marchat?'


Inside a large old stone house on the fabulously expensive Avenue Foch in Paris, a large tall man sat behind a Louis Quinze desk. The walls of the room were lined with bookcases but the lighting was very dim, the room mostly in darkness. He spoke in English to his visitor, seated on the far side of the desk and shrouded in gloom.

'I think you ought to start on your travels again. Take an early flight to Heathrow tomorrow, hire a car, drive down to Dorset. Specifically, to Wareham. Clear?'

'As far as it goes, yes,' replied the visitor. 'What am I looking for in Dorset?'

'Trouble. It may be a clean-up job you have to undertake. If so, do it. No loose ends, please.'

'I'm an expert at locating them, tying them up.'

'Which is why I'm sending you. I've explained what has happened, as far as I know it. Certain people will be running all over the county like ants. Watch your step.'

'I always do that,' the visitor replied, pushing back his chair prior to leaving.

'I repeat, watch your step,' Leopold Brazil emphasized. 'You don't know the details, but a world is at stake.'


In the bar of the Priory Eve Warner tilted her glass, knocked back her fourth large vodka. Newman watched her cynically. As far as he could tell the amount of alcohol had no effect on her. She had a head like a rock. Philip was sipping the last of his single glass of wine.

'Bed for me,' Eve announced. She yawned without putting her hand over her mouth. 'It's been an exciting day.'

'I wouldn't call it exciting,' Philip objected. 'I think tragic is a better word.'

'Well. It isn't as though we'd known either of the victims. Good night, Bob. See you in the morning, I hope?'

'Possibly,' Newman replied.

'Tap on my door, Philip, when you come down. Just to say good night.'

'Your rooms are close?' Newman asked Philip when she had gone, leaving the bar empty except for the two men.

'I'm not in the main hotel. There's what they call the Boathouse down by the river. You get to it through some French windows in the lounge. Eve's got the suite across from mine.'

'Convenient,' Newman commented with a dry smile. 'How did that come about?'

'By chance. Tweed, who knows this place, booked me the suite. Eve was booked into the one opposite. I have just met her,' Philip ended with a note of protest.

'Don't mind me. Just joking. *How* did you meet her?'

Philip explained the circumstances, leaving out any mention of the red Porsche which appeared to have followed him from Park Crescent. He'd first seen it close to Baker Street underground station.

'Well, it will make a change from being on your own in that empty house. You're not moving, then? It's over a year since Jean died, isn't it?'

'Yes.' Philip paused. 'That house was our home and I am definitely not leaving it. Tweed sent you down here as back-up, didn't he?'

33

'Yes. He's very worried about something which happened since you arrived. He didn't say what. The barman has gone. Open your jacket so I can get at the pocket.'

Philip obeyed the suggestion without comment. Newman produced a Walther eight-shot 7.65mm automatic with spare mags, slipped the weapon into the pocket.

'Your favourite weapon. It was Tweed's idea. So he has to be worried.'

'Something you ought to know. As Eve told you, I met General Sterndale in this bar much earlier – before she and I drove out to the cliff at Lyman's Tout. Sterndale told me that despite having a servant who lived in, a man called Marchat . . .'

'Spell that, please.'

Philip did so. He'd asked the General the same question.

'Did Sterndale tell you where this Marchat came from? To me the name sounds Mittel-European.'

'No, he didn't. I was going to say Sterndale told me his house was so isolated he personally closed and locked up every shutter over windows each evening.'

'So he created his own fire-trap, poor devil. Tweed gave me all the details he'd got from Buchanan. I called him from a phone box when I was close to Wareham. I'll walk you down to this Boathouse place, if you don't mind. It sounded fascinating . . .'

The garden beyond the French windows was illuminated with lanterns at intervals. As they walked together along a pebble path Philip told Newman about Marchat.

'The weird thing is,' he went on, 'this servant, Marchat, seems to have vanished without trace. Tweed was quite definite only two bodies were brought out of the ruins.'

'So in the morning we'll start tracking Mr Marchat. As

he lived in the mansion the local pubs would be a good place to start. In the country they know all about who is who. This is quite a place.'

They had arrived at the Boathouse. It appeared to be a modern building, designed to fit in with the ancient Priory, or there had been skilful renovation. Newman peered in through tall glass doors as Philip took out his key. Beyond was a large hall with a stone floor, very spacious and with several doors leading off.

'My suite is the one at the end on the left, overlooks the River Frome. Eve's is the one on the other side of the hall.'

'See you in the morning for breakfast – if that isn't getting in the way of a friendship,' Newman suggested. 'You need some female company.'

'I'll join you for breakfast.' Philip paused. 'I've only just met her. She's attractive but I keep getting danger signals flashing. And she told me she was – I'm quoting her exact words – "I'm in security. And it's rather special . . ." I got the impression she'd let that slip out.'

'Said something similar to me.' Newman slapped him on the back. 'It's just possible she's on our side.'

'Then why is she so aggressive?'

'Because she's clever and that attitude makes for a good cover. Sleep well . . .'


The outer door to the hall, illuminated by bright lamps, closed and locked automatically. Reaching Eve's closed door, Philip paused. Would she think he was trying to move too fast? But it had been her idea. He rapped on the door which was unlocked and opened a few inches almost at once.

'Just saying good night,' Philip told her.

'Good night to you. I'll be up at seven o'clock. You sleep in and we'll meet later.'

The door was closed and he heard her lock it. Inside

35

his own suite he began exploring again. He'd spent only a few minutes inside earlier, opening his case, hanging up jackets and trousers. Jean had always told him to do this. 'Even if you're in a rush, do open your case and take out the things which could get creased . . .'

At the recollection of this memory his eyes filled with tears. He could hear how she spoke, a rather deep timbre, but her voice was soft and she had always spoken so clearly.

'Get a grip on yourself, you bloody fool,' he said to himself.

He hurried to the bathroom, turned on the cold water tap, and sluiced his eyes and face with water, drying himself vigorously with a towel. He knew what the trouble was. This was the first time since she had died he had come away on his own and stayed by himself in a hotel. Except for his vengeful excursion into Europe, hunting down the men who had killed her.

All thoughts of Eve had gone out of his head. Still feeling alert he prowled round the spacious suite – Tweed had been generous in choosing his accommodation. Entering the suite he walked straight into a large and comfortable living room with French windows looking out on the River Frome. One of the staff had closed the curtains. At the end of the room he turned into a corridor with the bathroom leading off it and the large double bedroom beyond.

He lit a cigarette, prowling from one room to another restlessly. In the living room he pulled back the curtains to look at the river which ran only a few feet beyond. In the moonlight he saw a towpath skirting the far edge.

A large man on a bicycle was riding along the towpath away from Wareham. He was staring across at the Boathouse. A very big man indeed, wearing a windcheater and a deerstalker hat pulled well down over his forehead. Impossible to see his face.

Suddenly the light on his machine was switched off. He had been cruising slowly past but now he increased speed, vanished. Philip's sixth sense came to life. He closed the curtain after checking the door locks. Then he toured the suite, checking all the window locks.

He forced himself to take a quick shower despite a wave of fatigue which unexpectedly came over him. Slipping into pyjamas, he flopped into bed, read a few pages of a paperback, then switched off the bedside light. Why was he oppressed with a sense of imminent doom?

# 3

Newman also was alert, restless, after he had left Philip. He wandered back through the garden where the lawn was coated with a white frost. The temperature was very low but cold stimulated him.

'I wonder if Tweed is still up,' he mused to himself. 'I'll give him a ring from that phone box Philip described, bring him up to date if I catch him . . .'

He entered through the lounge doors, thought of going up to his room, decided his windcheater would protect him enough. The night man behind the counter gave him a key to get back in.

'Feel like a walk. Not sleepy,' Newman remarked and closed the door, locking it as he stood in the cobbled courtyard.

He met them as he walked into the old square. Wareham was a town of Georgian houses, originals. They were cluttered all round the square. A group of six motorcyclists sat astride their machines near the exit from the square into the South Street.

As he appeared they began drinking beer from cans and several lit cigarettes. Why did he get the impression they were putting on an act as soon as he appeared? One, who had his gloves tucked under his arm, was blowing on his cold hands. Several wore their large crash helmets, watched him through huge goggles.

'You won't find any street ladies in this dump,' one of them called out in a sneering tone.

'You never know,' Newman replied amiably and kept walking.

He turned right into the deserted South Street and saw the phone box. Once inside he lifted the receiver, inserted coins, and dialled Park Crescent. Three of the motorcycle gang had wheeled their machines into South Street and stood watching him. After dialling Newman turned with his back to the phone so he could watch the gang. If they started anything he'd crack a few skulls with the barrel of his Smith & Wesson .38. Monica took the call, put him straight on to Tweed. Newman reported tersely, hung up the phone.

He walked back slowly, hands swinging slowly by his side. His very deliberate march seemed to worry them. They backed away to their original position. Newman walked on back to the Priory. A crop of the usual macho types. Then he remembered the motorcyclist Philip had told him had followed Eve and himself back from Kingston.


Tweed put down the phone after listening to Newman. He told Paula and Monica the gist of Newman's conversation. It's going to be an all-night session, Paula had been thinking.

'Well, at least I'm glad Philip at long last appears to have found a woman friend,' she commented.

'There could be something significant about Eve Warner's reference to being in security,' Tweed remarked. 'And her reference to it being "special". I just wonder.'

'Wonder what?' Paula probed.

'She could just be Special Branch.' Tweed glanced at the wall clock. 1.30 a.m. 'I think I'll call my old contact in that outfit, Merryweather. Like Philip, he's an owl. Doubt if it will work but it won't if I don't try. Could you get him, Monica? If he's there . . .'

'What is it, Tweed, at this hour?' Merryweather demanded when Tweed picked up his phone.

'Come off it, Sam,' Tweed chided him. 'You can't work until night has fallen. And you are there behind your desk. I need a favour.'

'You always do. What is it?'

'I'm going to give you a name. If she's employed by you I don't expect you to tell me.' Tweed paused to let that sink in. 'But if she is *not* on your staff it would be a great help to me to know. Her name is Eve Warner.'

Now it was Merryweather's turn to pause. Tweed waited patiently, winking at Paula. It was a very long pause before the reply came.

'Tweed, if I tried to get the name of someone on your staff – or tried to check that they were *not* on your staff – would you tell me? Like hell you would.'

'This is serious. I'm working on something which has involved three murders in the past few hours.'

'Try Scotland Yard. I can recommend Chief Inspector Roy Buchanan,' Merryweather added wickedly.

'You're a big help.'

'I always try to be. Keep in touch. Good night. Or rather good morning . . .'

Tweed put the phone down, shook his head.

'He wouldn't cooperate?' Paula enquired.

'There was a very long pause before he stonewalled me. It could be significant. Or he may have been reading a document. He does that, I know, when he's talking on the phone. So we just don't know.'

'Did Bob give you any opinion of this Eve Warner?'

'No, for some reason he was terse, as though he also had something else on his mind.'

'I've completed the profile you asked me a few days ago to draw up on Leopold Brazil,' Monica said brightly. 'It's a bit limited, with big gaps, but he's really a very interesting man.'

That was when the phone rang again.


'It's Chief Inspector Buchanan,' Monica said, masking the phone's mouthpiece. 'He doesn't sound in a particularly good temper. Shall I tell him you've gone home?'

'I'll take the call . . .'

'Tweed, I need a direct answer to a direct question.'

Buchanan's normally well-modulated voice had a hard rasp. Tweed settled himself more comfortably in his chair.

'Where are you calling from, Roy? The Yard?'

'No! From police headquarters at Wareham in Dorset.'

'Really? The early bird catches the worm . . .'

'This isn't funny. You know from my earlier call that two people have been brutally murdered at the Sterndale mansion. Did you know he had a living-in servant – chap called Marchat?'

'Could you spell that, please?' Tweed requested.

Buchanan obliged. 'Well, did you?'

'I do now. You've just told me.'

'This Marchat character – sounds foreign to me – has gone missing. His body was not found in the relics of the Sterndale mansion.'

'I expect you'll track him down.'

'I will,' Buchanan replied grimly. 'But not in the middle of the night. Now for the direct question – to which I expect a direct answer.'

'You said that before. You must be tired,' commented

40

Tweed, baiting him. If he could get Buchanan to lose his temper he might let something slip.

'How many men have you got down here already? And why?'

'That's two questions,' Tweed responded mildly.

'Damnit . . . ! Excuse me, I'll start again. I've been checking on hotel registers. At the Priory Hotel I find not only is Philip Cardon registered in a suite – in addition Bob Newman is staying at the same hotel in Room Four. I want to know why.'

'Philip,' Tweed replied smoothly, 'was sent on holiday by me. The first he's had since his wife, Jean, died – in case you've forgotten what happened.'

'You know I haven't.' Buchanan's tone had softened. 'I liked Jean, a remarkable woman. May I ask why Newman is also at the Priory?'

'Philip was very reluctant to go on his own, but I persuaded him to do just that. After he'd gone I thought it might be a bit traumatic for him, so Newman is there to keep him company.'

'Tweed, you should have been a barrister . . .'

'No, thank you. Lawyers make their money out of other people's misery. Court cases involving bitter domestic disputes, just to name one example.'

'I must warn you that nevertheless I shall have to question both of them during tomorrow. No, today.'

'That's your prerogative. Why don't you snatch a few hours' sleep? It's almost two in the morning.'

'And yet you are still at your desk. I'll be in touch again soon. Good night. Or rather, good morning . . .'

Tweed put down the phone and sat bolt upright in his chair. He was frowning, staring into space.

'From what I could gather you fended him off brilliantly,' Paula commented.

'When you're talking to a shrewd man from the Yard you stay within the truth as far as you can. I know he didn't believe me, but he couldn't fault me. He must be feeling frustrated, poor chap.'

'Do you – or do you not – wish me to read the profile I've taken days compiling on Leopold Brazil?' asked Monica.

'I'd like to be fresh when I absorb that. Unless there is something in it you think very significant concerning what has happened during the past few hours.'

'One thing is,' Monica replied with satisfaction. 'Brazil owns a large old house in Dorset, at a place called Lyman's Tout, whatever that means. It's called Grenville Grange and looks out from the clifftop over the sea. He's tried to conceal the fact he owns the place.'

'How on earth did you find that out?'

Tweed was suddenly exceptionally alert. He stared at Monica as she replied.

'Well, I've got contacts all over the place, as you know. Some of them are clerks in the offices of your beloved lawyers. They shouldn't gossip, but of course they do. He bought it in the name of Carson Craig. Eventually I contacted your friend, the money tracer, Keith Kent – he was on a short visit to Paris. He told me Brazil has a Carson Craig as a deputy on his staff, that Brazil often uses him as a front.'

'You've done well.'

'I wasn't satisfied with that. I have a friend, Maureen, who lives in a remote village called Kingston up in the Purbecks. We've had lunch several times at a nice old inn called the Scott Arms. She described the location of Grenville Grange. Says the place gives her the willies. She had no idea who owned it.'

Tweed jumped up, walked over to look at the Ordnance Survey map of Dorset Paula had earlier attached to the wall. He traced with his finger the route from Wareham to Kingston, then the narrow road which led to the Sterndale mansion and another track to

Lyman's Tout. He walked quickly back to his desk, sat down, drummed his fingers on his desk.

'That does it,' he decided 'At the moment all roads seem to lead to Dorset. Philip and Bob are down there on their own and I sense the situation is pretty explosive. Monica, I'm sending them reinforcements. Call Marler now, then Butler and Nield. They're to start driving – separate cars – down to Wareham before dawn. They must not stay at the Priory . . .'

'The Black Bear,' Monica said promptly. 'I know Wareham and it's in South Street, a five-minute walk from the Priory. Do they know each other when they arrive?'

'Marler keeps away from Butler and Nield – unless they're facing an emergency. All three can stay at the Black Bear Inn. Marler is a sales representative for something plausible. Butler and Nield are taking a holiday – their hobby is bird-watching. That will explain the high-power binoculars they'll be taking . . .'

Monica was reaching for the phone.

'Wait a minute,' Tweed rapped out. 'All three are to be armed – as is the case with Philip and Newman. And your first call is to Newman at the Priory. You'll probably wake everybody up, but they're used to it. Phrase the message to Newman like this. "The Buchanan Brothers are in town. Suggest an early breakfast for Philip and yourself, then push off somewhere. If the brothers contact you then you're in for a boring day." '

'Got it,' Monica replied, picked up the phone and dialled the Priory from memory.

While she was making her urgent phone calls Paula left her desk, sat in a chair close to Tweed.

'These are very heavy reinforcements you are sending. What triggered off your decision?'

'Monica's news that Brazil owns Grenville Grange, which is in the same area as Sterndale Manor. And I want a dragnet out to find the missing Marchat before

43

Buchanan gets to him. He could be the key to what really happened.'

'You've got something else on your mind too. I can sense it.'

'Something I've only told Philip so far. I phoned Maggie, the General's niece, earlier. I met her at a seminar – very boring. But when she found out I knew General Sterndale she opened up with something that was worrying her. Sterndale kept the bulk of the bank's capital in a safe at the manor. Ran his own show. The capital was in the form of bearer bonds.'

'Which can be turned into cash anywhere in the West – they have no one's name on them. What sort of money are we talking about?'

'Three hundred million, Maggie said.'

'Oh, my God! Sterndale Bank's capital has gone up in flames.'

'If the bonds *were* still in the safe . . .'


At Devastoke Cottage on the edge of Stoborough, a hamlet not far south of the River Frome and Wareham, Marchat locked his packed case and looked at his new tenant, who hurried in with three cases. Partridge, a bachelor from nearby Poole, dumped the cases and smiled.

'Phew! That's the lot. Funny time to move in. Three in the morning. But when I got your phone call I just wanted to get here. Love this place.'

'You're satisfied with the agreement we've drawn up ourselves?' Marchat asked anxiously. He looked at the document on the table.

'Well, it didn't take long to make an inventory. Not a lot here, if you don't mind my saying so. Which suits me. How do I get in touch with you?'

'I'll write to you when my aunt confirms I can take over her flat in London. Do keep the place locked up.'

Marchat sounded anxious. It occurred to him Partridge looked very like himself. Strange he had not noticed the close similarity when Partridge had visited the property a few days earlier. Marchat had put an advertisement in a Poole newspaper, saying his cottage was available for renting.

'You said over the phone your aunt was unwell when you called me this evening, that is, yesterday,' Partridge remarked. 'Nothing serious, I hope?'

'No. She fusses. She probably rushed about too much getting ready to leave her flat. I know she'll move out when I have given her a hand with packing. You seem to have a lot of stuff to move,' remarked Marchat.

Partridge had already brought in five suitcases from his car earlier. He smiled, made a dismissive gesture.

'As I told you, I work from home. I've got a PC – personal computer, fax machine, you name it. I'm a financial consultant. I'll start getting everything fixed up in a few days. I want to explore round here. Lovely remote spot.'

'I'd better go then,' Marchat said, checking his watch. He pointed to a row of keys laid out on a table. 'All the security keys are there. Do make sure windows and doors are locked at night – or if you go out.'

'Don't worry,' Partridge assured him. 'I'll keep a close eye on the place.'

He had already decided Marchat was the nervous type. Taking an envelope from his pocket he handed his landlord a fat envelope of banknotes – the deposit and three months' rental in advance.

'You ought to check that,' he suggested.

Marchat had stuffed the envelope in his breast pocket. He shook his head, said he trusted Partridge, picked up his two cases, and hurried out to his old Austin.

He would drive through the night to Heathrow, park the car in 'Long Stay', and be ready to board his flight. He had an open flight ticket in his pocket and had phoned Heathrow to make a firm booking. His destination: Europe.

The early morning flight from Paris was disembarking its passengers at Heathrow. A tall man was the first to leave the plane. He hurried to the car hire counter, produced the requisite papers for the Volvo he had hired over the phone from Paris, paid the necessary money, and within minutes was driving away. His destination: Wareham.

A few minutes later another tall passenger off the same flight approached the same counter, went through the procedure for obtaining the car he had hired by phone from Paris. Once outside the airport he drove at speed, heading south. Destination: Wareham.

# 4

It was still dark when Philip heard the tapping on his window which overlooked the Boathouse entrance. By nature a zombie when he woke, he had trained himself to wake quickly. Careful not to switch on a light – which would make him a perfect target – he checked the time by the illuminated hands of his wristwatch. 7 a.m.

As he slipped out of bed his right hand grasped the Walther P38 from under his pillow. He pushed the safety lever upwards. He had loaded the weapon the night before. The tapping was repeated more urgently.

He approached the window, stood to one side, his weapon ready, slid back one of the curtains. Outside, illuminated by the lamp over the outer door, Newman stood, holding up a sheet of paper with a message

46

in block letters. The sheet was pressed against the window.

> Get up now. See you at b/fast in fifteen minutes. We must be away from here for the day. Show a leg. Order from T.

Philip switched on his bedside light, went back to the window, nodded agreement. Newman disappeared.

Taking only a few minutes to wash and get dressed, wearing his hip holster with the automatic nestled inside, Philip opened the door from the suite, closed and locked it quietly. He looked across at Eve's door, left the Boathouse, and hurried to the breakfast room which he found on the ground floor.

'Buchanan is likely to call on us,' Newman explained as the waitress disappeared with Philip's order. 'Tweed wants us to avoid meeting him as long as we can. The bad news is that Buchanan arrived in Wareham last night.'

'He won't be a fun person,' Philip remarked after the waitress had brought rolls, marmalade, butter, a pot of coffee, and a jug of cold milk. 'Anyway, what's the programme?'

'We get out of here pretty damned fast. Then we drive round in the country in my car to waste time. We get back into Wareham just after ten.'

'What's the significance of ten o'clock in the morning?'

'The pubs round here open at ten. We'll try the Black Bear in South Street first. Barmen listen to gossip and know just about everything that goes on locally. I want to find out something about this weird character Marchat . . .'

They drove round slowly in Newman's Mercedes 280E, a big car he was very fond of. The roads into the

47

Purbecks were quiet in February. Philip kept a lookout for the Porsche Eve drove but saw no sign of it. Overhead dark brooding clouds threatened more rain. They returned to Wareham just after ten.

Newman avoided parking his car in front of the Priory wall where he had left it overnight. Instead, crossing the bridge over the Frome back into Wareham, he turned a sharp right. Philip looked round as they entered a small square closed in with Georgian houses. On the fourth side was the river front and the water was high, almost lapping the square.

'We're tucked away here from Buchanan,' Newman said as he put money into a meter. 'Now for the Black Bear . . .'

Philip saw you couldn't miss the hotel. Above a square porch was perched a large black bear, reared up, made of metal and painted a grim black. The entrance was a long narrow corridor with the opening to the bar on the right. The corridor continued under a glass roof. Marler stood leaning against a wall as he lit a king-size. He took no notice of Philip and Newman as they entered the bar which had no customers until they walked in.

'Two glasses of French dry white wine,' Philip ordered, and left it to Newman to ask the questions. The barman was a genial type who greeted them pleasantly.

'Just visiting?' he enquired.

'We're looking for a place in the country for my sister,' Newman said. 'A bit early for customers? By the way, I wonder if you could help me? A friend of mine lives in the area. Chap called Marchat. I'd better spell it . . .'

'No need.' The barman studied Newman before replying. 'You obviously haven't heard. Your friend often comes in here for a noggin one evening a week. He worked for General Sterndale, who lived out in the wilds below Lyman's Tout. Sterndale Mansion went up in flames last night. Horrible tragedy. The General and his son, Richard, were burnt to death. The rumour is it was deliberate. Arson.'

'Sounds awful,' Newman agreed. 'Not what you expect in peaceful Dorset.'

'No, it isn't.'

'What about Marchat?' Newman asked. 'I hope he wasn't there when that happened.'

'He wasn't. He was in here. His evening off. Drinking his usual noggin. We heard the police cars and ambulances screaming their sirens as they went past here. Later, a constable who had come off duty told us what it was all about. We were shocked, I can tell you.'

'Was Marchat here when the constable came in?'

'Yes, he was. He left very quickly without saying a word. In shock, I suppose.'

'Marchat lived in at the mansion, then?' Newman asked.

'Five days a week. He had the weekends off. A friend, you said?'

'Yes.'

'Then you'll probably find him at his cottage outside Stoborough. Know where that is?'

'We drove through it this morning.'

'Difficult place to find. I'll draw a map . . .'

Newman had just pocketed the map when a very large man clumped into the bar. His hair was thick and black, he had wide shoulders and large hands. His aggressive jaw was smeared with a dark stubble. He wore a shabby windcheater and denims. Philip was reminded of the large man riding a bicycle along the towpath the previous night.

'A pint of mild and bitter. Make it quick. I can't 'ang around here all day. Give me space at the bar,' he snapped at Newman.

'There is plenty of space.'

'Sassy, are we?' The newcomer glared. 'You look

familiar. You look just like that newspaper peeper, Robert Newman.'

'Maybe because I am.'

'I'm Craig. People keep out of my way.' He rested his elbow on the bar close to Newman. 'I said people who know me keep out of my way. 'Eard me, did you? Or are you bleedin' deaf?'

The barman had placed the drink Craig had ordered on the counter in a tankard. Craig shifted his elbow, knocked it over. Philip heard the *vroom-vroom* of motorcyclists arriving. Three of them entered the bar and he thought of the experience Newman had told him about when he'd gone out to find a phone the previous evening. He turned to face them as Craig faced Newman.

'You just knocked me pint over. Order me another.'

'Knocked it over yourself,' Newman replied mildly.

'You asked for it . . .'

Craig clenched a huge fist to slam into Newman. The foreign correspondent's hands moved in a blur. Then he was gripping both Craig's arms at a certain point where nerve endings were located. Craig froze, gulped with pain as Newman pirouetted him round, forced him back against the wall, released one hand, grasped the head of his opponent, slammed it against the wall.

'Now grow up. Otherwise you might get hurt. In fact I think it might be wiser if you cleared out. Like *now!*'

During the confrontation Philip had stood between the two men and the three motorcyclists who showed signs of taking Newman from the rear.

'Have you come in for a drink or a barrel-load of trouble?'

'Let's make mincemeat of the boy,' one of them suggested.

'I wouldn't cause any trouble if I were you,' a voice drawled behind the three youths.

As they swung round Marler stood in the doorway.

He was holding a Beretta, a small automatic just over four-and-a-half inches long in his right hand. He kept tossing it a foot or so in the air and then catching it. Each time he caught it he held it for a moment so it was aimed at a different man point-blank.

'It's really a toy, in my opinion, but it's loaded with real bullets. And I have a certificate to carry this neat little weapon. Why don't you all shove off back to your silly machines and take off?'

It was the silky tone in which he spoke as much as the gun which scared them. Marler stood aside as they walked out, leaving Craig to cope by himself.

'Sue you for GBH,' Craig mumbled.

When Newman had thrown him back his skull had hammered against the wall. He was dazed, but his look was venomous.

'I won't forget this,' he mumbled again.

'I agree,' Newman responded. 'Take you a few days before your head stops hurting. Forget your pint.'

'Screw . . . you.'

Craig walked unsteadily out of the bar and into the street. The barman waited until he had left the hotel before he commented.

'I don't want any more visits from him and he didn't pay for his beer.'

'He's been in here before?' Newman asked.

'A couple of times over the last week. And he asked me the same question you did. Had I heard of a man called Marchat, and if so where did he live.'

'What did you tell him?' Philip enquired.

'Nothing. Said I'd never heard the name, so how could I know where the chap lived. I never said a word about Marchat's place, Devastoke Cottage.'

Marler had disappeared as swiftly as he had appeared by the time they finished their drinks, thanked the barman, and went over to where Newman had parked his Mercedes. Philip looked up and down South Street, which was almost deserted except for the odd woman carrying a shopping bag. No sign of the motorcyclists he had heard leaving near the end of the fracas.

'Where to now?' Philip asked as he glanced round the small square close to the bridge and the river.

'Don't say anything or stare when you look in the back of the car,' warned Newman, who had automatically checked the rear as he stepped into the vehicle. 'And we're going to find this Devastoke Cottage where Marchat lives. Time we had a word with him, to find out what he knows about the fire at Sterndale Manor.'

Philip glanced back quickly as he climbed into the front passenger seat. Coiled up in the back on the floor was Marler. He was holding a canvas sheath and Philip guessed that resting inside it was Marler's favourite long-distance weapon, an Armalite rifle.

Stoborough was little more than a hamlet with a few houses and a tavern. Glancing down at the map the barman had drawn Newman turned along a country lane, hedge-lined and with open fields under water on either side.

'You know who Bully Boy was?' Marler called out from behind them.

'Chap called Craig.'

'They call him "Crowbar" Craig. His real Christian name is Carson.'

'Why Crowbar, then?' Philip enquired.

'You're going to like what Bob did to him when I tell you. When friend Craig wants information from someone and they don't cough up he uses a crowbar to smash their kneecaps. A real charmer.'

'How do you know this?'

'Archie, an informant I met over lunch at an out-of-the-way bar, told me. He said if he ever saw Craig coming he'd run like hell. The intriguing thing is he's deputy to a rich man called Leopold Brazil.'

'A thug like that?' Philip's tone expressed disbelief. 'Brazil is a man who mixes in top society.'

'I thought his Cockney way of speaking was phoney,' Newman commented. 'What makes you so sure he was this Crowbar Craig?'

'Archie gave me a good description of him to put me on my guard. He's good at descriptions, is Archie. What he gave me fitted Bully Boy perfectly.'

'Slow down!' Philip called out. 'You just passed the place. There's a signboard stuck in the hedge.'

Newman glanced in his rear-view mirror, backed the car, saw why he hadn't noticed Devastoke Cottage. It was set well back from the road behind a thorny hedge. The cottage was small with a thatched roof and a single dormer on the first floor peering out between the thatch, which was a greenish colour.

Marler came with them as Newman opened a small wooden gate, which creaked. Not much sign of main-tenance, Newman thought as he led the way up the path dense with weeds, noted the colour of the thatch. He was bothered – all the curtains were closed.

'I wonder what we shall find here,' he said, half to himself.


He had to press the bell four times before the ancient heavy wooden door was opened. A man stood framed in the entrance, small with a plump face, clean-shaven with a smooth skin. His brown hair was all over the place and he wore a dressing gown over pyjamas.

'Sorry to get you up,' Newman opened. 'I believe you are Mr Marchat.'

'No. I'm Partridge. Mr Marchat has rented Devastoke

Cottage to me. I arrived early this morning and I was short of sleep.'

'Could we have a word with you about Mr Marchat? I apologize again for the inconvenience but it's very urgent.'

'All three of you?' Partridge asked nervously.

'This may reassure you.' Newman produced the Special Branch pass skilfully forged by the boffins in the basement at Park Crescent.

'Special Branch. I've never met anyone from your outfit. Please come in. Sorry about the mess. Let's go into the sitting room. I'll open the curtains . . .'

He ushered them into a small room on the right overlooking the front garden and the road beyond. When he had pulled back the curtains he invited them to take seats. The room was furnished with chintz armchairs, which matched the curtains. Newman and Philip sat down while Partridge occupied another armchair. Marler, as was his habit, leaned against a wall by the windows. He took out a king-size, put it between his lips, then paused.

'You may smoke,' Partridge assured him. 'Please do. I think I'll have one myself,' he went on, producing a packet from one of his dressing-gown pockets. 'How can I help you, gentlemen?'

'We expected to find Mr Marchat in residence,' Newman explained. 'Could you tell us where he is?'

Despite obvious lack of sleep, Partridge, a man Newman estimated to be in his forties, explained tersely the whole series of events which had brought him to Devastoke Cottage.

'The extraordinary thing is,' he concluded, 'we look very like each other. I was quite startled when I first met him.'

'You think he selected you as a tenant for that reason?' Newman probed.

54

'Oh, no. We practically agreed I would take this place over the first phone call when I answered his ad in the local paper. Subject, of course, to my liking the place.'

'How long ago is it since you first spoke to him?'

'About a week. No more. Has he done anything wrong?'

'Nothing like that,' Newman assured him. 'He may just be able to help us with our enquiries. He gave you the address of this aunt in London whose flat he was taking over?'

'No, he didn't. He said he would phone me all details as soon as he knew she would definitely be moving. He had no doubt about that.'

'I hope you won't mind my asking this,' Newman said at his most tactful, 'but could you give me proof of your identity?'

'Not at all. You did expect to find Mr Marchat here. So would my driving licence do?'

'That would cover everything.'

While they waited for Partridge to come back Marler, who was still standing to one side of the window, suddenly stepped back against the wall and peered out from behind the folded curtain.

A grey Volvo was cruising very slowly past the cottage from the direction of Stoborough. The windows were misted up but the driver had earlier rubbed a hole in the blurred surface. Marler had a fleeting impression of a tall man behind the wheel. Newman's Mercedes was parked on the grass verge outside the hedge. The Volvo speeded up once it was past the cottage.

'Something wrong?' asked Philip.

Marler had no time to reply as Partridge returned, handed a driving licence to Newman. Glancing at it he saw it was made out in the name Simon Partridge. He handed it back as he stood up.

'Thank you, Mr Partridge. Again, very sorry to disturb your beauty sleep.'

'That's all right.' Partridge glanced at a couch pushed against a wall. 'Think I'll lie down there and leave the curtains open. Otherwise I'll sleep until Heaven knows when. And there's so much to unpack . . .'

'Strange,' Newman remarked as they walked back down the footpath, 'that Marchat should push off so quickly after the tragedy at Sterndale Mansion.'

'He did start trying to let the place a week ago,' Marler reminded him. 'Seemed a harmless enough cove, that chap Partridge.'

'Funny that business about his likeness to Marchat,' Philip commented.

'Oh, they say we all have a double somewhere,' Newman replied.

The weather had changed while they were inside Devastoke Cottage. The windows on Newman's car had misted up and he began cleaning them with a wash leather. He set the wipers going to clear the windscreen, squeezed out the leather, and dried his hands on another cloth.

'We'd better get back to Wareham. We'll have to face the music sooner or later, the music with a nasty rasp played by Chief Inspector Buchanan. We'll forget we paid a visit to Partridge. Marler, I suggest you keep out of the way, slip back to the Black Bear Inn. No point in letting our favourite policeman know how many of us are down here. That really would rouse his suspicions . . .'

Marler again coiled himself up on the floor in the rear after retrieving the Armalite he'd hidden under a travel rug. As they headed back for Wareham Philip was thinking about their colleague tucked up in the back. Marler had stood with a faraway look while Newman had cleaned the windows, as though he had something on his mind.

They had passed through Stoborough and were close to the bridge over the Frome when Marler called out.

'Bob, turn back now, please. Drive back to Devastoke Cottage.'

'What the hell for?'

'Trust me. Just do it.'

'Oh, all right. You might give me a reason,' he growled as he executed a three-point turn on the straight stretch of road, which was deserted.

'A Volvo cruised slowly past the cottage while we were inside. I didn't like the look of it. The more I think about it I still don't like the look of it.'

'I noticed that car,' Philip recalled. 'It crawled past while Partridge was fetching his driving licence. I thought the driver could be a woman.'

'Hard to tell. It – he or she – was little more than a silhouette,' Marler responded. 'And why are *we* crawling?'

'Because,' Newman explained as though speaking to a child, 'there's a farm tractor ahead of us with a car behind it. And there's traffic in the opposite direction. I can't overtake. Contain your impatience, we'll soon reach the turn-off lane.'

'And the tractor will go down there,' Marler snapped.

An air of tension was rising inside the car. Newman also was beginning to get worried. He'd had experience of Marler's intuitions and too often they had proved to be well founded. The tractor and the car ahead continued straight on towards Corfe and he turned down the lane where there was no traffic. He accelerated.


'Everything looks the same as before,' Newman remarked as they left the Mercedes parked outside Devastoke Cottage.

'No it isn't,' said Marler and produced his Beretta,

holding it close to his side. 'Partridge clearly told us he wasn't going to draw the curtains over the living room while he had some more kip. Well, they're closed now.'

'Could have changed his mind,' Newman pointed out.

'There's a path leading round the side of the cottage, probably to a back door. I suggest we go and see . . .'

Their feet made no sound on the moss-strewn path and at the rear of the cottage they found the back door. They stopped abruptly as Marler pointed, raised one finger for absolute silence. The back door was slightly ajar, had been jemmied open forcibly, shown by splintered wood in the door jamb. He pushed it open slowly, his gun raised. They crept into a darkened kitchen with an old iron cooker in a setback.

Newman was gripping the .38 Smith & Wesson in his hand and Philip had produced his Walther. They walked slowly into a narrow hall. The door to the sitting room, now on their left, was half open. Marler stood to one side, slowly pushed it wide open. By now their eyes were accustomed to the semidarkness.

'Oh, my God!' Philip whispered.

Partridge was lying half on and half off the couch, his head on the floor, twisted at a bizarre angle. Marler walked in, bent down, checked the carotid artery, looked up.

'Dead as a dodo. His neck is broken. I think I know whose work this is. There's a new assassin on the loose in Europe. Kills for big sums. Simple technique. He comes up behind his victim, slips his arm round the target's neck in a certain way. This is the result. They call him The Motorman.'

'Weird name,' Philip said quietly. 'Why The Motorman?'

'Because he moves like greased lightning. As I'm sure he did here. He thought he was killing Marchat . . .'

# 5

'So you think this assassin believed he'd killed Marchat?'
Tweed asked.

He was sitting in his office at Park Crescent when
Monica told him Newman was on the line. He had
listened with a poker-face while Newman related tersely
what had happened, including the encounter with
Crowbar Craig. This was the first time he interrupted
Newman's narrative.

'That could be the deputy of Mr Leopold Brazil, a
man called Carson Craig. But Monica has dug up more
data on this gentleman. He usually sports a business suit
and a sophisticated accent.' His tone became ironic. 'The
sort of chap you could invite to your club.'

'Except that I don't waste my time belonging to any
club,' Newman retorted. 'But I thought his Cockney
accent was a fake. "Gentleman" is not the term I'd use.
Basically he is a sadistic tough. Nicknamed "Crowbar".
Uses one to smash people's kneecaps if they annoy him.'

'I see. Bob, Monica has also found Brazil owns
Grenville Grange, in the vicinity of the Sterndale house.
Perched near the cliffs at Lyman's Tout. Check that place
out. Not by yourself. Take Philip and Marler with you.'

'If you insist.'

'I do. Three murders in Dorset is three too many. Try
to avoid Buchanan as long as you can. Also send Butler to
this Partridge's previous address in Poole to check him
out. I presume you noted his address when he showed
you the driving licence.'

'I did. I'd better get moving before Buchanan hoves
up on the horizon.'

'Do that. I sense the momentum of something is

building up. Continue to stay with Philip at the Priory. Anything further with Philip's new friend, Eve Warner? I can't confirm whether she's Special Branch or not.'

'Nary a sign of the lady so far this morning. Signing off.'

'Take care . . .'


'Why don't I keep my big mouth shut?' Newman said to himself as he emerged from the phone box in South Street in Wareham. Standing on the kerb, leaning against her red Porsche, was Eve Warner. Dressed in a clean white windcheater with the hood hanging on her shoulders, she waved to him. She had a small frame, he noted, and even wearing drainpipe blue denims with the windcheater she looked very attractive. No wonder Philip seems to be falling for her, he thought.

'Top of the morning to you, Bob,' she called out cheekily. 'I see your Merc parked behind me. Going someplace? I'll come with you. Hello, Philip. Sleep OK, all on your ownsome?'

'Very well,' snapped Philip, who had just walked out of the Black Bear. He thought her remark tactless, as he'd told her that this was his first holiday on his own since Jean's death.

'Then don't sound like a sorehead,' she rapped back. 'Where are we off to today?'

'You're not invited,' Newman told her bluntly as she came up close to him.

Marler had slipped out of the hotel and into the back of Newman's car without her noticing. She was too busy flashing her seductive smile at Newman, intent on persuading him.

'Don't be an old spoilsport,' she challenged him. 'I need company.'

'Look elsewhere, then. Excuse me . . .'

'I can always follow you!' she shouted at his back as he disappeared inside the hotel. It took him only a few minutes to locate the burly Harry Butler, to give him Tweed's instructions about checking on Partridge and the address in Poole.

'What about my sidekick, Pete Nield? He's in his room.'

'Tell him to stay here and keep a discreet watch on the Priory Hotel for any sign of Chief Inspector Buchanan. He's round here somewhere. I'll come back here for your report later in the day.'

When he came out on to the street Eve was leaning up against her car, arms and legs crossed.

'You don't get rid of me as easily as that,' she told him.

'We'll see about that.'

Being careful not to show his annoyance at her persistence, he got behind the wheel. Philip was already in the front passenger seat; Marler was secreted in the back. He drove off towards the bridge, heading for Corfe and then Kingston, recalling that Philip had told him about the route over breakfast. In his rear-view mirror he saw Eve take off after him.

'I'll lose you, hellcat,' he said aloud.

'She's all right,' Philip protested.

Newman made no reply.


Back in his office at Park Crescent Tweed had relayed to Paula and Monica the gist of his conversation with Newman.

'The Motorman?' Paula repeated. 'He does sound a bit sinister. From what you've told me he must have moved jolly fast to commit that foul murder at Devastoke Cottage.'

'Hence his nickname, I presume. The Motorman,'

Tweed said grimly. 'I've heard mention of him before. I know who it was. Arthur Beck, Chief of Federal Police in Switzerland. Get him on the phone, Monica – you should find him at his headquarters in Berne.'

Monica was reaching for her phone when it began ringing. Answering it, she nodded to Tweed.

'It's Lasalle from Paris again. Sounds urgent.'

'Tweed,' Lasalle burst out the moment he knew he was talking to him, 'we've just discovered another top-flight scientist and his family have disappeared. Over a month ago. From Grenoble. He was on leave, hence the delay in his unit realizing he'd gone missing.'

'Another one? That makes a total of twenty of the world's most important scientists missing from Europe, here, and America. Details, please. What was this one's speciality?'

'Advanced satellite communication. Very secret work – probably the top man in his field anywhere. Georges Blanc. Like the others, his wife has disappeared too.'

'Kidnapped?' Tweed suggested.

'No evidence of that. Before vanishing he instructed his lawyer to sell his house and contents – antiques included. The lawyer has to send the proceeds to a numbered account in a Belgian bank. The President is raving mad. We were leading the world in that field.'

'Any clue as to how Blanc left Grenoble?'

'His chauffeur – I'm having him flown to Paris so I can interrogate him myself – told me on the phone he had driven Blanc, his wife, and a load of luggage over the border to a remote airfield in Germany. He was ordered to drive back to Grenoble after Blanc handed him a handsome bonus to keep his mouth shut. Blanc's story was he was on a top secret mission.'

'Any type of aircraft waiting on the airfield while this chauffeur was there?'

'No. Blanc is brilliant. He was working on an

advanced satellite – for comunications between the Earth and the orbiting satellite.'

'I'll add him to the list. While you're on the phone, have you ever heard of The Motorman?' Tweed enquired.

'God! Why do you ask?'

'Because this reputed assassin may be operating over in this country.'

'He's a new, highly skilled killer. Very expensive, so the underworld rumours have it. He's assassinated two bankers in Paris. That's confidential. We've kept very quiet about him while we track him. Not a clue so far.'

'What sort of bankers?' Tweed asked quietly.

'Both owned small, very exclusive banks. One founded in the time of Napoleon. Family banks.'

'How can you be certain The Motorman was responsible?' Tweed pressed. 'He leaves a calling card?'

'Of course not. It's the technique. Both bankers had a lot of security round their houses. It was bypassed, God knows how. They both died of broken necks. One was killed in his library while his wife was in the adjoining room. She never heard a thing.'

'Any money missing?'

'Strange you should ask that,' the Frenchman commented. 'In each case a lot of the capital was held in bearer bonds. They've vanished. How the hell am I supposed to trace bearer bonds?'

'The banks have gone bust?' Tweed enquired.

'No. Enough cash was kept in each branch to keep them solvent. Tweed, I'm up to my neck, over my head.'

'You'll swim to the surface,' Tweed assured him. 'You always do. Keep in touch . . .'

Tweed sighed to himself as he put down the phone. Monica asked him whether she should still call Arthur Beck and he nodded. She began dialling immediately.

'Beck here. What is it, Tweed?'

The Swiss police chief, normally genial and calm however fraught a situation, sounded brusque.

'Arthur, a little while ago you mentioned an assassin, a professional, called The Motorman. Have you had any luck identifying him?'

'Why?'

'He's been operating in France . . .'

'I know that . . .'

'Well, what you probably don't know is that he's now in this country as far as we can tell. He tried to kill a key witness to a double murder but by mistake murdered the wrong man.'

'First time he's made a mistake.' There was a pause. 'I don't like this – he's becoming very international. I've got nowhere tracking him down. He just disappears into thin air. He's responsible for killing three Swiss.'

'What were their professions?'

'Bankers.'

'Owners of small private long-established banks?'

'How on earth did you guess that? We've kept silent about his activities. I thought that might throw him off his guard.'

'And you know it was The Motorman because with all his three victims he broke their necks?'

'Yes. He's the bloody Invisible Man. No amount of top security can keep him out. You can imagine how security-conscious bankers are.'

'He bypasses their security in some weird way?'

'Oh, I think I've now worked that out. Tweed, he *talks* his way in. In all three cases the security was still intact. I'm wondering now if he has an attractive woman with him when he calls to help get him inside.'

'Could The Motorman be a woman?' Tweed speculated.

'She'd have to be pretty strong. One of the bankers was built like a bull. Didn't save him. And there's no sign

64

of a struggle in all three cases. Except with the bull, whose feet scuffed up the carpet.'

'To change the subject, do you know anything about a Leopold Brazil?'

Another pause, a long one. 'Tweed, I've been warned off making any enquiries about him.'

'I don't believe it. Nobody warns you off. Who are you talking about?'

'That I can't tell you. Damn it, no one pushes me up against the wall. He has an expensive villa along the lake in Zurich. Between you and me I am watching discreetly. Very discreetly. Something strange about that man with all his power. I'll tell you he flew off in his private jet from Kloten, Zurich, on his way to Paris.'

'What kind of a jet?'

'Well, here's the tricky part. He has two private jets, both Lears. One has *Brazil SA*, the name of his Swiss company, in huge letters along the fuselage. The other, painted white, has no markings identifying that it belongs to him. He uses the white jet to confuse watchers whether he's aboard or not. Both have aircrews standing in rotas twenty-four hours round the clock. It was the white job which flew to Charles de Gaulle. That's it.'

Tweed put down the phone. His concentration on what Beck had told him was so great he hadn't noticed Monica was holding her phone, staring at him impatiently.

'Lasalle is back on the line from Paris. He's asked me twice to make sure you're on scrambler.'

'I still am,' Tweed said, and picked up the phone again. 'Sorry to keep you hanging on,' he said into the mouthpiece.

'I told you I was warned off investigating Leopold Brazil. Which is why I omitted to tell you he flew in yesterday from Zurich. A limo with tinted windows met him and drove him to his villa in the Avenue Foch. One of my best men identified him as he left the limo.'

'So why tell me now.'

'Because I'm sure now he's on his way to Britain within the next two hours.'

Tweed half-closed his eyes. Paula noted the mannerism, which told her he was tense.

'How do you know that?'

'The pilot of his white Lear jet just filed a flight plan for two hours hence.'

'To where?'

'Bournemouth International Airport. In Dorset . . .'


Tweed thanked Lasalle briefly, jumped up from his desk, ran to a cupboard, hauled out two cases kept packed for emergency departures – one for himself, the other for Paula.

'We'll take the Ford Escort,' he snapped. 'I'll drive. You'd better bring your Browning automatic. Monica, phone the Priory Hotel. Book us each a room. Indefinite stay. You can reach me there, but wrap up any message.'

'What's the emergency?' Paula asked.

She had already opened a locked drawer, taken out her Browning .32 automatic, slipped it into the special pocket sewn into her shoulder bag which gave her instant access to the weapon. Tweed was studying the map of Dorset on the wall.

'Monica,' he rapped out before she could dial, 'if Newman phones tell him to post one man at the roundabout just south of Stoborough Green. Not Stoborough. Stoborough *Green*. I want another man posted to watch the ferry across the exit from Poole Harbour. Both are watching for a limousine with tinted-glass windows. If either man spots it they are to follow it with caution. My guess is it will be headed for Grenville Grange, in the Purbecks near Lyman's Tout. Leave you in charge . . .'

Paula caught him up as he jumped in behind the

wheel of the Ford Escort parked outside as she slid into the front passenger seat.

'What is the emergency?' she repeated.

'Leopold Brazil is headed our way – flying within two hours from Paris to Bournemouth International Airport.' He was already driving towards Baker Street as Paula fastened her seat belt. 'From Bournemouth International he has to drive by one of only two routes – and we'll have watchers checking. Which means we should beat him to Wareham.'

'What is happening? Everything has suddenly moved.'

'I think Dorset is about to explode . . .'

# 6

'It's no good,' Newman said as he drove up the steep, winding hill to Kingston, leaving Corfe behind. 'Your Eve Warner is a damned good driver and I'm not going to lose her.' He checked his rear-view mirror. 'She's just come round that snaky bend like a pro at Brand's Hatch.'

'In that case,' Marler drawled from his curled-up position on the rear floor, 'my hiding is a waste of time. Warn me when you come to another bend and I'll get up, perch in a corner. When she sees me she may think I was sitting like that all the time.'

'Then get ready . . . *Now!*'

Newman had accelerated suddenly, swinging round a dangerous curve. In the back Marler scrambled up, settled himself in a corner of the seat, eased the ache out of his legs.

'Perfect! She didn't see you,' Newman reported.

'I still think we ought to have come in my four-wheel-drive,' Philip protested.

'And you'd have risked running into Buchanan if you'd tried to collect it from outside the Priory.'

'Your Merc will never make it along that track across Lyman's Tout.'

'Who said we were going to try?' Newman enquired.

'Then where the devil are we going?'

'Straight to Grenville Grange, residence of a certain Mr Leopold Brazil.'

'Asking for trouble . . .'

' "L'audace, toujours l'audace," as Danton once said, or something like that. I checked the map. We turn out of Kingston here to reach the entrance to his drive.'

'And when we're challenged by a posse of guards?'

'I bluff our way in. You seem to have forgotten that once I was a foreign correspondent,' Newman said jauntily. 'In that game you learn to get in anywhere.'

'Prepare for battle,' Marler commented.


The entrance to Grenville Grange appeared suddenly off a lonely road on the heights of the Purbecks. Two massive wrought-iron gates were thrown back and an open pebble drive stretched beyond them. Philip saw the dark hulk of Grenville Grange half a mile beyond. No sign of any guards, no sign of life.

'Stop the car a minute if you're going in there,' Philip said.

'All right. But why?' asked Newman, pulling up.

'I want to go back and persuade Eve to wait for us back down the road. You heard what Marler said.'

'Good idea. She'll only get in the way. I'd been thinking about that same problem myself . . .'

Eve had stopped her Porsche a dozen yards behind them, behind the high grey stone wall which bordered the road. She raised her dark eyebrows as Philip approached and flashed him her inviting smile.

'I'll bet Bob Newman could horsewhip me. Tell him it's a free country.'

'Eve.' Philip perched his elbows on the edge of her open window. 'This could be very tricky. Dangerous, even . . .'

'But you'll protect me, won't you? If it came to a pinch I think even Bob would come to my aid. Who is the chap in the back? Haven't seen him before, have I?'

'Eve, I'm asking you to reverse the way we came. We'll come back for you.'

'Bet you will,' she said sarcastically. 'Tell Newman I'll be on his tail. I'm bloody stubborn.'

'You are,' snapped Philip.

'Now don't lose your temper.'

Philip shrugged, hurried back to Newman, climbed in beside him.

'She's not having any,' Newman remarked.

'I couldn't persuade her. How could you tell?'

'Her expression. Yours. Now what's she up to? She's running towards us. I suppose I'd better try and make her see sense.'

Eve poked her head in at Newman's window. She looked back at Marler.

'Hello, nice man. Who are you? Maybe you'd buy me a drink soon. My favourite tipple is vodka.'

'Go home,' said Newman.

Eve lit a fresh cigarette from the one she had been smoking. She blew out smoke, away from Newman's face. Her manner became serious.

'Bob, I could be useful. I have cat's eyes.'

'And cat's claws no doubt.'

'I'll pretend I didn't hear that. Are you calling at this place or just checking on it? If the latter, you see where the drive forks, one bit going up to the big terrace entrance, the other section curving round the back of this architectural masterpiece? That second fork would take you round the back and then away from Bleak House down a slope to the sea. Near the cliff's edge – and you'd better watch that – it curves round the end of a drystone wall on to Lyman's Tout.'

'How do you know that?'

She had Newman's attention now and he gazed straight at her, his curiosity aroused.

'Because when Philip took me up Lyman's Tout I noticed the drive coming round the house through a gap where the drystone wall had crumbled. I'm observant. Trust me . . .'

She ran back to her Porsche. Newman drove forward at a slow pace, studying the dark house, which was very big. All the shutters were closed but as they got closer he noticed they had been painted black recently. Black. Awful!

The dark hulk seemed to move towards them and Philip saw that at the end they would pass round were several large barns – very like the barn General Sterndale's old Bentley had been partially parked inside. Here the great doors were all closed.

'Let's hope she knows what she's talking about,' Newman commented. 'She's on my tail – if she drops back I'm going to get suspicious . . .'

Ever since they had left Wareham the weather had been unpredictable. And there had been no more rain overnight. Philip was pondering these factors as they cruised past the barns.

'You might make it back along the track over the top of Lyman's Tout even in your Merc,' he remarked. 'I think the mud might have hardened. I don't promise anything.'

There was still no sign of anyone occupying Grenville Grange. Newman was not reassured as he rounded the end of the house and saw a pebbled track continuing towards the sea which petered out into ruts halfway down the slope towards the cliff edge. He turned off the engine and the car slid slowly down the slope and inside the ruts, which were hardened, probably due to the lack of rain and the severe frost.

'What do you think?' Marler asked.

'Something's not right. Those wide-open gates bother me.'

'Why?' asked Philip.

'They suggest someone is expected. So *I'd* expect there to be staff inside the house. Everyone shut up. We're close to the cliff edge . . .'

He switched on the engine for more control. The wind off the sea had hit them like a hammer blow as they came round the end of the house and started down the barren slope. The sea gleamed an intense blue and great white horses showed on mountainous waves thundering in.

Reaching the end of the drystone wall, Newman eased the car round the end, glancing to his left. The cliff edge was very close. Behind him Eve drove her Porsche slowly, a few feet from his tail. As he negotiated the turn inland onto Lyman's Tout he watched her in his rear-view mirror. She had the sense to ease her way round, following Newman's example. He parked the car close behind the drystone wall, which was higher than his roof. Eve parked behind him.

'What now?' Philip asked.

'We watch that place for awhile. You and Marler stay a distance behind me to guard my rear. Take Eve with you if you have to drag her.'

He lifted the large pair of 'birdwatcher' binoculars he had borrowed from Butler, got out, found the ground *was* hard, wandered back, and lay down on the ground at a point where he could see the house round the end of the wall.

He could feel the cold seeping through his clothes as he focused, waited. Marler, Philip and Eve had disappeared behind huge rocks some distance to his rear. Patiently, he waited. He heard nothing above the whine of the wind, the dull thud of the monstrous waves against the cliff base far below. Then something round and metallic pressed against his neck, the muzzle of a gun. He froze.

'I'm holding a loaded shotgun, *chum*,' a familiar voice said. 'Blow your head off. My head still aches from your catching me off guard in that bar. Now, what are you doing here on private property? Might as well talk before I pull the trigger . . .'

The voice of Craig, a more sophisticated voice now, and even more menacing.


Pete Nield, Harry Butler's partner, was a great contrast in appearance and manner to the man he worked closely with. Whereas Butler dressed in denims and a shabby windcheater, Nield, unlike the burly Butler, was slim and a snappy dresser.

Nield wore a check sports jacket and fawn slacks with a razor-edged crease. His white shirt was spotless, bisected by a smart grey tie. He had returned from watching the Priory for any sign of Buchanan to contact Tweed, to bring him up-to-date on Newman's trip to Grenville Grange.

'Pete,' Monica interrupted him, 'Tweed is away.'

'Where?'

'He didn't say.'

'Paula there?'

'No. Listen. I have instructions for you and Harry. I assume you're calling from a phone box.'

'Monica, you have the most amazing intuition.'

'Flattery will get you nowhere. I said listen . . .'

Nield kept quiet while she relayed Tweed's instructions. After the brief conversation he hurried back to the

Black Bear in the hope that Harry Butler would call him from Poole.

Fat chance of that happening now I have to leave to watch the roundabout at Stoborough Green, he thought. Life was not like that. As he turned the key in the door to his room he heard the phone ringing. He rushed across to the instrument – knowing it would stop ringing as he picked it up. He grabbed it.

'Yes. Who is it?'

'You sound breathless. You're out of training,' Butler's heavy voice mocked him.

'Very funny . . .'

'Partridge is OK for tonight's meal? Partridge is OK.'

'My favourite dish,' Nield replied, playing along with Butler's cryptic message. 'You're still in Poole? Good. New instructions. An important client is possibly coming via the ferry at the exit to Poole Harbour . . .'

'Sandbanks this side, Shell Bay on your side. Go on . . .'

'He has to be treated like royalty. If he travels that route he'll probably be inside a limousine with tinted windows. You're his escort – a *very* discreet escort. He could just arrive within an hour, maybe longer.'

'Got it. I'd better get moving.'

'Me too.'


At Sandbanks Butler eased his sturdy bulk out of the phone booth, ran to his parked Ford Fiesta. Pete Nield would have grasped the gist of what he had reported: that he'd checked out Partridge.

Using the phone directory on arrival, he'd torn round in his car, calling at four different addresses where a Partridge lived. Apologizing at the first three of them, explaining he was looking for a friend, he hit gold dust at the fourth, a small detached house with a notice in a

73

window. *Room To Let*. The landlady, a portly woman, was forthcoming.

'I'm sorry, but your friend has just moved to a cottage near Wareham. Very quick it was. I'm sorry to lose him, he was a quiet tenant. Worked in his rooms – had a lot of funny equipment. Computers he called them. And a machine which chattered and spewed out typed sheets of messages.'

'Probably his fax machine,' Butler guessed.

'He was such a nice quiet man. No trouble at all. He wanted a quiet place in the country. Some people like that, you know. Wouldn't suit me. I like a bit of life . . .'

'Just to make sure I've got the right man, could you describe him,' Butler interjected to halt the flood of words. He waited. People were terrible at describing someone they even knew well.

'Small. Much smaller than you. Less well built, if you don't mind my saying so. I wondered if he was a foreigner. Mind you, he spoke perfect English, but his appearance. He had such smooth skin that I used to wonder if he ever had to shave . . .'

'Could you give me the actual address he's moved to?' asked Butler in desperation.

'Devastoke Cottage, near Stoborough. That's south of Wareham. You take the . . .'

'Many thanks.' Butler was backing away to escape the barrage. 'I know how to get there. I'll be on my way . . .'

He hurried to the phone booth he'd noticed, confident he'd get across to Nield that Partridge seemed genuine. Then he drove to the car ferry point.

Butler had already decided where he would wait. He had driven to Poole via the ferry from Shell Bay and had noticed a car park near the beach on the far side. A ferry, a large craft controlled by a chain from shore to shore, was just about to leave. The only other vehicle aboard was a local bus. The ramp was elevated as he parked behind it.

The crossing took only a few minutes and in the distance Butler could see the curving ridge of the Purbecks. He drove off, paused at the toll-booth to pay the fare, then turned left into the car park a few hundred yards away from the crossing point. His was the only car on the sunny but bleak bitter February day.

'Perfect,' Butler said to himself. 'Perfect – cars passing don't notice this park unless the drivers are very observant.' And coming from Sandbanks he would be invisible to any traffic from Bournemouth and beyond. He opened a flask of coffee, had a hot drink, settled down to wait. Butler had the patience of Job.

The muzzle of the shotgun pressed deeper into Newman's neck. He lay quite still as Craig taunted him.

'Boot's on the other foot now. My head still aches. Better than having it blown right off. Who sent you?'

'I sent myself,' Newman mumbled, his chin pressed into the ground. 'I'm a reporter, in case you've forgotten.'

'Don't get sassy with me, *chum*! I'll ask you just once more. Then my nervous finger will pull the trigger. Come to think of it, this is an ideal spot. Afterwards I can dump your body over the cliff. Tide's about to go out. Why the two cars parked by the wall?'

'Porsche is my girl friend's. Motor conked out. She's been gone awhile on foot for help.'

'And you're about to conk out. I'll do it like they do on the films. Start counting up to ten. Who sent you? One . . . two . . . three . . .'

Huddled behind a huge boulder, Philip crouched shoulder to shoulder with Eve. Marler was behind another rock further back. He had his Armalite aimed at Craig's back, but Philip realized he dare not shoot. He'd get Craig but the brute might press the shotgun trigger as a reflex action when the bullet hit him. Newman's neck would be blown to pieces.

'I'm going to try and creep up on Craig,' Philip said, gripping his Walther.

'I'll try and create a distraction,' Eve replied, her teeth chattering, with cold or fear: maybe with both.

'If you do think of something, for God's sake time it so I'm close enough to ram my gun into the bastard's back.'

'I'm not an idiot . . .'

Philip stood up, began walking forward, keeping to the soft arid turf which carpeted the Tout on either side of the track. His footsteps made no sound as he clenched his teeth and came closer to Craig. If the brute turned round the range of his weapon was still greater than that of his Walther. He narrowed the gap, wondering what on earth Eve had in mind.

Behind the boulder Eve searched quickly among a pile of stones, found a large round one. She took a firm grip on it, stood up while Marler, puzzled, watched her.

Philip was within a foot of Craig when Eve hurled the stone with all her force against the drystone wall. Its impact made a sharp crack.

Startled, Craig moved the shotgun away from Newman as he began to turn. Newman grabbed the barrel, thrust it well away from himself. At that moment Philip rammed his Walther into Craig's back.

'My bullet will smash your spine. Keep very bloody still. That's a good boy. Now let go of the gun slowly . . .'

As Craig released his grip on the weapon Newman, still gripping it by the barrel, hauled it well out of his attacker's reach. He stood up as Marler ran up to them.

'Are you all right?' Marler asked.

'Fine.' Newman flexed his right hand. 'But I do have a little unfinished business.'

He suddenly clenched his hand into a fist, hit Craig with a haymaker to the jaw. The big man collapsed. Newman checked his pulse.

'Out cold, but that's all. I guess he'll stay that way for half an hour.'

'We continue watching?' Marler asked.

'Of course.'

'Then I'd better tie up the parcel . . .'

He produced one of several handcuffs he carried, bent down, turned Craig over on his back, clasped both wrists behind him, handcuffed them together. He next took out two pieces of cloth from his capacious pocket. He tied the dark handkerchief round Craig's eyes, looked up.

'That will disorientate him when he comes to. This will keep him quiet as a babe.'

He twisted the white cloth into a makeshift gag and applied it across Craig's mouth. Then he dragged his 'parcel' across and shoved it against the drystone wall. Newman turned to Philip, who was slipping his Walther inside its holster.

'Thank you, Philip. You probably saved my life – and even I didn't hear your silent approach.'

'You should thank Eve,' Philip explained as she came up to them. 'She created the diversion that caused Craig to shift his weapon away from you.'

'Really?' Newman stared at Eve in surprise. 'Well . . .'

'Glad you approve.' Eve made a pantomime of studying her long shapely fingers. 'Maybe there'll come a time when you realize a woman can be useful.'

'That time has come.' Newman held out his hand, gripped hers. 'Thank you. You're something else again.' His tone became brisk. 'Now we resume watching Grenville Grange, knowing it's not as unoccupied as it looks. Incidentally, how did Craig come up behind me?'

'Because we weren't watching closely enough,' Eve

said bluntly. 'Philip and I were whispering to each other.'

'And I was checking my Armalite,' Marler added. 'Out of the corner of my eye I did see Craig slip through that gap where the wall has crumbled. God, for a man that size, he moved quickly. It only seemed to take him an instant to come up behind you and jab his gun into your neck.'

'That's all right,' Newman replied. 'But I suggest from now on, Marler, you take up a position by that gap. Philip, you find a boulder close to Marler and back him up. Take Eve with you. Now I resume watching.'

He dropped to the ground at the end of the wall as though nothing had happened. Reaching for the binoculars he'd let go of he checked the focus on the house and began waiting. No point in telling the others, but he was pretty sure now something was going to happen.

# 7

Butler, seated behind the wheel of his Fiesta, jammed the top on his coffee flask, thrust it into the door pocket. Still waiting in the car park, he had the window open to hear anything coming from the ferry and the wind off the sea was raw. He could hear the crash of waves on the nearby beach, see a fleet of black clouds approaching the Purbecks.

What had alerted him was the arrival of another bus. Shortly afterwards he heard motorcyclists coming at a steady pace. Three men clad in black leather astride their machines headed towards the Purbecks. Butler started his engine, then paused.

A gleaming black stretch limousine with amber-tinted windows glided past. Behind it followed two more outriders.

'Jesus!' he said to himself. 'Nield did say royalty.'

He waited a short time, then drove out after the limo, keeping well back. No view through the rear window, which was also tinted. This stretch of road was lonely with a bleak stretch of swampland to his right. Reed islands protruded above the water. To his left a thorn hedge blotted out the sea.

'You should have waited a mite longer,' he told himself.

In his mirror he saw a single motorcyclist in black leather thundering up behind him. Like the earlier outriders he was astride a powerful machine, a Fireblade. As he drew up alongside him Butler saw the word *Police* painted on his jacket. The newcomer waved to him to pull over and stop. Butler obliged.

The motorcyclist shoved off his helmet, exposing a tough, hard-jawed face with eyes too close together. Butler said nothing as the cyclist shouted at him through his open window. His head was practically inside Butler's car.

'You following that limo?' the rider demanded.

'I'm going home. It's a free road.'

'That's an important personage.'

'What's the difference between a person and a personage?' Butler asked innocently.

'Police business. Turn round, drive back to the ferry.'

'Why should I?'

'Because I say so. Get that machine turned round now.'

Butler lit a cigarette. He leant his arm on the edge of his open window.

'Can I see some identification, please? That you really are police?'

The rider took off his right glove, he shoved his hand inside his jacket. As Butler saw the hand coming out gripping the butt of a large gun he leaned over, pressed his cigarette on the back of the man's bare hand.

There was a yelp of pain as Butler reached out, grabbed the gun. It was a 7.65mm Luger. Not a handgun the British police ever carried. He opened his car door and shoved with great force. It hit the motorcyclist. Everything toppled over sideways. Man and machine.

The rider was trying to get out from under his machine when Butler tapped him over the skull with the butt of the Luger. Unconscious, he sprawled back in the road.

Butler, checking there was no other traffic, went through every pocket swiftly. No sign of a warrant card or anything else confirming he was a policeman. Butler heaved him up by the shoulders, dragged him across the road, hurled him into a thick patch of gorse bushes. His cargo disappeared. It took Butler no time to find him, to unbutton the jacket and haul it off the inert body by sheer brute force. As Butler had estimated, they were about the same build. Ripping off his windcheater, he slipped on the black jacket. Not a bad fit, he said to himself, and zipped up the front. Then he pushed the thug's body further into the gorse.

For a well-built man Butler could move with great speed. He had already switched off the engine of the Fireblade and he folded his windcheater, opened the pannier at the rear of the machine. Under a spare black jacket he found an assortment of handguns, five in all with spare ammo.

'We have a different type of policeman these days,' he muttered under his breath.

Putting on his gloves again, he carried the handguns, using the spare jacket as a makeshift tray. A few feet along the grass verge he found a gap in the hedge with a lake of muddy ooze beyond. He hurled each gun and saw them sink. The jacket followed the guns.

Hurrying back to the prone motorcycle, he lifted it upright, kicked out the prongs which held it in that

80

position. He had already detached the black helmet from the thug's head and he pulled it over his own head.

En route from the ferry he had noticed several sandy tracks leading off towards the sea on his right and he saw another one a few yards away. No wheel tracks. Who would want to drive down to sit on the beach in this weather, at this time of the year?

It took him barely a minute to back his Fiesta down the track out of sight, to park it behind some bushes. Locking it, he ran back to the Fireblade, pulling the visor of his helmet over his face. He slipped the Luger into the pannier. You never knew when it might come in handy.

Astride the Fireblade, he checked his watch. Three minutes since he had knocked the outrider unconscious. He fired the engine, took off at high speed along the deserted road. He was anxious to catch up the limo before it reached the turn-off to Swanage. He rode through the sleepy hamlet of Studland like the wind, saw the limo in the distance.

Butler breathed a sigh of relief. The limo was still proceeding at a civilized glide, showing no sign of speeding up.

'Must be a big egg inside that,' Butler said to himself. 'Doesn't like being shaken up into an omelette.'

He slowed down as the limo with its distant outriders drove straight on, passing the turn-off to the small seaside resort of Swanage. Soon, to his left, Butler saw the steep slopes of a range of the Purbeck Hills sweeping up just behind the country road, shaped like great barrows.

'Corfe next,' Butler said to himself. 'Next point is where do you turn there? On to Wareham or up into the hills?'

His question was answered as the limo turned left at the base of the mound on which the great stones of the ancient castle reared up, then through the old village of Corfe itself. Just at the end of Corfe the limo swung off to the right past a signpost that pointed to Kingston.

'Looks like Grenville Grange,' Butler commented under his breath as the wind hammered down a steep hill against his visor. 'I wonder where everybody else is? Tweed would be interested in this development . . .'


'You do realize we've been followed all the way from Park Crescent?' said Paula.

Behind the wheel of his car Tweed nodded as he came close to Wareham.

'A blue Vauxhall,' he said. 'One man, the driver. Now he's disappeared and we have a grey Jaguar keeping us company. Maybe they do it in turns, hoping to fool us. The Jag is probably a coincidence. It appeared only a few miles back.'

'You don't normally believe in coincidences,' she reminded him.

'Because behind the Jag is a blue Renault which, I think, is using the Jag to mask himself. All this is very promising.'

'Promising?' Paula queried in surprise.

'Yes, it means my wide enquiries into the activities of Leopold Brazil have triggered off anxiety.'

'It sounds as though you've provoked suspicion deliberately.'

'Well, I did ask a few contacts to spread the news that I was asking leading questions about His Lordship.'

'I might have guessed. Heavens, look at those fields. They are just lakes.'

They were crossing a bridge over a river into the main street of Wareham, which looked dead. Paula gazed at the ancient Georgian terraces, each house with its door painted a different colour.

'In good weather this looks like a nice sleepy place, I expect.'

'Very sleepy,' Tweed commented. 'Three murders within twenty-four hours. Which reminds me, I think it's vital we track down the real Marchat. I have a hunch he was heading for Heathrow on his way out of the country.'

'So we've lost him.'

'Not necessarily. While you were out of my office for a few minutes freshening up I called Jim Corcoran, Security Chief at Heathrow, gave him Newman's description of Partridge – apparently looks very like our will-o'-the-wisp, Marchat. I asked him to check all the early morning flights out of Heathrow. Especially to Europe.'

'Why Europe?'

'Because so many things are happening in Europe. That's where The Motorman has been most active. Don't mention him to anybody. And Brazil has at least two houses in Europe we know about. One in Paris at the Avenue Foch, another on the lakeside in Zurich.'

'Why are you worried about Leopold Brazil?'

'Because of rumours from sources I trust that he is planning some huge operation. Because he has such power – with his contacts at the highest levels. Because I have been warned off investigating him – and so have Lasalle in Paris and Arthur Beck in Berne. Here we are . . .'

Tweed turned left off South Street at a point where, beyond a bridge, Paula could see the grim-looking sweep of the Purbecks in the distance, their summits lost in a blanket of black clouds. He arrived outside the Priory, parked the car in a slot up against a stone wall near the entrance. As he did so the grey Jaguar pulled up alongside. The driver waved to Tweed.

'We have pleasant company,' Tweed remarked. 'You do know Bill Franklin, ex-member of Military Intelligence?'

'I call him Uncle Bill . . .'

Paula jumped out of the car as a tall man climbed out from behind the wheel of the Jaguar. She ran across and hugged him.

'I've been following you, Tweed,' Franklin said over her shoulder.

Franklin was a well-built man in his forties without a trace of fat on him. He was constantly smiling, and was clean-shaven with a strong jaw and a quizzical expression. He hugged Paula, released her from his embrace.

'Such a warm welcome on a day like this. Are you and Tweed having a rare holiday? You could both do with one.'

He gave her an infectious grin. Franklin spoke slowly with a public school accent that came naturally to him. His movements were slow, giving the impression of a lazy man who never hurried. Paula knew that in his quiet way he was very active. She had always been fond of him.

'So, you've been following us,' Tweed said with mock severity. 'May I ask why?'

'You just did.' Franklin smiled warmly. 'I've been busy. For a change. Decided to take a few days off. I was driving around looking for a decent hotel and spotted you passing me at a side turning. I said to myself, I'm in need of some good company and there it is. You could have knocked me down with the proverbial feather when I saw Paula with you.'

'Well, the Priory here is a very good hotel,' Tweed replied. 'Why not stay here? When I have a minute we can talk over old times.'

'Great idea. Let me . . .' He took Paula's bag off her. She remembered he was always courteous and kind. Inside reception they registered and the three of them were given rooms in the main hotel.

'Tell you what,' Franklin suggested, after registering, 'why don't we dump our bags in our rooms and meet up in the lounge? I could do with a cup of coffee.'

'Black and strong as sin, you used to say,' Paula reminded him.

'Did I? But I remember you have total recall for conversations.' He smiled his slow smile again. 'So I will have to be careful what I say to you. It's a bit early in the day for me to compromise myself.'

'When you two have stopped flirting . . .' Tweed interjected. 'And yes, Bill, we'll meet up in the lounge. Say in five minutes?'

Well beyond Kingston Butler slowed down, stopped his Fireblade. Some distance ahead of him the cavalcade – outriders and limousine – was entering a drive between high drystone walls. As it disappeared he eased his machine forward slowly – just in time to see huge wrought-iron gates closing slowly. No sign of anyone shutting them, so he guessed they were automatically operated by remote control.

Parking his machine on a grass verge, he walked slowly up to the gates, then quickened his pace. As he passed them he saw the limousine pulling up at the end of a long curving drive beyond where it forked. He stopped, bent down as though to adjust his footwear.

The outriders gathered round the limo. A large door in the grim dark house perched on a terrace was opened. A tall man he couldn't see clearly emerged from the rear of the limo, hurried agilely up the steps, disappeared inside the house, followed by the outriders who had parked their machines and removed their helmets. They tucked them under their arms and followed the tall figure like a military escort. The door closed.

Now the gates were closed he read the two words inscribed in gold, one on each gate. *Grenville Grange.*

'I guessed right,' he said to himself. 'They don't seem to have noticed they have one man missing. Or maybe his job is to stand sentinel outside. I'll wait awhile and see if anything more happens, then report to Newman . . .'

Newman, cold and stiff from lying on the ground at the end of the wall, raised his binoculars again. At the point where the drive curved he had a glimpse of the main drive coming up from the gates, had seen the cavalcade arrive.

'Go and tell Marler to hide in the back of my Merc,' he told Philip, who was lying alongside him. 'Tell Eve to get behind the wheel of her Porsche. Warn them both we may have to be ready for instant take-off down that track over Lyman's Tout. Order Eve that she is to come behind me. No arguments from her. Our lives may be at stake.'

'Will do . . .'

Newman waited a few more minutes, then raised his binoculars again. A terrace ran the full length of the back of the house and double doors had opened near a flight of steps.

A tall well-padded man with greying hair appeared. He was holding a huge dog on a leash, some kind of ferocious-looking wolfhound which tugged at the leash and then stood for a moment, sniffing the air.

'Damn!' Newman muttered. 'The wind's behind me and that nasty-looking beast may pick up our scent.'

'Horrible brute,' replied Philip, who had returned and dropped to the ground next to Newman. 'Imposing sort of chap. Oh, Lord, he's coming this way.'

The figure with the dog had descended the steps and was beginning to walk with brisk strides down the track where earlier Newman had driven towards the cliff edge.

As he drew closer Newman let his binoculars drop so they were looped round his neck and stared in disbelief.

'It can't be,' he said. 'We might as well stand up. He's going to see us.'

Despite the raw wind, the low temperature, the man coming towards them wore an expensive-looking midnight-blue suit, a white shirt, and a pale grey tie. His large head was held erect, his complexion was ruddy, his features were strong with a Roman nose and a wide mouth above a firm jaw. He walked with an air of complete self-assurance and had a commanding presence. He was very close when he left the track and stood on a large flat rock, the dog straining at the leash.

'Heel, Igor,' the tall man ordered.

The dog immediately sat beside its master, its mouth open, teeth showing, gazing at Newman as though it hoped it was supperlime.

'Mr Robert Newman, I presume,' the tall man remarked. 'I think as Stanley said to Livingstone, or was it the other way round?'

'One or the other,' Newman replied calmly. 'And you are right. Robert Newman.'

'Welcome to Grenville Grange. I am Leopold Brazil.'

# 8

Newman studied the large man before reacting: an aura of power seemed to emanate from him as he stood calmly, steady as the rock beneath him, with the full blast of the wind battering him. He had startlingly blue eyes and Newman realized he was in the presence of a most unusual and forceful personality.

'I once tried to interview you,' Newman recalled.

'Indeed you did.' The ghost of a smile crossed Brazil's

face. 'I rarely give interviews but now that I have met you I almost wish I had granted your request. Have you seen a minion of mine, a certain Carson Craig?'

'Yes. He's tied up behind the wall. He made a mistake. He threatened me with a shotgun.'

'Oh, Lord.' Brazil sighed. 'Actually he is one of my most able deputies. A brilliant administrator, but he has an evil temper. I am constantly telling him that he must control it. Could your friend beside you kindly release him and I will send him back to the house.'

'Do it,' Newman said quietly to Philip.

'I also observe you have two cars with you, one with a woman behind the wheel . . .'

Newman then realized that from his vantage point on the rock Brazil could see the vehicles over the top of the wall. He glanced at the Porsche. Eve, seated behind her wheel, had wrapped a scarf round her head and was now wearing tinted glasses.

'I trust you were not thinking of driving back down the track along Lyman's Tout,' Brazil continued in his amiable tone. 'I see they are pointed that way. It is a dangerous route. I urge you to return the way you used to come here – along my drive. The gates are shut but I will order Craig to open them for you.'

'I'm not sure that route might not be more dangerous,' Newman told him bluntly.

'Ah, a man of my own heart. Cautious, taking no chances unless compelled to.' Brazil chuckled. 'Mr Newman, I will sit with you in the front passenger seat and escort you to the road. We have to give Craig time to reach the house and operate the automatic gates.'

Inwardly, Newman was again taken aback, although nothing in his expression showed his surprise. Philip, who had earlier been given the key by Marler before hiding in the back of the Merc, had removed the blindfold and the gag and then unlocked the handcuffs.

Craig staggered to his feet, blinking, saw Newman, began stumbling towards him.

'You . . .'

'Craig!' Brazil's tone was like a man addressing a child. 'Don't make bad worse. Kindly keep your mouth closed. Go back to the house and open the gates. Mr Newman and his companions are leaving. I shall be sitting with Mr Newman before I bid him a safe journey and return to the house. *Move, man!*' he suddenly thundered.

Bewildered, Craig stumbled past the end of the stone wall, paused when he saw his shotgun lying on the ground.

'I . . . said . . . move . . . Craig,' Brazil ordered in a soft tone which seemed to scare his deputy.

As Craig was passing him Brazil handed over the leash holding the wolfhound, said nothing while Craig took charge of the dog and tried to hurry back to the house.

'We won't want this,' Brazil said briskly.

Leaping very athletically off the rock, he picked up the shotgun, checked it, took hold of it by the stock, and hurled it towards the sea. It vanished over the edge of the cliff. Newman was impressed by Brazil's physical strength – it had been a long way to hurl a heavy object.

'I'll travel in the Porsche,' Philip suggested, to Newman's relief.

He was thinking quickly in this bizarre situation, Newman noted. He had realized he couldn't travel in the rear of the Merc with Marler still curled up under the travelling rug.

'I'm riding with you,' Philip called out as he approached Eve. 'Newman leads and we follow. We're going out the way we came in.'

'What the hell is going on?'

'Just get ready to turn the car round and follow Bob.'

89

'You are bossy.'

'When it's necessary,' Philip rapped back.

Newman opened the front passenger door of his car and Brazil slipped into the seat, fastening his seat belt. He laughed.

'That's a precaution in case you get it wrong and take us over the cliff.'

'I'll try and avoid doing that,' Newman responded jocularly. 'How did you know there was someone behind the wall – that I was there?' he asked as he eased his way back into the grounds.

'Elementary, my dear Watson. I like neatness. When I was last here I gave orders for the pebble track we are about to drive onto to be raked over. When I came out on to the terrace I noticed wheel marks. A simple deduction.'

The wheels were crunching over the pebbles now with the Porsche close behind them. Brazil clasped his large hands, very relaxed.

'You see, the gates are open,' he remarked as they drove slowly round the corner of the house. 'Mr Newman, would you mind if I asked you an important favour?'

'Ask away. It depends on whether I can help you.'

'I am very anxious to meet Mr Tweed during the next week.'

For the third time Brazil had thrown Newman off balance. It only took him seconds to phrase a reply.

'I think Tweed will want to know why you wish to see him.'

'Naturally. He is a most formidable man. I would like to discuss with him the present state of the world. To get his views on what should be done to correct a chaotic situation. I am talking globally, you can tell him.'

'If he's willing, how does he contact you?'

'If it does not seem impolite I will contact him. Then I will suggest a mutually convenient rendezvous.'

'I'll certainly pass the message on when I next see him.'

'Thank you. I am grateful.'

In his rear-view mirror Newman was checking for signs of activity outside the house. There were none. Again the place looked unoccupied. He pulled up when the two cars were outside the gates and safely on the road. Brazil climbed out, kept the door open, stared straight at Newman.

'If you still want that interview, I may some day feel able to oblige. I bid you a safe journey. I can say with sincerity I have enjoyed your company, brief as it has been.'

He held out his hand and Newman took it. Brazil gave him a warm smile and Newman noticed he had a strong grip. He waited a minute while Brazil made his way back up the drive with long, vigorous strides as the gates closed behind him.

A short distance along the road to Kingston, Butler stood by his Fireblade on the verge. He had removed his helmet so they would recognize him. Newman waved him on.

Butler took off on the machine, staying thirty yards or so ahead of the Mercedes with the Porsche following it. This time Butler was acting as outrider, on the lookout for any signs of an ambush. Newman could have told him there wouldn't be one. As the Mercedes rounded a long curve he called out to Marler to get up and sit in a corner while the Porsche was briefly out of sight.

'You have just met Leopold Brazil,' he told Marler as his companion settled himself in a corner.

'At least I've heard his voice. Very striking. But he didn't know you had company back here.'

'I'm perfectly sure he *did* know. It would be a great

91

mistake to underestimate Brazil,' Newman warned. 'But he hasn't seen you, which is an ace up our sleeve.'

'How can he possibly know about Tweed?'

'Oh, you haven't caught on.' Newman smiled. 'I am quite sure Mr Brazil knows just about everything that is going on . . .'

# 9

In the lounge at the Priory Hotel Paula sat with Tweed as they waited for Franklin to join them. Coffee, cakes, and biscuits had been served for three people. There was no one else in the large comfortable room with French windows overlooking the spacious garden and the path leading to the Boathouse.

'Actually,' Paula whispered, 'I saw Bill Franklin in his car at the side turning where he spotted us. I didn't say anything to you because you were talking, explaining something to me.'

'Your eyes met?' Tweed queried.

'Very definitely.'

'Then maybe it was a genuine coincidence. Bill is fond of you,' he teased her.

'That's all there is to it,' she said sharply.

'I want to find out how he's spending his time nowadays since—'

He broke off as Franklin entered the room. He looked very handsome, wearing a heavyweight safari jacket and trousers. He smiled, sat next to Paula on the couch with Tweed beyond her.

'Sorry to keep you waiting. Coffee. Just what I need to wet my whistle.'

'What are you doing now, Bill?' Tweed asked immediately. 'Or are you ex-ex-Military Intelligence?'

'Now what, I wonder, does that cryptic remark imply?'

Franklin smiled, thanked Paula as she handed him a cup. He began munching a cake, leaning forward so he could see Tweed, who replied quickly.

'It means, Bill, have you gone back into Military Intelligence?'

'Now would I tell you if that were the case?' Franklin joked. 'Actually, I decided it was time I made a little money. You know how extravagant I am. Over a year ago I established a small chain of private detective agencies in Europe. They're thriving. I call the outfits by what I thought was rather an original name, *Illuminations*.'

'That's a very clever name,' commented Paula. 'I guess it means you find things out people are trying to conceal. You *illuminate* a situation.'

'Spot on,' Franklin told her. 'And with the contacts I established when I *was* Military Intelligence I'm doing rather well. Why don't you use me, Tweed, some time?'

'Where are you based?'

'Geneva, Paris, and Rome.'

'Must be an advantage,' Paula said between bites out of a cake, 'that you're fluent in French, German, and Italian.'

'It helps. Finding good staff was the problem.'

'What about London?' Tweed asked.

'I toyed with the idea, but there's a flock of outfits over here. I'm still thinking about it. *Are* you two taking a break?'

'We're down here investigating three weird murders – my interest was triggered off by something odd which happened on the Continent.'

'Playing it close to the chest, as usual.' Franklin grinned at Paula. 'Getting blood out of a stone is a piece of cake compared with getting Tweed to open up.'

'You are muddling your metaphors,' Tweed pointed out.

He looked up as the proprietor appeared at the door and beckoned to him. Excusing himself, he joined the proprietor in the privacy of the hall. His host had a worried look, which was unusual.

'Sorry to interrupt your conversation, Mr Tweed, but a Chief Inspector Buchanan from Scotland Yard called here and asked me if Mr Robert Newman was staying with us. I had to say he was and this Buchanan wanted to know if he was in his room. I told him he'd gone out, that I didn't know where or for how long.'

The proprietor paused, clearly embarrassed. Tweed said nothing, gave no indication that he had heard of Newman.

'He then went on,' the proprietor continued, 'to ask me if a Mr Tweed was registered with us. I told him no – because at that moment you had not appeared. I saw no reason to tell him you had stayed with us before.'

'Thank you for telling me. We are just going out to keep an urgent appointment. And *I* have no idea when we'll be back.'

'I'm sorry to . . .'

'Think nothing of it.'

Tweed walked casually back into the lounge. Franklin was joking with Paula who looked very relaxed.

'I'm afraid we'll have to leave immediately,' Tweed told them. 'We may not be back until it's time for dinner.'

'Mind if I accompany you?' asked Franklin. 'But if it's hush-hush I'll steer clear.'

'You can come. You'll hear about what's been happening sooner or later. But I'd like us to move now . . .'

The wind seemed even more bitter as they crossed the cobbled yard outside and went to their cars. Franklin reached into his Jaguar, brought out a heavy fawn raincoat, which he donned. It had wide lapels and broad belt; Paula thought he looked very much a military type.

Tweed put on the new coat Paula had pushed him into buying but she felt quite comfortable in her windcheater.

'What is our destination?' Franklin called out.

'Just follow us.'

Tweed dived behind the wheel of his car, turned on the engine, and began backing at speed. He turned, headed for the small square which led into South Street.

'Where are we going, then?' Paula asked.

'Anywhere outside Wareham. Buchanan put in an appearance. Asked for Newman, then for me.'

'For you? That's strange.'

'He's very shrewd is our friend, Roy Buchanan. I think he was aiming a shot in the dark. Hang on, there's Bob coming back, with Philip in Eve Warner's Porsche on his tail. And Butler, dressed like a gangster, on a Fireblade behind them.'

Tweed pulled up in the Georgian square tucked away from South Street. Other cars were parked but no one else was about. Jumping out, Tweed ran over to Newman, who had braked.

'Don't ask any questions. Don't go near the Priory – just follow me. That's Bill Franklin in the Jaguar. He turned up unexpectedly and is coming with us. Wait a sec . . .'

He ran to the Porsche and Eve lowered her window. Tweed addressed Philip across her.

'Get out. Move. Then get into Bob's car.' He looked at Eve, studying Philip's new friend as Philip left to join Paula. She stared straight back at him. 'I assume you are Eve Warner,' he began, and she interrupted him.

'And how, may I ask, do you know about me? My name?'

'Newman mentioned you when he phoned me. I hope that you won't mind, but we are all going to a meeting.'

'Who are you to try and push me around?' she asked cockily.

95

'My name is Tweed,' he said reluctantly. She was going to find out anyway, staying at the Priory. 'I would appreciate it if you would wait at the Priory – Philip will be back later.'

'I don't feel like staying on my own,' she informed him. 'And we've had an adventure. You might like me to tell you what happened . . .'

'Later. Excuse me.'

Tweed, feeling like a grasshopper, ran across to Butler.

'Harry, follow us.'

'News to tell you. And Pete Nield is still probably at that roundabout you told us to send him to. Or Monica did . . .'

'We've got to get away from here.'

'OK. But Pete is wasting his time.'

'Then we'll drive there and you can tell him to drive back to watch the Priory again. He's to resume looking for Buchanan to arrive.'

Tweed tore back to his own car, jumped behind the wheel, took off, turned left into South Street, across the bridge over the Frome, and out into the country.

'You *are* fit,' Paula remarked. 'You weren't even puffing when you came back.'

'Probably my frequent walks from my flat in Radnor Walk and back again in the evening. This isn't good,' he said, glancing in his mirror.

'What isn't good?'

'We have a regular convoy – first me, then Bob, followed by Franklin. And would you believe it? The Warner girl is coming up behind him in her blasted Porsche. At least Butler is keeping well back. Imagine if we run into Buchanan driving in the opposite direction. He'll spot us, do a U-turn when he can, and come after us.'

'Then let's hope we don't see Buchanan,' Paula said calmly.

'Don't be too hard on Eve,' Philip called out from the back. 'She practically saved Bob's life, maybe my own, too.'

'Really? And I thought I told you to get into Newman's car.'

'You did. But I've a lot to tell you.'

'Tell me now. While the attractive Eve isn't bending an ear to our conversation . . .'

Philip, keeping his recital of events terse, began with their drive to Grenville Grange and what had happened afterwards. Tweed's expression didn't change when he came to the arrival of Leopold Brazil with his wolfhound, Igor.

'So Mr Brazil would like to meet me,' Tweed commented when Philip had concluded his description of their experience. 'Well, he will have to wait.'

'Why?' asked Paula.

'Because I need a lot more information about what he is up to.'

He slowed down, cruising. He had reached the roundabout south of Stoborough Green, had spotted Pete Nield parked in his Sierra, apparently reading a newspaper. Tweed continued cruising so Butler wouldn't lose them after instructing Nield.

Behind them Eve had been aware of the motorcyclist following the Jaguar behind her. The rider had kept his visor down so she couldn't see his face. She also missed seeing Pete Nield as she forced herself to drive like a snail behind Newman's car.

As soon as Butler caught them up Tweed increased speed. Reaching the junction below Corfe Castle and before entering the village he turned right onto a quiet country road signposted *Church Knowle – Kimmeridge*. He slowed down. At intervals along this road he knew there were isolated cottages and very little traffic. The sort of road where children ran out without looking.

'Where are we going now?' Paula asked.

'Didn't you see the signpost? Eventually it is a dead end if the firing range operated by the Army is being used for target practice. Mostly tanks. Kimmeridge is a tiny place near the edge of the sea. Buchanan certainly won't be using this road.'

He was almost crawling round sharp bends and then on into open country. To their right a range of the Purbecks climbed steeply in grassy slopes, hemming in the road, which was little more than a tree-lined lane.

Tweed was passing a house, back from the road with land in front of it, when he signalled, stopped the car.

'What is it?' Philip called out.

'Well, I'll be damned,' replied Tweed, who rarely swore even mildly. 'I'm sure that chap outside this house is Keith Kent, the money tracer. I'd no idea he had a place down here. Let's go and have a chat with him . . .'

Newman switched off his engine, got out, and stood, as Tweed went down the long path to meet him. He recognized Keith Kent too, despite the fact that previously he had only seen him immaculately garbed as a City gent. He frowned as he watched.

Kent, despite the cold, wore a check shirt rolled up to his elbows and a pair of old corduroy trousers. He was chopping wood, slicing up a tree trunk. His arms were sinewy and he swung a heavy axe high into the air without any apparent effort. The axe thundered down, split a huge log into two. He was lifting the axe again when he saw his visitor.

'Hello, Tweed.' He greeted him in an upper-crust accent which was entirely unaffected. 'Good to see you. I'd stay where you are for a moment. Wood chips can fly off at an angle and do you no good at all.'

The large axe was whipped up in a fresh arc, brought

down with great speed, sliced straight through a huge log. Interesting, Newman was thinking to himself. Kent laid down the axe, turned to greet his visitors with a broad smile.

A slim man, of medium height, he was in his late thirties, early forties. Clean-shaven, he had thick dark hair, neatly trimmed, and shrewd grey eyes. He shook hands after wiping them on his trousers while Tweed made introductions. Suddenly aware that someone was standing close behind him, Tweed turned to find Eve waiting with a bleak look.

'Oh, and this is Eve Warner, a friend of Philip's. Keith Kent.'

Eve held out her hand after Kent had extended his own with an apology.

'Hope my mitts aren't sticky. Welcome to Bradfields. Excuse the attire. We ain't given to puttin' on nice duds down 'ere,' Kent explained with a grin as he mimicked a Cockney. 'Coffee, everyone? I could drink a litre. Come inside . . .'

The old house was built of brick covered with whitewash and with a thatched roof above the first floor. Inside Kent ushered them straight into a large living room with ancient leather armchairs scattered about, invited them all to sit down.

'I'll just make the coffee. How do you like it?'

'Black for me,' Eve chimed in quickly. 'No sugar.'

'I'll give you a hand,' Paula said, following Kent. She noticed Eve had sat down in a chair with her legs crossed, obviously with no intention of giving her host any aid. She heard Tweed say something which struck her as odd because she had seen him complete the task.

'Don't think I locked the car. Be back in a moment.'

With all the others inside he hurried down the path into the road. Butler was perched astride his machine just out of sight of the property. Tweed walked briskly up to him.

'I hoped you'd come out,' Butler said. 'I left my car hidden down a track near Studland. I'd like to go back there now and retrieve it.'

'Do that. Then go back to the Black Bear and I'll be in touch. Where did you get the Fireblade?'

Butler explained what had happened briefly when he had seen the escorted limo with tinted windows pass him after coming over via the ferry.

'You did well. Very well. Look after yourself . . .'

When he returned to the house he made for the kitchen. It struck him as odd that there was no sign with the name Bradfields. Paula was pouring coffee from a large jug into cups on a tray.

'Look,' she said, 'Wedgwood. Keith has some lovely chinaware.'

'Keith indulges himself when he can't afford to,' Kent said and grinned. 'If you can put some work my way it would be welcome.'

'Investigate where Leopold Brazil gets all his money from,' Tweed whispered. 'It's urgent.'

They went into the living room with Kent insisting on carrying the heavy tray. Paula served coffee, not looking at Eve as she filled her cup. Not that Eve noticed: she was too busy chatting up Bill Franklin. Philip didn't look too happy at her enthusiasm.

Tweed sat in an armchair, sipped his coffee, and let the others do the talking. He noticed Philip's annoyance but he also noticed that he was scanning the room, looking for clues to Kent's personality and interests. He was doing his job.

Newman appeared relaxed, glancing first at his host and then at Franklin and was unusually quiet. Along one wall were shelves crammed with books from floor to ceiling. He had just seen that a number dealt with the history of old British banks when the house shook. *Thump! Thump! Thump . . . !* Six times altogether.

'What on earth is that?' Eve cried out. 'It sounded like thunder but then again it didn't.'

'Not to worry,' their host assured her. 'It's the tank range at nearby Lulworth practising. Gunfire from the tanks. At Bovington Camp, to be precise.'

'I wouldn't like to live here,' she said tactlessly.

'Oh, you get used to it. Like living near a railway line.'

Tweed leaned across, laid a finger on Kent's arm to attract his attention. He kept his voice low while the others continued chattering away.

'Keith, could we go for a short walk? I'd like to stretch my legs and get your opinion on an insurance problem.'

The reference to insurance was for Eve's benefit. Already Tweed suspected she had the gift of listening to one conversation and eavesdropping on another. Kent asked her, as he stood up, had she got a good job in London.

'A very good job.' Her eyes gleamed. 'In security. I can't give you any details. I had to sign a piece of paper.'

The Official Secrets Act? Tweed wondered. He stood up as Kent prepared to leave, opening a cupboard and taking out an expensive suede jacket which looked as though it had not been worn before. He apologized as he slipped it on.

'Hope you don't mind my leaving you for a few minutes. I am the host, I know . . .'

'I'll look after everyone,' Paula said quickly.

'Then I'd like some more coffee,' Eve said casually.


As they walked down the path from the house Kent gestured towards the land on either side, scruffy grass which was waterlogged.

'Step off this path and you're into a quagmire. I hear it's been raining solidly for a week. Dorset is under water. Lucky I've got that stone patio near the house or I

101

wouldn't have been chopping logs. Now, what is it you really want to talk to me about?'

'You've heard about Sterndale Manor going up like a torch?' Tweed asked.

'No, I only got down here from Heathrow soon after the crack of dawn. You were lucky to catch me.'

'Heathrow? Been on your travels again, Keith?'

'Just a short trip to Paris. Waste of time. My potential client wouldn't give me enough data to go on. I insisted he paid my expenses. Bloody nuisance. I came back on the first flight and hared down here to get away from it all. But you've something on your mind. Is it to do with my checking on Leopold Brazil?'

'Yes. Of course you know about bearer bonds?' Tweed enquired.

'Usually issued by the big international oil companies. Other large conglomerates, too. They're a way of moving – or storing – really large sums of money. A single bearer bond can be worth a huge amount of money. The weakness is you have to guard them like gold – they have nothing on them to show the owner. So they're totally negotiable anywhere in the world. One bond could be worth six figures in pounds. You know this. Why are they significant?'

'Because General Sterndale, who perished in the inferno along with his son, Richard, kept the bulk of the bank's capital in a large old safe in his house.'

'God! Does that mean Sterndale will go bust if the bonds have been reduced to ashes?'

'No. Apparently he kept enough funds at his different branches to keep them solvent.'

'How do you know this?'

'Someone I trust who was close to him told me. But I'm wondering if the bonds were no longer in that safe. A number of other private banks in Europe have had bearer bonds stolen, especially in France and Switzerland . . .'

'That's true.'

'Check out what form their capital was in.'

'This is concerned with my checking out Leopold Brazil?'

'Yes. Where did he get all this money from is the big question. And watch your back.'

'Will do. I'd better warn you this is going to cost you.'

'Bill me.'

'When you leave you ought to drive on to Kimmeridge. An interesting chap lives in a tiny cottage called the Bird's Nest. Useful bloke. I bumped into him in Paris. He's called Archie . . .'

# 10

When they returned to Bradfields Tweed had decided that a visit to Archie, the informant Marler also had met during his trip to Paris, would have to wait.

Marler had stayed in the back of Newman's car while the others were Kent's guests. Tweed had not invited him, which was enough to tell him, 'Stay under cover . . .'

The Mercedes was parked several yards behind Tweed's car and Marler had remained huddled in his corner. Now he wore wrap-around dark glasses and a deerstalker hat, which would make it impossible for someone who had not met him to recognize him.

Going into the house Tweed was surprised to find Eve in the kitchen with Paula, helping her with washing the dishes. Had Paula bulldozed her into giving a hand? The two women seemed to be chatting amiably. As Tweed entered Eve looped a tea towel over a wire hung above an old-fashioned stove to dry.

'Job's done,' she said cheerfully. 'What's next?'

'Back to the Priory for lunch, if we're not too late. Which I hope is not the case . . .'

As Kent accompanied them into the front garden Newman walked along a paved path leading to the patio where Kent had been chopping wood. Lifting the axe, Newman swung it high, brought it down on a very large log and split it into two smaller pieces.

'One more for the fire,' he said to Kent.

They thanked him for his hospitality and headed for their cars. Newman led the way alongside Tweed a short way ahead of the others.

'That's a very heavy axe,' he commented as they went out on to the road.

'Who is that chap who likes to keep to himself?' Eve asked chirpily. 'The man in the back of Bob's car.'

'A friend who came along for the ride,' Tweed said quickly.

'If it's all right with you I think I'll travel back with Eve in the Porsche,' Philip suggested.

'Why not?' said Tweed agreeably.

Paula joined him in his car, Tweed did a three-point turn and headed back for Corfe and Wareham, leaving the others to follow.

'Did you have to drag Eve into the kitchen by the hair?' Tweed asked.

'Not at all. She volunteered to help, just came in with me. She's a funny girl. She can be warm and friendly, and at other times she's almost rude.'

'She feels the need to assert herself, particularly in the presence of a number of men, would be my guess. I noticed Newman was very quiet while we were in the house.'

'So did I. He was studying our host and Franklin.'

'So, which one intrigued him – and why? Was it Franklin, or Kent?'

*   *   *

104

They parked their cars on the Quay, the small square on the edge of the Frome. After putting money in the meters they walked the short distance to the Priory. They met trouble the moment they entered the hotel. In the shape of Chief Inspector Buchanan.

'Tweed, Newman, I need to talk to you both. On your own. *Now.* The lounge is empty. Follow me . . .'

'Really?' Tweed exploded. 'We've had no lunch and if we don't get it now we go hungry!'

'That's your problem.'

Buchanan was a tall lanky man in his forties, slim and normally with a languid manner. His grey eyes glared at Tweed. Behind him stood his assistant, Sergeant Warden, a tall clean-shaven man who always reminded Tweed of a wooden Indian. This time Warden came to life.

'It is essential the Chief Inspector questions you now.'

'Who asked you?' Tweed rapped out with a rare burst of apparent aggression.

'The lounge,' Buchanan said firmly, fingering his neat brown moustache.

'You have a warrant for our arrest?' Tweed demanded.

'No, of course not . . .'

'Then we're having lunch first.' Tweed glanced into the dining room where a waitress was hovering, wide-eyed. 'May we, please, all have lunch? Sorry we are rather late.'

'That's all right, sir,' the waitress replied. 'The chef is ready when you are.'

'I said the lounge,' Buchanan repeated, rasping. 'I have a very busy day.'

'Then you have two alternatives,' Tweed told him. 'If you have business elsewhere I suggest you go about it. Otherwise wait in the lounge and we will come in when we have finished a leisurely lunch.'

'You're supposed to cooperate with the police,' Buchanan snapped.

'Not at the drop of a hat – and when we're hungry. I am not arguing the point one moment longer.'

'There have been three murders I am investigating,' Buchanan said after he had come close to Tweed.

'Then what are you hanging about here for?'

'I'll expect you in the lounge after you've had your lunch. Don't take too long . . .'

'We'll take as long as we like. I'm not getting indigestion for anyone. Incidentally, you can get coffee in the lounge, and it's very good here . . .'

On this note, spoken in a genial tone, Tweed entered the dining room.


He skilfully manoeuvred the table placings so that he would be seated at a table by the rear wall with Paula, Newman, and Philip. Taking Eve by the arm he ushered her to another table some distance away, overlooking the garden.

'Bill,' he said to Franklin, 'would you mind looking after Eve?'

'It will be my pleasure,' Franklin agreed with zest.

'Afterwards,' Tweed went on as they sat down, 'we'll be grilled by Buchanan. I don't think you'd enjoy that, so Bill, why not take Eve for a drive out into the country? Leave the dining room quietly before we do.'

'What about Philip?' Eve demanded.

'In a few minutes I'll send him over to join you at this table. Then he can come with you on your jaunt. Don't come back too early . . .'

'What are you up to?' Paula asked quietly after they had ordered. 'I saw you scribble a brief note before you left the car when we arrived. You screwed it into a ball and tossed it into Marler's lap as you passed Bob's car.'

'The note instructed him to go straight back to the Black Bear and stay under cover with Nield – and Butler when he gets back with his car. Now, Philip, if Buchanan should grab you, you're down here with a girl friend on holiday. Don't tell him anything else. I suggest you now go and join Eve and Bill – and later go with them for a ride in the country.'

'I'll go over to their table now, then.'

'He didn't need much encouragement,' Newman commented. 'What's the strategy in coping with Buchanan? He's on the warpath.'

'You and I – with Paula – came down here because we thought Philip would be on his own. You, Paula, insisted on coming. We found he'd met a girl only after we got here. Buchanan knows how deeply affected Philip was – is – by the death of his wife, Jean.'

'And what about people like Marchat?' Paula queried.

'Never heard of him. I'm surprised Buchanan knows about Marchat . . .'

'Partridge,' Newman warned.

'Quite right. But Buchanan has caught on to Partridge very quickly – he did refer to *three* murders.'

'That's because of me,' Newman explained. 'Before I left Devastoke Cottage with Marler I slipped into the kitchen, where the phone is. I called Dorchester police anonymously, put a silk handkerchief over the mouthpiece to disguise my voice. Simply told them there was a dead body there, at least I thought the man was dead, so would they also send paramedics. I couldn't just walk out and leave the poor devil to rot for days.'

'You were right, again. But why Dorchester?'

'I guessed Buchanan would have established his base at Wareham police station on West Street, on the outskirts. We needed time to get clear. Dorchester would have to phone Wareham and ten-to-one Buchanan would be out.'

'Good thinking. Ah, here's the main course. I could eat a horse.'

'Let's hope you're not going to,' joked Paula.

'Not here. This is a first-rate hotel. Fuel up – we need full stomachs before we face my old friend, Buchanan . . .'

'You were right, Tweed,' Buchanan greeted them with a dry smile. 'The coffee here is excellent. Do sit down and relax.'

Tweed went on full alert inwardly. He had not expected such an amiable approach. Buchanan was a dangerous opponent, experienced at throwing people off guard. He had arranged the seating cleverly.

With Sergeant Warden, notebook at the ready, Buchanan was ensconced on a couch, long legs crossed behind a wide table. Chairs for his guests were arranged on the other side of the table, upright chairs with arms.

Tweed, Paula, and Newman had just sat down when Buchanan leaned forward. He stared at Tweed.

'Ever heard of a man called Marchat?'

'March-what?'

'I'll spell it,' Buchanan snapped and proceeded to do so. He suddenly switched his gaze to Newman.

'You know a man called Partridge.'

It was a statement rather than a question, a typical Buchanan ploy.

'I have never in my life spoken to anyone with that name,' Newman said blandly.

'Made any anonymous calls to the police?' Buchanan rapped out almost before Newman had finished speaking.

'Not since this morning,' Newman said with a broad grin. 'It isn't really one of my pastimes.'

'I'm serious,' Buchanan snapped. He turned to Tweed. 'So why are you down here with such a heavy back-up?'

'Heavy?'

'There's three of you here and Philip Cardon was with you. Where has he disappeared to? Paula, maybe you would care to enlighten me.'

Paula gave the explanation Tweed had suggested. Coming from her the story carried conviction and Buchanan looked frustrated.

'You're all lying,' he said grimly. 'I suppose you're going to say you haven't heard about the three murders.'

'Are you talking about General Sterndale and his son, Richard?' Tweed enquired, jumping in.

'That's two of them. How do you know about them?'

'It's local gossip,' Tweed said in a bored tone. 'I have even heard the Sterndale mansion was burnt down, that it was arson . . .'

'It was! The place was sprayed with petrol and then set alight while Sterndale and his son were inside.' He switched his attention suddenly to Paula. 'You know a place called Devastoke Cottage?'

'How do you spell that?' she asked sweetly.

'Never mind.' Buchanan reached in his pocket, pulled out a small cheap wooden frame with a photograph, and tossed it into Tweed's lap. The frame slipped down between his legs under the table and came apart. As he bent down to retrieve it Tweed saw there were two photographs of the same man, one behind the other. He fiddled with the strut at the back of the frame, slipped one photo out, put his foot on it, brought the other photo and the frame above the edge of the table. He spent a short time re-assembling it so the full-length picture of a man in a garden fitted back inside the frame. Then he studied it.

'You've seen him somewhere before?'

Buchanan stared hard at Tweed. He'd made it sound like an accusation.

Paula slipped her shoulder bag onto the floor, rubbed her shoulder as though the strap had been uncomfortable. While Buchanan's attention was concentrated on

109

Tweed she bent down, picked up the photo as Tweed raised his foot, slipped it inside her shoulder bag. Her hand came up holding a handkerchief and she pretended to blow her nose.

'You've had enough time to study it,' Buchanan rasped.

'I've never seen this man in my life,' Tweed said truthfully. 'But he has an interesting face. Who is it?'

'Marchat. We're sure of that. We found that framed photo tucked under some foreign newspapers at the back of a drawer.'

'*Three* murders, you said,' Tweed reminded him. 'Who is the third victim? This man?'

'It was supposed to be, we think. Marchat lived on his own at Devastoke Cottage. We found a body there. But it was the body of a man called Partridge. We found an agreement to lease the cottage in Partridge's favour, as a tenant of Marchat. We believe the murderer made a mistake, thought Partridge, who had just moved in, was Marchat.'

'Why?' asked Newman.

'Because Marchat was a servant at Sterndale Manor, the only one. Normally he lived in five days a week and spent his weekends at the cottage.'

'Still don't understand,' Newman commented.

'We think Marchat could have given us a clue as to who torched Sterndale Manor, that he was supposed to have perished in the flames with the Sterndales.'

'I suppose it's a theory,' said Newman.

'So,' Buchanan said, taking back the framed photograph, 'none of you know anything? Is that it?'

'We know what you've told us,' Tweed said placidly. 'Oh, you mentioned you found that photo under some foreign newspapers. What country were they from?'

'Copies of the *Journal de Genève*. At least a fortnight old. Geneva. Switzerland . . .'

# 11

After talking to Tweed outside Bradfields, Keith Kent's remote house, Harry Butler headed back on the Fireblade through Corfe and Studland to where he had hidden his car.

He left the motorcycle perched on the grass verge and walked the last hundred yards to the entrance to the sandy track. He held his own Walther by his side, approached the Sierra cautiously. It appeared to be just where he had left it.

He listened for several minutes, heard only the endless crash of the waves on the invisible shore. He next got down on his knees, dropped flat, crawled under the car. No bomb had been secreted under the chassis. He ran back to the Fireblade.

Pushing it on the opposite side of the road, he found the disturbed gorse where he had left the unconscious body of the fake policeman. The body had gone.

'Probably hitched a ride to as near to Grenville Grange as he could manage,' he said to himself.

He became very active. He wheeled the machine back to a gap in the gorse hedge he had noticed, pushed the machine through to the edge of the quagmire beyond. He gave the Fireblade a hard shove, watched it enter the marsh, the front wheel sinking first, followed by the rest of the machine which disappeared under the evil ooze.

He had taken his windcheater and the Luger out of the pannier before getting rid of the Fireblade. He took off the black leather jacket, hurled it into the quag, then threw the Luger with his gloved hand. The gun vanished in seconds.

He returned to his car, was about to switch on the engine when he heard motorcycles coming from the direction of Studland and towards the ferry. Wishing he'd kept the Luger a little longer, he left the car, crept forward, hid behind a thick bush.

He was just in time to see the stretch limo with tinted windows cruise past, bound for the ferry. A single outrider, clad in black leather like the others, brought up the rear.

I think Tweed will be interested, Butler was thinking. Mr Big-Wig didn't spend long at the old dark house . . .

He waited a few minutes, then drove out, turned left for Studland and Wareham way beyond.

'I feel in need of some fresh air,' Tweed had remarked pleasantly to Buchanan when the interview ended.

They were walking up to the square leading to South Street when Buchanan, at the wheel of an unmarked car with Warden alongside him, passed them.

'I think we all coped with that rather well,' Paula mused.

'Certainly he couldn't get a handle on us,' Tweed agreed. 'But he didn't believe one word we'd said. Let's call in at the Black Bear . . .'

There was no sign of Buchanan's car when they crossed South Street. They found Marler leaning against the bar when they entered the hotel.

'This is Ben,' Marler said, introducing the barman, who greeted them cheerfully. 'He's standing in for a friend who's away on holiday. What are you drinking?'

'I need a double Scotch,' said Newman.

'A small glass of white wine, please,' Paula requested.

Tweed had ordered orange squash when he looked back at the doorway and saw Butler, standing in the corridor and beckoning to him. Saying he'd better go to the loo, Tweed joined him outside.

He listened while Butler told him about the motor-cade he'd seen returning the way it had come when he'd first spotted it.

'Tell Newman on the quiet I'll be back later. I'm on my way to that public phone box. I live in them . . .'

He was surprised when he dialled the private number at Heathrow of Jim Corcoran, security chief, to find his old friend was in his office.

'Any news about Marchat?' he asked.

'Yes. Good job it's February.'

'Why?'

'Not many passengers. So I had fewer passenger manifests to check. I even found the check-in girl who dealt with him. She remembers him. He seemed nervous.'

'I'm waiting for you to get to the point.'

'Always want everything yesterday. Anton Marchat was the passenger's full name.'

'I have his photo now. When I get back to London I'll send a copy to you by courier. See if the girl agrees the photo is of Marchat.'

'You never stop plaguing me. OK.'

'He caught a flight to Geneva,' Tweed said.

'Via Swissair. So why the devil do you ask when you know?'

'It was an educated guess.'

'Who said you were educated?' asked Corcoran.

'I have another favour to ask you. Now, don't blow a gasket. Do you know the security chief at Bournemouth International?'

'Yes, I do. Jeff is a pal I sometimes visit. Nice part of the world down there. What is it this time?'

'I'm pretty sure that Leopold Brazil will be taking off from that airport in his private jet – may already have done so. He'll have filed a flight plan, or his pilot will. It's very important I know his destination. If I could know it before he lands that would be marvellous.'

'Marvellous is the word,' Corcoran said cynically. 'I call you at Park Crescent?'

'Yes. And give the destination to Monica.'

'You owe me . . .'

Corcoran had gone off the line. Tweed knew he was very quick. He'd already be calling Jeff at Bournemouth International. Tweed dialled Park Crescent, explained the situation briefly to Monica.

'If Corcoran calls you, leave a message for me at the Priory. Just the destination.'

'Understood. Don't go, I've got a message for Marler. From someone called Archie. He asked for General and Cumbria Assurance, so I don't think he knows who we really are. Message was, could Marler go and see him urgently? Address, The Bird's Nest, Kimmeridge. I ask you! The Bird's Nest. Sounds cuckoo to me.'

Tweed chuckled briefly at one of Monica's rare bursts of humour.

'How would this Archie know Marler is down here?' he asked.

'I was going to tell you. He saw Bob Newman somewhere down there, thought Marler might be with him.'

'Did he? I'll pass on the message . . .'

Tweed *never* looked smug. It wasn't in his nature. But as he hurried back to the Black Bear he looked pleased. Everything was on the move, the momentum was building up.


Re-entering the bar, Tweed found Paula and Newman with Marler seated at a large table near the bay window overlooking South Street. Ben, the barman, was sitting between Marler and Newman. He started to get up but Tweed waved him back into his seat.

'I've still got my orange juice.'

'Ben,' Marler began, 'was waiting for you to come back. He's got something interesting to tell us about Marchat, apparently.'

'Really?'

Tweed sat down, relaxed. Ben was a small tubby man with a ruddy complexion and a mop of sandy hair. He smiled at Tweed, cleared his throat before speaking. Paula was amused. There was something about Tweed's appearance, his personality, which made people tell him things they wouldn't normally speak about.

'Ben is a stand-in, as I mentioned earlier,' Marler explained. 'For a friend, the normal barman who has gone off to the Caribbean for a month's holiday.'

'Marchat,' Ben started, 'came in about a week ago and had more to drink than usual. I wouldn't say he was tipsy but he wasn't sober either. He told me that he was worried. He'd spotted prowlers outside Sterndale's house several nights running. Always after dark. He reported what he'd seen to Sterndale but the General pooh-poohed his fears, said nobody could get into his house after he'd locked up.'

'About a week ago?' Tweed said thoughtfully.

'Yes, it would be that,' Ben agreed. 'I told him to tell the police, to go to the station in Worgret Road—'

'That's the name,' Newman interjected. 'I said West Street earlier.'

'Lot of people make that mistake.' Ben was still talking to Tweed, rubbing a hand over his plump face. He struck Tweed as a likeable, decent chap, not over-endowed with brains but shrewd in summing up customers. 'You see, West Street runs into Worgret.' He paused. Tweed waited, sensing Ben was wondering whether to tell him something else. He was sipping his orange juice when Ben started talking again, keeping his voice down even though no one else was in the bar.

115

'He told me something else which sounded important – Marchat thought it was very important—'

He broke off as two men entered and stood by the bar. One rapped a coin on the counter.

'Have to go serve them.' Ben looked indecisive. 'You know Bowling Green?'

'I do,' said Newman. 'A grassy bowl beyond the far end of North Street, or near the end. There's a footpath on the right past St Martin's Church . . .'

'That's it,' said Ben. 'I live near the River Trent, take my dog for a walk at eleven o'clock at night. Could we meet at Bowling Green? Mind you, the forecast is for a cold frosty night.'

'We'll be there,' Newman promised him. 'We may come along the East Walls . . .'

'That will get you there.'

The two men were getting impatient at the bar and again the coin was rapped on the counter. Newman glanced at them as Ben ambled back to the bar. He lowered his voice.

'I suppose they couldn't be more of Mr Brazil's kindly friends?'

'He might have left a couple behind to keep an eye on things, but I think it's unlikely.' Tweed was speaking very quietly. 'Butler has told me he saw the limo which brought Brazil to Grenville Grange was on its way back to the ferry. I think he's leaving the country again.'

'So we've lost him,' said Paula.

'Maybe . . .'


'I'd like a quiet word with Marler,' Tweed said as they left the bar and entered the corridor.

'We could walk further along this passage to what they call the Beer Garden,' Marler suggested. 'It won't be very comfortable at this time of year – wooden benches and a cobbled floor.'

'Ideal.' Tweed looked at Paula and Newman, but Paula spoke first.

'I noticed a place called the Old Granary down on the Quay. We'll wait there for you . . .'

'Good idea. Near where the cars are parked outside the Priory . . .'

Tweed was being cautious. He suspected Archie was very careful to keep his clients, the people he acted as an informant for, separate and unknown to each other. He doubted whether Newman knew Archie was Marler's informant.

Seated on a cold hard wooden bench, he told Marler about Archie's urgent call to Monica. He asked whether Marler would sooner drive there on his own.

'I don't think so,' Marler decided. 'You come in your own car, following me, and Newman and Paula can come in the Merc. When I get there, drive past the cottage a short distance and I'll consult Archie.'

'We'd better get moving.'

'Just so long as you don't mind if I drive like the wind to Kimmeridge. Archie sounds worried.'

'We might just manage to keep up with you.'


It was still daylight as the three cars drove along the winding road well beyond Corfe Castle. They had to slow down as they approached Keith Kent's house because of a bend just before they reached it. As they passed Tweed saw one of the curtains in Kent's living room twitch. They had been observed.

They turned left later where a narrow road was signposted Kimmeridge. They had been hemmed in on both sides with hedges and the odd copse of trees. Now the landscape opened out and in the gloom of the afternoon they saw the sea below them.

'Looks very rough,' Paula commented to Tweed. 'Think I'll suggest to Bob behind us he goes for a swim.'

'Tiny little place, Kimmeridge,' Tweed observed. 'It's one short lane with cottages on either side and the road stops at the sea.'

'Seems a good idea,' Paula joked. 'Lord, it looks like the end of the world.'

She thought she had never seen such a bleak outlandish coast. They had descended several hairpin bends to reach Kimmeridge and beyond was a large bay with grim-looking cliffs enclosing it. Not a sign of life anywhere.

Marler pulled up outside a dark two-storey brick cottage, very small and undistinguished. The other two cars cruised past, pulled up further along the street as Marler got out.

He walked briskly up to the front door which opened immediately. Archie stood in the doorway.

'Those two cars which followed you . . .'

'The safest people in the world. One is my chief.'

'Tweed,' said Archie. 'And Bob Newman. Is the lady Paula Grey?'

Marler stared at him in astonishment. He had never revealed any of the names to his host. Archie's knowledge was unnerving. He thought quickly.

'Yes, you're right.'

'Invite them in,' said Archie.

Again Marler was astonished but he didn't show his reaction. Going back into the road he beckoned, was about to introduce them when Archie closed the door, locked it, led them into a small untidy room with worn-looking armchairs and piles of books on the floor.

'Please sit down, Miss Grey, Tweed, Mr Newman.'

'He knew who you were,' Marler said hastily, catching a certain expression on Tweed's face.

'I'm in need of protection,' Archie explained. 'So the

more of you who know me the better. I'm making some coffee on the stove. Any takers?'

They all refused politely.

Paula was studying Archie with fascination. Small and lean, his face was pallid and he sported a small dark moustache which reminded her of pictures she'd seen of Hitler, but the resemblance ended there. At the corner of his mouth was a half-smoked dead cigarette and she suspected it stayed with him all the time he was awake. He had kindly, shrewd grey eyes and his movements were quick and nervous. It occurred to her he would be easy to recognize, which surprised her. He had a shock of grey hair which kept falling over his head. He spoke very fast but every word was clear. He sat down on a small wooden stool with his mug of coffee. From that moment on he was very still and all traces of nervousness disappeared.

'I'll get right to the point . . .' He addressed Tweed but included Paula in the conversation courteously at intervals.

'I'm talking about a man you will have heard of. Mr Leopold Brazil, the so-called billionaire. You've heard of the missing scientists who are the top men in their fields?'

'Yes,' said Tweed.

'They disappear overnight – with their wives – but often it is months before it is known they have gone. Always a good reason is given to their neighbours, their friends. It is a very well organized operation. Directly or indirectly they are all concerned with communications – especially with the so-called information superhighway.'

'Yes,' said Tweed.

'Brazil hires them for fantastic salaries. Somewhere he has established a high-tech laboratory with advanced equipment.'

'You really *know* this?' demanded Tweed, leaning forward.

'I have an informant. I can say no more at the moment.'

119

# 12

Tweed sat silent, made no attempt to press their host for further information. Paula had noticed that Newman had acted as though Archie was a stranger, someone he had never met before. It was the safety valve operating between an agent and an informant. Obviously Archie had kept Marler and Newman in separate compartments.

She really was intrigued by their host. Well dressed in a blue business suit, he wore surgical gloves. She tried not to look at them and glanced round the room. It hadn't been dusted for months. Archie seemed to read her mind.

'The gloves I wear intrigue you,' he said to her. 'By always wearing them I leave no fingerprints. The people who are searching for me are very skilled. Also, you have observed the room is covered in dust, does not look as though it has been inhabited for months. Which is the impression I wish to leave behind in case someone breaks in.'

'You're very thorough.'

'It is the secret of survival.'

'But what about the neighbours?' she persisted. 'Supposing someone questioned them?'

'They would say the place was empty for months, that it was a holiday home. In a tiny village like this the locals do not take kindly to strangers.' He looked at Marler. 'Do I get protection?'

'We haven't the manpower to guard you wherever you go night and day. What sort of protection?'

'Just for the next few hours. Tomorrow I need to be driven to Heathrow, but tomorrow is a long way off.'

'The boot of my car,' Newman suggested. 'It won't be

comfortable but you could stay overnight at the Black Bear in Wareham. Marler is staying there.'

'Comfort?' The cigarette at the corner of his mouth wobbled as he chuckled. 'Comfort is something I can live without. I have often slept rough – especially on the Continent. It is getting dark.' A frown creased his forehead.

Paula had noticed that dusk was beginning to fall. And there were no lights so Archie was becoming a silhouette in the gloom. He stood up.

'I will meet you all on the beach. Drive straight on through the village. I will join you. I have to clear up here. This mug has to be washed out. And there are other things to attend to. I will join you in a few minutes.'

'Can I help clearing up?' asked Paula as everyone stood up.

'Most kind, but I work faster alone.'

'Would I be inquisitive if I asked who you are afraid of?' coaxed Paula.

'Leave now. To answer your question, The Motorman is active. He killed the wrong man at Devastoke Cottage . . .'


They drove slowly down to the shore along a narrow road with arid fields on either side. It was dusk but the moon was up and Paula shuddered. The end of the world.

Pulling up in a flattened area above the sea which probably served as a car park during the season, Tweed switched the engine off. Paula got out, fastened the top button of her windcheater.

The bay was deserted with cliffs rising on both sides. A bitter wind blew off the sea, which was a chaos of churning waves. She looked back at Kimmeridge and saw specks of light. Newman was already busy with his open boot. She walked over to him and Marler stood watching.

Newman had hauled the travelling rugs out of the rear of his car, was arranging them inside the boot as a makeshift bed.

'He'll be able to breathe all right?' Paula queried.

'Plenty of air in there,' Newman assured her. 'I'll give two hoots on the horn occasionally,' he informed Tweed, who had joined them. 'Wait for me. I'll be checking to make sure Archie is OK. You can get him a room at the Black Bear?' he asked Marler.

'Easily. He'll probably want to stay in it. I'll tell the staff he's feeling exhausted and get a meal sent up to him. You'll be over from the Priory in the morning to take him to Heathrow.'

'I wonder where he's off to?' Paula mused.

'Don't ask him,' Tweed warned. 'He's one of the most remarkable characters I've encountered in a long time. And it's uncanny how he knows everything that's happening. Marler, you escort Newman back to Wareham.'

'Where are you off to?'

'I'm driving with Paula to Sterndale Manor.'

'The place will be a ruin,' Newman reminded him.

'Yes. But I like to observe for myself the scene of the crime. Probably goes back to the old days when I was a superintendent at the Yard.'

'And the youngest superintendent with Homicide in its history,' Paula piped up. 'What do we expect to find there?' she asked when Tweed shrugged at her remark.

'An old friend. Who the devil is this coming?'

Marler slipped a Walther out of its holster, held the weapon by his side. A scarecrowlike figure was cycling down the road towards them.

*   *   *

Paula gazed in disbelief at the man who jumped off his bicycle. He wore a battered old hat, a pair of glasses perched at a cock-eyed angle on the bridge of his nose, a shabby raincoat smeared with oil. It was only the dead cigarette at the corner of his mouth which told her this was Archie.

'Have to get rid of the bike,' Archie said urgently. 'I'll shove it off that cliff over there into the sea. Tide's on the turn.'

'I'll do that,' Paula said firmly.

'Thank you. Mind how you go.'

Archie stripped off the hat and the raincoat, exposing the same blue suit underneath. From a pannier at the rear of the cycle he took a travelling bag and joined Newman to climb into the boot.

Paula, by the light of the moon, pushed the bike a distance to her left uphill. Reaching a point where the cliffs were higher she took hold of the saddle, pointed the front wheel towards the sea, gave it a strong shove. As it went over a huge wave crashed against the cliff, threw spray high up in the air, and the cycle was gone. She hurried back as Tweed was instructing Newman and Marler.

'When Paula and I get back we'll have dinner at the Priory. Don't forget our eleven o'clock appointment with the bartender, Ben. Bob, you do know the way to Bowling Green? It will be dark.'

'There's a moon. Have fun with your mysterious friend at the manor . . .'


Leaving Corfe behind, Tweed accelerated up the steep winding hill, slowed to pass through Kingston, then drove higher. In his head he carried a map of Dorset and turned on to the tarred drive leading to Sterndale Manor. In the distance they saw arc lights shining on the wreckage. Policemen in uniform were moving about and a crane on the back of a small lorry was lifting something out of the carnage. Tweed slowed down as a policeman stood on the drive, hand held up.

'So that's your friend,' said Paula.

Behind the policeman Buchanan had appeared. He came up to the car and Tweed prepared for an argument. Instead, Buchanan looked at both of them and smiled cynically.

'As usual, your timing is perfect. Now you're here you might as well see.'

'See what?' asked Tweed, getting out of the car with Paula.

'The crane. What it's holding in its grab. The old General's safe. The trouble is the heat burst open the door a crack so everything inside will be burnt to ashes . . .'

A strong wind was blowing along the valley direct off the sea. They watched as the safe was lowered to the ground. Immediately a squad of men erected round it a large high canvas screen with a roof to ward off the wind.

'They're well organized,' Paula whispered.

'Buchanan always is,' Tweed replied.

He had just spoken when the Chief Inspector beckoned to them and they followed him inside the canvas tent as a policeman lifted a flap, closed it behind them. Buchanan put on a pair of asbestos gloves and carefully lifted the door open. Inside was a mess of black ashes. Nothing had survived.

'We'll send them to the experts,' Buchanan remarked, 'but I'm not hopeful we'll ever detect what was inside the safe.'

'Maybe I could help?' Tweed suggested. 'My people have been working on a very advanced technique for detecting what was written or typed on papers burnt to ashes. They've had a lot of success.'

'Really?' Buchanan thought about it as Sergeant

Warden entered the tent. 'Then supposing I do give you a sample and you crack it? As a quid pro quo would you explain the technique to us?'

'Agreed.'

Buchanan carefully used a scoop to extract some of the ash, putting it into a samples bag Warden handed him and sealing it. Warden gave him a larger bag and Buchanan put the smaller one inside it, sealed the larger bag. He handed it to Tweed.

'That would be safer inside my shoulder bag,' Paula suggested.

'Here it is, then.'

Emerging from the tent Tweed and Paula, with Buchanan standing beside them, gazed at the wreckage. One chimney stack had survived and was surrounded with barbed wire. Buchanan pointed to it.

'Unstable. It will have to come down.'

'What a lot of history we're gazing it,' Paula said. 'Generations, some of whom probably feuded with each other. The end of an era.'

'It was very professional,' Buchanan informed Tweed. 'We know now that not only was petrol used but that it was backed up with thermite bombs. Ruthless.'

'I'll keep in touch,' said Tweed, 'whatever the outcome of our experiments. It may take a few days.'

'Is that all?' Buchanan sounded surprised. 'Maybe you are on to something . . .'


Tweed was driving off South Street, entering the Georgian square where the short lane led off it down to the Priory, when a parked car flashed its lights at him twice. He stopped. Paula produced her Browning automatic, touched Tweed's sleeve with her left hand.

'Be careful. There's no one else about. And this place is dark.'

Which was true. It was dimly illuminated with lanterns suspended from wall brackets.

A slim figure emerged from the car, which Tweed now saw was a Rover. He recognized Keith Kent, dressed in his suede jacket and well-creased grey slacks. He had his window lowered as Kent peered in, nodded to Paula.

'A word in your shell-like ear,' he said to Tweed.

'Shall I take the wheel and drive on to the Priory?' Paula suggested, relieved that it was Kent.

'Not necessary, my dear,' Kent assured her. He smiled. Because, unlike Franklin, he only smiled occasionally, when he did he gave the impression he genuinely liked someone. 'I'm sure you know at least as much as Tweed about what is going on.'

'We'll get out and wander round the square with you,' Tweed decided.

'Good idea. I prefer the three of us on our own. I phoned the Priory from a box in South Street. They told me you were still not back so I waited here. I've seen Bob Newman come back in that old Merc of his. A little while afterwards that chap Franklin returned with the girl, Eve Warner, and Philip Cardon in the back.'

It was eerily quiet as they walked over the cobbles round the deserted square. Tweed waited for Kent to speak.

'This investigation of Leopold Brazil you asked me to undertake. I could start in London – he has a place in the City. But my instincts tell me to fly over to either Paris or Geneva.'

'Geneva,' Tweed said.

'You'd like any other information I can pick up concerning Brazil? Apart from where he's been getting funds from, I mean?'

'Every crumb would be useful. You have carte blanche.'

Kent paused under a lantern, cocked his head on one

side, a mannerism Paula had noticed when he was concentrating on every word.

'Carte blanche,' Kent repeated. 'That can be an extremely expensive item on the menu.'

'Spend what you have to,' Tweed said as they resumed walking. 'By the way, have you ever heard of a man called Marchat?'

'No, I haven't,' Kent said promptly.

A shade too promptly, Paula thought. And he was the first person who hadn't asked how it was spelt.

'Should I have heard of this character?' he enquired.

'I'd have been surprised if you had. I should tell you that Franklin runs a small chain of detective agencies, one in Geneva. The firm is called *Illuminations*. I'm telling you so you don't stumble over each other. He's also probably going to be checking out Brazil although I haven't asked him yet.'

'Will he know I'm investigating the same target?'

'No,' said Tweed. 'If he did it could become a muddle – and he'll be going about his enquiries in a different way from you. He hasn't your financial expertise.'

'So *I* know about him but he won't know about *me*?' Kent emphasized.

'You've got it.'

'Franklin struck me as a very able sort of bloke,' Kent remarked as they continued walking slowly round the square.

'He's ex-Military Intelligence.'

'A good background to run detective agencies. So if by chance I run into him, I'm there on private business?'

Which was typical of Kent, Paula was thinking. To dot every '*i*' and cross every '*t*'. In the past he had proved to be enormously reliable.

'That's your best cover,' Tweed agreed.

'Did you find that odd little character Archie I mentioned to you at Bradfields?'

'Yes, we did. It was a short visit. I gathered Archie is on his way out of the country. Don't ask me where to – he's not very forthcoming.'

'That's Archie. Never lets his left hand know what his right hand is doing. I rather like him. Gutsy.'

'You use him now and again for some purpose – or shouldn't I ask?' Tweed enquired.

'I wouldn't tell anyone else, but he makes a living, so he told me, by selling interesting news about important people to newspapers all over the world. Not sex scandals or any of that sort of dirt. Financial data – about some big company that's in deep water and no one else has caught on. He can spot the defect in a balance sheet as quickly as I can.'

'How did you get to know him?'

Kent paused, cocked his head on one side again, gazing first at Tweed, then at Paula.

'*He* got to know *me*. A friend in Paris couldn't give me what I was after but said Archie would contact me. For a price. I was shaving in my room in Paris at the Georges Cinq and he tapped on my door. He knew what I wanted to find out. And his fee was reasonable. Cash, of course. I don't think he believes in paying taxes.'

'You know how to contact him in Paris, then?'

'Heavens, no!' Kent chuckled. 'Not with Archie. When I go over there I'll be walking along the Rue St-Honoré and suddenly he's strolling at my side. It's uncanny. I have wondered whether he has a pal at Charles de Gaulle Airport with access to the passenger manifests. That's a guess. I really like, admire him. Now, I've got the picture, so I'd better vanish. Do the Invisible Man trick – like Archie.'

'Keep in touch.'

'If you're away whan I phone your office – which means probably Paula will be away, too – can I give a message to Monica?'

128

'Tell her anything. Keith, be careful. The Motorman is on the loose.'

'That's right, build up my confidence . . .'

Kent slipped behind the wheel of his Rover and was out of the square before Tweed and Paula entered the lane to the Priory.


'Could I have a word with you, sir? It's rather confidential, I gather.'

The proprietor leaned over the counter inside the hotel as though he'd been waiting for Tweed to appear. Paula, tactfully, nipped up the stairs to her room.

A moment later Eve appeared out of the lounge, holding a glass of vodka. She had changed into a green form-fitting dress, clasped at her waist with a gold belt and with a high collar.

'Come on, Tweed!' she called out. 'We're all about to feed our faces down in the dungeon. Want me to get you a drink?'

'Not just at the moment, thank you. I'll join you soon.'

The proprietor waited until they were alone again, leaned closer to Tweed.

'The caller, a lady, emphasized I must not write down the message, that I was to pass it to you verbally when you were on your own.'

'I think I am now.'

'The caller's name was Monica. She said the destination was Geneva. She repeated the name. Geneva.'

# 13

Tweed had mounted the stairs, thinking he was moving silently, when Paula's bedroom door opened. She was wearing a dressing gown and she beckoned him inside, then closed the door.

'It's all right. I'm decent. I'm just taking a quick shower and my new outfit is in the bathroom. Has there been a development?'

'Monica has reported that Brazil has flown to Geneva.'

'Geneva! You guessed right. How did you do it, when we know Brazil has HQs in Paris and Zurich, but no one has mentioned Geneva?'

'Partly for that reason. I'm beginning to get the measure of Mr Brazil. He's very secretive. So he's likely to conceal his real HQ. Plus the fact that Geneva is so international. And one other element you know about.'

'That's right, tease me. What element?'

'The photograph of Marchat Buchanan told us about. It was wrapped in copies of the *Journal de Genève*.'

'I should have remembered that. Incidentally, I'll wear my dove-grey suit—'

'You look good in that. Eve is dressed to kill. I saw her downstairs.'

'To kill Philip. What I was going to say was my dove-grey suit is warm. With a windcheater over that I'll be OK, however arctic it is outside, for our trip to see the barman, Ben, at Bowling Green after dinner.'

'I wasn't going to take you with us. It could be dangerous.'

'Which is why I insist on coming. I'll knock on your door when I'm ready. Five minutes?'

'Fine. I'm just going to have a quick wash. I have a lot to think about. Particularly a remark someone made to us today.'

'Which you won't tell me.'

'Not yet.'

'You are going to ask Franklin to check on Brazil – as well as Keith?'

'Yes, I decided when I got Monica's message.'

'You're throwing quite a net round Mr Leopold Brazil.'

'Big fish need a big net to catch them . . .'


At Cointrin Airport, Geneva, a white jet landed away from the main runways. A limousine with tinted glass drove up to the aircraft in the darkness. Brazil, accompanied by Carson Craig in an expensive business suit, descended the ladder and got into the back of the limo.

Bypassing Customs and Passport Control, the limo left the airport and drove out past the office blocks of famous international conglomerates. It cruised for a short distance, then speeded up as it drove onto the main road.

A plain-clothes detective at the airport phoned Arthur Beck, Chief of Federal Police, at his office on Kochergasse in Berne.

'Inspector Carnet here, sir. Talking from a phone booth at Cointrin. The subject has arrived, was met by a limousine as soon as the private jet landed.'

'And now you've lost him?' Beck suggested calmly.

'No, sir. Two unmarked cars and a motorcyclist are following the limo. It's headed east towards Ouchy and Montreux.'

'Keep me informed,' Beck instructed. 'But, as you have done, always call me on my private line . . .'

*　　*　　*

In the large stone-walled cellar at the Priory where dinner was served Eve, at the head of a long table, was holding forth. Tweed observed her bravura performance over Paula's shoulder as they descended the curving stone-flagged staircase.

'With that party,' Tweed told the head waiter.

'Welcome to the shindig,' Eve called out, waving a glass which, Tweed noted, had been refilled. In her other hand she held a cigarette. 'We've had a most super day,' she went on, flashing her smile at Tweed and ignoring Paula. 'Bill is a superb driver . . .' She paused and flashed the same smile at the man on her right. 'He's as good as Philip.'

Eve was flanked by Bill Franklin on one side, by Philip on the other. Tweed took hold of Paula's elbow to guide her.

'Paula can sit next to Bill,' Eve called out as though she would be obeyed as a matter of course. 'Tweed, your place is next to Philip . . .'

'You're paying the bill?' Tweed enquired, still standing with Paula.

The question threw Eve. She was drinking more vodka when Tweed propelled Paula next to Philip and walked round the head of the table to sit next to Franklin. Newman occupied the chair at the other end of the table.

'You're in the wrong seats,' Eve said with vehemence.

'I'm sure we are.' Tweed smiled. 'But you see *I* am paying the bill. You really look rather relieved now,' he teased her.

'Oh, well. Sit where you like.' She looked sulky. 'I suppose you're not going to tell us what you've been up to with Paula,' she said suggestively.

'No,' Tweed responded amiably. 'As a matter of fact, I'm not even going to give you a clue.'

He saw Paula's expression tighten, about to say

something. Under the table he touched her foot, signal-
ling *Let me handle this.*

'Sounds as though you've really made the most of
your time together,' Eve remarked, determined to pursue
the subject.

'Can it,' said Philip.

Eve looked astounded. She turned to him. Her head
was held high as she stared straight at him.

'*What* did you say to me?'

'I said can it,' Philip repeated. 'And go easy on the
vodkas.'

Eve reacted by emptying her glass, calling for a refill,
and lighting a fresh cigarette from the one she had just
been smoking. Franklin, with a broad smile, intervened.

'We also had a busy afternoon. I took Eve for a tour of
the Purbecks. We ended up in Worth Matravers, which,
as I guess you know, is perched high up. We called in at a
small pub which has a dramatic view of the sea. I was
glad I wasn't sailing – the sea was a cauldron.'

'Funny little place, that inn,' Eve joined in. 'They
didn't have vodka.'

'That didn't matter.' Franklin laughed good-
humouredly. 'You made up for it drinking cognac. This
lady,' he told everyone, 'has a head like a rock. I suspect
she could drink me under the table . . .'

My God, Paula was thinking. Vodkas, then cognac,
then more vodkas.

They had a leisurely dinner and Eve devoted most of
her attention to Franklin. Philip seemed unaffected,
turned instead to Paula and conversed with her and
Tweed.

The atmosphere became jovial and jokey while Tweed
was doing two things on the quiet. He checked his watch
in his lap – they had to leave in good time to meet the
barman, Ben, at Bowling Green. He was also observing
Eve.

He decided she felt she always had to be the centre of attention. He suspected this was due to a well-hidden inferiority complex. And yet there were times when she was charming, turning to chat animatedly with Philip over coffee. Or was it that she didn't like him paying too much attention to Paula?

'I hope you won't mind,' he said as he signed the bill, 'but Philip and Paula are coming with me to a meeting with someone. I doubt if we'll be away more than an hour. Bill, could you once again entertain Eve?'

'It will be my pleasure,' Franklin assured him, and beamed.

'Can't I join you?' Eve pleaded. 'I've hardly been able to talk to Philip all evening.'

'Sorry. I really am,' Tweed told her. 'But it is about a confidential insurance problem which turns out to be urgent.'

'That's all right, then.' Eve gave him a smile. 'I will wait up for Philip to get back.' She turned to Philip. 'Don't be too long, darling. Bill and I will be getting sozzled in the lounge.'

'I'm sozzled already,' Franklin said as they all stood up. 'But I'll keep up with Eve. My reputation is at stake . . .'


Tweed, after collecting his coat, followed Newman along the corridor on the ground floor of the Priory leading to the exit. Paula was behind him as Newman spoke to the proprietor, who had been studying sheets of figures behind his counter.

'We're going for a walk,' Newman explained to the proprietor. 'We need it after our excellent dinner. But we'll be walking along that towpath on the other side of the Frome . . .'

'It will be muddy, very slippery,' the proprietor warned, glancing at their shoes.

'That's what I suspected,' Newman continued. 'Have you by any chance any spare gumboots?'

'Loads of them. Visitors leave them behind, forget them. I'll bring a selection.'

'Any for me?' Paula called out.

'I think we can oblige . . .'

They were all equipped with gumboots in minutes. Newman asked for a spare pair of gumboots, slightly smaller than his own.

'We're meeting a friend,' he said. 'And we'll leave our shoes in my car – that way we don't trample mud all over your carpets when we get back . . .'

Newman led the way to the Black Bear to collect Marler. The spare pair of gumboots fitted him well.

'Archie has gone to sleep and Butler is keeping an eye on his room,' Marler reported as Newman took them back the way they had come.

'As we're not going along the towpath why the gumboots?' Paula asked. 'And what's inside that canvas bag you're carrying?'

'You'll see when we climb East Walls,' Newman told her. 'And' – he opened the canvas bag – 'everyone should carry a powerful torch, so here you are. I always carry them in the back of the car.'

'And a very uncomfortable pillow that bag made,' Marler commented. 'I presume we're all armed. I've brought a Walther. Lord knows who we'll meet at this hour and at this time of night. Maybe The Motor-man.'

'Don't make jokes like that,' Paula protested. 'It's eerie enough here at night.'

Wareham was dead at that hour. There was not another soul in sight as Newman led them back into the square and by a complicated route past the spired church which loomed up close to the Priory. Tweed pointed to it as he walked with Paula.

'That's hundreds of years old. The hotel used to be a nunnery. Wareham is steeped in history.'

'What are these East Walls you mentioned?' Paula asked Newman.

'They're supposed to be the walls the Saxons built to keep out Danish invaders. They run along the eastern side of the town. Then there are North Walls and West Walls. They pretty much join up so you can walk round on the top of them and get a bird's-eye view of Wareham.'

'And South Walls, too?' Paula enquired.

'No. The River Frome provided a barrier to invaders so no walls were needed there.'

'It's very dark and quiet,' she commented.

'It will get darker and quieter. Here we are . . .'

Newman had been striding it out, occasionally switching on his torch, which he did now. Across a street Paula saw a steep muddy path mounting a high grassy hump.

'I don't see any walls,' she said as they began a slippery ascent.

'They're supposed to be underneath us,' Tweed told her. 'Actually the so-called walls are more like a huge embankment circling three-quarters of the town.'

Below them on their left was a deserted road. To their right were some miserable allotments beyond a few houses. Paula pointed down to the road.

'Wouldn't it be easier walking along the road? It seems to run parallel to this slimy track.'

'More dangerous,' Marler called over his shoulder, walking just behind Newman. 'Easier for someone to lie in wait for us. Always take the high ground.'

She noticed Marler had slipped the Walther out of his holster and was holding it by his side. As she took out her Browning Tweed called out quietly.

'Our interview with Ben will probably be uneventful.'

'Famous last words . . .'

They continued along the narrow path, descending every now and again from one hump to a track or road, then climbing again up another treacherous path. By the light of the moon Paula saw that beyond the outskirts of Wareham the fields everywhere were inundated under water. They trudged along further under a star-studded sky and Paula clasped her windcheater round her neck. It was bitterly cold even without a wind. Suddenly Newman raised a hand for them to pause.

'We're there. The path swings to the left and has now become North Walls. There is Bowling Green.'

He flashed his torch down into a grass bowl to their left. It was deserted as Marler took the lead, turning a right angle. Newman swivelled his torch over the whole bowl.

'No sign of Ben and his dog. He's probably on the footpath further along.'

'Look at all that water,' Paula remarked. 'There's a river and it looks as though it's overflowed.'

'It has,' said Tweed. 'There are two rivers hemming in Wareham. The one we came over when we crossed the bridge entering Wareham is the Piddle or – if you wish to be politer – the Trent.'

'Stay exactly where you are!' ordered Marler. Paula's heart began to thud at his tone of voice.

Marler was perched on a section of the path above Bowling Green where it turned to the west. He was aiming the powerful beam of his torch down into a swamp beyond the path where the Trent had flooded a huge area.

'Oh, Lord,' said Philip, who had walked behind Paula and Tweed, guarding their rear. 'It's Ben. He must have slipped.'

'Slipped, my foot,' said Newman grimly, 'and that's not meant as a joke.'

'No one else around, is there?' asked Tweed quietly, recognizing the most important factor.

'Not at this hour,' said Newman.

He held his torch steady and in the beam Paula saw part of the figure of a man protruding above the watery ooze. He was submerged to his waist and one arm was held still and upright, as though calling for help. The head was bent back at a grotesque angle.

Using his own torch and Newman's beam to light his way, Marler slithered down a steep bank, reached the edge of the flooded area, carefully trod one leg into the mud, found it sank halfway up his gumboot and then settled on something firm below.

Paula sucked in her breath as Marler reached out with one hand after taking off his glove, gently pressed a finger against the carotid artery. Hauling out his leg on to dry land to join the other, he made his way back up the slope.

'Well?' said Tweed.

'It's Ben. His neck is broken.'

'What about the dog?' Paula asked.

'Oh, he'd throw it into the quagmire as soon as he'd killed Ben. He wouldn't want it running round drawing attention to this place too quickly. So, everyone, there we are.'

'Where are we?' Paula asked in a dazed tone.

'The Motorman. Again,' said Marler.

# 14

Everyone – except one man – had returned to London from the Priory Hotel early the next morning. Tweed had been electrified by the discovery of the corpse at Bowling Green.

'We're getting out of Dorset fast,' he had informed his team, at a brief conference held in his room.

'Why the haste?' Paula had asked.

'Because that's the fourth murder, and one way or another several of us have witnessed the killings. We can't risk staying here until Buchanan asks some very leading questions. Also, I'm going to speed up the tempo from Park Crescent . . .'

Only Pete Nield had been left behind, with orders to keep his eyes open and report any developments. By ten in the morning Tweed was in his office with Paula, Newman, and Marler. Newman was telling Tweed how he had handled Franklin and Eve.

'I saw them separately. I explained to Franklin you had received an urgent message recalling you to London and left it at that.'

'How did he react?'

'That it suited him to get back to London to check the progress of several investigations . . .'

'And Eve?'

'She also said she would be glad to leave. Apparently she had a nasty stomach upset soon after we left to meet Ben. She retired immediately to her suite, she thought it was something she ate which disagreed with her.'

'Too many vodkas and cognacs, more like,' Paula said caustically.

The phone rang. Monica answered it, then motioned to Tweed.

'Arthur Beck is on the line from Switzerland. Says he'd like to speak to you urgently . . .'

'Trouble, Arthur?' Tweed enquired.

'I tried to get you last night. About eleven, your time, Monica had just gone home someone told me. Brazil landed at Cointrin Airport, Geneva, last night. Had a limo waiting for him. One of my men watching the airport saw him leave with that aggressive bastard,

Carson Craig. The car was followed by two unmarked cars and a motorcyclist. It headed east for Ouchy and Montreux—'

'Curious. I've heard he has offices in Paris and Zurich but not—'

'Let me finish. In Ouchy both unmarked cars lost him. I've had an unkind word with the drivers. But the chap on the motorcycle was brighter. He saw Brazil and Craig switch to another identical limousine in Ouchy – with the same number plates as the one which left Geneva. He followed it to Berne, to here. Brazil has a secret HQ not a hundred yards from where I'm sitting – in my own HQ.'

'Tricky chap,' Tweed commented.

'I think he'll be on the move again soon. You know we have a small airport at Belp, outside the city. Well, the executive jet which flew him to Geneva has landed here. And the pilot has filed a flight plan for guess where?'

'I never guess.'

'You do it all the time. The flight plan is for the jet to fly to Geneva this evening. I have watchers at Belp Airport.'

'Like a perishing grasshopper, our Mr Brazil.'

'Must go now. Will keep you in touch – even if it does cost me my job . . .'

Tweed sighed, put down the phone, told the others the gist of Beck's call.

'What do you think?' he asked.

'That Geneva keeps cropping up,' Newman said.

'I'm suspicious after what you've told us,' Paula said slowly while she drew faces on her notepad. 'If I were Beck I'd have someone waiting at this Belp Airport who can definitely recognize at least Brazil – and Craig if possible. To make sure that if two men board that jet they really are who they're supposed to be.'

'I think you've just had a flash of inspiration.' Tweed thought for a moment, then looked at Monica. 'Would you call back to Beck and give him Paula's idea? Tell him it came from Paula – he respects her – and that I'm in full agreement with the suggestion.'

He had just finished speaking when the phone rang yet again. Monica answered, frowned, looked at Tweed.

'Bill Franklin is waiting downstairs. Says he'd like to see you briefly if you have the time.'

'Then we'll make the time for Bill. Call Beck after he's gone . . .'

In a small stone villa on Kochergasse in Berne, not far distant from Federal Police Headquarters, Brazil sat behind a huge Louis Quinze desk. The only other occupant of the room, its walls covered in ancient tapestries, was José, a tall lean man wearing a grey business suit. He sat in a corner behind his own much smaller desk.

'Well, José,' Brazil boomed cheerfully, 'would you say I fooled them all last night? Your idea of changing limousines was brilliant.'

'From what I've heard of Tweed I would assume it was dangerous to feel too confident.'

'I was talking about Beck, not Tweed,' Brazil said sharply.

'My comment stands.'

Brazil stared at his most trusted confidant. In his late thirties, José came from French Guiana, the one-time French colony in South America, now a *département* of France. José had a poverty-stricken childhood but, working hard, he had saved enough money for a one-way ticket to the States.

There he had sold newspapers on the streets, washed up in restaurants, living in one slum of a room while he studied in the early hours to be an accountant. Achieving top marks in his exams, he had applied to a conglomerate run by Brazil in America for the job of junior accountant.

Brazil had wandered into the office where José was being interviewed, had taken over the interview himself. He was so impressed by José's intelligence, by his ethics, he had appointed him as his deputy, a post José had held ever since Brazil had moved to Europe.

His skin was coffee-coloured. Clean-shaven, he always dressed impeccably and was the only man who didn't hesitate to disagree with his chief. It was a quality which Brazil admired.

'Now you have a moment free,' José began, 'I can tell you of a phone call from England which came in early this morning, our time. It was from the informant you nicknamed the Recorder.'

'Interesting information?'

'The Recorder told me a few names of key personnel on Tweed's team. Robert Newman, Paula Grey, and – subject to confirmation – William Franklin.'

'Is that all?' There was an edge to Brazil's voice. 'I must have at the earliest possible moment the names of *all* the key members of Tweed's team. That reminds me, I must put in a phone call to England.'


Paula thought how smart Franklin looked as he came into the office. He wore a thigh-length navy-blue coat and a matching pair of well-tailored slacks. Taking off the coat, he revealed a navy-blue blazer with gold buttons, a blue-striped shirt, and a pale grey tie.

'Morning all,' he greeted the occupants. 'It's cold enough outside to freeze an Eskimo. Thank you,' he said as Tweed invited him to sit down.

'A cup of coffee?' Monica suggested. 'No sugar and with a dash of milk.'

'You have angels on your staff,' he said with another smile, looking at Paula. 'Yes, please, Monica.'

'Where is Eve now?' asked Tweed.

'I think Philip dropped her off at her flat in South Ken. Not far from your pad,' he told Newman.

'I gather she was unwell soon after we left,' Tweed continued quickly.

'She was. She'd had a big meal and no sooner had you gone than she said she felt ill. She had some stuff in her suite which she said settled stomachs, so off she went. So I was left on my ownsome. I lit a cigar and a few minutes later went outside for a drop of fresh air in the square. Felt like a bit of silence and what did I get? A motorcyclist roaring at top speed up South Street towards North Street. He must have been doing sixty.'

'How long was that after we had left?' pressed Tweed.

'Ten minutes at the outside.'

'And how long,' Tweed asked, looking at Newman, 'do you reckon it took us to reach Bowling Green?'

'Twenty-five minutes at the outside. I checked the time we left and looked at my watch again after we found what we did.'

'And what did you find?' Franklin asked after thanking Monica for the cup of coffee she handed him. 'Or is it a state secret?' Tweed shook his head.

'Sorry!' Franklin raised an apologetic hand. 'Guess I shouldn't have asked. Also, I shouldn't waste your time so I'll get straight to why I'm here. You said down in Dorset you might want to use me. A big job has just landed on my desk. It's boring and I'd just as soon give it to one of my staff – that is, if you want me to carry out an investigation.'

'I do. Just a small one.' Tweed smiled grimly. 'A man called Leopold Brazil.'

'I see.' Franklin smiled back drily. 'A mere nothing. What do you want to know about that gentleman, where do you suggest I start?'

'I want to know everything you can dig up. Especially all the places he operates from. Geneva is the place to start. You said you had an agency there.'

'Geneva, here I come.' Franklin swallowed the rest of his coffee, stood up, slipped on his coat, looking across at Paula. 'Tweed, if you have to send someone out there to meet me I'd be quite happy if it was Paula.'

'And Paula would be quite happy to come,' said Paula.

Franklin gave everyone a little salute. He looked now at Marler, who was leaning against a wall, smoking a king-size, and had said nothing.

'I don't think I know your name.'

'No, you don't,' Marler replied.

'Another state secret,' Franklin said to Tweed, grinned, and left the room.

'He doesn't waste much time,' Paula remarked.

'And you find him interesting, don't you?' Tweed teased her.

'Yes. He's courteous, intelligent, and good fun. And he likes women.'

'What more could you ask for?'

'Why were you so interested in the timing of that motorcyclist Bill heard just after we'd left the Priory to go and meet poor Ben?' she asked, changing the subject.

'Because I think that could have been The Motorman, getting to Bowling Green to kill Ben before we arrived.'

'But how on earth could anyone have known the timing and place for our meeting him?'

'You've forgotten,' Tweed told her. 'When we did make the arrangement Ben lifted his voice several times – and there were two strange men waiting at the bar, the ones who tapped on the counter with a coin. They could have told someone else who instructed The Motorman. I feel I should have spotted the danger.'

'You can't think of absolutely everything. And I wonder how Philip is getting on with Eve?'

\*     \*     \*

144

Philip had driven back from Wareham in his Land Rover with Eve behind him in her Porsche. Whenever she could she overtook him to be in the lead. Philip then waited until the road ahead was clear and would overtake her, waving a hand at her as she had waved to him. They continued this leap-frogging until they ran into London's traffic.

Philip was surprised at how close her flat was to Bob Newman's. Eve lived in a large red-brick house which had been converted into flats and looked expensive. Inside her first-floor flat she threw her coat carelessly on to the end of a long couch.

'The drinks cabinet is that thing over there,' she informed him. 'Make me a large vodka while I go to the loo.'

He opened the cabinet, took a glass, and put a modest amount of vodka in the glass – modest for Eve. Then he went over to the bay window and looked down into the South Ken road. In midmorning it was quiet.

At the Priory Eve had arrived very late for breakfast, had then eaten two fried eggs with bacon and tomatoes. She had explained her lateness between mouthfuls.

'I hardly slept all night. Just sat up in bed and read a paperback . . .'

Which, at the time, had seemed odd to Philip. Before going to bed he had wandered round the outside of her suite and there had not been a light on in any room.

He was thinking of this as he stared down and she came back into the room. He handed her the glass.

'Call that a large vodka? For God's sake.'

'Isn't it a bit early . . .'

'No, it isn't,' she snapped as she filled up the glass. 'Aren't you drinking? You could always pour yourself an extra strong orange juice.'

She flopped down on a long couch, stretched out her

legs. He sat down at the far end, watched her while she drank her vodka in two separate gulps. She had calmed down. He reached out and clasped her hand.

'Not yet. We hardly know each other, darling.'

Jumping up, she sat in a nearby armchair, flashed him her warm smile. She leaned forward.

'I don't even know anything about your job.'

'I'm in insurance,' replied Philip, suddenly guarded.

'What kind of insurance? Who are the key people? Is Tweed the top man in your outfit? He's nice. Who does he work with besides yourself? I'm interested.'

'You don't tell me anything about your job,' he reminded her. 'Except to say it's hush-hush . . .'

'Is yours hush-hush?' she asked quickly.

'No, it's boring to talk about. And I told you before I was in insurance.' He looked at his watch. 'I have to get to the office now I've seen you safely home.'

Annoyed with her swift changes of mood, he just wanted to get out of the place. She leapt up from her chair, threw her arms round him, kissed him full on the mouth, and then broke away.

'Call me tonight, Philip. Before six. I may have to go abroad on a job.'

'Where to?'

'God knows, but my boss does. I'll know when he tells me.'

'I'll give you a buzz . . .'


Tweed was pacing round his office, his mind racing as he played with the pieces of the jigsaw he was trying to assemble.

'You're putting an iron curtain round Leopold Brazil,' Paula commented. 'First Keith Kent going off to Geneva. Now Bill Franklin heading for the same Swiss city to activate his detectives.'

146

'It will need an iron curtain to pin down what Brazil is up to.'

'You're sure he *is* up to something?'

'I am after what Beck told me. Otherwise why go to all that trouble to elude anyone following him – switching cars at Ouchy, arriving in Berne, summoning his jet to Belp Airport? He's putting up smokescreens to hide something. The question is what? By the way, Bob, you came here early after delivering Archie to Heathrow. How was he?'

'I collected him from the Black Bear.' Newman pulled a face of resignation. 'It seemed like the dead of night – it was early morning. And Archie was freshly shaved and perky as a squirrel. We arrived at Heathrow in good time for him to catch his flight.'

'Did you check quietly where he was going?'

'You don't play games like that with Archie – he expects to be able to trust you. When we reached the concourse he told me to wait by the bookstall. I saw him heading for the Swissair check-in counter and thought that would be the last I'd see of him. Then I was going to drive here.'

'Something happened then?' Tweed enquired.

'Something unexpected. Archie *did* come back to me. He showed me his flight ticket – the copy and his boarding card. Just guess where he was flying to. He'll have arrived several hours ago.'

'Just tell me,' Tweed said impatiently.

'Geneva.'

# 15

There was silence in the office for a few minutes after Newman had reported Archie's destination. Tweed sat in his chair staring at a map of Europe Paula had earlier attached to a wall at his request.

Tweed had stuck pins with coloured heads in the map marking certain cities. Paris, Zurich, Berne, Geneva, Ouchy, and Montreux. Paula had the impression he was not looking at the map at all, that his mind was miles away. Suddenly he sat up very straight.

'Monica, call Butler at his flat, tell him to pack a bag for cold weather, and then come over here. When Pete Nield calls from Dorset tell him to make record time getting here. If he doesn't phone within the hour keep trying him at the Black Bear.'

'What about us?' asked Paula.

'Be ready at a moment's notice to fly to Europe, all of you. Cold-weather kit.'

'Why cold weather?' enquired Marler, still standing against the wall.

'Because the moment I arrived back here I checked in a newspaper the temperatures in Switzerland. They're way below zero and there's been heavy snow. Because of the latter factor pack footwear for snow – and for ice.'

'Action this day,' said Paula. 'We're going on our holidays.'

'Not yet,' said Tweed. 'But I want everyone *ready* to go.' He stood up. 'And now I have to keep appointments I've made with two people . . .'

He paused as the phone rang. Monica answered, looked surprised, and it was rare for her to show any emotion. She covered the mouthpiece.

'Tweed, you won't believe this but I have on the line Leopold Brazil. Not an assistant – the great man himself. He wants to speak to you.'

'Take down this message which I want you to repeat to him word for word. Mr Tweed is away for the whole day . . .' Monica scribbled in swift shorthand on a notebook the exact wording as Tweed continued. 'I know Mr Newman passed on your request to him to meet you but at the moment he is heavily involved. That's the message. Begin the conversation by saying it's a bad line and you're transferring to another phone. Then pause and start talking as soon as I lift the phone so I can listen in . . .'

Tweed picked up his phone when Monica nodded, listened with great concentration. When she had finished passing on the message Brazil began speaking again.

'Could you kindly tell Mr Tweed when you see him that I need to see him urgently before there is a catastrophe. I have an executive jet at my disposal which can pick him up from Heathrow and fly him to any airport in Europe of his choice. I would prefer him to come alone. I shall be on my own. Thank you so much . . .'

Tweed put down the phone at the same moment as Monica. He repeated to the others what Brazil had said, then looked at Newman.

'I once met him but it was quite awhile ago and it was a brief conversation. Listening to him on the phone I had the impression of a man of great charm, also one of great authority but without a trace of arrogance. His voice has a strong timbre. I also detected a ruthless streak. What was your impression on the day you met him at Grenville Grange?'

'Exactly the same as yours.'

'Interesting. And I'm glad I've taken the precautions Monica is about to put into action.'

'I'll have to make a quick trip to my pad,' said Marler.

'Better go now then.'

'You're not going to meet him under those conditions, for heaven's sake, are you?' protested Newman. 'Travelling aboard his jet he'll have you in the palm of his tough hand.'

'We'll see . . .'

'You must have back-up. Very heavy back-up,' Newman insisted.

'We'll see,' Tweed repeated as he stood up and quickly put on his coat. 'Now I must hurry . . .'

'You didn't tell us who you were going to see,' Paula said anxiously.

'Sorry, I had my mind on something else. My first outing is to see Miss Maggie Mayfield. I've reserved a room at Brown's Hotel so we can have privacy.'

'Who on earth is she?'

'General Sterndale's niece and only surviving relative. She was due to stay with him on the night the mansion was burned down – but had a bad cold so she never went.'

'And your second appointment?' Paula went on.

'With Professor Grogarty in Harley Street. Does that name ring a bell with anyone?'

'Greatest living all-round scientist,' said Newman.

'Which reminds me,' Tweed said to Monica. 'I'll need that list of twenty missing scientists you drew up which shows each one's speciality.'

Monica handed him a file. He looked round the room as he tucked it under his arm.

'When I return we may have a better idea of what exactly is going on. Grogarty is eccentric, but a genius . . .'


In his Berne office Brazil had put down the phone after attempting to speak to Tweed and stared into space. His

150

reaction was oddly like a mannerism of Tweed's. José kept quiet for a few minutes before speaking.

'He was not available then, sir?'

'I can't be sure, but I think Tweed was listening in to every word. I sensed his presence while his assistant fed me lies, said he was away.'

'A very elusive man, our Mr Tweed,' José remarked.

'It makes me even more anxious to meet him again – and for a really deep conversation this time. I suspect he knows that. I'm counting on the word "catastrophe" I used to fester in his mind.'

'And in the meantime we wait?'

'We do not!' boomed Brazil, standing up behind his desk and gazing down at his assistant. 'We proceed with our project which will not be ready for a few days at the earliest. I want you to phone Konrad and tell him all is proceeding according to plan. Konrad, a peculiar code name for a Russian, for Karov, the real man of power.'


Tweed shook hands with Maggie Mayfield in the private room at Brown's. A plain woman in her forties, plump but with a strikingly intelligent face and shrewd brown eyes, she smiled.

'I'm sorry to have kept you waiting,' Tweed began.

'I always arrive ten minutes early for appointments.' She grinned wickedly. 'I have been known to turn up at an embarrassing moment. Now, how can I help you?'

They sat down and she poured coffee for both of them. Tweed had taken off his coat and they faced each other across a small oblong antique table.

'After the tragedy at Sterndale Manor I was present when the police retrieved the large safe you told me about. The contents had been burned to ashes but my people are working on a technique to bring up what was written on them.'

'Rubbish. It will be rubbish.'

'Why are you so certain of that?'

'Because when I phoned my uncle to tell him I could not come to his home I also asked him if the bearer bonds had been returned. After all, he told me they were on loan to a remarkable man to finance a project which would make Europe a safer place.'

'He gave you the name of this so-called remarkable man?'

'No. He refused point-blank. Said that was his affair. But he did tell me the bonds would be back in the safe by the end of the month. It's nearly the end of February now.'

'How long ago was this phone conversation you had with the General?'

'Two days ago. I'm recovering from my cold, but as you can probably tell it's still with me.'

'So you doubt very much whether the bonds would have been in the safe when the fire took place?'

'Absolutely certain. I know – knew – him well. And to reassure me I think he said the end of the month when he probably meant the end of March.'

'You did once see that the bonds were kept in the safe?'

'Yes, as I told you on the phone he once opened it in my presence. I can remember his exact words. "Would you like to see three hundred million pounds, the bulk of the bank's capital?" He then opened the safe, which was stuffed with folders. He opened one and showed me one of the bearer bonds. I was staggered at the amount one bond alone was worth. Issued by some huge oil company – I forget which one. That, of course, was before he loaned them to this unknown man.'

'Can you remember the colour of the folders?'

'Yes. They were the old concertina type – with separate sections. The colour was a faded green. I had the feeling they'd lain there inside that safe for years.'

'And you still think this enormous sum wasn't the total capital of the bank?'

'No, the General went out of his way to explain that all the different branches had their own funds and assets, more than enough to keep them going.'

'And you believed him?' Tweed asked quietly.

'Oh, yes.' She smiled wanly. 'My uncle was an honest man. He'd never have deprived the branches of their own funds. He'd feel he had a duty to the depositors who used the branches to guard their security.'

'If you had been able to accept his invitation to stay at the manor that night am I right in thinking his only remaining relatives would have been there? And the only three people who knew he had loaned the bonds to someone?'

'Yes, you are right. Richard, his son, also knew about the bonds and didn't like what he had done.' She drank more coffee and stared at Tweed as she put down the cup. 'You're thinking that if I'd been there no one would have been left who knew about those bonds, aren't you?'

'Well, yes.' Tweed was admiring her as a gutsy lady. 'So who else knew you were coming?'

'Only Marchat, who acted as butler, cook, cleaner – you name it. A nice, very quiet little man.'

'Could he have talked to anyone about your visit – and the fact that what remained of the family would be in the manor that night?'

'I don't see why not. Marchat used to visit a pub in the evenings, a pub in Wareham. He wouldn't see any reason to keep it a secret. I gathered that after a couple of drinks he'd become quite talkative.'

'Miss Mayfield, I'd better warn you that a man from the Yard, Chief Inspector Roy Buchanan, is bound to interview you sooner or later. Tell him everything you've told me – except the last bit you've just told me about Marchat. And emphasize the bank will stay solvent, that

153

the branches are all right. Once information like that –
about the bonds – starts getting known it could cause a
panic.'

'I'll tell him. He's already phoned me at my home and
said he'd like to see me soon.'

'Thank you for giving me your time,' Tweed said, and
he helped her on with her coat. 'You've been very
helpful.'

She turned round and stared at him. Her lips
trembled, then her mouth became firm and she had a
very determined look.

'I've heard rumours, Mr Tweed. Read accounts in the
newspapers. Was my uncle murdered?'

'Yes. There's no doubt about that. Sorry to put it so
bluntly, but I think you're the sort of woman who prefers
frankness.'

'I do. And I thank you for being frank.' She hesitated.
'Is there any chance that the person or people responsible
will ever be brought to justice?'

'I'm working on it personally. If I ever do prove who
did it I'll see they pay the ultimate penalty. Don't ever
repeat what I've just said.'

'I won't. Again, thank you,' she said, holding out her
hand.

'One final question. Have you any idea of the
nationality of Mr Marchat?'

'Yes. He was Swiss. Very hard workers, the
Swiss . . .'


On his way in a cab to see Professor Grogarty Tweed's
mind was in a whirl. He liked Maggie Mayfield. She was
the sort of woman he suspected he could marry if she were
willing. But of course his wife, who had long ago deserted
him overnight to live with a Greek shipping magnate, was
still his wife. He had never bothered with a divorce.

It was a subject his staff never brought up. The only person he occasionally talked to about it was Paula. You're an idiot even to contemplate the idea, he told himself.

He thought of Philip, enamoured with Eve. Maggie Mayfield would be a much better choice but he had no intention of interfering. Philip must make his own decision, for better or worse.

Marchat. He couldn't get the name out of his head. He still thought that Marchat could be the key to solving the mystery. If they ever found Marchat. If he was still alive . . .

'Hello, Tweed,' Professor Grogarty greeted him in his high-pitched croaky voice. 'Grab a chair, if you can find one unoccupied. Care for a Scotch? No? I permit myself one each day after eleven in the morning. Never a minute before . . .'

Tweed took off his coat, looked round the room, which had once been a consultant's. Armchairs everywhere, the covering worn and faded, and all piled up with books and files of papers. He removed a pile of newspapers, placed them carefully on the floor.

'Bet you wonder how I find anything,' Grogarty croaked. 'Well, I can lay my hand on a specific sheet of statistics, go to it within seconds. Cheers! Sorry you won't join me with a Scotch . . .'

Tweed was sitting in an armchair, studying his host. He never ceased to be fascinated by his extraordinary personality, his appearance.

Grogarty was a bulky man, six feet tall with wide, stooped shoulders. He had a large head, a mop of unruly grey hair, thick brows, pouches under intensely blue eyes, and a prominent hooked nose on which perched a pair of *pince-nez* at a slanted angle – so one eye peered

155

through the lens while the other gleamed over the top of the second lens. His mouth was broad and below it he had a couple of jowls.

'You always come to me with a problem, Tweed, and I am thinking you have done so today. Why not surprise me sometime and drop in for a chat and a tot? All right, what is it?'

With his free hand he shoved books off a chair onto the floor and sat down.

'Now your filing system's gone to pot,' Tweed chaffed him.

'No it hasn't.' Grogarty lowered his bulk into the chair, sat upright. 'There are twelve books down on the carpet and I can see from here which is which. I am ready, sir!'

'You've heard, I'm sure, that twenty top-flight scientists have gone missing. Despite the weird fact that the news has been kept out of the newspapers – even in the States, which is quite something.'

'I have indeed heard. Most sinister. I called Joe Katz, astrophysics, in South Carolina. A stranger told me he owned the house, that Mr Katz had gone to live abroad. Indeed, a top man. Katz had invented a system whereby a satellite in orbit two hundred miles up can be guided by the star constellations.'

'He's on this list of everyone missing – with a note of his particular speciality.'

Grogarty took the folder Tweed had handed him, opened it, adjusted his nose clip so both eyes peered through a lens and ran down the list in a matter of seconds. He gave Tweed back the folder. The speed with which he could grasp every single item on a close-packed sheet of typing never ceased to astonish Tweed. Grogarty took another sip.

'You're looking for a pattern, something which would make these sixteen men and four women a team, I would suspect.'

'You've got it first time. I've looked at that list for hours and sense something, but I'm damned if I know what it is,' Tweed confessed.

'There is something, I agree.' Grogarty stared at the moulded ceiling as though the answer were there. 'Of course it's communications. Global. Worldwide. The system upon which we are becoming far too dangerously dependent. The Internet. The information superhighway, a stupid phrase invented by ignorant journalists. But this list is more than that.'

'What is it then?' Tweed prodded.

'Give me time, my friend.' Grogarty was still gazing at the ceiling. Somehow he managed to sip more Scotch with his head bent back. 'One man in that list is the key player in the game. Would that I could identify which name triggered something off at the back of my mind.'

Tweed kept silent. He glanced round the large room which overlooked Harley Street. The furniture pushed against the walls consisted of genuine antiques. The framed pictures on the walls were priceless. One was a Gauguin. Grogarty was a wealthy man.

No one would have thought so from the way he dressed. He wore an old grey cardigan with loose skeins of wool at the hem and two buttons missing, a third ready to join its lost fellows. His blue check shirt was open at the thick neck and the collar was crumpled. His fawn trousers had not seen a trouser press for years.

'Odd that Irina Krivitsky, the world's greatest authority on lasers and their adaptation to controlling satellites, should be on that list,' Grogarty said suddenly. 'You will excuse me if I talk to you while I'm thinking.'

Tweed stared quizzically at Grogarty. He knew that he sometimes adopted this weird mental technique when he was working on a tough problem. One part of his brain would converse while another part concentrated furiously on the problem he was wrestling with.

'You can talk back to me,' his host reminded Tweed. 'I won't be distracted. Indeed, rather the reverse.'

'What's odd about this Irina Krivitsky?' Tweed asked.

'The last I heard of her – by devious means and routes – was that she was working in one of the secret Russian laboratories behind the Ural Mountains in Siberia . . .'

Grogarty paused. He shook his head and his *pince-nez* went askew again over the bridge of his nose. He didn't seem to notice but he was nodding to himself. Something was coming.

'Go on,' said Tweed.

'Those hidden laboratories – buried underground, beneath the tundra – can't be spotted by Yank satellites from the air. They are as heavily guarded as they'd have been in Stalin's time. So why should they let her leave to work outside Russia?'

'If she *is* outside Russia,' Tweed pointed out.

'Oh, but she must be. Several of the names on your list would never agree to cross the frontier into Russia, let alone work there.'

'They may have been kidnapped,' Tweed suggested.

'Oh, but they weren't. Reynolds, an American, talked to me just before he disappeared. Over the phone. Said he'd received an offer he couldn't refuse so he was leaving his company in California and taking his wife with him. He said it was rather secret but Ed never could keep a secret.'

'This is all science fiction to me . . .' Tweed began.

'No! It isn't. Science is advancing by leaps and bounds. That's what worries me. The momentum is insane. Lord knows where we're going to end up.'

'We'll find out in due course—'

He never finished his sentence. Grogarty suddenly seemed to wake up, as though coming out of a trance.

158

'Ed Reynolds!' he almost shouted. 'Ed Reynolds – he's the key player. His speciality is sabotage of the whole communications network.'

'*Sabotage?*'

Tweed's nerves were tingling already for another reason. But the word made him sit on the edge of his chair. His host looked excited.

'I mean he worked on techniques which *could* sabotage world communications, throw the world into chaos. His objective was to find means of *countering* any such techniques. Like a doctor working on a vaccine to protect people against a certain disease. Do you understand me now?'

'Yes. But does that link up with the other scientists?'

'Yes, it does. If the *real* secret of the research going on somewhere *is* sabotage.'

'That's it, then?'

'That's it,' Grogarty agreed, standing up. 'Nice to see you, Tweed. Better get cracking – this thing is global. May be a complete change in the balance of world power.'

# 16

Philip was on the verge of leaving Eve's flat, reluctantly, when he closed the outer door and came back into the living room.

'That was a quick trip to the office,' Eve said perkily.

Her looked down at her, seated in an armchair, her shapely legs crossed. She was wearing dark blue trousers and a pale blue sweater, her arms rested on the chair's arms as he came towards her.

She saw a man in his thirties, dark haired and clean-shaven with thoughtful eyes. Philip was again in a state of inner turmoil – enormously attracted towards this

159

lively woman but still grief-stricken for his dead wife. He wasn't sure where he was.

'Well, I've got your number . . .' he began, to tell her he would call her that evening.

'And I've got *your* number, Mr Philip Cardon,' she replied, meaning something quite different as she jumped up and kissed him on the cheek.

He was advancing closer when she held up both hands and waved him away. She stood, folded her arms.

'Maybe we could go away on holiday to somewhere really exciting. Bermuda. When I have the time.'

'That's a great idea,' Philip said.

'I did say *maybe.*'

'If you have to go abroad how long will you be away?' he asked.

'No idea.' She stood in front of a wall mirror, used both hands to smooth down her jet-black hair close to her head, then swung round to face him. 'Absolutely no idea at all. But I'll ring you. When I can,' she added. 'What is your office number? I may only be able to call during the day.'

'That I can't give you. They frown on personal calls at the office.'

'Stuffy old insurance bods. Then you'll just have to sit each evening in that empty house of yours in Hampshire and stare at the phone.'

The remark hurt, the reference to the empty house, but Philip didn't show a trace of his reaction. He watched her pick up a burning cigarette from an ashtray, use it to light a fresh one. He found himself admiring her slim figure.

'Giving me the once-over?' she enquired. 'You should know what I look like by now. Philip, I've got to take a shower.'

'I was just going . . .'

He closed the outer door behind him, walked slowly

down the stairs, his emotions chaotic. Eve had a habit of lifting him up and then putting him down. He knew that some women used the tactic on men but Eve was an expert.

Tweed walked into his office to find only Monica and Newman there. Newman was just lifting the phone.

'Hello, Archie. Yes, it's Bob. How are you getting on?'

'News, Bob. I'm speaking from Geneva. Tricky city. People are trying to follow me. Think I've shaken them off. The news – Brazil appears to be compiling a list of all the members of Tweed's staff. So far he knows about you and Paula Grey – and he's got down Franklin as a possible member.'

'You're quite certain about this?'

'My informant is totally reliable. He doesn't even do it for money, which is reassuring. Must go now. I gather help is on the way . . .'

Newman stood up, gave Tweed, who had taken off his coat, the chair behind his desk. He repeated what Archie had told him.

'You think he's targeting my staff – Brazil?' Tweed asked slowly.

'Does sound like a hit list,' Newman agreed cheerfully.

Tweed stood up again, began to pace round the office as he counted on his fingers.

'Yourself, Paula – and Franklin possibly, who isn't on our team. The absentees are significant. Marler, Butler, and Nield.'

'I don't get you,' observed Newman.

'Dorset. There are only three people who could pass on that list. Franklin himself, Eve Warner, and Keith Kent.'

'Why would Franklin add himself to that list?'

'As a cover. I know it's thin.'

'I'm still half asleep after my early morning,' Newman admitted, 'but I can't see how you come up with those three people as a suspected informant to Brazil.'

'Think! Dorset. Marler kept under cover all the time. None of my three suspects saw him – and when Marler was in the office when Franklin was here he refused to give Franklin his name. Also neither Butler nor Nield appeared.'

'It's creepy,' Monica commented.

'Oh, what was that bit about I gather help is on the way Archie ended up with?' Tweed asked.

'Archie phoned before Bob arrived,' Monica explained. 'You'd told me about him and he said he desperately needed back-up. Paula volunteered. She dashed off to Heathrow to catch a flight to Geneva.' Monica saw the expression on Tweed's face. 'She was excited about the idea . . .'

'*You let her go! On her own!*' Tweed exploded. 'She's going into the cauldron and *won't be armed. Will she?* I leave the office for a couple of hours and you allow this insanity to happen!'

Tweed was in one of his very rare rages. Monica looked appalled. In all the years she had worked for him he had never spoken to her like this. He was pacing round his office.

'I couldn't . . . have . . . stopped . . . her,' she stuttered.

Newman, calm as always, lit a cigarette. He watched as Tweed went round his desk and thudded into his chair. For a moment Tweed said nothing, then stared at Newman.

'Could I have a cigarette?'

Newman gave him one, lit it for him. Tweed, who hardly ever smoked, handled the cigarette in the fumbling way of people not used to smoking, taking short puffs.

'You've forgotten something,' Newman said.

'Have I? What?'

'Some time ago you gave orders that if you were not here Paula was empowered to act in your stead, to take any decision on her own without reference to anyone. You weren't here when the emergency came. Neither was I.'

'That's true. You are quite right.' Tweed had quietened down as swiftly as he had blown his top. 'Monica, a thousand apologies for my totally unreasonable outburst. I am very sorry.'

'Thank you,' said Monica. 'I appreciate what you've just said. But you are quite right – Paula couldn't have taken her Browning automatic when she was flying. But Archie covered that in his earlier call.'

'He did? How?' Tweed asked anxiously.

'He gave me the name and address of an illegal dealer in arms Marler uses. She'll go there first from the airport.'

'That's a relief.' Tweed studied the end of the cigarette he had hardly smoked, stubbed it in the crystal-glass ashtray Monica had perched on his desk. 'But how will she find Archie?'

'He covered that, too, in his first call. Whoever goes out meets him in a restaurant in the old city across the Rhône. A place called Les Armures. Archie said any cab driver knows it.'

'I know it,' said Tweed. 'You get the best kir royale in the world there.'

'Archie also said,' Monica continued, 'he'd be there from nine o'clock onwards this evening. So Paula does know how to contact him.'

'I'm still bothered. The Old City is a labyrinth of old alleys and narrow streets near the cathedral – where Les Armures is. And it will be very dark – that area is not well lit. What time does Paula fly out to Geneva?'

'She'll be in the air now.'

'What time is the next flight?'

'A couple of hours from now,' Monica said from memory.

'Well, in that case—'

He broke off as Philip walked into the room clad in a heavy coat with a fur collar which he immediately took off. He looked at Tweed.

'I left my case packed for the Arctic downstairs.'

'Book Philip on that next flight to Geneva, Monica,' Tweed said with an air of crisp decision. 'Give him all the data Archie provided. Including the details about that underground arms dealer. Philip, Paula may be running into more trouble than one person can handle. The fact that she's a woman has nothing to do with it . . .'

# 17

Leopold Brazil stood at the window of his spacious office in the villa in Berne. He was protected from view by thick net curtains. Behind him stood Carson Craig, clad in a grey suit which had cost him a thousand pounds.

'Time I left for Belp Airport, sir,' Craig reminded his chief. 'I've got your double standing by to board the jet with me. We should land at Cointrin, Geneva, in no time.'

'You said my double, Craig.' Brazil turned round and stared at him. 'Some bosses would resent the idea that they had someone who looked exactly like him.'

'I'm sorry.' Craig's brutal face crinkled into what he hoped was an apologetic expression. 'He doesn't look exactly like you.'

Brazil was amused. He didn't give a damn how closely the so-called double resembled himself, but he liked confusing his minion, who lacked a sense of humour.

'I wouldn't worry too much about it, Craig. But now I mean what I say. Go easy in Geneva.'

'We have reason to believe that trouble is on its way from London,' Craig said stubbornly. 'Our watcher at Heathrow has reported that one of Tweed's lackeys – the woman, Paula Grey – boarded a flight for Geneva. He had a good description of her from The Recorder. I'm going to wipe up Tweed's troublemakers before they can start anything.'

'Like you did at Sterndale Manor?' Brazil's tone had sharpened. 'Nobody told you to kill everybody in that house. My order was to raid the safe, make it look like a robbery.'

'We couldn't get into the house,' Craig persisted. 'I used my initiative.'

'I said go easy in Geneva. That is all.'

Craig left the room and joined his henchman, Gustav, who was waiting in an anteroom. Gustav was a fat, mean-looking man with a thin, cruel mouth.

'He's on again about us going easy,' Craig growled as they descended a wide curving marble staircase to the ground floor. 'You've got your kit?' he asked, glancing at the canvas bag Gustav was carrying.

'Everything, boss. Black leather jacket and trousers and helmet. The machines are waiting for us in Geneva with the rest of the team.'

'Good. We'll give them hell. They're getting just too close to the laboratory.'

'Where's that?'

'Shut your face,' snarled Craig.


The call to Tweed from Arthur Beck in the Federal Police building came an hour later.

'Tweed, I think you should know the jet left Belp with three men a few minutes ago. My man reported Carson

Craig was definitely one of the passengers. Another looked superficially like Brazil, but wasn't.'

'How could he tell?' Tweed asked.

'Body language. He observes how people move.'

'And where was this jet flying to?'

'Geneva. It should arrive there in no time. Trouble, savage trouble would be my guess – as Craig is with them. That's all for now . . .'

At Park Crescent Tweed put down the phone, looked at Newman and Marler with a grim expression. He told them what Beck had said.

'It looks as though Paula could be walking into an inferno,' he said bleakly.

'Then it's a good job you sent Philip,' Newman told him. 'And don't look so worried. Philip will have left his emotional baggage on his doorstep. And he likes Paula.'

'If I'd known earlier I'd have sent both of you to back up Philip. But I wanted to discuss my interview with Professor Grogarty. What do you both think is the significance of what he told me, in his mixed way?'

'I think,' Marler said, 'if it can be arranged safely you should now meet Leopold Brazil as soon as possible. I repeat, if it can be arranged so your safety is guaranteed. By us.'

'What do you suggest?'

'That at least four of us, disguised, are in the vicinity of the meeting place, which must not be a hole in the wall. By all of us I mean Bob, myself, with Butler and Nield.'

'Pete Nield is expected back from Dorset any moment,' Tweed told him. 'I overlooked one thing – I should have put a tail on Eve Warner.'

'Not to worry,' Newman replied cheerfully. 'I knew you were up to your neck so last night I called on Philip briefly in his suite at the Priory and asked him for Eve's address. She lives in a flat near mine. Quite posh. That's why Marler arrived late.'

'Get to the point, Bob.'

'Marler followed her when she left her flat after Philip had gone. Followed her to Heathrow where she boarded a flight. Bound for Geneva.'

Thank Heaven I brought arctic clothing, Paula thought.

The aircraft was flying lower over Switzerland. It was dark but the sky was star-studded and the moon shone brightly. They were passing over the Jura Mountains, which were snow-bound, and a small lake was a gleam of solid ice.

As some flights did, the plane flew east, then south, then west over Lake Geneva. It landed smoothly at the airport and the American beside her she had chatted with got up. She was in Business Class and quickly put on the fur-lined coat a stewardess brought her from where it had hung during the flight.

'Say, I can remember this airport when it was pretty small,' said the American who had come up next to her as they walked along an endless corridor. 'Now it's too goddamn big – and gettin' bigger all the time.'

'I can remember it in those days too,' Paula replied. 'It was cosy and no distance at all to walk.'

'You're on your own, lady. Care to join me for dinner this evening? No strings attached. I mean that.'

'That's very kind of you but I do have a date for this evening.'

'Enjoy your date. Nice to have met you . . .'

He walked more quickly and Paula heaved a sigh of relief. The American was a nice man, it was pleasant to realize she was still attractive, but she had no time to waste.

Leaving Cointrin, she took a taxi to the Hôtel des Bergues, booked a room, and tipped the porter when he'd carried her heavy bag up. The spacious room overlooked the River Rhône and a blaze of neon lights on the far side advertising this and that. The lights were reflected in the water as wavy distortions. She dialled Park Crescent and Monica answered.

'Paula. I'm at the Hôtel des Bergues, room number . . .'

'Got it,' said Monica.

Paula put down the phone, unpacked her bag swiftly, went back down into the lobby wearing her fur coat again.

'Be careful, miss,' the commissionnaire warned as she was about to step into the street. 'It's like a skating rink out there . . .'

She paused outside, tested the grip of her fur-lined boots, found it was good. She was wearing a pair of boots with special soles which had tiny spikes. After being inside the warm hotel for a few minutes the cold air hit her and she adjusted the coat's hood over her head.

On the plane she had checked the address of the dealer in arms and found she was familiar with the street which ran parallel to the Rhône across the water. She started walking across the footbridge, which zigzagged over the river. A raw wind froze her exposed cheeks, a wind blowing all the way from the distant Rhône glacier down the lake into Geneva. Despite the heavy gloves she wore, with her hand on the rail to keep her balance, she felt the cold penetrating the gloves. It was way below zero.

Leaving the bridge, she walked a short distance, turned into the right street, checking the numbers. Her destination turned out to be a shop with the word *Antiquateren* over the fascia. No sign of the name Rico Sava.

She had checked several times coming across the bridge to make sure she hadn't been followed. And the street she was in was deserted. So, it appeared, was the shop. The windows were in darkness with a grille over them. The door was ancient, heavy, and had a Judas window with bars. She pressed the bell beside it, pressed it several times when no one came. God, has he gone home, she thought. But I do need a gun.

There was a rattling sound and the Judas window opened. She couldn't see who was behind it.

'Rico Sava?' she asked.

'*Oui.*'

'Do you speak English?' she asked; although she was fluent in French, she thought Sava might be more convinced of her identity. 'A friend of mine, Marler. Marler,' she repeated, 'sent me here. He said you could supply me with something special.'

'I speak English. Are you alone? You say you are. Now close your eyes.'

Mystified, she did so, and a glaring light over the door came on. It was so powerful she was aware of it even with her eyes closed. She heard several locks being unfastened, bolts drawn, then the door opened. She kept her eyes shut.

'You can open your eyes now.'

The light had gone off. She blinked, stared at a small figure silhouetted in the dark. Sava told her to come in, took her elbow, warned her about a step down, then closed the door, made it secure, and switched on a normal light.

Rico Sava was small, had the beginnings of a paunch, was dressed in corduroy trousers, a dark waistcoat which was unbuttoned revealing a clean white shirt, open at the neck. In his sixties, she guessed, he had a turnip-shaped head with the short end his chin. His swarthy skin was lined but his eyes were bright, very alert.

'Describe Marler,' he said, hands on his hips.

She did so, emphasizing his upper-crust accent and languid manner.

'Mimic his voice,' Sava suggested pleasantly.

169

Paula did so, exaggerating the drawling manner Marler spoke with. Sava nodded, satisfied.

'You're careful,' Paula commented.

'In my business I have to be. So tell me how I can help you,' he said with a smile which lit up his previously sombre face.

'I want a .32 Browning automatic in perfect condition. And spare mags. Have you got one?'

'You know, I think we might be able to oblige.'

Sava walked quickly to a bookcase on a wall hidden from all the shop windows. He opened the case after unlocking it, took another key from the ring in his hand, and inserted it into a keyhole Paula, even with her sharp eyes, could not see. The entire interior of the bookcase from floor to ceiling revolved open like a giant door, revealing another compartment behind it. On the shelves, neatly stored, was a large collection of handguns. He turned round to hand her a Browning.

'In perfect condition, you said. That fell off the back of a lorry on its way to a police armoury.' He chuckled. 'That is a British joke, is it not?'

'It is,' replied Paula with a smile.

She made sure the weapon was not loaded, then checked its mechanism. Sava handed her a magazine. She slid it inside the butt, rammed it home with the heel of her hand, then lifted the gun in both hands, raised it to test its weight and feel, staring along the shallow gunsight. It nestled in her hands like her own weapon back at Park Crescent.

'Great,' she said. 'Just great. How much – with the spare mags?'

'For you, three thousand francs. Including the mags.'

'And for someone else?' she teased him.

'Three and a half thousand,' he said seriously, and she believed him. 'Because you are a friend of Marler's,' he explained.

She paid him in thousand-franc notes, slipped the gun into the hip holster she was already wearing. She normally carried the weapon in a special pocket inside her shoulder bag but her fingers were so cold, as she had anticipated might be the case, she knew she could reach the gun quicker out of the holster.

She turned to speak to Sava and he had already closed and locked the fake bookcase. A very careful man.

'Thank you for your help.'

'Give my regards to Mr Marler when you next see him.'

'I will – and I'll tell him about the generous discount.'

'It was nothing.'

He spread his hands, then crinkled his brow and Paula waited, guessing he was wondering whether to say something else.

'I would never dream of asking you why you are here,' Sava began, 'but I hope you are not going near the Old City tonight.'

'Why the warning, if I may ask?'

'Of course you may. There is a murderous gang we have nicknamed the Leather Bombers patrolling that area. They are men in black leather on motorcycles and the other night they knocked down a woman crossing one of the old streets. They just picked up her body, slung it over the rear of one of their machines, and drove off.'

'That's horrible, and thank you for the warning . . .'


Paula hurried back to the Hôtel des Bergues and had dinner at the Pavillon restaurant leading off the lobby. Tonight, she felt, was a very unknown quantity and she was more alert after a light meal.

Leaving the restaurant, she hailed a cab and asked the driver to take her to Les Armures. The driver nodded that he knew where it was and crossed the Pont du Rhône, the bridge over the river.

From that moment they left behind the bright lights of the international city of Geneva and climbed into the dark of the Old City, perched high up. Although he was driving on snow tyres the cabbie proceeded cautiously. He was climbing ever more steeply, veering round dangerous bends, and on both sides of the narrow cobbled street Paula looked out at ancient stone buildings which gave her the impression of an abandoned district. He skidded three times but managed to regain control. Higher and higher they mounted until, to Paula's relief, the cathedral, built on the summit, came into view, a menacing edifice in the moonlight.

He pulled up beside a weird stone platform and looked over his shoulder.

'The restaurant is over there. I can't get any closer,' he said in French.

She paid him off, standing on treacherous cobbles covered with ice. Then he was gone. An uncomfortable silence she could almost hear descended. No one else was about. She checked her watch. The illuminated hands registered 8 p.m. She had deliberately arrived one hour before the earliest time Archie had said he would be at Les Armures. She wanted to check out the area.

Philip's flight landed at Geneva and he went immediately to a phone and called Monica.

'Philip here. Calling from Cointrin Airport. I've just arrived. Any news of Paula?'

'Yes. Staying at the Hôtel des Bergues, room number...'

'Thanks. Must go.'

'Put that phone down and you're fired.'

Tweed's voice, grim.

'To hell with that,' Philip snapped. 'I've arrived late. Plane held up at Heathrow. Something about engine maintenance. It's eight o'clock here, for God's sake . . .'

'Information you need.' Tweed's voice was calm now. 'I had Beck on the line over an hour ago. Carson Craig has flown to Geneva. Beck reported a motorcycle gang which is careering round the city. Killed a woman and took her away. The police can't locate the gang.'

'Got it. I'm going now . . .'

'Good luck,' said Tweed but Philip didn't hear the words. He had slammed down the phone.

He was in a desperate rush to reach Les Armures by nine. But he had vital jobs to do first. He ran out of the concourse, grabbed a cab, asked to be taken to the Hôtel des Bergues.

At the hotel he registered for a room quickly, left his bag for a porter to take up to his room. He paused to enquire whether his friend Paula Grey was in the hotel.

'No, sir. She went out . . .'

'Thanks.'

Philip dashed out, nearly lost his balance on the ice even though he was wearing special boots with soles to grip ice. He dived back into the cab he'd kept waiting, gave the driver the address of Marler's dealer in arms. Reaching his destination, he gave the driver an amount far exceeding the fare.

'Wait for me and there's a large tip. For God's sake don't go away. I'm late for an appointment with a girl friend.'

'I'll be here.' This driver had a sense of humour. 'Never keep a woman waiting is my motto . . .'

Philip had spoken in French, which he found came back to him easily. He nearly went mad as Rico Sava put him through the same procedure he'd adopted with Paula, taking centuries to open the Judas window, then the door. Asking for a description of Marler.

'I need a 7.65mm Walther automatic, the one with eight rounds capacity.'

'You may need more than that.'

173

'What do you mean?' Philip asked, controlling his growing impatience.

'I had a very nice lady here. She purchased a Browning automatic . . .'

'She did?'

'I warned her not to go into the Old City. I think she was going to ignore my warning. If you're here to protect her you'll need more than that,' Sava repeated.

'Supposing I was here to do that?'

'There's a villainous motorcycle gang . . .'

'I've heard about them . . .'

'After the lady had gone a murderous-looking man with a mean face called here and spent a fortune. I heard his motorcycle stop further down the street.'

'What about it?'

'I'm breaking my golden rule' – Sava looked regretful – 'never to inform on one customer to another, but you come from Marler. And I didn't like this man.'

'He spent a fortune, you said. What did he buy?'

'A large supply of stun grenades. Also a number of Army grenades. Lethal. Twelve handguns, plenty of ammo. And this, which puzzled me.'

He took Philip across the shop into another room, showed him a huge searchlight-like lamp. It wasn't cumbersome. Sava handed it to Philip, who was surprised at how little it weighed. Sava showed him how easily it was switched on.

'Motorcycles,' Sava reminded him. 'What do you want? I can put the searchlight into a canvas bag with a strap to hang from your shoulder.'

'What about both types of grenade?'

'They would go into separate pockets inside the bag.'

'How much? Don't forget the Walther with spare mags.'

'Expensive, especially the searchlight. Fifteen thousand francs.'

'Pack them quickly. Everything in the bag except the Walther. Very quickly, please . . .'

Thanking God that Tweed always insisted key members of his staff carried a lot of money in high-denomination Swiss francs and Deutschmarks, Philip peeled off fifteen notes.

'Excuse me,' Sava said as Philip was leaving, 'but you are a brave man . . .'

Canvas bag over his shoulder, Philip dived back into the waiting cab, told him to drive to Les Armures.

'I'm sorry, sir,' the driver said as he drove off, 'but I can only drive you as far as the cathedral. There is big trouble in the Old City. The police have got it wrong – they are watching the outskirts of Geneva to check everyone entering. The people they are after are already here.'

'All right, then. The cathedral.'

Philip checked his watch. Ten minutes to nine. Everything had taken too long. He had an awful feeling he was going to be too late.

# 18

As her cab vanished into the dark Paula climbed the few steps onto the elevated platform of old stone, roofed in and open on three sides. She walked past two ancient cannons, descended the steps on the other side, and a waiter opened the door of Les Armures.

'Good evening, madame. Are you by yourself?'

'I won't be. My friend is meeting me here later.'

'A drink at the bar while you wait?'

'No, thank you. I want a quiet table in a corner.'

Which is what Archie would want, she thought. Leading the way, the waiter showed her a small table for two in the angle where two stone walls met. Paula looked back at the entrance and saw it was hidden from view.

'This would be perfect. He may not arrive for awhile.'

'That does not matter, madame. The table is yours . . .'

She looked round the restaurant as the waiter left her. The place was as she remembered it when she had once dined there with Tweed, very old with an arch leading to another cavern. The atmosphere was lively. Most tables were occupied, there was a babble of voices, laughter, the tinkling of glasses. The cloths on the tables looked brand new and waiters were dashing back and forth. No sign of Archie in the cavern beyond the first room. But she was very early. She turned, went back to the door. Her waiter ran up.

'Madame is not going out again?'

'Madame likes the fresh air . . .'

'Fresh air! It is like the North Pole out there! I must warn you there is solid ice on the cobbles.'

'I know.' She smiled. 'I'll be careful . . .'

After the glorious warmth of the restaurant the air hit her like a blow. I should have taken off my coat while I was in Les Armures, she thought. She mounted the steps on to the strange platform which was very wide and deep. Behind the two cannons there was solid stone wall, well back from the narrow roads surrounding it.

She walked down the steps into the main street where the cab had left her, nearly lost her balance. 'You watch it, my girl,' she told herself.

This was the main street, which led away from the cathedral and dropped steeply, she recalled. The only lighting came from lanterns attached to brackets protruding from the street's walls. She listened. The absolute quiet was disturbing.

She walked down the street, which was cobbled, stepping carefully. On either side there were ancient

176

buildings with shops on the ground floor. Mostly antiques dealers and picture shops. She paused in front of one, looked at the single framed picture in the window of a waterfall. No price.

She began to explore the side-streets and alleyways to her right, all of which dropped steeply. Still no one about. It had been like this the time she had walked back down into the main part of Geneva with Tweed. As though no one lived there.

The atmosphere was eerie, her favourite word for such surroundings. She went back later, explored a narrow side street opposite to the platform. When she checked her watch she saw it was nearly nine o'clock. She had walked further than she realized. Archie might have arrived.

She was mounting the steps to the platform where the floor was not covered with ice, on her way back to Les Armures, when the first motorcyclist arrived, roaring up the hill, headlight glaring. She pressed herself against the rear wall, took off her glove, tucked it under her left arm and hauled out the Browning automatic. The headlight on the machine shone on her briefly, the motorcyclist, clad in black leather, slowed down, threw something towards her.

The pineapple-shaped object, seen briefly in the headlight, curved in an arc, landed on the far side of the platform, rolled down the steps, exploded with a deafening crack. Stun grenade, she said to herself. He was a rotten shot.

The machine drove on past her and then she saw a small army of headlights speeding up the road towards her. No time to run for Les Armures. No guarantee the men screaming towards her would be equally rotten shots.

The second motorcyclist saw her in his headlight, lifted his arm. By now Paula had grabbed a pair of sunglasses out of her shoulder bag, had put them on to neutralize the headlights. She raised the Browning and pressed the trigger. The motorcyclist froze in his saddle, still holding what he'd been about to hurl at her. His machine went out of control and as he fell the grenade exploded with a different sort of crack. Shrapnel peppered the buildings on either side but she guessed most of its deadly contents had blown into the still body now lying motionless in the road.

Another motorcyclist appeared, followed by others. At the same moment a powerful arc light came on from the last side-street she had explored to her left. She was splotlit like a star on stage in a musical. It had become a bloody nightmare.

She stood with her shoulders pressed hard against the wall behind her. There was nowhere to run. She'd glanced at Les Armures, seen a waiter dropping a grille over the inside of the door. Gritting her teeth, she had one idea – to bring down as many of them as she could. Her nerve was colder than the ice on the roads. She took aim at the next oncoming motorcyclist, who again had one hand lifted, holding something. She was aiming at his headlight. It suddenly went out. His machine skidded on ice, threw him like a bomb against a stone wall as the machine slithered, fell, its wheels still spinning. It was the searchlight from the side-street, illuminating her, which bothered Paula most.

A shadowy figure appeared to her right on the platform. She swung round her Browning.

'It's Philip,' a voice yelled.

His arrival had distracted her for vital seconds. A new motorcyclist appeared, hurled something which landed at her feet. A grenade. Philip dived forward, grabbed it, lobbed it at the searchlight. She heard it explode, the sound of shrapnel flying against the nearby buildings. That would have killed her. But it was the searchlight which died. The lamp's glare vanished, its light faded into nothing. She thought she heard a shriek from the same direction. The man who had switched on the searchlight. Another motorcyclist was approaching.

'I'll take him,' Philip said. 'Give them some of their own medicine . . .'

He took the pin out of the grenade he'd grabbed from his canvas bag, counted, hurled the missile. It dropped into the lap of the approaching motorcyclist, detonated with a roar. The explosion lifted the rider off his machine, then he dropped into the street, a crumpled corpse riddled with shrapnel. The machine toppled over sideways in the middle of the narrow street.

'That's blocked it for the rest of them coming,' said Philip.

He quickly hauled the searchlight out of his bag, set it up between the cannons, switched it on. Its powerful beam shone a long way down the street. Paula saw the front rider throw up a hand over his goggles, stop his machine so suddenly that the one coming up behind him smashed straight into it. The street was a chaos of ruined metal. In the distance, at the extremity of the beam, they saw more motorcyclists stopping, then turning, heading away.

'Time to go,' said Philip.

'Time to check whether Archie is inside Les Armures . . .'


The waiter who had reserved Paula a table recognized her, lifted the grille, opened the door. Paula had slipped a full magazine into the Browning as they walked across the platform. Inside the restaurant there was now dead silence. Customers sat like waxwork figures. No one was eating as they entered. Philip spoke quickly.

'A gang was trying to kill someone. Don't know who,' he continued in French.

He was gambling on the assumption that no one would have had the nerve to look out of the window.

'Has my guest arrived?' Paula asked briskly.

'He's over there,' the waiter replied. He swallowed. 'Are you all right?'

'Fine.' She handed him a banknote. 'But after that we won't feel like eating. We'll just collect our friend . . .'

Archie was sitting at the corner table with a kir royale and a glass of water in front of him. He had a dead, half-smoked cigarette in the corner of his mouth. Paula bent down to whisper.

'Time to go. We'll have dinner sent up to my hotel room.'

'OK.'

That was all Archie said. Most people would have wasted time asking 'What has happened? It sounded terrible out there . . .' or some such enquiry. Not Archie.

He stood up, took the cigarette out of his mouth, put it in his pocket, his hands swathed in surgical gloves. The waiter brought his coat and he slipped it on and wrapped a scarf round his face so his small moustache wasn't visible. All in seconds. Paula realized he was disguising his normal appearance.

'Down this alley,' Paula said as they went outside. 'It leads to the footbridge over the Rhône. The police will be arriving any moment . . .'

With Paula leading, Archie following, and Philip bringing up the rear they slithered, slipped, slid their way down over icy cobbles. Since Paula had first arrived the ice had become a diabolical sheen.

She kept moving, shivering as the cold penetrated her clothing. Crossing the footbridge over the Rhône they all clung on to the rail to keep themselves upright. As they reached the hotel entrance they heard an endless screaming of police sirens. With lights flashing, car after car crossed the Pont du Rhône to their right, heading for the Old City.

They entered the hotel and went up to her room, which was really a suite, with living room, bedroom, and bathroom. Paula, hands frozen, took off her coat and flung it on a chair.

'I'll be with you in a few minutes,' she said and fled into the bedroom, leaving the door half closed. Then she broke down.


Philip heard her, told Archie to sit down and make himself at home. He pushed the bedroom door open, shut it behind him. Paula was sitting crouched in an armchair, shaking, shuddering, crying uncontrollably.

He went into the bathroom, found a glass, filled it with water, took a flannel, held it under the warm-water tap, put it on a towel, and went back to her as she looked up at him through fingers over her face.

'Use this warm flannel,' he said firmly. 'Then dry yourself with the towel. Then have a drink.'

'What is it? I could do with a brandy.'

'No, you couldn't. Spirits are the last thing you need when you're in a state of delayed shock. Come on.'

'Thank you, Philip. You are kind.'

She applied the flannel, used the towel to dry herself, then started to gulp down the water.

'Not so fast,' he told her. 'Sip it first.'

'I will . . .'

She drank all the water, took a deep breath, stood up, walked over to a wall mirror.

'I look a mess.'

'You look great. I'm not kidding.'

'What's Archie doing?' she asked.

'Smoking a cigarette.'

'He's doing what! I thought he didn't smoke.'

'He doesn't. He lit one, took a couple of puffs to get it going, then left it in the ashtray. I think he'll stub it out when it's half-smoked, then stick it in the corner of his mouth.'

'Philip, that's ridiculous . . .'

She began to laugh, a high-pitched laugh, couldn't stop. He walked over, slapped her on the face hard. She blinked, stared at him, but she had stopped laughing.

'You were hysterical,' he said quietly.

'That's the first time a man has done that to me and I haven't fought back. Philip, I haven't said thank you – you saved my life.'

'We're a team.'

She came forward and buried her face in his chest. He put his arms round her, held her tightly as she cried again, quiet tears. Eventually she pulled gently away from him, used a handkerchief to dab her eyes. When she spoke her voice was normal.

'How are you getting on with Eve? Or perhaps I shouldn't ask.'

'Don't see why not. I'm all at sea with her.' He waved his hands helplessly. 'I can't get her out of my mind but I'm still stricken with grief for Jean. It could be affecting my judgement.'

'I've never met anyone like her.'

'Neither have I. She can be intimidating and that worries me.' He felt the atmosphere was becoming emotionally overcharged, changed the subject. 'I suppose we ought to call Tweed about this evening.'

'Not until I've had a shower and a good dinner. My tummy is rumbling. Incidentally, they made copies of Marchat's photograph before I left and I've got one with me. Do you think we ought to show it to Archie?'

'I doubt if he's ever even heard of him. We might try it – after dinner. Go and have a good relaxing shower.'

182

'I'll only be ten minutes. Order dinner from room service for us, would you? You know what I like.'

'Make it twenty minutes, then you can have your shower and change into something else. That will help your morale.'

'Philip, you know one hell of a lot about women . . .'

# 19

'Beck is on the phone for you from Berne,' Monica informed Tweed as he sat back in his swivel chair. 'And he sounds in a bad mood.'

'Just what I need.' Tweed glanced at Newman and Marler, who had returned from having dinner together. 'Still, I'd better take the call . . .'

'Tweed?' Beck's voice verged on the harsh. 'Have you any of your people on my patch – in Geneva, to be exact?'

'Why?' asked Tweed, concealing his anxiety. 'I don't make a habit of reporting to all and sundry where my staff are.'

'Because there's been slaughter in the Old City outside a restaurant called Les Armures. The target was a woman.'

'Tell me what's happened, then. Don't beat about the bush.'

Tweed was gripping the phone tightly. His expression was grave.

'A gang of motorcyclists attacked her. They've been terrorizing that area for a couple of days. I've only got first reports but they say six bodies have been recovered.'

'And what happened to the target? Give me a complete story, please.'

'You sound concerned. The woman apparently escaped unscathed, disappeared. She was aided by a man. There was gunfire, grenades exploding, you name it.'

'How do you know all this?' asked Tweed, to divert his caller.

'The usual source. An old busybody woman who lives nearby watched the massacre from behind her curtain. Tweed, I'm flying to Geneva as soon as we've ended this call. I'm going to find out what's going on. I'm going to question the staff of Les Armures, who have been told to stay there until I arrive.'

'Good idea. Arthur, you say this gang has terrorized the Old City for two days. How on earth did you allow that to go on for so long?'

As he'd hoped, his provocative question enraged Beck.

'Because the fool of an inspector in charge at Geneva took it into his wooden head to station his men outside the city to watch all entrances into Geneva. He should have had them patrolling the Old City itself – it never occurred to him they might be holed up there. That's why.'

'A bad mistake.'

'And don't think I haven't noticed you never answered my question as to whether you have any of your people in the city!'

The phone at the other end was banged down, the connection broken. Tweed had never known Beck treat him like that. He sat back, sighed with relief, told the others what had happened.

'At least it looks as though Paula got away,' he said. 'And I'm sure the man he mentioned was Philip. The meeting place with Archie was Les Armures.'

'Do you want me to call Paula at the Hôtel des Bergues?' asked Monica.

'I think it might be more tactful to see if she calls me tonight. It sounds as though she and Philip had to cope with one devil of a firefight. Let's give her a couple of hours. Incidentally, while you were all out Fred, from the basement, came up. He has cracked what was on those ashes from General Sterndale's safe.'

'So what was on them?' Monica prodded him.

'Telephone numbers. And remnants of a thicker material of a pale green colour. Maggie Mayfield – I told you I met her at Brown's earlier today. Was it today? Of course it was. The past few hours have seemed like a week. She told me he showed her the real bonds he once kept in faded green folders, the old concertina type. Fred said he was sure the remnants show traces of pale green concertina-type folders.'

'And the telephone numbers?' Marler enquired.

'Obviously relics of old telephone directories – they would pack out the folders, make them look as though they still had the bonds inside. Clearly the bearer bonds were *not* any longer in the safe.'

'Three hundred milllion smackers.' Newman whistled. 'That ain't hay, as they say in educated circles.'

'But it might go a long way to financing whatever project Brazil is working on,' Tweed pointed out. '*If* he is the man Sterndale loaned the bonds to.' He sat up. 'I've just remembered, in an earlier call Beck said Carson Craig was flying to Geneva earlier this evening.'

'Just the gentleman to direct a massacre,' Newman commented.

The phone rang. As Monica picked it up Tweed raised his eyebrows.

'Something tells me this is going to be a long night. And that I'll be glad Butler and Nield are waiting and raring to go downstairs.'

'It's Keith Kent on the line,' Monica called out.

'Getting anywhere, Keith?' Tweed asked quickly.

'I'm speaking from a phone at the airport, Geneva, so it's safe to talk.' Kent's cultured voice paused. 'I think I've hit pay dirt. I called a man in Zurich who knows what's going on there. A bank, private, called the Zurcher Kredit, nearly went bust. A large number of bearer bonds had gone missing. Guess who was a consultant, a non-executive director on its board? Leopold Brazil. What happened to the chairman will intrigue you.'

'Go ahead. Intrigue me.'

'The chairman of Zurcher Kredit was murdered. Someone got into his villa while his wife was away and broke his neck.'

'Broke his neck?' Tweed noticed both Newman and Marler were staring at him. 'Any suspects?'

'Beck,' Kent continued in his rapid-fire speech, 'thinks it had to be someone good at talking their way in. The chairman had fearsome security on his villa and it was intact.'

'How do you know that?'

'From a friend of a friend who knows Beck. Same story as with Sterndales – although no one bothered to talk their way in there. I'm starting to check on another private bank. Will report any findings.'

'Keith, there's a motorcycle gang operating in Geneva and—'

'I know. Bunch of rowdies. Macho kids who get their kicks frightening old ladies.'

'More than that. There was a shoot-out in the Old City tonight. Six dead bodies. All motorcyclists. They are more than macho kids.'

'Really . . .' For once Kent paused. 'Geneva doesn't sound very healthy. Thanks for the warning. I'm off to Berne in the morning. *Early* in the morning after what you've told me. Be in touch . . .'

Tweed put the phone down, told Monica and the two men what he'd heard.

'Now we have a direct link between Brazil and missing bearer bonds,' Newman commented.

'It would seem so,' Tweed replied.

186

'You didn't mention The Motorman to Kent,' drawled Marler.

'It slipped my mind.' Tweed took an envelope off his desk, extracted two photos, handed one to Newman and one to Marler. 'Those are copies of the photograph of Marchat we brought back from Dorset. Just in case we ever find him. Monica has told me Paula took her own copy with her before she flew to Geneva.'

His office door opened and Howard, the pompous Director, strolled in. A tall man, well padded, in his late fifties, he was immaculately dressed, as always.

He was clad in a blue business suit with a chalk stripe which was a Chester Barrie bought from Harrods. He had a pink face, clean-shaven, and a lordly manner.

'Good evening, everyone,' he opened in his public-school voice, 'all quiet on the Western Front?'

It was a joke. No one smiled. Tweed stood up, walked over to the window, pulled aside a curtain, and stared out into the night.

'You could say that,' he replied.

'Not chasing after Mr Leopold Brazil any more, I trust. The PM was very annoyed we'd started to investigate him. He's expecting Brazil to join him for drinks soon at Downing Street.'

'How nice for the PM,' Tweed responded.

Howard sat down, draped one leg over the arm of the chair, adjusted the razor-edged crease in his trousers.

'The computer equipment I've had installed on the floor above is working like a dream. Reginald is very good.'

'Reginald?' Marler queried.

'He's the communications wizard in charge of bringing us into the twenty-first century. You'll be able to throw away your old card-index system, Tweed.'

'I shall keep it going,' retorted Tweed, his back still to the room – and to Howard.

'What on earth for?'

'Because I know any storage system of vital data operated by computers can be penetrated.' Tweed swung round to face his chief. 'Hacked into, is the jargon phrase.'

'I was going to suggest . . .' Howard paused, glanced at Newman and Marler who were staring at him with blank expressions, as though he wasn't there. 'I was going to suggest,' Howard started again with less confidence, 'we should use the computer to store the names of all our informants . . .'

'No,' said Newman.

'No,' said Marler.

'It's hardly up to you gentlemen to . . .'

'It *is* up to these gentlemen . . .' Tweed went round his desk, sat in his chair and gazed grimly at Howard as he went on. 'It is up to these gentlemen never to reveal to anyone – not even to me – the names of their secret informants. Haven't you realized yet that lives are at stake – the lives of our informants?'

'Well . . .' Howard stood up, tucked a finger inside his shirt collar as though it felt uncomfortable. 'Well, if you feel so strongly about it I suppose we can postpone including them . . .'

'For ever!' snapped Tweed.

'Yes, I see. It is after all your responsibility.'

'All the time,' replied Tweed, refusing to give an inch or to bother about saving Howard's face.

'Appreciate it if you could keep me informed. When you can, of course . . .'

On this defensive note Howard retreated out of the office. He closed the door behind himself very quietly.

'That's seen him off,' piped up Monica with unconcealed glee.

'He hasn't a clue,' growled Tweed. 'In that big office

on the next floor up near the head of the staircase there's enough equipment to run the Pentagon. Reginald, a wet, has a number of personal computers, laptops, a staff of three, cables linking the stuff to the telephone, those horrible green video screens. It must have cost a fortune. Howard was counting on our records being the show-piece of his new toy department. Now I've killed that idea Heaven knows what they'll play about with to justify their existence.'

'I have a friend, Abe Wilson, who works from home,' Newman said. 'He had a lot of this junk. His wife told me that when he comes down at night he heads for the living room and gazes at television. Then he promptly falls fast asleep. She asked me on the quiet would I take her out to dinner.'

'Attractive?' enquired Marler.

'Very. I turned down her invitation as tactfully as I could. Abe is going round the bend.'

'Bob,' Tweed interjected, 'what is your impression of how Philip is getting on with Eve?'

'The poor devil doesn't know whether he's coming or going. She's playing him on a long string. But he becomes the old Philip we know when he's involved in his work.'

'I wonder where Eve Warner is at this moment?' Tweed mused.


Alighting from her flight at Geneva, Eve moved quickly after going through Passport Control and Customs. She went straight to the car-hire counter, identified herself, signed the papers for the Renault she had hired over the phone from Heathrow, paid the girl behind the counter. Then she lingered nearby, smoking a fresh cigarette, glancing casually round at the few passengers hurrying out. Near the end of February the airport was quieter than in the season.

She was looking for anyone who might have followed her. Eve had a photographic memory for faces, even those seen for a fraction of a minute. She saw no one who aroused her suspicions. She walked briskly back to the counter, told the girl she had dealt with she was ready to leave.

Escorted to the waiting Renault, she took the keys from the girl and glared at her.

'It's red,' she snapped, slapping her gloved hand on the bonnet. 'I distinctly asked for a neutral colour.'

'I'm sorry, Madame, but you were insistent over the phone that you wanted a Renault. This is the only one we had left.'

'I suppose it will have to do. Thank you for nothing.'

Taking off her camel-hair coat, she flung it in the back. She wore a scarf over her hair which hid her jet-black hair and was wearing tinted glasses. Only her walk identified her.

She drove off out of the city and hit the highway which headed north-east. Keeping just inside the speed limit, she overtook one vehicle after another. A truck driver blared his horn at her as she swept past him on a long bend. She waved a hand at him over her shoulder.

An hour later she pulled in at a small hotel on the edge of a town. She had a quick meal and rationed herself to one vodka, then, nervous, spilt perfume down her front to mask any faint alcoholic fumes. The Swiss police were bastards about drinking and driving.

Before leaving the hotel she found a phone, dialled a number from memory. When a man answered the phone she pulled a face. That creep.

'Eve Warner speaking from Geneva. I'll be driving and will reach you this evening. Pass the message on . . .'

She slammed down the phone, went outside and again she was driving north-east on a main highway.

Earlier she had passed the Jura Mountains, their snow gleaming in the moonlight, passed attractive villages with church spires like needles, illuminated. She had seen none of this. Magnificent scenery didn't interest her. As she drove she kept lighting another cigarette and overtaking, overtaking, overtaking. She couldn't bear to have another vehicle in front of her. She felt very good, leaving them behind her, showing them what a marvellous driver she was. She would arrive at her destination early. She liked surprising people.

Inside his office in Berne Leopold Brazil was in a towering rage. He strode round the room, hands clasped behind his back as he thundered. Igor, the wolfhound, watched him, then watched the target of Brazil's anger.

Tall and lean, the dog had a small head and its ears were lifted, sensing the mood of its master. Craig, who had flown back from Geneva to Belp, then had been driven by a waiting car to the villa in Kochergasse, kept glancing at the dog, which had its mouth open, its teeth bared.

Craig had reported to Brazil the ghastly fiasco in the Old City of Geneva – although he had been careful not to use the word 'fiasco'. Only by grilling him had Brazil got the truth out of his deputy.

'You are the world's greatest idiot!' Brazil shouted. 'Corpses lying in the street – your men – just when we need no adverse publicity, to say nothing of the dead you are responsible for. Did I or did I not warn you after the Sterndale Manor massacre that we must maintain a low profile?'

'They had a lot of men waiting for us,' Craig lied.

'I have independent sources to check that statement. Are you under the impression you are running Murder Inc.? I experienced this sort of thing in the States, which is why I left that violent country. You are supposed to

191

frighten people, to intimidate them, not kill them,' Brazil roared.

'They started shooting first,' Craig lied again.

'Who is "they"?' Brazil demanded.

'Tweed's men, I presume . . .'

'You presume! Now you're lying. I know something of Tweed, met him once briefly. He's not the sort of man to operate in that way . . .'

'You can't be sure of that—'

'*Don't you dare interrupt me!* I *am* sure of that. And soon I have to meet Tweed, if he will ever agree to do that after this horror . . .'

Brazil tightened his hold on the leash. The hound had started to move towards Craig, who backed away.

'And another thing,' Brazil raved on. 'Up to now, with the aid of certain powerful Swiss banker friends, I have neutralized Arthur Beck.' He stood quite still, hands on his hips. 'In case your memory has gone Beck is the Chief of Federal Police, his headquarters a mere stone's throw from where I'm standing. If he can find the smallest link between what happened in Geneva and myself he'll be on my back – just when the project I am directing is about to be launched.'

'If I knew what the project was—' Craig began unwisely.

'You don't – and you won't. Not until zero hour. I would greatly appreciate it if you would get out of my sight, get out of this room. I'll instruct you in the morning. Go! For God's sake . . .'


Arriving at the villa, Eve had been admitted by José, and had run up the curving staircase to Brazil's office with José rushing up behind her. Even through the heavy door to his office she heard Brazil's voice and guessed he was roaring at Craig.

This I must see, she thought. She detested Craig, who ignored her most of the time. Her hand was on the doorknob when José grasped her from behind.

'You can't go in there . . .'

'Yes, I can. I have information . . .'

'You must wait.'

She detested the smooth-skinned José and struggled to get free. She raised her foot and scraped it down his shin. She heard him grunt but he wouldn't let go.

'Let me go, you Colombian turd . . .'

'I am from French Guiana,' José said calmly.

He held on, pinioned her arms to her side. She hadn't realized he was so strong. She swore at him but he continued holding her in his grip and didn't bother to answer the insult. Then the door opened. Craig, his face flushed, closed the door behind him. He stared at her.

'Listening at keyholes again?'

'Sounds as though you had a proper thrashing,' she retorted with a wolfish smile.

Craig walked off. José released her. She took off her coat and scarf, opened the door and went inside, followed by José, who took his normal place behind his corner desk.

'Didn't expect you so quickly,' Brazil commented, now quite calm.

'I'm a good driver,' she said as he sat down behind his large desk. 'Did he . . .' She gestured towards José without looking at him. 'Did he remember to give you the names of key members of Tweed's team I found out? Bob Newman, Paula Grey – and possibly William Franklin?'

'José always remembers. He did give me the names.'

'I have another one to add to the list. Philip Cardon.'

# 20

In Paula's suite at the Hôtel des Bergues the three of them had just finished an excellent dinner brought in by waiters wheeling two tables which they put together.

'That sole was wonderful,' Paula said. 'I feel a new woman.'

'The food was superb,' said Archie. 'Thank you very much.'

He produced the half-smoked cigarette from his pocket and tucked it into the corner of his mouth. Philip had wondered whether he would eat his meal with the stub still in place.

'Let's sit on that long couch to drink our coffee,' Paula suggested.

She waited until they were settled, then produced the copy of the photograph of Marchat from her shoulder bag. She handed it to Archie.

'I don't suppose you've any idea who this is?'

Archie studied the photo, held it under a lamp on the coffee table. He stared at it for almost a minute. He doesn't know, Paula thought. Nice try. Archie handed back the picture to her.

'Is he important?' he asked.

'He could be very important.'

'I see.'

Archie picked up his cup, sipped coffee with his cigarette still in his mouth without spilling a drop. He put the cup down carefully. Paula had already observed all Archie's movements were deliberate. He used a napkin to dab at his mouth.

'Something wrong?' asked Philip.

194

'Is the man in the picture in danger?' Archie asked.

'He could be in great danger. He was supposed to have been burned to death in the fire at Sterndale Manor in Dorset – as were General Sterndale and his son, Richard. Also the only remaining relative who would have been there but was indisposed.'

'I see,' Archie said again.

'No hurry,' Paula assured him. 'Take your time. I mean that.'

'Anton Marchat,' Archie said suddenly. 'A Swiss. He lives with his wife in the Valais.'


Paula was briefly stunned. She had not expected a positive reply.

'The valley?' she repeated. 'Which valley?'

'I meant the canton of the Valais. Well to the east of where we are sitting.'

'How stupid of me,' Paula said, annoyed at herself. 'I do know French but we've been speaking English. He disappeared from England. We know he flew to Geneva, but that was all.'

'Rugged country, the Valais,' Archie ruminated. 'The people are hardy. They have to be to live there – especially now in winter. It will be at its worst.'

'Will he have gone back there, do you think?' Paula pressed.

'Was he frightened?'

'I'd say he was scared stiff,' Philip told him. 'An assassin tried to murder him but got the wrong man.'

'Then if he flew to Geneva . . .' Archie paused, working it out. He sat up straighter, the dead cigarette wobbled. 'If he flew to Geneva,' Archie repeated, 'it's more than likely he boarded one of the international expresses at Cornavin Station. Then he'd get off in the Valais and go home and stay there.'

'You wouldn't know his address?' Philip asked casually.

'Is someone going to visit him, to protect him?'

'I am,' said Philip.

'*We* are,' said Paula.

'I know what happened outside Les Armures,' Archie said slowly. 'One of the waiters crouched behind a table where he could see. He said there was just one woman and one man. Imagine those two finishing off that gang of murderous thugs.'

He glanced first at Paula, then he glanced at Philip.

'You had a pretty grim time when that motorcycle gang attacked.'

'Let's say we had a lively evening,' Philip replied cautiously.

That seemed to be answer enough for Archie. He took a hotel notepad off the table, tore off a sheet, turned the pad over and began writing with the pencil which had lain next to the pad.

Paula noted how he wrote very lightly. No pressure which could imprint something of what he was writing on the cardboard back of the pad. He held the sheet after dropping the pad back on the table.

'Sion,' he said.

'Where?' asked Paula.

'Sion.'

'It's deep in the middle of the Valais,' Philip told her. 'The international expresses from Geneva, bound for Milan, make only three stops in the Valais. At Martigny, Sion, and Brig.'

'The weather will be terrible,' Archie warned them while still holding the sheet of paper. 'Heavy snow, a lot of ice. It's rugged country, the Valais. Anton Marchat lives in an old house on the edge of the town. It lies under a great hunk of rock, a grim hill like a small mountain with the castle – or is it the cathedral? – perched on top.

You can see that precipitous hill as the train approaches Sion. Here is the address.'

He handed it to Paula, who showed it to Philip. Archie sat thinking some more, clenched his cigarette.

'If you go you had better be arrmed . . .' His eyes twinkled at Paula. 'But then the two people outside Les Armures had weapons. One important point. If you go. If you meet Anton Marchat or his wife, you must mention my name. Otherwise you get the door slammed in your faces.'

Philip kept the sheet, folded it, put it in a secret pocket in his wallet. Archie stood up, looked round for his coat.

'You're not going out tonight?' Paula asked anxiously. 'I found a couch here – that one over there – and it turns into a bed. That way you can sleep here overnight and there'll be no trace in the hotel register that you were ever here.'

'I must go now, but thank you for the invitation.' Archie was putting on his coat, helped by Paula, who had brought it from her bedroom. 'My work never ends. I have to catch a night train.'

'Where to?' enquired Philip. 'Or shouldn't I ask?'

'There is going to be great activity in a certain city tomorrow. I must be there to see what happens. Perhaps you should be there, too.'

'Where then?' Philip persisted.

'Berne.'


Monica, who had answered the phone when it rang, looked taken aback. Everyone in the room noticed – they had never seen anything throw her off balance.

'General and Cumbria Assurance,' she had said.

'Good evening. I apologize for the late call. This is Carson Craig,' the voice continued courteously. 'Mr Brazil has asked me to see if we can arrange a meeting

197

between himself and Mr Tweed. At Mr Tweed's convenience, of course.'

'Please hold on. I may be a minute. I'm not sure you have got the right number . . .'

'Please do not think I am being impolite, but I *know* I have the right number. I will hold on. There is no rush.'

Masking the phone with her hand, Monica told Tweed what Craig had said. She looked at Newman and Marler.

'I thought he was a roughneck. He sounds like a highly educated man.'

'I'll talk to him,' Tweed said to everyone's surprise.

He gestured for Monica to hand her phone to Newman so he could listen in.

'Good evening, Mr Craig. Tweed speaking. I don't believe I've had the pleasure of making your acquaintance,' he said smoothly.

'That's true. But it's a small world, as they say, Mr Tweed. I hope we can remedy that situation one day. Mr Brazil has flown to Bonn to meet the German Chancellor. I gather he also works late hours. But Mr Brazil will be back in the morning early.'

'May I ask where you are speaking from?'

'Of course. My apologies. I am in Mr Brazil's office in his villa on the Kochergasse, Berne. Mr Brazil has thought over his earlier offer to meet you and thinks you may not wish to take up his offer to travel in the executive jet he was prepared to put at your disposal. If you prefer to make your own way to the rendezvous he is quite happy with that idea.'

'I do,' said Tweed. 'So what rendezvous are you suggesting?'

'We now feel it might be more courteous if you told us where you could meet him. Wherever that might be Mr Brazil will travel there.'

'Zurich,' said Tweed.

'Certainly . . .' There had been a brief pause before Craig agreed. 'Could you possibly tell me the location and the time?'

'At the Hotel Schweizerhof . . .' Tweed paused and saw Newman give the thumb's-up sign, indicating his full approval. 'It's opposite the main station – in the Bahnhofplatz. Do you know it, Mr Craig?'

'I most certainly know where you mean, although I've never been inside that particular hotel. Had you a specific time in mind?'

'Yes. Seven tomorrow evening. Swiss time. I will be waiting for Mr Brazil in the lobby.'

'Mr Tweed, I can tell you Mr Brazil will not only be pleased, he will be greatly relieved. I doubt if I will be with him, but I hope to meet you for a drink, even for dinner, at a time and place at your convenience.'

'Thank you for calling. Good night, Mr Craig . . .'


'*Was* that Craig?' Tweed asked Newman when he had put down the phone.

'Yes. Most definitely.' Newman looked bemused. 'Dr Jekyll and Mr Hyde. I met the evil Hyde in Dorset, you've talked with the suave Jekyll a moment ago. It's quite incredible. I've never encountered such a dual personality.'

'Anyone want to let me in on this?' enquired Marler.

'You saw – and heard him – during the fracas at the Black Bear.' Newman had twisted round in his chair to address Marler standing against a wall. 'How would you have described him?'

'A rough, foul-mouthed, brutal thug.'

'Not the sort of chap to invite to your club,' Monica commented, mimicking Howard's upper-crust voice.

'Something like that,' Marler agreed. 'So?'

'Well, on the phone just now,' Newman continued, 'he was the polished, well-educated businessman. Courteous and deferential to Tweed.'

'Why did you select Zurich?' Monica wanted to know.

'Because,' Newman answered her, 'I think Tweed recalled how well we know that area.'

'Tweed is still here,' said Tweed. 'We have to get moving. We'll probably be here all night. Monica, book tickets for the earliest flight tomorrow to Zurich. For myself, Newman, Marler, Butler, and Nield. Then book us rooms at the Hotel Schweizerhof – that is for myself and Newman. Then book rooms for Marler, Butler, and Nield at the Hotel Gotthard.'

'Which is just behind the Schweizerhof,' said Monica.

'Exactly. And I'd better repack my case in that cupboard over there with cold-weather clothing.'

'I can do that,' urged Monica.

'No, you can't. Get on with booking the flights and hotel reservations. This is the development I have been waiting for. Brazil's patience has cracked. Which means that whatever project he has planned is about to be put into action. Remember in a previous phone call to me he used the word "catastrophe"? The balloon is going up . . .'

# 21

Eve had been buffing her fingernails while Craig talked to Tweed. She listened to Craig and sneered to herself. When he had put down the phone she tried to put him down. After all, Craig was in trouble with Brazil so this was the moment to kick him.

'How smarmy can we get?' she started. 'You certainly did crawl to Tweed.'

200

'We can get as smarmy as we have to – when we have to,' Craig told her amiably.

She had her legs crossed, open to view where the slash in her skirt exposed them. He eyed them as he lit a cigarette. I wonder if I could hook him and then drop him with a bang, she thought.

'Well, you had a job to do.' She flashed him a smile. 'And actually you did it pretty well. The fish has taken the bait?'

'Tweed is meeting the boss tomorrow over here, if that is what you're getting at.'

'You'll earn medals instead of brickbats yet.'

'At least my job isn't to lure powerful men into the pit,' he remarked.

'*What did you say?*' She was furious. She sat up very erect. 'Are you implying I'm a high-class call-girl? Because I have a clear understanding with Brazil that I don't go to bed with any man he may ask me to target.'

'I know that,' he said quietly. 'You do blow your top at the drop of a hat. And I haven't even got a hat to drop.'

'Haha! Very humorous. If you go for cheap gags no self-respecting comedian would dream of using. Now, Carson, we could be friends instead of scrapping with each other all the time. And Leopold doesn't like it. By the by, that animal over there shouldn't be here. He was in England when the boss visited Grenville Grange. Six months in quarantine is the British rule.'

'The chief was careful. Igor was smuggled off the jet at Bournemouth International, then kept in Brazil's limo. While we were at the Grange Igor never even saw another animal of any kind.'

'He broke the law,' Eve insisted. 'But that's his affair,' she said hastily. 'If you sneak on me to him I'll say you made it up.'

'You would, too. Maybe you and I could go out some

time, have a few vodkas, shoot the breeze, as they say, whoever "they" may be.'

'Maybe,' she replied. 'Where is this meeting with Tweed taking place?'

'That's classified information.'

'I heard you say a hotel. Which one?' she coaxed.

'It's still classified.' He got up. 'Don't blame me and start yelling. The boss's orders. I get paid to do as he tells me.'

'Bet you don't get paid as much as I do.'

'I wouldn't know. José hands out the bread.'

'I don't trust José,' she said and watched Craig with her eyes narrowed.

He was walking towards her. She waited for him to lay a hand on her leg. The moment he did he'd get her full glass of vodka in his face, down his nice suit. Craig walked past her to stroke the wolfhound. Igor was sitting in a corner, tongue hanging out, a dreamy look on its face. Igor had recently had its supper. It stood up and snarled as Craig came close.

'Watch it.' Eve swallowed her vodka, stood up, and walked towards the door. She looked at Craig over her shoulder. 'I'm going to bed. On my own,' she said sweetly.


In her bedroom at the Hôtel des Bergues Paula couldn't get back to sleep. She switched on the table lamp, checked her travelling clock. 2 a.m. Great.

She used the phone to call room service, ordered coffee for two, although she felt sure Philip would be fast asleep. Putting on a dressing gown and belting it, she opened the door into the living room quietly. Philip was not asleep.

Sprawled out on the couch bed, his table lamp alight, he was reading a paperback. He put it down as she came in, slipped on his dressing gown over his pyjamas, sat with his feet on the floor.

'You, too?' he said.

'Afraid so. It was a pretty exciting evening. I've ordered coffee, some for you on the off-chance you would be awake – although I didn't expect it.'

After the waiter had tapped on the door, brought a wheeled table in with coffee and cakes, and left with his generous tip, she poured for both of them.

The phone rang just as she was about to start drinking hers.

'A man on the phone for you, Miss Grey. He wouldn't give a name but insisted you'd want to speak to him.'

'I'll take it . . .'

'This is your dinner guest, Paula. Very sorry to call you at this hour but I've reached my destination. I checked with a friend . . .' He paused and Paula realized he meant an informant. 'He gave me one word, which I don't understand. A girl's name. Ariane . . . Said it was very important. Good night . . .'

She told Philip. 'A girl's name. Ariane. Ring any bells?'

'None at all. Archie must have thought it was important to call you back at this hour. I get the impression he has an informant in a really key position.'

'He did say it was very important. Damn it, I'm wide awake and so are you. I'm going to call Tweed . . . He might still be up.'


Tweed came back into his office, towelling his hair, then combing it in a mirror he borrowed from Monica. He looked at Newman and Marler.

'I feel good for another twenty-four hours. Amazing the way a bath freshens you up. I can recommend it.'

He stopped speaking, went behind his desk as the phone rang yet again. Monica took the call.

203

'It's René Lasalle from Paris. Sounds urgent.'

'Put him on. Good morning, René. So you, too, are burning the candle at both ends . . .'

'Tweed, this you should know. I've just heard it myself. Brazil sent a team to Cayenne – French Guiana. I heard about it, sent my own team with special cameras. You know about Ariane, our rocket-launching system in Guiana. Ariane. Brazil has had his own satellite flown out by plane for launching by Ariane into orbit. You know we make money by renting out the system for anyone with the funds to use Ariane to launch a satellite into space.'

'I know.'

'Well, something tricky took place. Brazil's team said they were checking the satellite, erected a canvas screen, but my team flew over in a helicopter just at the right moment and took a lot of pictures. A different satellite was substituted and we have the pics flown back from Guiana. They don't make sense to my so-called top experts, even though they have shots of what's inside the satellite.'

'Strange,' said Tweed.

'I know you have that weird man who has cracked scientific problems when no one else could. I have taken the liberty of sending you copies of the photos. A courier is in the air now, is being flown to Heathrow in a light aircraft.'

'When may I expect them?'

'Within an hour or two. At Park Crescent. I've phoned Heathrow and arranged for a car to be standing by.'

'I'll call Professor Grogarty now.'

'Won't delay you. I was summoned to the Elysée again and given a dressing-down by the President himself. Threatened with instant dismissal if my people went anywhere near Brazil. That's it . . .'

Tweed put the phone down, told Newman, Marler, and Monica what Lasalle had said.

'What on earth is that man up to?' Monica asked.

'We may know more if Grogarty can detect something from the photos. He's invented an extraordinary microscope which can read three-dimensional ciphers of a minute size. Monica, try and get Grogarty on the phone. He works through the night.'

The phone rang once more before Monica could start dialling. She listened, called out quickly.

'It's Paula on the line for you . . .'

Tweed grabbed the phone. He took a deep breath to hide his anxiety.

'Very good to hear from you. I've been thinking a lot about you.'

'Thank you,' said Paula quickly. 'I'm speaking from the Hôtel des Bergues,' she warned him. 'From my bedroom. I had a call recently from our friend who smokes cigarettes but doesn't smoke. You know who I mean?'

'Yes.' Tweed was careful not to mention the name Archie.

'He's had information from a reliable source. It's odd. Just one word. A girl's name. Ariane . . .'

'I know who she is, what he is talking about.'

'Thank heavens. Philip is with me, trying to sleep on the couch in the living room. Neither of us can go to sleep. Too alert.'

'Are you all right? I know about the Old City. Beck has called me in a rage. Don't worry. How are you?'

'OK. Quite OK. So is Philip. Our competitors seem to know every move we make in advance.'

'They're well organized and have plenty of money at their disposal. It helps.'

He was listening carefully to every word she said, trying to detect any signs of strain and stress. There were none.

'Has a certain important man Newman met in Dorset a base in Berne?' Paula asked.

'Yes, he has. Why?'

'We'll be going there tomorrow.'

'In the Kochergasse,' Tweed said swiftly. 'You're both going? Good. I want you both to try and see me at the Schweizerhof late tomorrow afternoon. We've stayed there before. Remember?'

'I'm sure we can make that. We *will*. Hadn't you better get some sleep?'

'I could say the same to you. I have to take another call. Take great care . . .'

He nodded to Monica, who dialled the Professor's number, said Tweed was on the line.

'Tweed! So, like me, you're an owl.' Grogarty gave a hoarse chuckle. 'My best work is done in the early hours. You have another problem. Of course! Otherwise you wouldn't be getting in touch.'

Tweed had a wild whim to ask him whether his *pince-nez* was crooked, but desisted.

'Yes, I do have a problem. A very strange one.' He explained about the call from Paris without mentioning Lasalle's name, ending with the fact that a courier was flying in with the photos of the satellite which had been secretly substituted for the original one.

'Sounds intriguing,' Grogarty commented. 'And you want my opinion yesterday?'

'No,' said Tweed, 'the day before yesterday.'

'Then why don't you hold the courier, look at the photos yourself, then send them straight on to me by the same courier.'

'I'm going abroad early in the morning. Soon after daylight.'

'Then you'd better send that courier over here pretty damned quick. Another thing, Tweed, it would help me if I knew its orbit – the areas of the Earth it passes over.'

Tweed put down the phone and swore aloud mildly, which he rarely did.

'Won't he cooperate?' asked Monica.

'He'll pull out all stops for me. But he wants now to know its orbit – what parts of the planet it is crossing. There's a problem for you.'

'Easy.' Monica began dialling a number from memory. 'I have the answer, with a bit of luck. Cord Dillon, Deputy Director of the CIA, and your old pal. He works late, and in any case the headquarters at Langley is on Washington time, so they're five hours behind us . . .'

'What would I do without her?' Tweed asked Newman as he stood up.

'Collapse,' Newman snapped.

'I'm going to the loo. Maybe you'd like to come up in a minute and we'll look in on Reginald and all his junk. I have a key to that room.'


Tweed found the door to the communications centre, as it had been called, was open and Reginald was inside with his staff of two. Newman entered the spacious room with Tweed, followed by Marler.

'Do come in, Mr Tweed,' said Reginald, seated in front of the largest machine in the place.

'I am in.'

'What I meant was I'm delighted you are at long last taking an interest in our work, that you have been converted to modern techniques.'

'I haven't.'

The three visitors looked slowly round the room which had smaller computers and PCs on metal tables against the walls. Green screens were flashing madly, some even showing wording, line after line of it.

Reginald was in his twenties, lean and wearing pebble glasses, his face almost cadaverous. He gestured towards the big machine he was sitting in front of, his fingers poised over the keyboard.

207

'This is the master computer, which is why it's bigger although the trend now is for computers to be smaller and smaller. The master computer I'm sitting in front of is linked to the telephone system – as are the others. And our security is foolproof.'

'No, it isn't,' said Tweed. 'I asked my bank director recently could he guarantee no one could hack into my account. He looked embarrassed, then agreed that it could be done, that it *had* been done on a number of occasions. Do you normally work so late?'

'Well, no. But since Monty arrived we're all keen to complete the link-ups.'

'Monty?' queried Tweed.

'That's what we call my master computer.'

'I'll leave you to get on with the good work . . .'

'Monty!' Tweed said with disgust as they went back down the stairs to his office. 'I wonder what those flashing lights will do to their eyes.'

As they went back into his office Monica was putting down the phone, looking pleased.

'Cord came up trumps. They're furious at Langley that Paris hasn't informed them they were launching a new satellite.'

'Paris?' queried Tweed. 'It's Brazil's satellite.'

'Obviously he has concealed his ownership by passing it along the line that it's a new French satellite. I suppose being on such good terms with the President in the Elysée he's got his support. Cord said they had heard about Ariane launching Rogue One and they've been tracking it.'

'Rogue One?'

'That's what Langley has christened it. Rather a good name, I thought.'

'A good name for Leopold Brazil,' said Marler.

*　　*　　*

'Mr Brazil has arrived back,' José told Eve. 'He wants to see you in his study.'

'I haven't had breakfast. I need my breakfast.'

'You've had sleep. Mr Brazil hasn't had any. When he does have sleep he only needs four hours. He has great energy, is a dynamic personality.'

'Shouldn't you wait until you're in his presence before you butter him up?' sneered Eve. 'Telling me isn't going to earn you any medals.'

The dark-skinned José's expression didn't change. It hardly ever changed. He told Eve Mr Brazil was waiting for her in his study.

She went downstairs to the first floor, didn't bother to knock on the study door, walked straight in. Igor, sitting alongside Brazil who was in his chair behind his desk, stood up, snarled.

'Igor prefers you to knock,' Brazil said mildly. 'He thinks it better manners.'

'Oh, I see.' Eve tossed her head. 'Would you like me to go out again, knock respectfully on your door, and wait for your command to come in?'

'Don't be impertinent. Sit down.'

Brazil was dressed in a smart heavy grey business suit with a regimental tie he had bought in Bond Street. He radiated an aura of power and purpose. On his desk was a fat envelope. He was amused to watch Eve trying not to look at it. He began talking again in his deep voice as soon as she sat down facing him.

'I am going to meet Tweed later today. I employ you because you have a flair for weighing up men, for spotting their weak points, for moulding them in your hands like putty. What sort of man is Tweed? Could you lure him so you had him in the palm of your hand?'

'He's an enigma.'

'Come. You can do better than that. You told me you had dinner with him one evening at the Priory Hotel.

Seeing someone at dinner is a good time to tell what they are really like.'

Eve frowned, forcing herself not to look at the fat envelope which was the only object on Brazil's desk. She was, as usual, trying to work out what reply would make her boss happy.

Brazil waited, appeared to read her mind.

'I don't want what you think I would like to hear. I want an honest assessment. You are supposed to be shrewd where men are concerned.'

'He's the most difficult man to analyse I ever met. He has changes of mood. Sometimes he's quite amiable, even jokey. At other times you can't tell from his expression what he's really thinking,' she said truthfully.

'He's insignificant?' Brazil suggested.

'No, far from it. I'd say he is cautious, likes to be sure of his ground before he moves. No woman could trap him. If they appeared to be doing so they'd get a nasty surprise. He likes women, but he's very discriminating in those he mixes with.'

'Go on. This is better. Much better.'

'Take Paula Grey. She's someone I'd say he trusts.'

'All right. What sort of woman is Paula Grey?'

'Attractive,' Eve said reluctantly. 'She's shrewd, probably very loyal to Tweed. I think they have a very special relationship built on mutual respect. Sometimes I thought she was in love with him.'

'And he with her?'

'If he is, he never shows it. At least I couldn't detect it.'

'You think they have ever been intimate together?'

'I'm sure they haven't. It's a very permanent relationship, but without that, I'm certain. A woman can tell.'

'Getting back to Tweed, if he was up against an enemy he regarded as very dangerous, what would be his reaction? I get a picture so far of a very intelligent, thoughtful man, very self-controlled and quiet. What would be his reaction?' he repeated.

'He'd be ruthless. He'd take decisions very quickly and move like lightning.'

'Interesting. You've done well. Now you can take the envelope on my desk you've had trouble keeping your eyes off. It's your salary plus a large bonus.'

'Thank you.'

The envelope disappeared inside her shoulder bag like a conjuring trick. She was dying to open it, had felt crisp banknotes inside it, but she knew opening it in front of Brazil would be a mistake. It would indicate greed.

She had no idea that when Brazil had originally hired her he had detected greed as the main motive in her makeup. Now she had the envelope she decided to ask the question which had been bothering her.

'After I'd got to know the chairman of the Zurcher Kredit bank I went to his house with a man you told me to meet at the station under the clock. You told me to introduce him as Mr Danziger Brown, the man I'd persuaded the chairman had an idea as to how the bank could make a huge profit. I introduced this man to the chairman after dark and went away, as instructed. Later, I read in the papers the chairman had been murdered.'

'So?'

'Was I introducing the chairman to the man who killed him?'

'Describe Mr Danziger Brown.'

'I couldn't make out whether he was tall or of medium height. He seemed very fat. The buttons of his overcoat were strained. He stooped, as though he was round shouldered. I couldn't see the colour of his hair – he was wearing a black beret. I couldn't see his face. It was a cold night and he had a muffler across most of his face.'

'He was a financial consultant. Whoever killed the chairman must have gained entry after he had gone.'

'The same thing happened when I made friends, on your instructions, with that banker in Geneva. And he was murdered the same night I took another man to see him.'

'A coincidence,' Brazil said blandly.

'I see.' She hesitated. 'Have you heard of someone called The Motorman?'

'Who?'

'The Motorman.'

'No. Sounds like a racing driver.'

Brazil was lying, but nothing in his expression gave away the fact. In this respect only he was like Tweed.

When Eve had left the room Brazil stroked Igor, began talking quietly to the dog.

'Tweed sounds very promising. If only I can persuade him we would make an unbeatable partnership . . .'

# 22

In the middle of the night in her suite at the Hôtel des Bergues Paula and Philip had an argument and for a while neither would give way.

'I say we ought to take an early morning train to Berne,' said Paula.

'Don't agree with the method of transport,' Philip rapped back. 'We are going to hire a car and drive there.'

'The roads will be hell,' Paula said vehemently.

'I'll drive. You're not questioning my ability to do that, are you?'

'Of course not! Don't be so touchy. A train will get us there. Swiss trains always do . . .'

'Then later we have to get to Zurich, in case you've forgotten.'

'I have not forgotten!' Paula began to pace up and

down the living room, like Tweed. 'But *you* have obviously forgotten there are express trains from Berne to Zurich.'

'I am aware of that . . .'

'Then why are you being so stubborn?'

'Not stubborn. Just looking ahead,' Philip shot back at her. 'We *can* drive from Berne to Zurich and get there by the time Tweed suggested.'

'I think a train will be safer . . .'

'No, it won't. If Craig's thugs have found out we're staying here they can board the same train we do.'

'How on earth could they find out we are here?' she demanded. She paused. 'Or maybe they could?'

'Yes, by impersonating detectives, asking to look at the hotel register downstairs. You believe Craig wouldn't have thought of that, provided some of his men with forged police credentials ages ago?'

Paula stood still, folded her arms. Philip poured more coffee for both of them.

'Thanks,' said Paula automatically. 'Philip, I think you are right. We'll hire a car. I wonder what on earth Ariane means? Tweed seemed to know.'


At Park Crescent the French courier had arrived with the photographs from French Guiana. Tweed asked him to wait downstairs and, taking out a batch of large glossy prints from the envelope, spread them out on his desk. Marler, Newman, and Monica came to stand behind him.

'They don't tell me anything,' Tweed said after examining them under a magnifying glass. He handed the glass to Newman, who studied the photos quickly.

'Just a jumble of nothing. Let's hope Grogarty is cleverer than us.'

'Monica, put these in an envelope addressed to the Professor, go down to the courier, who I found when I

213

saw him speaks English. Get Butler or Nield to drive the courier to Grogarty in Harley Street, tell the courier to wait if Grogarty wants to send them back quickly.'

'I've got the envelope ready . . .'

Marler spoke up when she came back and reported the courier was on his way with Butler driving him.

'I've just decided I want to fly to Geneva – not to Zurich. I have a contact there I'd like to visit. We'll need an armoury of weapons.' He was thinking of Rico Sava, the arms dealer. 'Then I'll catch an express to Zurich and be there in good time before the meeting with Brazil . . .'

'Monica, please change Marler's ticket for a flight to Geneva. The earliest possible,' Tweed requested.

She had just put down the phone after calling Heathrow when it rang again. She raised her eyebrows.

'You said it would be a long night,' she told Tweed.

'It's Keith Kent, long distance,' she told him after answering the call.

'How's it going, Keith?' Tweed opened.

'I'll probably have that information about the Geneva bank tomorrow – no, today. Where can I reach you?'

'Hang on . . .' Tweed called across to Monica. 'What is the phone number of the Schweizerhof in Zurich?'

She gave it to him instantly. He repeated it to Kent.

'Zurich?' Kent chuckled. 'Checking up on me about the Zurcher Kredit?' he joked.

'Of course. I always double-check you,' Tweed joked back. 'Now you know where you can get me. After five in the afternoon, Swiss time.'

'Be in touch . . .'

'Keith Kent is in Geneva,' Tweed told the others after putting down his phone. 'Seems to be a popular place.'

He had hardly finished speaking when the phone rang once more.

'Bill Franklin is on the line,' Monica informed Tweed.

'No one sleeps these days,' Tweed greeted Franklin.

'I doubt if you ever did,' Franklin replied with a chuckle. 'Your stamina never ceases to amaze me.'

'Don't do so badly yourself. What's happened?'

'Hoped I'd get you. My phone is safe.' Franklin paused. 'But *is* yours?'

'Come off it, Bill. You know I'll be on scrambler.'

'Good for you. That you remembered to press the button,' Franklin chaffed him. His voice became businesslike. 'My agency team has been very busy. Mr Brazil, at this moment, is in his villa in Berne. On Kochergasse. Almost opposite the Bellevue Palace Hotel. A woman arrived there earlier last night, driving herself in a Renault. A red job.'

'Description?'

'Difficult. She had a scarf over her head, another one round the lower half of her face. She walked very slowly from the underground garage when she'd parked her car. The garage is just beyond the eastern end of the Bellevue Palace. My chap guessed she was in her fifties, maybe sixties. By her walk.'

'Unless she's very cunning,' said Tweed.

'What does that mean?'

'Nothing. Just a random thought. Any more?'

'Yes. Carson Craig, Brazil's deputy, arrived before the woman. He went inside the villa with an ugly-looking thug, a small lean man. Tell you more when I know more.'

'Take down this number . . .' Tweed gave him the phone number of the Schweizerhof in Zurich. 'I'll be there tomorrow evening.'

'Going on your travels again. So you're launching a big offensive?'

'Not necessarily. Keep me informed of developments.'

'Don't go yet,' Franklin said quickly. 'One more item. My chap watching Brazil's villa said that soon after Craig and Co. had arrived a team of ten motorcyclists came purring along Kochergasse. They parked their machines

215

in the garage and then came out and walked into the villa. They were dressed all in black leather and wore their helmets. In Geneva last night there was a battle in the Old City between similar motorcyclists and someone else – don't know who. The locals, scared out of their wits, have nicknamed them the Leather Bombers. It appears they've now turned up in Berne.'

'That's very interesting. Thank you, Bill . . .'

As Tweed told the others what Franklin had said, Marler, standing against a wall, was twiddling a king-size between his fingers, not lighting it. He was frowning.

'That last bit of news from Franklin gives me an idea,' he said slowly. 'You'll need protection, Tweed, when we get to Zurich.'

'Yes, you will,' Newman said vehemently. 'I still think this could be a trap.'

'I don't agree,' Tweed replied. 'I'm getting the measure of Leopold Brazil. Despite what villainies he may have been responsible for I think he has his own peculiar code of honour. Now, I'm going to have a doze for thirty minutes. Unless the phone rings to remind us it's there.'

He had taken off his jacket and tie, loosened his shirt collar, when Pete Nield came in.

'Wrong moment?' he said, looking at Tweed.

'No. What is it?'

'I haven't had a chance to tell you what I found out while I was on my own in Dorset. Buchanan is going berserk down there. He's got it into his head the key to the four murders is the missing Marchat and he's turning Dorset upside-down to find him.'

'Thanks for the information. I wish him luck.' Tweed commented, 'Marchat is somewhere in Switzerland.' He shut his eyes and fell asleep.

*　　*　　*

216

It was snowing as they left Geneva early in the morning with Philip behind the wheel of a hired Audi he'd collected from the airport. Paula, sitting by his side, was thinking I told you so, but refrained from saying anything.

They were light flakes, drifting down, creating a weird luminosity as the moon faded for another day. To her left Paula gazed at the high white outline of the distant Jura Mountains, the old villages across the fields with snow piled on their rooftops.

'The scenery is beautiful,' she remarked. 'Incidentally, and just for the record, do you think we are being followed?'

'No sign of pursuers so far.'

'What time do you think we'll reach Berne?'

'In time for breakfast at the Bellevue Palace. I have been wondering what Archie had in mind when he mentioned Berne.'

'He's probably after another piece Tweed can fit into the jigsaw he's building up.'

'I've also been wondering where The Motorman is now.'

'Don't go and spoil the journey. I'm enjoying it.'

Which was true. Paula, an expert driver, loved being driven by someone who could really handle a car and she assessed Philip as a superb driver. She'd just had the thought when they skidded. Philip went with the skid, pulled out of it before they hit the barrier.

'This light snowfall is masking the ice,' he commented.

'You did all the right things,' she replied. 'And it was clever of you to ask the receptionist at the hotel when we were leaving the best route to Basle.'

'Well, if anyone enquires where we've gone they'll waste a lot of time searching for us.'

'I guessed that was the idea. You know, I have a

feeling our trip to Berne will prove to be very uneventful.'

'Famous last words . . . ?'


Tweed woke up, stretched his arms, stood up, put on his jacket after buttoning his shirt and straightening his tie in a mirror Monica held up for him. He felt as fresh as a daisy.

'You did have a deep sleep,' Monica told him. 'Thirty minutes. Cord Dillon phoned back from CIA HQ at Langley and you never batted an eyelid.'

'What did he say?'

'As far as they can tell – subject to double-checking – Rogue One, Brazil's satellite, is describing an orbit which takes it over Asia, Europe, London, the Atlantic, Washington, San Diego, and across the Pacific. He said the orbit seems to vary spasmodically, which doesn't make sense. He is also furious because he says the main orbit seems to pass over the Pentagon. He'll come back with more later.'

'Curious.'

Tweed went over to a globe of the world standing on a corner table, used his finger to follow the orbit Cord had detailed. The phone rang as he was studying the globe.

'Professor Grogarty,' Monica called out.

'He's been quick. Or maybe he has a query.'

'Tweed?' Grogarty gave a hoarse chuckle. 'I've cracked it – with the aid of the microscope I invented. A sticky one, this. The photos show your satellite is a travelling telephone exchange. Most ingenious. Thousands of numbers, but I recognized one.'

'Which one?'

'The top secret one at the Pentagon – linked, I know, to their computers.'

'You know that number?' Tweed asked sceptically.

'Of course I do, man. They're always asking me questions so I need their number to call them when I've worked out the answer.' He chuckled again. 'I spotted another – *yours*! What's the orbit of the damned thing?'

Tweed told him, adding that Rogue One appeared to vary its course.

'That's Irina Krivitsky. Remember I told you one of the names on the list you showed me was a top Russian? She specializes in the control and manoeuvre of satellites by laser. Well, it has a laser mechanism embedded into it. But somewhere there has to be a ground station on Earth and another laser system to activate the one in the satellite. I've never seen anything like this bag of tricks.'

'Would it need a team to produce it?'

'Definitely. The kind of team made up by the missing scientists on your list. They could do it. And it's very advanced, is this little baby rotating over our heads. I've sent the courier back to you with the photos.'

'Can't thank you enough . . .'

'Yes, you can. Send me a bottle of Château d'Yquem.'

Tweed put down his phone, thought for a minute, and then asked Monica a question.

'I suppose my personal phone number isn't linked up with that rubbish upstairs?'

Monica looked embarrassed. She got up and beckoned for Tweed to look behind her desk at the lower part of the wall.

'I was going to tell you, but we've been so busy. No, the truth is I didn't know how to tell you. I thought you'd blame me.'

'Blame you for what?'

'While you were in Dorset Howard came in with some men and said they were installing a cable to link your phone number with that crazy junk they've got upstairs. I protested, but Howard overrode me.'

'Did he now? Well, I certainly don't blame you. Howard obviously chose a time while I was away to pull that trick. He knows my number – the private one – is the most secure in the building.'

Tweed examined the thick grey cable which almost merged with the grey skirting board and disappeared through a well-concealed hole into the hall outside.

'Howard's getting crafty in his old age. But we can't waste time on that . . .'

He told the others the gist of what Grogarty had reported.

'It's beyond me,' said Monica. 'Didn't he explain it more clearly?'

'I purposely didn't ask him to. I'd have been here all day—'

He broke off as Monica answered the phone, then pulled a wry face.

'Grogarty is back on the line.'

'Hello again,' said Tweed. 'Keep it short, please. I have a plane to catch.'

'You always have. I just wanted to remind you that one of the team on that list – Ed Reynolds from California – is an expert in sabotaging communications. You hear me?'

'Yes. Go on . . .'

'The too-clever-by-half scientists have invented a global communications system. They've *centralized* communications. I think your satellite tearing about the skies over our heads could be a very efficient instrument for sabotaging world communications. The question is why would they want to do that? And *when*? *Bon voyage* . . .'

Again Tweed tersely reported to the others what Grogarty had said. Marler nodded, looked at his watch.

'I've got to go now to catch my flight. I'll be having a chat with my friendly arms dealer in Geneva.'

He gave a little salute, slipped into a smart cold-weather coat with an astrakhan collar, picked up his bag, and left.

'What we have to do,' Tweed said after he had gone, 'is to locate the ground station controlling that satellite.'

'And how do we do that?' asked Newman.

'I've no idea.'

# 23

Arriving in Geneva, Marler took the same route Paula had followed. He travelled in a taxi, asking to be dropped outside the Hôtel des Bergues. There, unlike Paula, he didn't enter the hotel.

Instead, carrying his bag, he crossed the Rhône, which was swollen, by using the footbridge. He paused several times, putting down his bag as though it was heavy, and changing it to the other hand. As he did so he glanced back. The footbridge was empty. For Rico Sava's sake it was important he was not followed.

It was supposed to be daylight but February had ended and March had begun. The worst time of the year for bad weather. Overhead dark clouds drifted over the city, which was just waking up. It was more like a dirty dusk than daylight and he had to watch his footing. The footbridge was a solid sheet of ice.

Leaving the footbridge, he threaded his way into the street where Sava lived and carried on his illegal business. It was almost dark despite the fact that the street lights were still on. He walked past the heavy door leading into Sava's shop. His instinct told him he was being watched.

And I'm not armed yet, he thought. He walked a long way, turned back suddenly. No one in sight. You are getting paranoid, he told himself. Arriving back at the heavy door he closed his eyes after pressing the bell, remembering the glaring light.

It came on. There was the usual wait. Then the Judas window was opened.

'We are closed,' Sava's voice said in French.

'Not to me. It's Marler. Marler,' he repeated.

The glaring light was switched off, the door was unlocked and he walked slowly into the dark. Sava closed the door, relocked it, switched on a light, took the hand Marler had extended, and clasped it between both his own.

'As always, you are most welcome. Not just for the business you bring me, but for yourself. Why do you never pay just a social call, have a drink with me?'

'I will do. One day. What's your tipple?'

'A fine old brandy.'

'You shall have one. When I have the time. Or maybe a couple?' Marler said with a smile.

'A couple, drunk slowly – so we have time to talk. And now, what can I supply you with?'

Marler rapped out his list, a long one. For the first time since he'd known him Sava stared in amazement.

'You are going to clean up Switzerland, start a small war?'

'The other side will start the war, we'll finish it.'

'But you need something to carry that cargo.'

Marler slapped his suitcase on a table top, unlocked it, took out two large flattened bags with shoulder straps which lay on top of his neatly folded clothes. He gave the canvas holdalls to Sava, who took them and began to accumulate what Marler had ordered. He packed them carefully away.

'Two friends of yours called here yesterday,' Sava remarked with a smile.

'I know.'

Twiddling a king-size between his fingers but not lighting it, Marler noted Sava had not mentioned one of them had been a woman. A very discreet man. Sava placed a tin ashtray on the table.

'You may smoke. Please do. I will not be very much longer.'

Every item was carefully wrapped in polythene, stacked so nothing would move. Which was important, Marler thought – considering some of the items he'd ordered.

'I seem to remember there's a taxi rank at the end of the street,' Marler recalled. 'Near the Brasserie.'

'That is so. You will be heavily weighed down.'

'One bag over each shoulder and I can carry the suitcase in my hand. Give me the Walther and a hip holster. I'll want that where I can get at it easily.'

'You are a wise man.'

Marler stripped off overcoat and jacket, fastened on the hip holster, checked the Walther's action briefly, slid a magazine Sava handed him in the butt, then slid the gun inside the holster.

Sava told him how much it would all be with a generous discount and Marler took a fat envelope from the breast pocket of his jacket, counted out thousand-franc notes.

'Take care of yourself,' Sava said as he helped Marler on with his overcoat.

Hoisting each of the holdalls on to a shoulder by the straps, Marler picked up his bag as Sava went to the door and started dismantling the fortress.

'And you take care of yourself,' Marler told him. 'I won't forget the two large brandies.'

It was a remark he was later to recall bitterly.

*　　*　　*

223

The man inside the darkened arcade on the opposite side of the street stayed in the shadows until Marler had disappeared. He then crossed the street, stood in front of the heavy door set back in an alcove. He glanced up and down the street. A few vague silhouettes trudging off to work in the distance. He reached up inside the alcove on his right, pulled at a small metal box which had been attached to the stone wall by suckers. When it came free he pushed aside the hood covering his head, held the box close to his ear, pressed the button which would activate the listening device.

*We are closed . . .*

*Not to me. It's Marler. Marler . . .*

The words came out clearly, quietly. He shoved the box inside the pocket of his overcoat, took a deep breath, then pressed the bell. A glaring light came on.

He had a long wait. He was used to waiting. Then the Judas window opened.

'Who is it? We are closed.'

'Marler sent me back. Marler needs something else,' the voice said in French, the language which had been used in the recording. The glaring light was extinguished.

Another wait while locks were unfastened, bolts drawn. The door swung inwards and the visitor stepped inside cautiously. Sava closed the door, switched on the light.

His visitor appeared to be of medium height, shoulders stooped. He looked fat, the buttons on his overcoat straining at the threads. He wore a scarf over the lower half of his face, a hat pulled well down over his forehead. He stood very still.

'Well?' Sava asked, an uncertain tone in his voice. 'I thought I had supplied everything.'

'A Smith and Wesson .38.'

'He wants a second one?' Sava asked.

'Yes, he does.'

'Odd.' Sava stood hesitantly. 'He's never forgotten anything before.'

'A gun like that one over there.'

The visitor pointed. It was a reflex action on Sava's part to look behind him, although his brain told him there was no weapon on view.

As he turned round, the visitor moved swiftly. One powerful arm locked itself round Sava's neck. The other fell on his victim's left shoulder, holding him still. The visitor's arm performed a certain movement. Sava sagged in his arms, his neck broken. He was lowered to the floor on his back, a corpse in seconds. Whoever found him would see his neck turned at a grotesque angle, his eyes open, seeing nothing any more.

The visitor removed his thick motoring gloves, exposing hands wearing surgical gloves. He swiftly fiddled with the security on the door, opened it a short distance, peered out. No one about. He pulled the door almost shut behind him after putting on his motoring gloves and shuffled off down the street. He didn't want too long to elapse before the body was discovered. After all, he was entitled to his fee.

# 24

'I'm asking you, Craig, why did you want those descriptions I gave you of Paula Grey, Bob Newman, and Philip Cardon – to say nothing of Bill Franklin?' demanded Eve.

She was in her own room at the villa in Berne, had met Craig on the stairs, and, flashing him an inviting smile, had asked him into her room. Craig, misunderstanding her completely – as she had intended he should – had gone into her room like a lamb to the slaughter.

Now she was raving and ranting at him. He was completely thrown off balance. That a mere woman should talk to him like that was beyond his comprehension. He glared at her and attempted to quell her verbally.

'What the hell do you mean, addressing me in that tone?'

'You haven't answered by question, you piece of rubbish!' she shouted at him, standing with her hands on her hips.

'And I'm bloody well not answering your question.'

'You bloody well are,' she stormed. 'I heard you on the phone in your office last night, giving those descriptions to someone on the line. Before you rushed off to catch a plane from Belp. Does Mr Brazil know who you were phoning? That you *did* make that call?'

Craig's aggressiveness faded like ice melting under a strong sun. He was appalled and his expression gave him away. Eve understood the expression and knew she had him just where she wanted him. With his back up against a wall.

'That was confidential,' he said, almost bleated. 'I have duties to perform and the boss gives me wide latitude . . .'

'So Brazil does *not* know about that phone call,' she hissed at him triumphantly. 'Who the devil were you calling?'

Inwardly Craig was fearful. He had never suspected what a hellcat this woman could be. Obviously she had listened at his door, had quietly opened it a fraction while he was making the call on his private line. It was impossible for him to reveal who he had called.

He wiped his sweating palms on his trousers, gave her an oily smile. She waited, her expression ugly, her hands still on her hips. She was enjoying herself – to see this thug who had always ignored her, crawling to her. She was controlling the situation now.

'I'm sure you have expensive tastes,' he began. 'So maybe a little personal bonus just between us would be a help.'

'Don't like the word little.'

He took out his wallet, peeled off two thousand-franc notes and held them out.

'Put them on the table,' she ordered.

He did so, hating her for the humiliation she was imposing on him, treating him like a servant. Glancing at the money, she cocked her index finger, beckoned. He began to move towards her.

'Stay where you are!' she screamed at him. 'Are you so stupid? Don't you realize I was beckoning for you to get out your wallet again?'

'It's not enough?'

'Not nearly. You're loaded.'

He sucked in his breath, brought out his wallet again, extracted three more thousand-franc notes, laid them on the table. Five thousand altogether. This was blackmail on a big scale. Eve spoke again.

'Leave them there and get the hell out of here . . .'


Mopping his sweating brow, Craig hurried back to his own office. He had hardly closed the door when the phone started ringing. He swore foully, sat behind his desk, picked up the phone.

'Craig here. So who is it?' he asked viciously.

'Someone you expected to call you,' a thin reedy voice said in English.

'Do you mind holding on a moment, please, while I secure the door . . .'

His tone had changed to one of businesslike geniality. He jumped up, ran to the door, locked and bolted it. He should have done that last time before Eve had opened it and eavesdropped on him, the little cow.

'Yes, I'm here,' he said, resuming the conversation.

'This is your private line?'

'Yes, don't worry . . .'

'I never worry, I double-check,' the reedy voice went on. 'The job is done. Mr Rico Sava is no longer with us.'

'I see.'

'So please make the necessary transfer of funds to my numbered account. I do prefer prompt payment.'

The connection was broken and Craig was sweating again. Something about the reedy voice always disturbed him. He had no idea of the identity of The Motorman and paying him was a headache. Craig had control over a large amount of funds – much of it going to pay his team of motorcyclists. But José conducted an audit at regular intervals, checking expenses on the orders of Brazil.

Craig also had no idea of how to contact The Motorman. He knew that he – or a member of his staff – would later in the morning get another call giving a phone number where Mr Brown could be reached. The number was always an answerphone which gave another phone number.

Craig went to a cabinet, poured himself a large Scotch, drank half of it, sat down again behind his desk. He had thought for a long time that Brazil was too soft in the methods he employed. On the quiet, Craig tried to rectify that.

Several months before he had contacted a friend who had buddies in the underworld. He had wanted a really tough assassin. Just in case. Eventually he'd been given the name, The Motorman, and a number where he might reach him. The Motorman had called him back a week later, had told Craig what a complete job on a target would cost. That had been the start of Craig's secret contact with the assassin.

There was an insistent tapping on the door. When he unlocked and unbolted it José was standing outside.

'Mr Brazil wishes to see you urgently . . .'


'Craig, I'm going to meet Mr Tweed later this afternoon at the Hotel Schweizerhof in Zurich. Just in case you wish to get in touch with me. José will drive me there. We shall leave shortly so I can call on a friend in Zurich before I meet Tweed.'

'You need protection,' was Craig's instant reaction.

'No. No protection. I trust Tweed. I met him once, briefly, at a dinner in London.'

'You need protection,' Craig repeated. 'I will fix it up immediately . . .'

He stopped speaking, pulled up abruptly. Brazil had hammered his clenched fist on his desk.

'I said *no* protection. Are you deaf? You can go now.'


Philip drove into Berne some time after the snow had stopped falling but the city was deep in snow. Paula pointed to a building.

'Look at that. Icicles hanging like a railed fence from the gutters. It's cold and I'm hungry.'

'Well, we're in Kochergasse and there is the Bellevue Palace. We'll park in that underground garage and order an English breakfast.'

'Good. My tummy's rumbling . . .'

They walked back to the large hotel and entered the lobby. The first person they saw was Archie, sitting at a table close to a window with a tray of coffee on the table.

'I don't believe it,' Paula said, going up to him. 'How could we run into you here?'

'Because,' Archie whispered to them, 'from where I

229

am sitting I can observe Brazil's villa. That old stone place set back from the street.'

'Then we'll have breakfast here,' said Philip. 'Just so long as that's all right with you.'

'Be my guests,' Archie said, his dead cigarette clenched in the corner of his mouth. He summoned a waiter. 'What do you want?'

They ordered and Archie's eyes never left the villa he had pointed to. Paula sat alongside him.

'Activity already,' Archie commented. 'I think that's Brazil's limo pulling up outside with José at the wheel. Yes, there's Brazil himself coming out. He looks very smart. Must be going to meet someone important.'

Paula exchanged a glance with Philip but said nothing.

'That's interesting,' Archie went on as the limo pulled away from the villa. 'He's travelling without the thugs Craig always provides him with. He must trust whoever he's off to see totally.'

Again Paula kept her expression poker-faced and this time she didn't look at Philip. Archie continued watching as he spoke.

'I think Brazil is anxious. I caught a glimpse of his expression. He had the look of a man who hopes he is going to succeed in some venture, but fears he will fail.'

'How can you tell all that – when he was across the road?' asked Philip.

'Because I have spent many long hours waiting for Mr Brazil to appear in different parts of the world. I have studied him carefully. A most impressive personality. No wonder he has the ear of presidents and prime ministers all over the world.'

'These eggs and bacon are good,' said Paula, concentrating on the most important activity.

'Coffee's good, too,' Philip commented. 'What is it?'

Archie's relaxed figure had become tense. He was leaning forward.

'Ah! Something very interesting is happening now. Very interesting indeed.'

'What is it?' asked Philip, who had his back to the villa.

'Another large car has pulled up in front of the villa. A Volvo. And, if I'm not mistaken, it's being driven by a particularly nasty piece of work. A certain ugly gentleman called Gustav. Craig's henchman.'

'Keep me informed,' said Philip.

He didn't want to twist round in his chair for fear the action would draw attention to them.

'Even more interesting,' Archie continued. 'His Lordship has appeared. None other than the great man himself. Mr Carson Craig, carrying a hold-all which from here looks heavy.'

'He looks like a heavyweight businessman in that suit,' Paula said. 'And I do mean heavyweight. That's odd – it's not at all how Newman described how he was dressed during the fight at Grenville Grange.'

'And here comes the gentle Gustav,' Archie remarked, 'also carrying a heavy bag. Probably weapons.'

'Two more tough-looking types are coming down the steps,' Paula observed. 'And they look as though they mean business. They're getting into the back of the Volvo. Gustav is driving, with Craig next to him. There they go . . .'

Philip saw the Volvo driving past the hotel in the same direction taken by Brazil's limo. Archie looked thoughtful.

'You know, my informant has told me a little about Craig. He's in charge of security, subject to Brazil's approval. But Craig thinks he knows best how to handle his job and has been known to go his own brutal way, regardless. I am thinking maybe Brazil didn't want an escort for this trip, but Craig is again following his primitive instincts.'

231

'I don't like this,' said Philip, glancing at Paula. 'I don't like it at all. I think we ought to get moving to our destination now.'

'So do I,' agreed Paula.

Philip paid for their breakfast and Archie's coffee. He stood up and spoke quietly as he put on his coat.

'Archie, you look after yourself. The wolves are on the prowl.'

'I want to remind you both of something,' Archie replied, ignoring the warning. 'Don't forget Anton Marchat down in the Valais . . .'


Standing at her window, which overlooked Kochergasse, Eve had watched Brazil leaving. Later she had been puzzled when she saw Craig and three other men, including the hateful Gustav, driving off the same way in a Volvo.

Why wasn't Craig driving behind the limo to act as protection for Brazil, which was the normal procedure? Was Craig up to something underhand, playing his own game again as she knew he frequently did, concealing his actions from Brazil. She rubbed her hands together. She would wait and see if she heard a rumour about what was going on. She might be able to claw another five thousand francs out of the detestable Craig.

Then she stiffened. Even though masked from the road by thick net curtains, she almost took a step back, then froze. Movement might betray her presence. She could hardly believe her eyes.

Philip and Paula Grey had emerged from the entrance to the Bellevue Palace. She heard someone come into the room, glanced over her shoulder. Marco, one of the guards, was unlocking a drawer. Swiftly he took out a long knife, slipped it into a sheath attached to his belt.

'Marco!' she called out urgently. 'Come here quickly. Don't disturb the curtains . . .'

'What is it?'

Marco was already by her side. She pointed to Philip and Paula as they walked towards the underground garage.

'See those two? Follow them. They are enemies of Mr Brazil . . .'

'I'm on my way.'


Paula was walking alongside Philip close to the ramp which descended to the garage where their car was parked, when she slipped. Philip saved her and then she froze. She kept him still under the lee of a wall, nodded.

On the opposite side of the road a tall man dressed like a Russian with a fur coat and a fur hat was striding along. Philip stared, opened his mouth to speak, but Paula spoke first.

'That's Bill Franklin. I recognize his walk. What's he doing in Berne? Let's find out.'

'He's gone into a pharmacy. There's a queue at the counter. I'm going to nip down and make sure our car is all right.'

'Berne is like a rabbit warren,' she protested.

But Philip had already run down the ramp and didn't hear her. She stood in a fever of impatience, sure that Franklin would come out before Philip got back. She was relieved when Philip reappeared a couple of minutes later, running back up the ramp.

Pretending to study the menu of the Bistro, the Bellevue Palace's restaurant, for a quick meal, Marco saw Philip disappear and frowned. Obviously he was going to check with the garage attendant to see if he could find out where Brazil was being driven to.

Marco, pencil thin with a face as white as death, was always suspicious, putting the worst interpretation on the actions of anyone he was following. His suspicion was confirmed when he saw Philip hurrying back up the ramp two minutes later.

The target had obviously bribed the attendant to tell him Brazil's destination. Otherwise he would have been in the garage longer if the attendant had been close-mouthed. There would have been a long argument.

'He's still inside the pharmacy,' Paula reported.

'Let's cross the street while we can. Trams come over the bridge above the River Aare.'

They had just crossed when a small green tram rumbled over the bridge. Franklin came out of the pharmacy, looked round, waited until there was no traffic where several roads met, then strode over to the Munstergasse, a quiet cobbled street which descended to the great stone bulk of the Munster, a towering edifice with a tall spire that dominated Berne.

On the side he walked were arcades roofed over the pavement. Philip and Paula followed him slowly, stopping briefly to look in shop windows. There were bakery shops, picture dealers, antiques shops, and a patisserie. Underfoot the cobbles were treacherous, coated with a sheen of ice. The temperature was below zero.

Behind them Marco, wearing a brown leather coat which hung open so he could reach his knife quickly, trudged along. They had all passed several ancient narrow alleys leading off the pavement when Franklin suddenly vanished.

'Where on earth has he gone?' wondered Philip.

'Keep walking and we'll find out,' Paula insisted.

They reached another very narrow alley, not wide enough for two people to pass each other. Peering down it into the gloom they saw the fur-coated figure appear to walk inside a wall. They moved faster inside the alley,

234

using their hands to hold against the walls to avoid slipping.

The alley had become very dark. Paula glanced up at the space between the roofs of the ancient buildings which leaned towards each other, leaving only little more than a slit. The sky above was shrouded in dense low clouds, black as pitch, and heavy snow began to fall.

'That's where he went in,' said Paula just before they reached a bend in the alley which concealed the street beyond running parallel to Munstergasse.

Inside a small alcove two stone steps, worn down the ages in the middle by generations of footsteps, led up to a closed door. The plate beside the door read *Emil Voigt – Sachwalter*. There were no windows above the door.

'He's gone to visit a lawyer,' said Paula. 'I think I ought to go ahead into the next street in case he goes that way when he comes out. You go back to Munstergasse. We'll meet up at the entrance to the garage when one of us finds out where he goes to.'

'Good idea.'

Paula had just disappeared round the bend in the alley, Philip was turning to go the other way when through the falling snow he saw a slim figure clad in a brown leather coat approaching him.

'You are a spy,' Marco shouted in heavy guttural German. 'You were trying to find out where Mr Brazil was going to. You are his enemy!'

Ever impetuous, Marco whipped out his long knife and lunged towards Philip. His action, Marco felt sure, would earn him praise from Craig, perhaps even promotion. Reaching for his Walther, Philip took several swift steps backwards, felt his feet slipping on sheet ice, toppled over backwards, saving his head by jerking his shoulders upwards. Marco raised his knife to plunge it into the sprawled body, took two steps forward, skidded on the same patch of ice, fell against the wall.

Paula appeared. She had heard Marco shouting his threats. As he began to scramble to his feet Paula brought down the butt of her Browning on his skull. Marco collapsed and this time he lay still, made no attempt to regain his balance. The snow falling matched his deathly white face.

'I think we'll forget Franklin,' Philip said quickly, climbing upright with one hand supporting himself by holding on to the wall. 'Time we moved off to Zurich. Franklin is going to have a surprise when he does come out. And thank you – for saving my life . . .'

# 25

Eve was fretting at being confined to the villa. It had been Brazil's express order that she should not leave the building. She had never been in Berne before and she was dying to go out and look at the shops. Besides, the five thousand francs she had taken off Craig was burning a hole in her shoulder bag. When Eve had money she spent it. And she had interesting news to tell Brazil – that she had spotted Paula Grey and Philip on Kochergasse.

She'd just had the thought when the phone rang. She ran to it, curious to know what was going on.

'Is that you, Eve? Good. Brazil here, speaking from a phone in a gas station. No, damnit! A service station. The Americans can't speak proper English to save their lives.'

'How can I help?'

'Get in your car with your suitcase. Drive immediately to Zurich. I've phoned ahead, booked a room for you at the Baur-en-Ville. It's in Bahnhofstrasse near—'

'I know where it is. I was once in Zurich.'

'Then please get moving. I'm in a hurry. Stay in your

room at the Baur-en-Ville from the moment you arrive. See you there . . .'

Then he was gone. *Stay in your hotel room* . . . He'd be lucky, Eve thought as she hurried to her bedroom to pack her case. With Bahnhofstrasse on her doorstep. All those wonderful shops . . .


'I wonder if I killed that thug in the alley?' Paula reflected aloud.

With Philip behind the wheel, they were driving along a main highway, had left Berne half an hour earlier. It was snowing steadily and they had passed several snowploughs keeping the road clear. Philip glanced at her, spoke firmly.

'No, you didn't kill him. I paused before following you out of the alley and checked his carotid. The pulse was beating normally. But what if you had killed the thug? It was him or me – and he'd have finished me off with that long knife. How would you have felt then – if you hadn't moved quickly enough? Just bear that in mind.'

It was Paula's turn to glance at Philip, whose strong face was concentrating on the road ahead. For the moment he was no longer in the toils of Eve, a beastly woman, in Paula's opinion. And although she had no doubt the grief for his late wife, Jean, was still strong under the surface he now had full possession of his faculties. She recalled something Tweed had said to her.

'Philip, in the end, will have to work it out for himself. None of us has had his grim experience, so none of us really knows what it must be like . . .'


Tweed had flown to Zurich with Newman seated along-side him. He had ordered Butler and Nield, also aboard

237

the same flight, to travel quite separately as though they had nothing to do with him.

'The point is,' he had explained to Newman when they were in mid-air, 'according to Archie, Brazil has an incomplete list of our team. He knows about Paula, about you, and has Bill Franklin as a possible member. But he doesn't know about Philip, Butler, or Nield, so let's keep it that way. Nor does he know about Marler.'

'And the only people who could have informed him from our stay in Dorset are Eve, Kent, or Franklin himself.'

'Not Franklin,' Tweed pointed out. 'He would hardly put himself on their list even as a possible. I'm curious as to why Brazil is so anxious to build up a list.'

'Sounds like a hit list,' Newman said calmly. 'Something for Mr Craig to attend to. Or maybe The Motorman.'

'I wonder where The Motorman is now,' Tweed mused as the plane began to descend to Kloten Airport, Zurich.

Keith Kent was driving his hired Audi at speed along the highway from Geneva to Zurich, window open – a fresh-air fanatic. Well muffled against the cold, he whistled a tune to himself as he overtook huge juggernauts.

He was listening to a cassette playing Sade, the pop singer. She had a mellow, enticing voice which suited his buoyant mood. He was making money again, always a most satisfactory feeling. Maybe he'd buy himself a really expensive suit made in Germany in Bahnhofstrasse. The Germans had become superb tailors.

Kent had left Geneva early and was on his way to the Zurcher Kredit Bank in Talstrasse, which ran parallel to Bahnhofstrasse. Most convenient. He was overtaking a Mercedes sports car when he glanced sideways. Driving it by herself was an attractive blonde. He smiled and waved. She smiled back – Kent was a good-looking man attractive to the opposite sex.

Pity we hadn't been in Zurich, caught up in the traffic, he thought. I might have persuaded her to have dinner with me. Always observant, he had noticed her left hand on the wheel wore no ring.

Kent was always careful not to get mixed up in an affair with a married woman. It was not so much a matter of ethics – but when there was a husband about it could turn messy.

He reached Zurich about lunchtime, drove slowly down Talstrasse, where there was very little traffic, stared, slowed down even more, still staring. Outside the Zurcher Kredit Bank a stretch black Mercedes with amber-tinted windows had pulled up.

Kent stopped by an unoccupied meter, sat very still, his hand cupping his jaw. A tall, imposing figure had stepped out of the limo, paused while he limbered up, then strode into the bank as a black-suited man greeted him and the two men went inside.


Kent's mind was racing. There was no doubt about it. The man who had entered the bank was Leopold Brazil. The last man in the world he would have expected to return to this bank.

Keeping an eye open for a parking warden, he thought about earlier events. The time when it had leaked out that the bearer bonds, assumed to be the bank's total capital, had disappeared. The murder of the bank's chairman. No, that was something not to dwell on.

When news of the missing bonds had leaked out Zurich had been shaken to its foundations. The city had been on the verge of panic with talk of a consortium of all

239

the major banks being formed to rescue Zurcher, followed by the realization that its branches all held more than sufficient funds to remain solvent.

Brazil had been a consultant to this bank, a non-executive director. Although how he had gained the latter position was beyond Kent – Swiss law was firm that only citizens of Swiss birth could be any kind of director of a bank.

'I'll have to postpone my visit while he's inside,' Kent said to himself.

A taxi pulled up in front of Kent's car, a very old lady clambered out slowly. The driver appeared round the front of the vehicle, carrying a huge case with both his hands. His passenger gave him some money. The driver looked at the money, made a contemptuous gesture, got back behind the wheel, and drove off. The old lady gazed round with a bewildered expression. Kent jumped out, spoke to her in German.

'You are worried about something?'

'My suitcase. It is heavy. I told the driver I live on the third floor of this building. How am I going to get my bag up to my apartment?'

'Third floor? Easy. Follow me at your own pace. No need to hurry . . .'

He lifted the bag, which felt as though it was full of blocks of cement. Slim as he was, Kent ran up the steps, mounted the darkened staircase beyond without a pause. He had to wait ages for the old lady to appear, a key in her hand. She unlocked a door and Kent followed her inside with the immense suitcase. He dumped it on a divan she gestured to. The interior of the apartment smelt musty, was crammed with old-fashioned furniture. The old lady sank into a chair, gazed at him without warmth.

'You'd better go now,' she said.

'I'm on my way. You're all right?'

'Just go. Now . . .'

He ran back down the gloomy stone staircase, wondering whether he'd got a ticket for parking without putting coins in the meter. The street was deserted – except for the parked limo. The chauffeur, a dark-skinned man, was polishing the windscreen. What had impressed Kent was the fact that, instead of waiting for the chauffeur to open the car door, the normal procedure for men who ranked themselves among the élite, Brazil had got out of the car himself.

Getting back inside his own car, Kent flexed the hand which had carried the bag. It didn't even ache. Kent was not only strong, he was very fit. He drove off, following a devious route through the city due to its one-way system. He eventually parked in the underground garage of Globus, the great department store near the top of Bahnhofstrasse.

Feeling the need to stretch his legs after the drive from Geneva, he walked up to Bahnhofplatz, the large square in front of the main station. Descending the escalator into Shopville, he walked across it, ascended another escalator into the main station.

He bought himself a carton of coffee from a stall, took it outside to drink it. Here there was traffic, nonstop, plus Zurich's large blue trams rumbling along in all directions. Across the square was the Hotel Schweizerhof.

He was drinking more coffee when he stopped and again stared. A taxi had pulled up in front of the Schweizerhof. Tweed and Newman stepped out.


The experience which greeted Tweed's arrival at the hotel was hardly the peace and quiet he had anticipated before meeting Brazil. As he walked into the lobby with Newman, a tall man in a dark suit with greying hair, grey eyes, a neat grey moustache, and a face with a grim

241

expression jumped up, came forward. Arthur Beck of the Federal Police.

'Tweed, I have to talk to you now. You, too, Newman. I have reserved a room where we will be quiet. This way.'

'I hope you're paying for the room,' Tweed said quizzically.

'No charge to the police,' Beck snapped as they entered an elevator and he pressed the button.

'We should have registered,' Tweed remarked.

'The concierge knows you well.'

'Damn it!' snapped Newman, irked by Beck's abrupt manner. 'We've had no lunch and I'm hungry.'

'That will have to wait.'

Beck had a key in his hand. Leaving the lift he went to a door, unlocked it, waited until they had walked past him inside.

'You may sit. Perhaps you'd better.'

'I was going to anyway,' Tweed observed after taking off his coat and settling in an armchair. He looked at Newman. 'Make yourself at home. Nice of Arthur to arrange all these comforts for us.'

Beck took a dining chair from under a table, placed it in front of Tweed and Newman, who had also occupied an armchair. He straddled his long legs over the seat, perched his elbows on the top of the back, gazed at them, and said nothing.

Tweed and Newman, who knew this police tactic, refrained from saying a word. Eventually Beck spoke, his eyes on Tweed.

'You had some of your team in Berne this morning?'

'Not to my knowledge,' Tweed answered truthfully. 'Why?'

'You know a thug called Marco? Handy with a knife.'

'No.'

'I had an anonymous call from a man at my HQ in Berne. He informed me that he was walking down an alley off the Munstergasse when he came across a man sprawled in the snow. The man reached for a knife so the caller kicked him in the head. The victim was Marco. Am I ringing any bells?'

'Did you hear a bell ringing?' Tweed asked Newman.

'Look,' Beck said aggressively, 'Marco is all right. He was discharged after we took him to out-patients. But I don't appreciate violence on my doorstep.'

'Move your doorstep, then,' Newman joked.

'There's nothing funny about the present situation,' Beck snapped. 'Switzerland is supposed to be a peaceful country. We have a murderous shoot-out last night in Geneva. Six bodies in the morgue now. Plus another strange murder just reported – also from Geneva.'

'What strange murder is that?' Tweed asked.

'An unsavoury arms dealer was killed in Geneva also. A man called Rico Sava.' He paused. 'He had his neck broken.'

'The Motorman?' Tweed asked quietly.

'It has all his trademarks. That makes seven corpses. Now this thug, Marco, in Berne.' He smiled. 'Now I've done it.'

'Done what?' Newman demanded.

'Given you both a dressing down, covered myself. Just in case someone influential – a friend of Brazil's – asks me about you.'

Beck's whole manner had changed. He stood up, swivelled his chair round, sat in his normal manner.

'There's a development you ought to know about. I can't prove they're employed by Leopold Brazil, but I know they are.'

'Who?' asked Tweed quietly.

'A whole army of tough-looking thugs disguised as skiers came into Geneva from France. They broke up into groups and boarded several different expresses heading east towards the Valais. God knows what there is for

243

them in that canton. The season is almost over – the slopes are dangerous and there's the risk of avalanches. Yet they've flooded in like a small invasion.'

Beck stood up, extended his hand. He shook hands warmly with both Tweed and Newman.

'Why not go and have a good lunch? At least Zurich is quiet. Incidentally, I'll be based for the next few days at Zurich Police HQ. You know where it is – close to this hotel, overlooking the River Limmat.' He paused. 'Have a care. We now know The Motorman is back.'

# 26

Tweed and Newman had finished an excellent lunch in the comfortable surroundings of the dining room on the first floor of the Schweizerhof. As always, whenever he visited the city, Tweed had spoiled himself by ordering escalope Zurichoise.

'Let's go for a walk,' Newman suggested. 'A quiet stroll will be welcome after the earlier part of our encounter with Beck.'

'He has his problems,' Tweed replied as he turned down a side-street off Bahnhofplatz. 'Which doesn't help us. Every time we've been here before he's been able to give us his full backing. We'll just have to cope on our own.'

They were passing a side door which led into the Hummer Bar, one of the restaurants in the Hotel Gotthard. Newman paused.

'I could pop in and see if they've arrived. Marler and Butler and Nield.'

'We know Butler and Nield have arrived,' Tweed pointed out, continuing to walk. 'They came on our flight. Marler has to get here from Geneva.'

'I know. I hadn't forgotten Butler and Nield. But we don't want them wandering round, checking out the city before you've met Brazil. At least *you* don't want that.'

'No, I don't . . .'

It had stopped snowing while they were eating lunch and they turned along another street into Bahnhofstrasse, the section which was car-free because of the trams. As they re-entered Bahnhofplatz Newman stopped, grasped Tweed's arm.

'Look. Paula and Philip have just arrived on foot – they're going into the Schweizerhof. Incidentally, was it wise to mention the hotel's name over the phone to Paula when you spoke to her at the Hôtel des Bergues from London? That line would pass through the hotel's switchboard.'

'There are several Schweizerhofs in Switzerland,' Tweed reminded him. 'A big one in Berne, for example. And I did not mention Zurich – Paula knew what I was talking about. What is it now?'

Newman had again grabbed Tweed's arm. They stood still as Newman gazed across the far side of Bahnhofplatz in front of the main station.

'That large Volvo. Craig is sitting in the passenger seat at the front. There are three other yobbos in the car. You still feel no need of protection?'

They were standing close to the pavement edge with Newman on the outside. The Volvo continued its slow glide round the *platz*, cruised slowly past the entrance to the Schweizerhof. Craig was now seated next to the pavement. The car almost stopped alongside Newman.

Craig grinned, suddenly swung the door open to send Newman flying. Newman grabbed the handle, shoved the door shut with all his strength. He saw Craig's face crumple into an expression of pain. The closing door had struck Craig's elbow. He glared with hatred at Newman, then the car moved on.

'I don't care what you say,' Newman snapped, taking over control, 'I'm going back to the Gotthard to have a word with our people.'

Before Tweed could protest he was gone.


Philip and Paula had registered as Tweed entered the lobby and a porter had taken their bags to a lift and disappeared. Relieved to see her, Tweed kissed Paula on the cheek.

'We've had lunch. That is, Bob and I.'

'You unpacked your suitcases first?' Paula enquired.

'Well, no,' Tweed confessed. 'A porter took them up to our rooms and we went straight to the dining room.'

'You should have gone up to your rooms first,' she chided him. 'At least you should have opened your cases, taken out jackets and hung them up. Everything will be creased and crumpled.'

'That's what Jean always insisted on,' Philip recalled. 'Tweed, I need to talk to you. There's a crisis.'

'I need food,' said Paula.

'You go and eat and I'll join you later,' Philip told her as they all entered a lift.

Tweed accompanied Philip to his room while Paula went along the corridor to hers in the opposite direction. Inside the bedroom, which overlooked Bahnhofplatz, Philip began unpacking swiftly as he talked while Tweed sat in a chair.

'We met Archie in Berne . . .' he began and then informed Tweed of everything that had happened in that city. When he had concluded by describing their experience with Bill Franklin and the thug in the alley, he turned to Tweed.

246

'I haven't unpacked everything because I'm leaving by myself soon.'

'Are you? May I ask why and where?' Tweed enquired with an edge to his voice.

'Archie's last words were that we shouldn't overlook Anton Marchat, who apparently lives in the Valais. At Sion. He gave me Marchat's address. We heard on the radio, driving here, that all the mountain passes are still closed. So I'll hand in my hired car and catch a train to Geneva.'

'Why Geneva? You could catch an express en route at the Lausanne stop.'

'No, Geneva,' Philip said stubbornly. 'Then I can board the express where it starts – that way I see who else gets on. If I'm followed I want to know who is after me – so I can deal with them later. I don't want you to tell Paula until I've gone. She'll try and come with me.'

Philip looked at the clothes he had hung up, blinked, walked to the window to gaze out with his back to Tweed and his hands in his trouser pockets. Tweed realized he was upset. Memories. Thinking back to the times he and Jean had travelled together. Philip blew his nose loudly.

Tweed was in a quandary. His instinct was to order Philip to stay in Zurich where he had the company and protection of his friends. But if he did that Philip would immediately think Tweed was pampering him, still did not trust him to strike out on his own because of emotional instability. I'll have to let him go, he thought.

'Philip,' he said when his team member had come back from the window, his mouth tight. 'There is information provided by Beck, Chief of the Federal Police, which I think you ought to know . . .'

He explained what Beck had told him and Newman about the influx of fake tourists into Geneva. How *they* had boarded expresses travelling east with their ultimate destination, Milan – but travelling via the Valais.

'There you are,' Philip exclaimed, 'again a reference to the Valais. And Archie so far has proved a most reliable informant. Marler wouldn't use him if he wasn't first class.'

'Yes,' Tweed agreed. 'I'd better tell you all the data we have.'

He tersely recalled Professor Grogarty's opinion of the list of missing scientists; his theory as to what such a team of the world's top-flight scientists could be used to create; about Lasalle's calls from Paris, the satellite launched by Ariane in French Guiana, the photos Grogarty had examined of the satellite prior to launch, his conclusions.

'I still can't imagine what significance the Valais could have,' Tweed mused. 'It's a wild, desolate region and there's nothing there.'

'So maybe,' said Philip, 'bearing in mind what you have just told me, it's the location of the ground station controlling the satellite which seems to worry so many people.'


When he entered the Hotel Gotthard and asked for Marler Newman was given a room number. The door was opened cautiously by the sturdy Butler, even though Newman had rapped on it with a familiar tattoo. When he got inside Newman understood why.

'Welcome to the arms dump,' said Marler, looking fresh as paint.

A cloth was spread out across a double bed and the contents of two large canvas bags were spread out. Newman stared.

'Are you getting ready to start a small war?' he asked.

'That's almost the same question Rico Sava asked me,' Marler said with a grin.

Newman's expression became poker-faced. He realized Marler would not have heard the news of the murder of Sava at the hands of The Motorman. And Marler had liked Sava. Bad news can wait, he decided.

Arranged on the cloth was a large array of tear-gas pistols with plenty of spare shells, a .38 Smith & Wesson Special revolver with ammo, five 7.65mm Walther automatics with an ample supply of magazines, a large number of grenades, both stun and shrapnel, a generous amount of smoke bombs, a .32 Browning automatic for Paula, several pairs of small high-power binoculars, and an Armalite rifle, Marler's favourite weapon.

'How the devil did you smuggle this lot here safely? Supposing you had been stopped by a patrol car? I assume you drove here?'

'I did. They'd have seen these.'

Marler picked up the two canvas bags he had zipped up. At one end of each of the bags protruded the heel of an ice-skate.

'I doubt if they'd have even asked when they saw those,' Marler remarked. 'If they had I'd have said it was equipment for a party going up into the mountains.'

'Clever, I'll give you that. And when I've told you what happened when I was walking with Tweed, not long ago in this city of peace, I think you'll hand out tear-gas pistols . . .'

A few minutes later Newman was equipped with his Smith & Wesson inside a hip holster Marler had provided. He also had concealed inside his bulky suede coat a tear-gas pistol, as had the others. He also carried certain extra armoury in a small canvas holdall Marler gave him.

'I'm off back to the Schweizerhof,' he announced. 'And Marler, I think it might be an idea if you and Butler mooched round Bahnhofplatz to give back-up.' He turned to Nield, who had sat in a chair smoking a cigarette and saying nothing. 'Pete, you stay here as a

249

reserve. If you want to peek into Bahnhofplatz every now and again that's your decision . . .'


Eve, on Brazil's instructions, had arrived at the Baur-en-Ville Hotel, located near Parade-Platz, roughly halfway down Bahnhofplatz before it reached Zurichsee, Lake Zurich. She approved of the luxury of the hotel. After unpacking her bag, and drinking several glasses of vodka from the bottle she'd ordered from room service, she felt bored.

Against Brazil's instructions, she had walked out into Bahnhofstrasse with a scarf wrapped round her jet-black hair. She also wore a pair of tinted glasses which, with the scarf, completely altered her normal appearance. She spent some time gazing into the treasure house of shop windows displaying jewels, watches, expensive clothes.

Eventually she bought a matching gold jacket and skirt. The cost took most of the five thousand francs she had prised out of Craig. With the carrier bag over her arm she walked slowly up towards Bahnhofplatz.

I'm going to have to get some more money from someone, she was thinking.

The large salary which Brazil paid her disappeared within days on clothes and cosmetics. She was strolling along slowly when she almost stopped, but forced herself to keep moving at a leisurely pace. Newman had just walked out of the Hotel Gotthard, carrying a small hold-all.

'So, I've got lucky,' she said to herself. 'Stuff Mr Brazil and his stay-in-the-hotel routine. I smell more money . . .'

She followed Newman as he turned into Bahnhof-platz and watched him enter the Schweizerhof.

*    *    *

250

Across the far side of Bahnhofplatz, standing just inside the station, Keith Kent munched a sandwich, then paused as he was about to take another bite.

He saw Newman appear, walking quickly, disappear inside the Schweizerhof. But what caught his attention was a woman in a headscarf who seemed to drift along until she reached the corner, pausing to peer round the corner as Newman entered the hotel.

Keith Kent had trained himself to be a first-class observer. There was something in the woman's movements which told him she was tailing Newman. She stood at the corner, adjusting her scarf, when a blast of bitter wind caught her and tore the scarf off her head; only her quick grab prevented her from losing it. But for a few moments her head was fully exposed. Kent gazed at the jet-hair moulded close to her skull like a helmet.

'Something is going on here,' he said to himself.


Newman checked with the concierge in the lobby.

'Miss Grey is in the dining room,' he was told. 'Mr Tweed is still upstairs. He went up with a friend.'

'Mr Cardon, you mean?'

'Yes, sir.'

'I've forgotten their room numbers . . .'

The concierge obliged, gave him both room numbers. On the second floor Newman first tried pressing the bell outside the door of Tweed's room. When he got no reply he went back to Philip's room. Tweed opened the door a few inches, then opened it wide.

'How are the others?' he asked. 'Have they all arrived? And what have you got in that holdall you didn't have with you when you left me?'

'Is Philip going somewhere?' Newman asked.

He posed the question because Philip was fully

251

dressed to go out and had just picked up his case. Tweed gestured for Newman to sit down.

'Yes,' he said. 'Philip is going to take the train to Geneva, then an express from there to Sion in the Valais. He feels he should visit Anton Marchat since Archie was so insistent Marchat was contacted.'

'By yourself?' asked Newman.

'Yes. Why not?' Philip demanded aggressively.

'Just a simple question, which you've answered. Are you armed? From the little I've heard the Valais is a lonely place.'

'I've got a Walther, thanks.'

'Here's another, with spare ammo.' Newman had opened his holdall. He paused as Philip took what he'd offered. 'If you run into trouble stun grenades can come in rather useful.'

He produced several, rewrapped in polythene by Marler. Philip unfastened his bag, carefully packed the grenades under clothes, closed the bag, looked at Newman.

'I'm grateful, Bob.'

'Have you a way of getting in touch with us?' Newman checked.

'Yes. Tweed is letting Monica know wherever he may be. Leaving her a phone number. All I have to do is to call Monica to get the number.'

'Then you're organized. Good luck.'

'See you both . . .'

Tweed waited until he had left the room before he said it to Newman.

'I hope to Heaven we *do* see him again.'

# 27

Keith Kent had decided it was time to revisit the Zurcher Kredit Bank. He felt confident that Brazil would have left some time ago. In any case, he could check to see if the limo was still waiting for him.

Driving out of the Globus garage, he followed another devious route. In Zurich you could hardly ever drive straight from A to B. The insidious one-way system was a guarantee against that happening.

Later, driving down Talstrasse for the second time, he saw the limo had gone. He parked his car, was careful to feed the meter with coins. You don't get lucky twice – not where parking attendants are concerned.

Walking slowly into the bank, he studied the tellers behind the counters guarded by grilles. He had deliberately left his coat in the car, and he was wearing the type of expensive business suit Swiss banks associated with reliable customers. He chose a dopey-looking girl at the end of the counter. She had just suppressed a yawn.

Smiling, he leaned on the counter, gazed at her with admiration before he spoke.

'My name is Benton. I shall shortly have to make a very large transfer of money into Mr Leopold Brazil's main account. He insisted it must be deposited in his main account.'

'That would be at Sion,' the girl informed him.

'In the Valais.' Kent gave her another nice smile. 'I am most grateful to you. So will be Mr Brazil . . .'

He left quickly before she had time to mention what he had asked to another teller. He had persuaded her by his easy manner to break all the rules of secrecy.

'Now,' he said to himself, 'where Newman is Tweed

cannot be far behind. So back to Globus once more, dump the chariot, walk to the Schweizerhof . . .'

Kent had almost reached the top of Bahnhofstrasse where it merged with Bahnhofplatz when he glanced across to the opposite side of the street. Standing on the corner so she could see the entrance to the Schweizerhof was the girl with jet hair he'd seen following Newman earlier.

He couldn't see her hair but he recognized the scarf round her head, the well-cut camel-hair coat. Kent was a man who made up his mind quickly. He waited for a tram to trundle past, crossed the street, stood in front of her, and smiled.

'Hello there, you look lonely. I'm Tom Benton.'

'Or Tomcat,' she replied instantly, eyeing him up and down.

'So we're both English, both on our own in a foreign city. I know the best place in town for dinner. It's in the Altstadt. What do they call you?'

'Sharon Stone. And I'm waiting for my boy friend.'

She had hardly finished speaking when Bill Franklin arrived out of nowhere. He grinned.

'Well, if it isn't Eve Warner. Long way from Dorset.' He looked at Kent and was about to recognize him when Kent spoke quickly.

'Hello, Bill. I've just introduced myself as Tom Benton to the lady, asked her out to dinner, but she's playing hard to get.'

'I told you my boy friend was on his way,' Eve replied swiftly. She took hold of Franklin's arm. 'I thought you were never coming. Let's go down to the lake.'

'Hold on. Half a mo',' Franklin responded, standing still. 'What is all this, Eve? I didn't even know you were in Zurich.'

'You're a big help!' she snapped and stormed off down Bahnhofstrasse.

'Funny lady,' Franklin commented, holding out his hand. 'What are you doing in the city of gold, Keith?' he asked when they had shaken hands.

'Business. Confidential.'

'Close-mouthed as ever.' Franklin grinned again. 'Well, since you've undertaken assignments for me in the past it does inspire confidence. Now I've got to slip into the Schweizerhof to visit a mutual friend.'

'The friend has a name?' Kent enquired casually. 'Because that's where I'm going.'

Franklin paused, then threw back his head and burst out laughing. Taking out a handkerchief he wiped tears from his eyes.

'Let's go there together. You sit in the lobby while I have a word with the concierge. This could be very funny indeed. And what a coincidence – meeting Eve Warner and you.'

'I'm lucky with coincidences. They've made me a lot of money . . .'

Eve was puffing furiously at a cigarette as she walked down Bahnhofstrasse back to the Baur-en-Ville. She was livid. No matter how she tried to dismiss the idea, she felt sure Bill Franklin would, sooner or later, phone Tweed in London and report her presence in Zurich. And I was so careful on the way out, she recalled. Then a thought struck her which stopped her in her tracks for several seconds.

She had seen Newman enter the Schweizerhof. Was it possible – even likely – that Tweed also was at the same hotel? She cursed under her breath, resumed walking. Twice she glanced back but Franklin and the man who had introduced himself as Tom Benton were nowhere in sight.

Inside her room at the hotel she threw her coat and

scarf over a chair. The coat slid to the floor but she ignored it. Her first priority was the vodka bottle. She poured herself a large glass, kicked her shoes off across the carpet, sprawled out on a couch, drank half the glass. Then she noticed the lighted cigarette she had dropped inside an ashtray had fallen on the floor.

Cursing again, she picked it up, used it to light a fresh one. There was a burn mark on the carpet but that didn't bother her. The place was costing a fortune to stay at, she felt sure. Lucky Brazil was paying the bill.

Settling herself on the couch again, she drank the rest of the vodka and concentrated as she smoked.

'How can I make some money out of what's just happened? I'd like to make a really big pile,' she thought aloud.


Franklin stood by the concierge's counter, holding the phone he'd been handed.

'Bill Franklin downstairs in the lobby. Can I come up, Tweed?' He took a deep breath. 'Oh, there's someone else also waiting to see you. Keith Kent. We met in the street.'

'Both of you had better come up then,' Tweed said without a pause. 'Get the concierge to give you the room number. I always forget them . . .'

In his room Tweed put down the phone and turned to Newman. He chuckled.

'Bob, I've been caught out. Franklin's on his way up. With Keith Kent. They bumped into each other in the street.'

'Does it matter?'

'I don't think it matters at all. Might help. They now know they're in competition with each other. And there's nothing like a bit of rivalry to give them both an extra edge.'

'I didn't realize they even knew each other,' said Paula, who had returned from lunch.

'Neither did I,' Tweed admitted. 'But I can see how it probably happened. Keith Kent has a great reputation as a money tracer. Franklin's detective outfit may well have had a request from a client to trace a large sum. Bill would immediately think of Kent, who has expertise he doesn't possess. Let's see what they have to tell us.' He stood up. 'And here, I think, they are . . .'

Paula and Newman knew both men so no time was wasted as Tweed ushered his visitors to seats. He invited Kent to speak first, knowing how terse he was.

'Leopold Brazil has now made his main bank the Zurcher Kredit branch at Sion. In the Valais.'

Tweed, who had just told Paula about Philip leaving for the Valais on his own, saw her mouth tighten.

'Earlier I also saw Brazil visit the Zurcher Kredit here in Talstrasse,' Kent went on. 'I'm guessing, but I think he was transferring the balance of his funds in Zurich to Sion. Which is very weird – Sion is a nowhere place. That's it.'

'It's more than enough,' Tweed said grimly. 'Bill, the stage is yours.'

'I was in Berne this morning. There's a lawyer there called Voigt who used to work for Brazil. He broke off all contact with him when Brazil tried to tell him how to run his business. But Voigt has sources of a curious nature all over Europe. He told me Brazil is bringing in all his troops from France and Germany. Their destination? Sion in the Valais.'

'I see,' said Tweed, not looking at Paula.

'I had an odd experience when I left Voigt's office,' Franklin continued. 'His place is in a narrow old alley off the Munstergasse. When I came out a thin man with a white face was lying in the snow. As soon as he saw me he reached for a long knife. Instead of waiting for him to

257

attack me I gave him a good kick in the head. That seemed to quench any enthusiasm for a fight. Why he was going to attack me I have no idea.'

'We have something else to tell Tweed,' Kent reminded him.

'Yes.' Franklin folded his hands behind his head. 'I was on my way here when I saw Keith talking to someone I'd never have expected to see here in a hundred years. Eve Warner.'

There was a sudden silence. Tweed looked at Paula who gave him a thumbs-down reaction. Newman shrugged before he spoke.

'The lady does get around.'

'And the lady knows you're here,' Kent informed him. 'Staying at this hotel.'

He explained how he had seen her twice, the first time when she had followed Newman from the Hotel Gotthard.

'The information you have both given us is invaluable,' Tweed told his visitors. 'May I suggest you both keep digging?'

'We won't waste time checking up on each other,' Franklin said with a broad grin.

'You both have different talents, different contacts,' Tweed said as he stood up. 'This affair is so serious I need all the data you can provide. Thank you for what you have done so far,' he ended, escorting them to the door.

Paula exploded the moment they had gone.


As Tweed sat down to absorb what he had heard Paula stood up, gazing at Tweed.

'Now look what you have done!' she told him bitterly. 'He, Philip, has been sent into the lions' den. On his own. Or maybe that is your way of letting him show he can prove himself. Is that it?'

'Philip can cope—' Tweed began quietly.

'Oh, can he?' Paula stood over him. 'When Bill Franklin has just told us that lawyer, Voigt, said Brazil has recalled all his troops from France and Germany – that this horde is bound for Sion. Sion! Where Philip is now on his way to see Marchat.'

'*Sit down, please.* Keep quiet for a moment.'

There was something in Tweed's expression which made Paula do his bidding. Tweed said nothing for awhile, watching her as she calmed down.

'I can understand your reaction,' he said, 'but, I repeat, Philip will cope. Have a little more faith in him.'

'Well, at least he doesn't know the Eve woman is in town,' Paula conceded.

'Paula does have a point,' Newman remarked. 'The trouble is, Paula, I dare not suggest we all head for Sion at once. Tweed has this vital meeting with Leopold Brazil here this evening. Tweed and I have already encountered Craig and three thugs in a car outside here. We all – including Marler, Butler, and Nield – need to be here in case of more trouble until the meeting is over.'

'Do we have Anton Marchat's address in Sion?' Paula asked in a normal tone.

'We do. From Philip. We also have copies of the photo of Marchat.'

Tweed opened a briefcase, took out a wallet, handed one piece of paper to Paula and four similar sheets to Newman. Then he extracted five photos, handed one to Paula and four to Newman.

'This hasn't got Marchat's name on it,' commented Paula.

'Neither had the original which Archie wrote the address on. Archie is very careful,' Tweed replied.

'Of course. I should have thought of that. Now I've taken a decision.' Paula stood up, her expression determined. 'I appreciate the main body of the team must stay here until Brazil has left, but I am catching the first express to Geneva. There I shall board another express for the Valais.'

'You should wait,' Tweed told her. 'It's just possible I may be able to persuade Brazil to abandon this project he's planning, whatever it may be. Then the danger has gone away.'

'I'm still catching the Geneva express,' Paula said as she went towards the door.

'I said wait,' Tweed ordered.

'In that case I'm handing in my resignation to you now.'

She had her grip on the door handle when Tweed replied in the same quiet tone.

'Your resignation is not accepted.'


Newman jumped up, accompanied Paula to her room. She turned to him when they were both inside.

'I have to pack.'

'I know,' said Newman and grinned. 'I gave Philip a little extra armament. I'd like you to be equipped with the same. Back in no time. I'll rap on your door with my usual tattoo.'

'It's getting a bit out of date, that tattoo. You should invent a new one,' Paula commented with a smile.

He returned very quickly as she was finishing packing her case. From a small canvas holdall he produced a cardboard carton wrapped in blue ribbon and with the word *Dumbo* on the outside. He handed it to her.

'What in Heaven's name is that, Bob?'

'A present for the nephew you don't have. Actually you will find a tear-gas pistol inside, spare shells, smoke bombs – and be careful with these. They're stun grenades. You've handled them before.'

'No need for you to send Marler and Co. after me,' she joked.

260

He waited until she had concealed the 'presents' he had given her. She put on her coat and gloves, smiled at Newman.

'Carry your bag, lady?' he said.

'I'd be grateful, porter. You may even get a tip.'

Arriving at the main station, Newman checked the departure board, saw there was an express leaving for Geneva in five minutes. He told her to find a compartment and rushed to get her a first-class ticket. She was leaning out of the window when he ran onto the platform, handed her the ticket. She leaned further out, kissed him on the cheek.

'That's your tip.'

The express began to move out and she waved to him from the window. He stood watching its last coach until it disappeared round a bend.

# 28

Newman was giving last-minute instructions in Marler's room at the Gotthard when the phone rang. He pursed his lips at the interruption, gazing round at Butler and Nield as Marler answered the phone.

'Who is it?' he asked abruptly.

'Mr Marler, I'm sorry to bother you,' the operator began, 'but I have a woman on the line who wishes to speak to Mr Robert Newman if he is there.'

'What made you call me?' demanded Marler.

'When Mr Newman came in I asked if I could help. I was on reception for a few minutes while my stand-in took over. I recognized Mr Newman from pictures I've seen of him in the papers in the past. I did not tell the caller he was here. I merely said I would enquire.'

'But who is on the line?' Marler asked brusquely.

'A Miss Eve Warner . . .'

'Hold on. I'll be back in a moment.'

'You won't believe this,' he said to Newman. 'On the line waiting to speak to you is Eve Warner.'

'How the hell does she know I'm here?' Newman thought for a moment. 'Well, she does – and I'd better find out how she knows that.'

'Where are you speaking from?' were Newman's first words.

'A call box in Bahnhofstrasse.'

'So what made you think I might be found here? Tell me or I'll put the phone down.'

'Don't be like that, Bob,' she coaxed. 'I'll be honest. I saw you coming out of the Gotthard earlier today. I have information you need urgently.'

'How much?' Newman enquired cynically.

'That's not nice. Not nice at all. I'm not asking for money. This time.'

'Then why are you calling? What information?'

'Tweed's life is in danger. I overheard Craig saying he was covering Bahnhofstrasse and the *platz* with his troops ready for when Brazil meets Tweed at the Schweizerhof.'

'Did Craig say the target was Tweed?'

'Well . . .' A pause. 'Actually, no. I think he may have plans to kill you.'

'Thanks for the information.'

'I may call again if I have more information. So,' she ended, 'you see you have misjudged me. Not everyone in this world is interested only in money . . .'

Newman put down the phone, reported what she'd said to the others. Marler lit a king-size, took a puff.

'Don't understand what she's up to. From what you've said about her, Bob, she's on the make. All of the time.'

'I still think she is. Maybe this was her opening shot.'

He clapped his hands. 'We can't waste any more time on her. Now, is everyone clear as to the positions they're going to take up in Bahnhofplatz while Tweed is holding this crazy meeting with Brazil?'

'I'm clear,' said Butler, 'and I'll have smoke bombs ready.'

'I'm clear, too,' said Nield. 'And I also have my smoke bombs. Why are we using those – if we have to?'

'Because if there's shooting, corpses in the street, Chief of Police Arthur Beck will be in deep trouble. So shall we.' He checked his watch.

'Not long now,' Marler remarked. 'Zero hour draws nigh . . .'


Eve emerged from the call box in a furious mood – furious with Newman. The very idea that all she was interested in was money! It was insulting. Still, the important thing was she had established contact with him.

She was so annoyed she failed to notice a man inside a doorway who had been watching her. Not that she would probably have observed him anyway. Gustav, who had followed her from the hotel, was an expert shadow.

An attractive woman glanced into the doorway, looked away quickly when she saw him. He scowled. He knew why she had averted her gaze. Gustav's face was not a pretty picture. His long nose had been broken in a fight, which gave it a hooked appearance. His mouth was thin, cruel. He was coming to dislike women, except for one purpose.

What was Eve up to? he wondered. Something underhand – or else why should she go out to a call box to phone someone when she could have used the phone in her room? He'd report what had happened to Brazil when the chance arose. Not to Craig – who would simply take all the credit, would probably say he'd ordered Gustav to keep an eye on Eve.

As Eve drew near the Baur-en-Ville she saw the limo with the amber-tinted windows glide to the kerb. She stopped, pretended to gaze into a shop window. Out of the corner of her eye she saw Brazil emerge from the rear, opening the door himself. He ran into the hotel, checking his watch as he moved swiftly.

Eve waited until José had driven away the limo to park it and hurried into the hotel and up to her room. It was, fortunately, on the same floor as Brazil's suite. Inside her room, she locked the door, opened a hanging cupboard, knelt down, and felt along her shoes scattered across the floor. She brought out the stethoscope she had purchased in a Zurich shop, tucked it inside her shoulder bag.

Returning to the corridor, she walked quietly to the door leading into Brazil's living room. She had her excuse ready as she opened it, peered inside. Empty. Closing the door after entering, she ran lightly over the deep-pile carpet, opened a cabinet, took out a bottle of vodka, poured herself a glass and left it on a table near the two closed sliding doors leading into the meeting room with a long table.

She pressed her ear to one door and the material was so thin she could hear voices. She took out the stethoscope, pressed one end against the door, the other ends to her ears. If she heard someone coming she'd ram the stethoscope into her shoulder bag and say she'd come to get a glass of vodka. With the aid of the stethoscope she heard clearly.

'So you arrived safely from Sion, Luigi. How is everything going down there?' asked Brazil, voice booming.

'The station is ready for operation. We tested laser

contact with the satellite and it was a tremendous success.' An unpleasant pedantic voice. Italian accent.

'Please be more specific. What exactly happened when they carried out the experiment?'

'We used the equipment inside the room in the old house on the mountainside. The laser was directed at the phone number in that room which was included in the satellite's circuitry. It was tremendous!'

'But what exactly happened when you returned to the room after sending the signal for that number?'

'Every piece of equipment was shattered. The tethered goat was dead – killed by the terrible screaming noise.'

'Then it does work. Let me think . . .'

Eve shoved the stethoscope back inside her shoulder bag. Drinking half the glass of vodka quickly, she held the glass as she left the room in case someone like Craig should be in the corridor. Back inside her room she sank onto a couch.

'What the hell was that all about?' she asked herself.

She didn't even know where Sion was. Then she had an idea. Jumping up, she remembered to hide the stethoscope before leaving her room. She had just quietly opened her door when she heard voices further down the corridor. She froze.

'How are the scientists behaving themselves, Luigi? It is vital none of them leave the laboratory. If one should escape . . .'

'No one will escape, Mr Brazil.'

She heard a door close. She rattled the key in her lock as though just opening it, walked out, locked it. A small fat man in an expensive grey business suit walked towards her. He had a plump face, sensuous lips and a dark moustache to match his thick hair. He looked at her with brazen interest as they passed each other, then stopped, came back alongside her.

265

'My name is Luigi, beautiful lady.'

'My name is I damn well don't know you . . .'

She left him with a nasty expression on his face and went down into the lobby. Strolling around, she checked to make sure none of Craig's thugs were about. Then she walked up to the concierge.

'A friend has suggested to me it might be interesting to visit Sion. I don't even know where it is.'

'In the Valais, Madame. Let me show you on the map.'

She studied the map as he went on talking to her.

'I can't recommend Sion at this time of the year.'

'Why not?'

'It is in the canton of the Valais. Very popular with winter sports enthusiasts during the season, but the season is almost over. The weather has turned bad down there. We have had several reports of avalanches. If you were thinking of walking in the mountains I would advise against it.'

'Thank you.'

Eve went back to her room, closed and locked the door. She lit a cigarette, folded one arm across her chest, supported the elbow of the other on her hand. She walked slowly back and forth.

It was curious that Brazil, always so security-conscious, should talk about scientists and a laboratory so publicly. Then she remembered the long corridor had been empty except for the fat man, Luigi. Doubtless Brazil had peered out before he began talking.

She recalled the weird conversation she had eavesdropped on. She could remember every word although she didn't understand the meaning. Newman and Tweed would, she felt sure, understand what had been said. It sounded like information they should have.

*   *   *

266

Tweed was waiting in the lobby of the Schweizerhof when Brazil arrived, stepped out of the limo, walked briskly into the hotel. He held out his hand and Tweed shook it.

'I have a room upstairs where we can talk,' Tweed said and led the way to the elevator.

Brazil wore a blue pin-stripe suit, a white shirt, and, unusually for him, a gaudy tie in exotic colours. He was brimful of energy, refused Tweed's offer of anything to drink.

'No alcohol when I'm discussing business.'

Tweed had arranged an armchair on either side of a long glass-topped table. They sat facing each other, like duellists. Tweed said nothing, taking off his glasses to clean them with his handkerchief.

'I've come to offer you a partnership with me in a great historic enterprise,' Brazil told him. 'A plan to change the whole balance of world power.'

'Sounds rather ambitious.'

'The West is going into a steep decline, is rendering itself defenceless, cutting its arms budgets almost daily. In Britain, as in other countries, people are demoralized, no longer have any sense of purpose. They are drifting, Mr Tweed. So law and order is breaking down everywhere. Criminals control the streets. We need the discipline we once had, the stability, the sense of purpose. We are collapsing into moral decadence, which produces a growing decay in our society. Or would you not agree?'

'So far what you have said makes sense,' Tweed replied as he put on his glasses. 'What is your solution?'

'We need strong, ruthless leadership. The only thing to wake people up is the return of *fear*. There was fear when Soviet Russia was strong. Then there was energy in the West, the building up of NATO. People were alert, on their guard. Only the revival of Russia as a great power will instil the sense of fear which is needed to give the

West a sense of purpose. The battle for survival. Do you agree, Mr Tweed?'

'Do go on.'

'America is a shambles. Its President is a lazy lunatic. I know. I have met him. There is a widespread belief that Russia no longer counts. *No longer counts!*' His voice rose to a crescendo. 'They have a vast armoury of intercontinental missiles – which can reach London, Chicago, the world. Each month a new nuclear submarine of the silent, undetectable type, is launched from the secret shipyards at Murmansk, their ice-free port. Behind the Urals they have underground factories which are involved in new advances in nuclear warfare. An American diplomat who ventured in that region was expelled recently as a spy. Why? If there is nothing to spy on? Russia is a slumbering giant which will soon awake.'

'They say the Russian economy is in tatters,' Tweed commented.

'If that is really true how can they afford to produce the armaments I have listed?' Brazil demanded.

'It is a puzzle,' Tweed admitted.

'It is a gigantic smokescreen to blind the West. Behind their bumbling President, Ivan Marov pulls the strings, manipulating the existing President like a puppet. To give the West the impression Russia is finished while he – Marov – works with the generals and MOVAK to rebuild Russian power. You have heard of Marov?'

'The name seems familiar.'

'You are not a man I would play poker with, Mr Tweed. I am sure you know a great deal about Marov. A Georgian, he changed his name. I have met him. A Georgian, like Stalin. He looks rather like Stalin – especially when he turns on the charm. At the moment he is very careful to stay hidden behind the scenes. The Americans don't know he exists,' Brazil said contemptuously.

'You spent time in America, I believe,' remarked Tweed.

'I was born in Britain and as a young man went to America. I became chief executive of a huge conglomerate. I soon saw it should be broken down into six quite independent units. With such a vast organization the people at the top had no idea what was going on further down the line. I worked night and day to bring about what I knew must be done. You know what happened?'

'Tell me.'

'The other members of the board combined to force me to resign. Why? Because as fatcats controlling this huge dinosaur they had enormous salaries, plus big share option deals to make them millionaires. Ignorant Yanks. I returned to Britain.'

'You mentioned some organization called MOVAK.'

'That is Marov's invention. A secret unit to replace the hopelessly corrupt KGB. I am sure he will shoot every KGB officer when he takes over power in his own time.'

'I am still listening,' said Tweed.

'So the West needs a terrible *shock* to force it to become strong again. That shock will be the sudden rise of Russia as a world force. The groundwork has been laid. All frontier and customs controls between Russia and the republic of Belorus have been abolished. That means, quite simply, Russia has absorbed Belorus. The next objective is Ukraine.'

'You are helping people like Marov to achieve his objective of a new all-powerful Russia?' Tweed asked.

'I can only tell you what I am doing if you agree to join me in a full partnership. The two of us would make an invincible combination. You must decide now. The hour is late.'

'Why me?'

'I have studied your track record. You are incorrupt-

269

ible, immensely determined, you keep your word.' For the first time Brazil smiled. 'You are a rare bird.'

'Thank you for the compliment.'

Tweed stood up, paced slowly round the room. Brazil watched him, was careful to say nothing more. His mind racing, Tweed thought over what Brazil had said. Some of it he felt compelled to agree with. The West was drifting like a rudderless ship towards a stormy sea. Eventually Brazil did speak.

'I can tell you think very much like I do. I know you won't deny it. The West needs an earthquakelike shock.'

Tweed stiffened his shoulders. He turned round and stared straight at Brazil, meeting the ice-blue eyes. A truly remarkable, intriguing man, he was thinking. In the mould of General de Gaulle, Winston Churchill, and Konrad Adenauer. He smiled.

'Mr Brazil. I have to refuse your offer.'

'Reluctantly?' Brazil enquired as he stood up.

'I have to refuse your offer.'

'I feared you would take that decision. I will go now.'

Brazil left, closing the door quietly behind him. It seemed to Tweed the room was suddenly empty, as though a remarkable force had left behind a vacuum.


Newman, clad in a military-style trenchcoat with large lapels, a wide-brimmed hat on his head, and a scarf half-covering his face, walked across Bahnhofplatz as light snow began to fall. Standing at the top of the steps, leading into the main station, stood a man also wearing a trenchcoat and a hat. He had the appearance of a passenger who had just got off a train and was waiting for the snow to stop.

Newman paused beside him, apparently to light a cigarette.

270

'Well, Marler, did you get the clothing needed for Butler and Nield?'

'Yes. They're waiting just round the corner in Bahnhofstrasse. The clothing is a perfect replica.'

'Good. I wonder if it will be needed. Any sign of that Volvo?'

'Not so far. If it appears I signal Butler and Nield. I'm sure the charade will work.'

'Let us hope so, if it's needed. I'm going back so I am near the exit from the Schweizerhof. At least we are ready for them . . .'

# 29

Brazil avoided the lift after leaving Tweed's room. He ran down the staircase, reached the lobby, crossed it to the secluded bar. As he had hoped, at that time of the year it was empty except for the barman and one customer. Craig.

'I'll have a Cointreau,' Brazil said to the barman. He laid a large banknote on the counter. 'I don't want any change but my friend and I have something confidential to discuss. Would you mind waiting in the lobby? You can see from there if any new customer comes into here.'

The barman had trouble not spilling the glass of Cointreau. His eyes were on the banknote.

'Thank you very much, sir. I'll be outside if you do need me.'

'Well,' said Craig as soon as they were alone, 'did he agree to come in with us?'

'No, regrettably. He refused.'

'Then he's for the chop.'

Craig wore a heavy overcoat and a white silk scarf. He had trouble concealing his satisfaction.

271

'Craig,' Brazil said quietly. 'If anything happens to Tweed I'll see you don't stay alive an hour. And the way you treat your henchmen it will be a pleasure for any of them to carry out my order.'

'OK.' Craig was shaken. He drank the rest of his Scotch quickly. 'I've got the message. But what about his team? They're going to get in the way. You can bet on that.'

'I fear you're right.'

'So I have your authority to eliminate the whole of his team off this planet?'

'Yes.' Brazil paused. 'I suppose it's the only sensible thing to do.'

'Right. You'll be waiting for your limo.' Craig took a mobile phone from his pocket, dialled, spoke briefly. 'Craig here. Come and get me. Work to do. Pack the car with troops . . .'

Standing at the corner where Bahnhofstrasse met the *platz*, Newman brushed snow off his trenchcoat. He never took his eyes off Marler, still standing on the station steps. Then he saw him stretch both arms as though weary.

The Volvo had appeared, began to cruise round the *platz*. Craig, standing in the hotel exit, walked a few feet up the street away from Newman. The Volvo, with three men inside, the driver and one man in front, a third man in the back, paused and Craig opened the rear door on the pavement side and slipped into the vacant seat.

Newman removed his scarf and hat, tucked them inside his coat, waited on the edge of the kerb. Craig saw him immediately, said something to the driver. The Volvo cruised slowly towards where Newman stood. At the same moment two men appeared, clad in black leather, wearing helmets, and walking towards the approaching car. One man banged on the back window.

272

Craig, confused, told the driver to stop. He was convinced that, without orders, two of his Leather Bombers had arrived. He lowered the window and Newman walked up to him.

'Not a nice evening, Craig,' Newman called out.

'Not for you. You're the first,' Craig snarled.

He reached down to the car floor, grabbed hold of a shotgun. The first of the two men clad in leather, Butler, produced a tear-gas pistol and fired into the back of the vehicle. At the same moment Nield, similarly clad, fired his own pistol across Butler's shoulder into the front of the car.

Choking, the driver panicked, pressed the accelerator as one of Zurich's blue trams, built like a tank, was turning to proceed down Bahnhofstrasse. Craig saw the huge shape looming up through streaming eyes. He grasped the door handle, threw the door wide open, tumbled onto the pavement, rolling so his shoulders took the fall like a paratrooper landing.

The Volvo continued its onward rush for only a few seconds. A few seconds too long. It collided into the massive tram. The car telescoped with the force of the impact. The three men inside disappeared, lost in the mess of crushed metal. The tram's passengers were shaken, but unhurt.

Craig staggered to his feet, dazed. He recovered, ran off in the opposite direction, vanished. On the pavement lay the shotgun Craig had been going to use. Newman nodded to Butler and Nield. They ran along the *platz*, turned down the quiet side-street where Tweed had walked earlier.

Tearing off their leather, they stuffed it with the helmets into a litter bin. Wearing normal business suits, they disappeared inside the Gotthard via the door leading into the Hummer Bar. Newman was already inside the lobby of the Schweizerhof, heading for the lifts.

'Hell of a crash outside,' he said to the concierge, who was moving towards the front door. 'Some drunken oaf drove into a tram – at least that's what I was told.'

He went straight to Tweed's room. Brazil, still in the bar, heard what he had said. He pursed his lips. If Craig had been involved he was becoming a liability. If he was still alive.


'I saw it,' Tweed said when he had let Newman into his room. 'So the war has really started.'

'Craig had a shotgun . . .'

'I know. I saw that, too. Lying on the pavement. I turned down Brazil's offer for me to work with him – in a partnership. Now, it can only be twenty minutes since Brazil left this room, and they've already tried to kill you. Brazil himself must have given the order. He is not only ruthless, he is brutal.'

Tweed sounded grimmer than Newman had experienced for a long time.

'What partnershp?' he asked.

Tweed sat down, told him everything Brazil had said.

'It's strange,' Newman commented, sitting in another chair. 'But I find myself agreeing with some of what he thinks. Only some of it.'

'So did I,' agreed Tweed. 'And he didn't mention one more aspect of the global situation – although I'm sure he had it in mind. If Russia becomes strong again it provides a barrier against the Chinese, who grow more aggressive every day. They have now had successful tests at Lop Nor, launching intercontinental missiles with a range of over five thousand miles. That means those missiles could reach London – or the West Coast of the United States. Brazil has logic on his side, he can think globally, which few of our feeble politicians are able to. It's his methods I find repugnant. He would argue that is the

274

only way to achieve a necessary change in the balance of world power.'

'So what do we do now?'

'Eliminate Brazil and all his works . . .'


Craig made his way back round the side streets until he came out in Bahnhofstrasse almost opposite the Baur-en-Ville. Entering the reception hall, he saw Eve coming towards him.

'Craig, I wanted to—'

'Drop dead.'

Craig marched on, surveying the visitors sitting and chatting over tea. He went up to a thin man with a dead white face and a bandage round the back of his head.

'Marco, come upstairs with me. We're going to have a conference in Brazil's board room – with Luigi. Move the feet.'

'Charming man,' Eve said to herself after he had insulted her.

Then she listened carefully. Above the subdued hum of the voices of the scattering of guests she heard every word he'd said to Marco. Eve had acute hearing and Craig, still in a rage, had raised his voice more than he had intended to. She watched them disappear into a lift, waited, then walked into an empty one.

She had turned the corner into the long corridor leading to her room when she stopped, stepped back a few paces. José was just entering Brazil's living room. Presumably Craig and his henchmen had already gone into the board room.

She went back to her own room but left the door ajar. She was still holding the fresh glass of vodka she had ordered from the bar when she had met Craig coming back off the street downstairs. She sipped it, standing close to the door.

A few minutes later she heard a door close. When she glanced out she saw José walking away in the opposite direction. She decided to take another chance. Collecting the stethoscope from the cupboard, she stuffed it inside her shoulder bag, left her room, walked back to Brazil's living room. She opened the door quietly, the glass of vodka, half-drunk, in her other hand. The room was empty. She tiptoed over to the closed sliding doors leading to the board room, put her glass on a ledge, took out her stethoscope, listened. Craig was speaking, his tone ugly.

'I repeat, only Tweed is not to be harmed. God knows why. But that is Brazil's personal instruction.'

'You said all this before,' Marco's voice protested.

'Shut your face! Listen. I am saying it again to get it into your thick heads. You are listening, Luigi?'

'With both my ears.'

'Don't get funny with me. Listen, damn you! Every member of Tweed's team is a target for extermination. That includes Paula Grey, Robert Newman, Philip Cardon, and, possibly, Bill Franklin. We leave Franklin alone until we have confirmation of his real status.'

'Excuse me,' Luigi said. 'But do they know about Sion?'

'I am coming to that. I said *listen*. There are two other members of Tweed's gang, identities unknown at the moment. They appeared in Bahnhofplatz late this after-noon dressed in black leather motorcyclist outfits. They also will be killed, when we know who they are. Any questions so far?'

'Do they know about Sion?' Luigi asked anxiously.

'I'm sure they don't. Even if they did they will never reach it. I now come to my plan. They will never leave Zurich alive. How do we guarantee that? By stationing a group at Kloten Airport, another one at the Hauptbahn-hof in case they attempt to leave by train. They will be gunned down. Make sure they are dead.'

276

'Supposing they drive out of Zurich?' persisted Luigi.

'All motorways will have motorcyclist teams ready for that contingency. Zurich will be sealed off.' Craig paused. 'As a final reserve, do you have motorcyclist teams at Sion, Luigi?'

'An élite team waits there . . .'

Eve slipped her stethoscope back into her shoulder bag. She was careful to remember her glass of vodka as she crept out of the room and returned to her own bedroom. She locked the door and leaned against it, breathing heavily with tension.

'So, that's more than enough,' she said to herself. 'And Craig's top three deputies are Marco, the expert knife-thrower, Luigi, who appears to be in charge of whatever is at Sion, and Gustav, crack shot with a handgun. I wonder why he wasn't there?'


Gustav entered the bar at the Schweizerhof to find Brazil checking his watch, looking annoyed. He looked up, saw Gustav, frowned.

Even men fear my face, Gustav thought. Even the top man.

He hurried forward, full of apologies for not arriving earlier.

'José has twisted his right ankle, which makes it tricky for him to drive. I have the limo waiting outside.'

'Then let's go immediately. And don't open the door for me. I hate fuss.'


Half an hour later the operator rang Newman in his room.

'I have a gentleman on the phone. He won't give a name. He says you know him well, that you last met him at a place called Kimmeridge. I made him spell that name. I hope I have pronounced it correctly.'

'You have. Put him through.'

'Mr Newman?'

Only two words spoken on the phone but Newman recognized the voice at once. Archie.

'Yes, speaking. Very good to hear your voice.'

'Mr Newman, I know where you are. I am speaking from a call box nearby. May I come to see you?'

'Of course, Mr Sullivan. The concierge will give you my room number.'

Archie had gone. He was quick enough to know he should announce himself as Mr Sullivan to the concierge. Newman felt sure that Tweed would wish to see him, but he went along to his room to check.

Tweed was surprised to hear Archie was in Zurich but he said he would certainly see him with Newman.

'In this room, I suggest,' he went on. 'It's larger. So you had better instruct the concierge.'

Newman met Archie at the lift, said nothing until he had escorted him to Tweed's room. Tweed greeted him warmly, showed him to a comfortable chair, asked him if he'd like something to drink.

'Just water, please.'

Archie wore a heavy fur coat which he removed, his battered hat and, as usual, he had the dead stub of a half-smoked cigarette at the corner of his mouth.

'May I ask how you knew Bob was here?' Tweed enquired amiably.

'Simple. I phoned Monica at Park Crescent. She was very thorough in checking me out, then she gave me the number of this hotel. Gentlemen, you are in very great danger.'

'What kind of danger?' asked Tweed.

'You are to be spared. Brazil has ordered you are not to be harmed in any way.' Archie paused, switched his gaze to Newman. 'My informant has just told me that Craig, with Brazil's backing, has ordered his thugs to exterminate every member of Tweed's team, including yourself.' He looked back at Tweed. 'They have names. Paula Grey, Robert Newman, Philip Cardon. They also know two other men exist but so far they have no names.'

'I see.'

Tweed stood up, thrust his hands into his jacket pockets to conceal the fact he was clenching and unclenching them to regain self-control. He was in a state of fury he rarely experienced. The idea that he was to be left alive while his team was wiped out filled him with venom. He walked round the room several times, then sat down opposite Archie.

'Is the word "exterminate" you used your own or, if you know, was it the word used by Craig?'

'Craig apparently used that exact word,' Archie replied, and took a sip of water from the glass Newman had given him.

'I see,' Tweed said again.

'The danger is grave,' Archie continued. 'My informant told me there will be teams of killers waiting at the airport, at the main station across the way, also teams of motorcyclists watching the motorways out of Zurich.'

'They've sewn us up pretty tightly,' Newman remarked.

Archie smiled, a warm smile. 'Now I must go.'

'How much do I owe you for your expenses and your fee?' Newman asked.

'Two thousand francs for expenses. This time I do not want a fee. Marler is always very generous with me. And this time, bearing in mind the grave news I bring, I am glad to do you a favour.'

Newman took out his wallet, peeled off four thousand-franc notes, laid them on the table in front of Archie. He picked up two of the banknotes and left their twins.

'Do not embarrass me. I should go now.'

'This hotel may be watched,' Tweed warned. He

stood up to go to the windows, realized the curtains had been closed. 'It will be dark outside,' he warned a second time.

'It was dark when I entered via the Bistro, the small snack restaurant open to the public with a door on to the street. I came in that way,' Archie explained. 'I shall go back that way, order a cup of coffee and wait until I see some girls leaving. I will leave with them, asking them in German how to get to the lake. When I arrived I came into the Bistro, as I have said, then I walked into the lobby by the door which leads into the hotel. Any watcher will have seen one man enter the café and the same man come out with a couple of girls. I am most careful.'

'Thank you for all your help,' Tweed said, standing up and escorting him to the door. 'You must take care of yourself. Wild animals are on the prowl.'

'Thank you. And do not forget Marchat in Sion.'

After Newman had returned from escorting Archie to the lobby, but without leaving the lift himself, he found Tweed pacing again.

'It looks as though we're trapped,' Newman commented.

'That is how it would appear,' Tweed replied.

# 30

Earlier on the same day Philip had caught an express from Zurich to Geneva. He would have liked to visit the dining car but felt he could not leave his case in the first-class compartment. The train was quiet and he had the compartment to himself during the journey diagonally across Switzerland.

It began snowing heavily soon after the train had left

Zurich. Watching the slanting fall of the white curtain he nearly fell asleep. He got up, opened the window, let ice-cold air sweep into the compartment for a few minutes, then closed the window.

After stopping briefly at Berne, the express moved on and the snow ceased. Later, to the east, he had a panoramic view as the sky cleared and the sun came out. He could see the western end of the massive Bernese Oberland range which guarded the entrance to the Valais.

'Doesn't look too inviting,' he said to himself.

Arriving at Geneva, he took a taxi to the Hôtel des Bergues, asked for a room overlooking the Rhône. He had an early dinner and by the time he returned to his room it was dark. He stood by the window looking across the Rhône where small ice floes drifted past.

He was recalling the firefight he had shared with Paula in the Old City. Lord, the lady had guts. He wished now she was coming with him. The silence in the room began to get on his nerves. He turned on the radio for some music. Ever since his wife's death he had not been able to stand silence inside a room on his own.

Setting the alarm on his travelling clock for an early rising, he took a shower, put on his pyjamas, and flopped into bed. He read a few pages of a paperback, turned off the bedside light, and promptly became alert. He was thinking of Jean.

He had stayed at this hotel with his late wife, had been careful on arrival they didn't give him the same room. He lay still, on his back. This room had a double bed. The room he had shared with Jean had also had a double bed. It was automatic for Philip to have chosen the right-hand side as viewed from the bottom of the bed. Jean had always slept on the other side.

Eve came into his mind. He suddenly realized that when alone he often thought of Jean – daily, in fact. But he rarely thought of Eve, despite the amount of time he had spent with her. And it was only when he was with her that she held him in her spell. He knew she was coming closer to him each time they met. He also knew now that he was not on the same waveband as her.

He turned over before he fell into a deep sleep. On one side the pillow was damp. The alarm woke him with a start. He had been dreaming he was with Jean, walking down the street of a strange town as they chattered with each other like magpies. They had never been short of something to talk about.

He washed, shaved, got dressed quickly. He took his coat and case down to the Pavillon restaurant with him. In the lobby a fat man with a bushy moustache was reading a paper. For a moment their eyes met.

Philip had checked the train times the night before as he ate dinner. He arrived at Cornavin Station some minutes before the express was due to leave. When it moved slowly into the station he was standing behind a pillar where he could see the full length of the express. The metal plates on the outsides of the coaches gave the destinations, ending with *Milano*.

No one else was about except for a couple of uniformed railway staff. He was also watching the second hand on the platform clock. Swiss trains always left dead on time. No one appeared to have boarded the express as he ran forward, climbed into a first-class coach. The automatic door closed behind him and the long international express glided out of Cornavin.

The one section of the train Philip had not been able to watch was the front coach, due to a curve in the platform. It did not surprise him he was the sole passenger. At this early hour, at the beginning of March, he had anticipated few passengers.

In the coach he sat in a seat for two, facing the engine

282

and two similar seats. He had chosen the left side of the train because on the other side it would soon be running past Lake Geneva. He did not wish to recall the memory of his previous journey with Jean when they had gazed out at the panoramic view of the lake and the mountains of France on the far shore.

Philip's emotional mood had changed. He was in a grim frame of mind.

'God help anyone who gets in my way,' he said to himself.

The coach door leading to the next section slid open and a man walked slowly towards him. A fat man with a bushy moustache and a ruddy, outdoor face. The man who had sat in the lobby of the Hôtel des Bergues the previous evening.

'May I sit down opposite you, sir?' the fat man asked.

He spoke in English, had an overcoat over his arm, wore a black suit with a pale yellow tie bisecting a clean white shirt. He remained standing while he waited for Philip's reply.

Outwardly, Philip was amiable – he even smiled. He gestured towards the seat.

'Please do.'

Inwardly he was totally alert, ice-cold. If this was the beginning of trouble so be it. He would render the newcomer unconscious.

'Most kind of you,' the fat man said as he settled himself. 'We appear to be the only two passengers on the express so far. I like a little company when I'm travelling. My card, sir.'

Philip took the small piece of pasteboard. He read it with a shock.

*Leon Vincenau. Inspecteur. Police. Genève.*

'Thank you,' he said quickly. He smiled again as he handed the card back to the fat man. Vincenau waved a hand.

'Please keep it. You might want to get in touch with me.'

'Why should I want to do that?' Philip asked as he tucked the card inside his wallet. The card had a phone number.

'Because you are travelling alone. Because the world – even Switzerland – has turned into a dangerous zoo. We collected six bodies off the street after a shoot-out in Geneva a day or two ago.'

'Then Geneva is a good place for me to leave. Are you, if I may ask, on business or pleasure?'

'I am never sure. A detective is on duty twenty-four hours a day.'

'You are travelling far?' Philip enquired.

Damn this for a lark, he thought. I'll be the one who asks the questions.

'To the end of the line. To Milano. A terrible city. You take your life in your hands when you cross a street. The lights are in your favour, they change when you are three-quarters of the way over. The armada of traffic comes straight at you. If you didn't hurry they would run you over.' He waved a hand. 'Different countries, different manners. Would it disturb you if I smoked a cigar?'

'Go ahead. I think I'll use up one of the few cigarettes I smoke in a day . . .'

The fat man took out a cigar case, extracted a cigar, neatly trimmed off the end which he placed in the ashtray, then used a match to light it, moving the match backwards and forwards.

For the next hour or so Philip, growing more and more intrigued – even fearful – by what he saw out of the window, said nothing. Vincenau, wreathed inside the smoke from the large cigar he was smoking slowly, also said nothing. Philip suspected it was the old police tactic – using silence to compel the suspect to start saying something.

After leaving Montreux, the express entered the vast and endless gorge which was the Valais. Philip looked out on a frozen world. On both sides the world was hemmed in by continuous ranges of high, rugged, grim mountains.

The mountains, their summits towering so far above the express he couldn't see them often, were covered in deep snow. At frequent intervals mysterious valleys disappeared inside the mountain walls, their entrances guarded by immense cliffs.

Every now and again there would be a sinister narrow gash, a crevasse enclosing a threadlike waterfall, now solid ice. He saw great rock outcrops over which, at one time, water had spilled. Now the water was frozen into dagger-like stalactites, often a hundred feet long. Dozens of them formed palisades of ice.

They passed through Martigny, a small town huddled beneath a menacing giant of overhung rock, gleaming like an enormous mirror as a brief shaft of sunlight broke through the low overcast. There was no sign of life and the streets were piled high with snow.

Philip thought he had never before seen such a wasteland, as though this part of the world had returned to the wilderness of the Ice Age. He knew Vincenau was watching his reaction through the smoke and kept his face expressionless.

The floor of the valley, along the centre of which the rail line ran, was a bleak expanse of snow. Here and there was a sign of life. From the chimney of a stone house, perched on a lip, rose a trail of smoke vertically to meet the overcast above them. Could Siberia be any worse?

Vincenau tapped ash from what was left of his cigar, used the cigar as a pointer.

'See that snail-like thing halfway up that mountain? It's a small train.'

Philip gazed in disbelief at the two tiny coaches which

appeared to be clinging to the face of the mountain as they crawled higher and higher.

'Where is it going to?' he asked.

'It ends near a glacier. There are villages which have to be served. That is their only communication with the outside world in March. It will have a small snowplough attached to the front.'

'All right, if you like the quiet life,' Philip commented.

'The people who survive here are a tough, sturdy breed. The trouble is all the young folk have left for the bright lights of the cities. There are villages up in those mountains which are deserted, the houses becoming derelict. Old wooden houses with shingle roofs. Apart from tourism and vineyards in good weather later the Valais is dying.'

It was a long speech for Vincenau and, once again, Philip had the feeling his companion, conducting the conversation in French, was studying his reaction. He checked his watch and stood up to lift down his case from the rack.

'You are getting off at Sion?' Vincenau enquired.

'Yes.'

'Look out of the window.'

They were passing more slowly through a small station. On the platform stood a group of what looked like young refugees, waiting for a stopping train. Several were holding broken skis. One girl was on crutches and had her right leg swathed in bandages. All of them looked in a state of misery. Vincenau sighed.

'They will do it.'

'Do what?' Philip asked.

'Go skiing when they have been warned that the weather is changing, that the ski slopes are treacherous.'

The express was slowing even more when Philip saw out of the window an airfield. It was quite close to the rail line and a snowplough stood motionless at one end of a runway it had just cleared.

'That's just outside Sion,' said Vinceneau. 'They must be expecting an aircraft to land.'

'Well, I'd better get to the exit door. These trains don't wait long.'

'One minute at Sion,' said Vincenau.

He stood up to shake hands after stubbing his cigar. He stood close to Philip, who noticed his fleshy nose had red veins. The Swiss detective obviously liked his wine.

'Do not go up into the mountains,' Vincenau said with great emphasis.

'Thank you for your company. I hope conditions in Milan are better.'

Philip was standing by the exit door when the train stopped and the door slid open automatically. He was the only one to step down onto the platform. He waited, seeing no sign of station staff, no sign of anyone. The express moved off and Philip watched it disappearing rapidly. He felt he had just lost his last link with civilization.


Vincenau did not travel on to Milan. He got off at the next stop, Brig. He hurried to a phone, dialled Beck's private number at police headquarters in Zurich.

'Beck speaking.'

'Inspector Vincenau here, sir. Speaking from Brig in the Valais. I accompanied Philip Cardon on an express from Geneva. He didn't give me his name but he fitted one of the descriptions you gave me. I will repeat it . . .'

He did so while Beck, in his office overlooking the River Limmat, listened carefully. He only spoke when Vincenau had finished.

'Yes. That would be Philip Cardon. Where was he going to?'

'He got off the express at Sion.'

'Who was with him?'

'No one. He was alone. Of that I am sure.'

'Alone! Oh, my God . . .'

After he had finished speaking to Vincenau and they had agreed Vincenau should catch the next express back to Geneva, Beck, who had been up all night, put down the phone and sat thinking. He was appalled at the news. Beck took quick decisions. He called the Schweizerhof, asked to speak to Tweed, told him he was on his way over.

In his room Tweed told Newman what Beck had said. He had also been up all night. He had held a conference with Newman, Marler, Butler, and Nield on the problem of leaving Zurich alive.

'I have a plan,' Marler had suggested. 'We take a train. Preferably an early morning express before commuters clutter up the station. I will lead a guard team – all disguised in station officials' uniforms.'

'How are you going to get hold of them—' Newman had begun, only to be interrupted by Tweed.

'No good. There *will* be some passengers about and if it comes to a shoot-out innocent people could end up as corpses.'

Whatever plan was suggested it always came up against Tweed's objection that innocent lives could be at stake. For the first time in his life Tweed felt check-mated.

They were all still in Tweed's room when Beck tapped on the door, came in with his fur coat, flecked with snow, over his arm. Typically, he came straight to the point.

'I've just heard that Philip Cardon has arrived – in Sion.'

He explained briefly the circumstances which, on his

288

orders, had led Inspector Vincenau to the Hôtel des Bergues.

'That is where Philip Cardon and Paula Grey stayed on the night of the massacre in Geneva. Some instinct led me to have the hotel watched.'

'Well, at least Philip has got there safely,' Tweed remarked.

'What the hell's wrong with you?' Beck had exploded. 'One man against all those troops Brazil has brought in from France and Germany!'

'He will cope . . .'

'You hope.'

It was not a remark which made Tweed feel any better. He then explained to Beck that they were trapped inside Zurich – and why. Beck listened, then sat down, frowning.

'That I will not put up with,' he announced grimly. 'So you wait here for two hours. Have a leisurely breakfast. Then walk into the station and catch the first express.'

'What have you in mind?' enquired Tweed.

'A horde of uniformed police, plus men in plain clothes, will check the identity of everyone inside and outside the Hauptbahnhof. They will be searched for weapons. Because from what you have told me any of Brazil's thugs *will* be armed. I shall arrange with several police stations to have cells ready for them.' He grinned. 'Mr Brazil no longer carries the clout with that group of bankers who were putting pressure on me.'

'Why not?' asked Tweed.

'Because Brazil promised them huge profits for certain funds they loaned him. Now these so-called clever men believe they have been tricked. They know that he has transferred huge funds to the Zurcher Kredit Bank in Sion. Undoubtedly to pay the army of mercenaries he has assembled there. They come expensive – mercenaries. Even if they had not changed their minds I would have put this clean-up operation into action.'

'You are a good friend,' Tweed told him.

'I am a good policeman. Now, I must rush back to headquarters to organize the operation. I shall supervise it myself.'


In his living room at the Baur-en-Ville Brazil was giving secret instructions to Gustav, one of the few men he trusted.

'I am sure there is a leak inside our organization. I want the informant tracked down, eliminated. You have those compact listening and recording devices which can be concealed anywhere. Use them.'

'I would like first to install one in José's office.'

'José? You really think so?'

'We can at least check. Also I have another suspect in mind. Again I can use a listening device. Have I permission to check on anyone I wish to?'

'I suppose it is the only way to be sure. Who is the second suspect?'

'That I do not wish to reveal at this stage.'

Brazil glared at him, stroked the wolfhound, Igor, which had stood up from the floor beside his chair, as though detecting its master's brief annoyance. It bared its teeth, subsided as its master kept stroking it.

There was a knock on the door and Brazil called out, 'Come in.' Marco appeared, wearing an overcoat, holding a dog's leash.

'Time for you to go for a walk, Igor,' Brazil said.

He had heard several owners of dogs say 'walkies' and he detested the word and all that it implied. For Brazil Igor was a guard dog, an attack dog if necessary. Igor showed excitement when it saw the leash, submitted to the leash being attached, and went out of the room

290

with a bounce in its step as Marco closed the door.

'That's a fierce animal,' Gustav remarked. 'And it can sense when you are annoyed.'

'It's just a dog,' Brazil said curtly. 'How do you propose to handle this secret check if you do detect an informant?'

'I will bring the cassette straight to you. Then you can listen to what was said for yourself on your recorder.'

'Do it.'

He studied the man with the hooked nose as he got up to go. Gustav was probably the most reliable of all the staff he employed. Even more reliable than Craig who had a tendency to blow his fuse. At that moment Craig entered the room as Gustav, without a glance in his direction, left. Craig, as always, had not bothered to knock before being told he could come in. He sank his bulk into a carver chair, which creaked under the pressure.

'All set, Chief,' Craig reported. 'And no one has left the Schweizerhof. I've had it watched round the clock.'

'So we have them penned up. I'm leaving Zurich. José and Gustav are staying here for the moment to check how the situation develops. One other person may stay to assist José.'

'Who?'

'It doesn't matter. My jet has been flown in from Belp to Kloten. You will accompany me.'

'What about Eve?' Craig asked.

'She will stay here, too. I have told her.'

'Where are we flying to?'

'Sion, of course.'

# 31

'Police.'

The man in plain clothes held up his warrant card in front of the hard-faced man who had been pretending to read a newspaper in the Hauptbahnhof.

'Identity papers, please,' the detective demanded.

Hard-Face stiffened, then slipped his hand inside his raincoat. The hand of another man behind him grasped the hand, brought it out slowly, then rammed his own hand back into the breast pocket, slowly withdrew a 7.65mm Luger from the shoulder holster.

'Take him to the wagon,' the first detective ordered.

There was a click as the second detective locked a handcuff round Hard-Face's wrist, clipped the other cuff round his own wrist, marched him off.

It was happening all over the main station. Detectives worked in pairs, even checked every member of the uniformed station staff. Within an hour the chief of detectives reported to Beck over the phone.

'All clear at the Hauptbahnhof. We're staying in case more rubbish turns up . . .'


At Police Headquarters Beck put on a coat, ran down the stairs, and walked briskly, avoiding ice, to the Schweizerhof.

Tweed had also been up all night. He had sent Marler with Butler and Nield back to the Gotthard to pack their cases and be ready for instant departure to the station when he called. They had arrived in his room separately and had left at intervals to fool anyone watching the hotel. So far as Tweed knew their identities were still completely unknown to Craig's gang. Newman was talking to Tweed when Beck rapped on the door. Again he carried his coat over his arm and again it was flecked with snow.

'Still coming down?' Tweed queried, glancing at the coat.

'The forecast is it won't stop. I came to stretch my legs, to tell you the station is clear. We arrested eleven men, all armed with various cannons. Where are you off to?'

'Geneva.'

'An express leaves in one hour from now. You need how many tickets?'

'Five, first class. Why?'

'I'll get them for you and leave them in a sealed envelope with the night concierge downstairs. You'll keep in touch with me? I'm staying at Zurich Police HQ.'

'I'll report to you if and when I can, certainly.'

Beck paused at the door, smiled without humour.

'One more small item you might care to know. Brazil has had his jet flown to Kloten from Belp. The pilot has filed a flight plan for take-off just after dawn. Guess for what destination.'

'Sion.'

'Give the man the money . . .'

When Beck had left Newman began talking again. Like Tweed, he showed no signs of strain.

'I'm surprised Beck has never questioned me about that car crashing into the tram.'

'He probably thinks we're under enough pressure. They cleared up the mess quickly. From my window I watched police cars arrive escorting a huge lifting machine. They were very careful how they attached the claws of the crane to what remained of the car. Then they took it away, presumably for examination.'

'I don't envy them doing that – with three bodies inside,' Newman remarked.

'They were probably hoping to find the registration plates but I'd say their chances weren't good.'

'But there was the shotgun Craig was going to use. It will carry Craig's fingerprints. He wasn't wearing gloves.'

'Again it would be a disappointment. I saw some fool of a pedestrian pick up the weapon, having a good look at it before a uniformed policeman arrived and took him away with the gun. Any prints of Craig's would be smudged out of existence.'

'Pity. That leaves Craig in the clear. He's more than a hired thug. He's amoral and enjoys his work, I'm sure. I'd like to meet him again.'

'Maybe you will, so be careful,' Tweed warned. He checked his watch. 'We'll have to leave soon to catch that express. Only another half-hour at the outside. It will be dark for a while, so let's hope it has a dining car.'


Brazil had just finished an early breakfast, brought to him by room service, when there was a knock on his door. He called out 'Come in,' and Gustav entered, with a small box in his hand.

'What is it?' demanded Brazil.

'My idea has worked already. May I put this cassette in your recorder so you can listen?'

Brazil tensed inwardly. He had hoped Gustav was wrong in his suspicions that an informant, a traitor, existed within his organization. He had always chosen staff so carefully, checking them out himself. He nodded his approval and listened as Gustav started the small tape.

*You know who this is?* José's voice.

*Yes. You have more information for me?* Another voice, also speaking in English, but with a guttural accent Brazil suspected was faked.

294

*Brazil and three key members of his team, Craig, Luigi, and Marco, are leaving by jet from Kloten this morning bound for Sion.* José's unmistakable whispering voice again.

*Thank you. I am still willing to make a payment to you.* The other voice.

*No. I want no payment. Brazil is a violent and evil man. I will keep you informed of developments.* José once more.

Gustav rewound the tape, looked across the desk at his boss, who was gazing out of the window where, through a slit in the curtain he could see snow falling.

'Shall I replay the tape?' Gustav suggested. 'I always was suspicious of José. Too smooth.'

'No! I don't want to hear the damned thing again. How did you manage it?'

Gustav showed him the miniature tape-recorder. It had four suckers attached to its base.

'I merely placed this under the surface of his desk so it would pick up phone conversations.'

'Very ingenious.' Brazil sounded disappointed. 'I'll summon José when you have left. He will be travelling with me aboard the jet now. Is there any point in your staying here any longer?'

'The helicopter which was going to transport me to Sion is still standing by at Kloten?'

'It is.'

'Please keep it waiting for me. There is still another suspect I wish to check out.'

'The name?'

'I still would prefer not to mention it. After all, I might be wrong.'

'As you wish.'

Gustav, he reflected as his deputy left the room, liked to be secretive, which probably accounted for his reliability. I hope to God there isn't another rotten fish, he thought as he forced himself to press his intercom to summon José.

There was another knock on the door and he braced himself not to show his feelings when José entered. But it was Marco, bringing in Igor, who loped forward and flopped on the floor beside Brazil.

'He's been fed,' Marco explained. 'He'll fall asleep in no time.'

'Thank you, Marco. I'm expecting someone else . . .'

Absentmindedly, his mood on what he had heard on the tape, Brazil took a cigarette from the gold box on his desk. He rarely smoked except in moments of tension. He called out after someone knocked on the door and José came in. He hurried forward, took hold of an onyx lighter on the desk, held it to light the cigarette. Brazil had to exert all his self-control not to dash the lighter out of José's hand. He let him light the cigarette, leant back in his chair.

'José, there is a limo waiting for me at Sion?'

'Yes, sir. I sent another driver with it as you instructed me.'

'I have decided I only feel comfortable with you behind the wheel. So you will fly with me in the jet to Sion.'

'It will be my pleasure, sir.'

'That is all.'

Igor had stood up when José had lit the cigarette, had given a low growl. It was extraordinary, Brazil thought, how the hound had sensed his own suppressed feelings of venom towards José. He stroked the dog.

'Igor, you'll soon have to work for your supper. Let's see whether you have forgotten your training.'


Tweed checked his watch again in his room and looked at Newman, who sat quite relaxed in a chair. By his side was his packed case and a canvas bag with a shoulder strap.

'Ten more minutes and we should go to the station,' Tweed remarked.

'Best not to get there too early,' Newman agreed. 'I know Beck has cleaned out the Hauptbahnhof but you never know – he could have missed one watcher. And we have the tickets,' he added, producing the envelope he had collected from the concierge's desk.

The phone rang. Tweed pursed his lips, picked it up.

'Yes? Who is calling?'

'The man from Kimmeridge,' said Archie.

'You have more news?'

'Yes. Our very important friend and top members of his team will be leaving this morning. They will fly from Kloten to the Valais.'

'Thank you. We will be leaving here soon. I do appreciate your keeping me up to date.'

He told Newman what Archie had said. Newman shrugged.

'We knew that already. Beck told us.'

'But it shows how closely Archie keeps his finger on what is happening. He's quite a character.'

He had just finished speaking when the phone rang. Tweed tightened his lips. Should he answer? They were due to leave shortly. He picked up the phone.

'Monica here. Thank heavens I've reached you!'

She was speaking quickly and Tweed detected great anxiety under the surface although, being Monica, she was calm.

'What's happened?' Tweed asked. 'If you could keep it brief.'

'Howard has panicked, gone right over the top. Someone is needed here urgently to take control.'

'What caused the panic?' Tweed enquired, checking his watch again.

'The rumours on the international grapevine – rumours that a major coup is imminent in Moscow.'

297

'Where are the rumours coming from?'

He received the answer he had least hoped to hear.

'That's the odd thing. *I* am sure they are deliberately being spread by some central organization. And not from Russia. Somewhere in Europe. But Howard is seeing the PM almost hourly, working him up with his panic. It's very serious.'

'What you're suggesting,' Tweed said grimly, 'is that the situation is bad enough for me to return to London at once?'

'They're running round like headless chickens. And the atmosphere is getting worse by the hour. Yes, I think you should return. Howard has no idea I'm making this call.'

'Where is Howard now? Could I speak to him for just a minute?'

'I'm afraid not. He's over at Downing Street, waiting to wind up the PM some more.'

'Monica, you realize you're talking to me in my room. There's an unimportant item I'd be interested in. You have obviously been checking these rumours carefully. Where did they start?'

'That's difficult to say.' Monica paused, then went on quickly. 'Zurich.'


After he had told Monica he would call her back when he had had time to take a decision, Tweed told Newman what she had said.

'Could all this come from a rumour factory?' he asked Newman. 'You've had a lot of experience as a foreign correspondent.'

'It could, easily. All you need is a top-flight organiza-tion, a big staff, and a brain like Brazil has for planning. You then arrange to phone the right man or woman at key radio outfits, TV – and the newspapers. You'd time it carefully so simultaneous calls were made – to London, Paris, Bonn, Madrid, Stockholm, and Washington. They would immediately start checking with each other and find the same rumours everywhere.'

'It would be the first phase of Brazil's plan. Some-times,' Tweed mused, 'I think Brazil hates America more than Russia – because of his being thrown out as chief executive in the States. The Americans frighten easily – imagine the panic in Washington if Russia overnight became rampant again.'

'What are you going to do about Howard?'

'I'm thinking of putting you in sole command of the team we're sending to Sion. That I'll have to fly back to London before Howard does any more damage.'

'I'm ready to go, then.' Newman stood up. 'I'll be looking for the ground station controlling that satellite, Rogue One.'

'That has to be Brazil's key weapon to spread chaos in some way. You know, Bob, if I didn't detest Brazil's violent methods, I'd have a sneaking sympathy for what he's trying to achieve – to wake up the West.'

'He's a villain who employs villains.' Newman looked at Tweed as he heaved the shoulder strap of his canvas bag over his shoulder. 'One thing I've been going to ask you. With both Bill Franklin and Keith Kent you haven't ever mentioned to either of them the existence of The Motorman.'

'Must have slipped my mind . . .'

'Oh, come on!'

'Well, I have a strong feeling that we have already met and know The Motorman.'

# 32

When Philip, standing on the platform at Sion station, had watched the express carrying Inspector Leon Vincenau disappear, he felt thirsty. Exploring the lonely station he found a restaurant, to his relief. He went inside, ordered coffee from the pleasant waitress he addressed in French.

He suddenly felt bone-weary, with a desperate need to talk to someone in this grim Valais. Apart from himself the place was empty and he smiled at the waitress. She began talking at once.

'I hope you are not thinking of climbing a mountain. The weather is closing in and we have already had a tragedy.'

'What tragedy is that?' asked Philip.

'Two Englishmen with an American girl went skiing on a slope. They had been warned it was dangerous. They were all killed in a snow-slide yesterday.'

'I'm sorry to hear that – even if they were warned.'

'There is a mystery, so we have heard. The American girl had a bullet in her back. The police have transported the bodies to Geneva.'

'A bullet in her back? You mean someone shot her? So where did the tragedy take place?'

'I will bring you a map.'

Obviously glad of someone to talk to, the waitress hurried away, came back with a map which she unfolded and spread on the table. She pointed to an area on the northern mountains rising up behind Sion.

'It happened near the Col du Lemac on the Kellerhorn. That is the name of the mountain, which means Wild Boar Mountain – because the summit is shaped like the head of a wild boar. To get there you have to drive up this dangerous road . . .' She pointed to a road which, marked on the map, looked like no more than a narrow yellow thread. 'That is where the new meteorological station has been built. It has been in working order for some time.'

'A weather station? A state enterprise?' Philip enquired casually.

'Oh, no! A very wealthy man had it built. He is interested in making weather forecasts more accurate. It was built very quickly before the snows came. It must have cost him a fortune. He brought in workers from outside and they worked in three shifts all day and all night.'

'How could they work at night?'

'He is clever. He had huge arc lights erected so the men could work easily in the dark. He brought most of the workers from the Balkans. Now they have returned to their homes with their pockets full of money.'

'And this weather station is close to the Kellerhorn?'

'It is built *on* the Kellerhorn, close to the summit. He has it well guarded against vandals. His security force patrols the area day and night.'

'And was it close to this station where the tragedy you have just described took place?'

'Yes, it was. We hear the police visited the chief of security but neither he nor any of his guards had seen the skiers.'

'Point out the site of this weather station to me on the map, if you would be so kind.'

The waitress made a small cross below the word Kellerhorn. She looked at Philip.

'You seem interested. You can keep this map. I have another one.'

'Thank you.' He took the map she had folded and put it in his pocket. 'I suppose you wouldn't know the name

301

of the man who had the station built? He must be very well known round here.'

'No one knows his name. He arrives in a private jet at the airfield outside Sion. A big car with tinted windows so you cannot see inside waits for his plane, then takes him up to his villa.'

'His villa? That is near the weather station?'

'Oh, no. It is in the mountains on the other side of the valley. He had it built when they were creating the weather station. The villa was completed first. It is very remote and overlooks a glacier. I could show you on the map.'

Philip took out the map again, unfolded it, spread it out. The waitress's finger followed another yellow thread of a road, again with frequent zigzags, like the road to the weather station. She marked the position of the villa and the glacier below it. The area was called Col de Roc.

'You want to see the villa? You will have to hire a car with chains. That road is as dangerous as the other one. But do not go now.'

'Why not?'

'Because we have heard this very important man is due to fly in to the airfield. A friend who knows the controller told me. He is always escorted with motorcyclists.'

'Do you know where I could hire a car with chains?' enquired Philip. 'I could go to see this villa when he has gone.'

'Wait a minute. I have a street plan of Sion . . .'

She rushed off again, eager to please this man she had taken a fancy to. He was so polite, so interested in the Valais. She returned with the street plan, pointed to a cross she had already marked.

'That firm will hire you the car you want. You will have no difficulty. All the tourists have gone. It is the weather – and the few who might have stayed heard about the tragedy.'

'And about the bullet in the American woman's back?'

'Oh, no! That is a secret. The police have told us we must not mention that to anyone who visits Sion. Really I should not have told you, but I got carried away talking to you.'

'I promise not to say a word about it. There, I have had three cups of coffee while we were talking. How much do I owe you?'

She told him. She also said he could keep the street plan of Sion. When he had given her a generous tip she frowned.

'It is too much. And you asked me for the name of the important man. I said I did not know. But I have just remembered the name of the unpopular man who supervised the building of the villa and the station.'

'Why was he unpopular?'

'He was a big man with no manners. An Englishman – you will excuse me for saying that. You are English, of course? I thought so. The English are usually polite but this man was very rude. He spoke to people as if they were slaves.'

'And his name was?'

'Craig.'


Philip left the restaurant in a bemused state. He recalled something Newman had once told him from his experience as a foreign correspondent.

'Philip, if you want to find out something when you are in a new town, don't ask leading questions. Simply mix with the locals – in a bar, in a café. Get them talking. There are a lot of lonely people in the world who will tell strangers things. Be a good listener. And if you are listening to a woman who likes you, then you will be surprised how much she will sometimes tell you . . .'

He was glad he had removed his fur-lined coat before sitting down in the restaurant. Ice-cold air hit him as he stood on the platform. A door opened, the waitress ran up to him.

'You left your gloves. Do put them on. The mist is with us. Otherwise you may get frost-bite.'

'Thank you. You are most kind.'

She had run back inside the restaurant. He realized his hands were freezing. He felt bemused again as he looked across to Sion. A dense white mist had descended on the Valais. It shrouded the town in a motionless layer. To his right what looked like a small mountaintop sat on top of the mist. Perched on its summit, probably a couple of hundred feet high, was what looked like an ancient castle. As he watched, the mist layer rose to cover the summit, leaving only the castlelike building which appeared to float in mid-air.

Carrying his bag towards the exit he almost paused, then kept moving. Three motorcyclists clad in black leather with their visors pulled down over their helmets had appeared, were swaggering towards him.

'You want a girl?' one of them shouted in French. 'Then come with us. She will warm you up.'

'I am afraid I can't understand you,' Philip replied in German.

The three louts parted to let him pass just as he reached them. The same man shouted behind his back in French.

'Bloody Kraut.'

Philip ignored the insult, left the station. It began to look as though Sion crawled with Craig's body-guards.

The mist swirled everywhere as he entered the town looking for a hotel, carrying his bag. Like the icy fingers of a ghost it smoothed over his face, a sensation he found distinctly unpleasant. Here and there it thinned, showing him the buildings.

This part of Sion, which he later realized was most of the town, was not what he had expected. Instead of old houses there were modern office blocks of concrete, shop fronts which were also modern and boring. Because he had walked straight out of the station along the Avenue de la Gare he quickly saw Hôtel Touring, a small block of white concrete.

He didn't hesitate. The hotel was near the station and the mist was growing thicker. He went inside, booked a room. While the receptionist took details from his passport he peered into a bar, which had a circular counter of wood, a wooden ceiling, wooden stools at the bar, wooden tables and chairs. They have a lot of wood in Switzerland, he thought.

Once inside his room he partially unpacked his bag, leaving underclothes inside to conceal his small armoury. He also took out two rubber wedges which he pushed under the door, a trick Marler had taught him.

'Hotels always have people with master keys,' Marler had reminded him.

Philip had hung up his coat but now he took off his heavy sports jacket. The hotel believed in keeping its visitors warm and the room was almost hot. He would have liked to go down and eat another breakfast but he was suddenly overcome with a wave of fatigue, the penalty of a disturbed night at the Hôtel des Bergues in Geneva and constant alertness since he had started the day – including never relaxing in the presence of Inspector Vincenau.

Kicking off his climbing boots, he flopped on the bed and began studying the map of the area the waitress had given him. Blinking, he forced himself to look at the two routes more carefully. He began talking quietly to himself. It was all right as long as you knew you were doing it, he reckoned.

'That road up to the Col du Lemac and the Kellerhorn where the so-called weather station is looks a real swine. Too many zigzags – which mean fiendish hairpin bends, probably with a drop into eternity on one side.'

He yawned, took in deep breaths, turned his attention to the route up to the villa Brazil had had built.

'That one doesn't look any better. And if the waitress was right in where she put her cross the villa hangs right above the glacier. Part of the road before you get there also is poised over the glacier. Great . . .'

He yawned again, took the Walther out of his holster to get more comfortable, slipped the gun under the pillow. Then he fell fast asleep, the map spread out over him.

When Paula boarded an express for Geneva at Zurich she chose an empty compartment at the rear of the train. From that position she could see any passenger who also boarded the express after she had done. No one appeared as the train moved out of the station.

Knowing that this express did not stop anywhere until it reached Berne, about an hour later, she stood up, inserted a small needle at the side of her case on the rack. This would tell her when she returned if someone had tampered with the case.

Then she strolled slowly along the full length of the express, glancing into each compartment. The train was almost empty. Midway along she looked into yet another compartment and almost stopped, but she forced her feet to keep moving.

Apparently asleep in a corner of an otherwise empty compartment was Keith Kent. On the seat beside him rested his case, touching him – as though he felt the need to be sure no one tried to examine it while he was sleeping.

As she passed more compartments there was evidence that other passengers were aboard. A coat folded on a seat, bags on racks, books left on seats. She would have loved to check what they were reading but there was too great a risk of the owner returning.

She reached the dining car, stopped. Through the glass window in the door she saw it was almost full. Waiters were serving a meal and she decided she would go back to her compartment – she would be too conspicuous walking the full length of the dining car.

Settling herself in her seat, she reminded herself to look out of her window at the few stops before Geneva. The presence of Kent on the train puzzled her. To avoid his seeing her she would have to leave the express last if he travelled all the way to Geneva – after seeing him disembark from her window.


Arriving eventually at Cornavin, she watched Kent leaving the train, carrying a case. She had her coat and gloves on and hurried off the express, carrying her own bag. Outside the station she told a cab driver to take her to a small hotel near Cornavin she had once stayed at.

It never occurred to her that Philip might be spending the same night at the Hôtel des Bergues. After dinner she borrowed a rail timetable from the receptionist and checked expresses to Milan which stopped at Sion for the following morning.

Again she didn't realize she had chosen the next express after the one Philip had planned to board. She undressed, had a shower, sank into bed, and fell asleep at once. When she woke in the morning with a start she recalled the dream she had had. The Motorman, a shadowy figure, had been pursuing her. He had almost caught her as she ran, when she woke up.

She ate a full English breakfast, remembering Newman's advice.

'When you're on a job you eat on the hoof. You get a meal wherever you can – because you never know where or when the next one will be available . . .'

She took a taxi back to Cornavin, boarded the express when it came in. She was making herself comfortable in an empty first-class compartment when someone hurried past to board the train higher up. Keith Kent.


As the express later entered the Valais she had the same reaction as Philip. She gazed out of the window with a growing sense of fascination and horror.

She felt she was entering a white hell. She saw the snow-covered mountains looming close to the train as it passed through Martigny, the valleys, the frozen waterfalls, the lack of life in the snow-deep plain hemmed in by the great mountains on both sides.

I'll have to buy more sweaters in Sion, she thought.

She had brought a fur-lined trenchcoat with a hood she could pull over her head, but when she opened the window for a moment the well-heated compartment became ice-cold in seconds. She slammed the window shut.

Gazing out of the window, she tried to work out a plan to locate Philip. She felt sure now he would have caught the earlier express. On an assignment, Philip was a very early riser. Then the idea came to her.

She was worried about getting off the train at Sion in case Kent also disembarked. It was only a one-minute stop. A man's voice on the internal tannoy announced they were approaching Sion. Standing up, she saw outside the window the airfield and then everything was blotted out by a white mist as thick as cottonwool.

Charming, she thought. Just what I needed. I don't think . . .

When the automatic door opened outside the end of the coach she stepped down on to the platform, paused. Further along the platform Kent had already got off, was hurrying towards the exit.

'That was a bit of luck,' she said to herself. 'Now I need a list of hotels in this place.'

She saw the restaurant, went inside, sat down after taking off her coat, ordered coffee from the same waitress who had served Philip earlier.

'Would you have a list of the hotels in Sion, please?' she enquired.

'I can give you a brochure.'

The waitress hurried away, brought back the brochure, handed it to Paula, and went away. She preferred men as customers, particularly if they were on their own. In her opinion women could be all right, but they could also be very awkward.

Paula studied the brochure while she drank her coffee. It was a street plan of the town, a map of the surroundings, and a list of the hotels, each with an alphabetical letter which was reproduced on the map. She counted the number of hotels.

Oh, Lord, she thought. Twenty-two of them. So finish your coffee and get moving. Blast the mist . . .

She left the station, carrying her bag, and found a hotel not far from the station. She had her script in her head as she walked in and spoke to the receptionist.

'I'm looking for a friend, Philip Cardon. He's staying somewhere at a hotel in Sion but I don't know which one. The trouble is his mother is seriously ill back in London and I have to tell him. Is he staying here? Philip Cardon. Shall I spell it?'

'No one with a name like that staying here, I'm afraid.'

She plodded on, the mist freezing her face despite her pulling her hood close to her face. She thought Sion was dreary, the buildings boring. Maybe it was because there was no one else about and the depressing atmosphere of the mist.

She went into another small hotel. A man stood behind the reception desk. He wore a shabby waistcoat, unbuttoned, and an open-necked shirt due for a spell at the laundry. His hair was greasy, as was his skin. She recited her story.

'Don't fool me.' He leered at her. 'Lost your boy friend, have you? Will I do? And hotel registers are confidential so there we are.'

With an expressionless face she extracted a ten-franc note from her purse, held it between her fingers. His small eyes gleamed. She thought he was going to lick his lips. He reached out, snatched the note and made it disappear in a flash.

'All right. He's not here. Show you the register . . .'

'Don't spend it all at once,' she snapped and walked out.

Still carrying her bag, she strolled further down the street, heard a motorcycle coming. The rider in black leather pulled up alongside her.

'Just arriving?' he croaked in French. 'On business or pleasure.'

'Just leaving.'

He said something she didn't catch and rode off into the mist. This place is beginning to get me down, she was thinking, when she saw a clothes shop. She went inside, wasted no time buying two polo-neck sweaters, one white, one pale blue.

'I'll be wearing both of them at the same time soon,' she said to herself. Then she trudged on, checking hotel after hotel.

She saw yet another which she hadn't ticked off on her map. Hôtel Touring. Taking a deep breath she walked inside, went up to reception.

'Paula!'

She swung round. Philip had just come down into the lobby. He rushed towards her. She dropped her bag and the carrier containing the sweaters. He flung his arms round her.

'Am I glad to see you.'

'You can say the same for me. This is the tenth hotel.'

She buried her head in his chest and burst into tears.

# 33

Philip carried Paula's bag up to her room after she had registered at reception. He was going to leave her by herself when she stopped him.

'Don't go. It will only take me minutes to unpack, so sit down over there.'

'You're exhausted, you need a rest.'

'I need a stiff brandy in the bar . . .'

He stared at her. Paula's voice had changed, had become strong, normal. He watched with disbelief as she unpacked swiftly. She paused when she had put away her clothes.

'Yes,' she said, 'I know where to hide them.'

'Hide what?'

'Rather lethal travelling equipment supplied by Marler.'

'I see. I hid mine beneath under-clothes in my case and left it open, very much on view. Anyone searching my room will be looking for an obscure hiding place.'

'Good idea. Don't suppose you've had time to find out anything interesting.'

'You'd be surprised.'

'Surprise me, then.'

He told her what he had learned from the waitress at the station restaurant. While he was talking she took out her small armoury, tucked everything away inside the big strong carrier the clothes shop had given her. Then she carefully put back both heavy sweaters, stood the carrier on a stool at the foot of the bed. She was moving quickly but efficiently but it took several minutes before she was satisfied. By that time Philip had finished telling her all he had learned. She perched against the bed and folded her arms.

'So your idea is to wait until the mist clears before we explore the Col du Lemac, the Kellerhorn, and this highly suspect weather station?'

'Yes. We can hire a four-wheel-drive with chains from a place I passed on my way here.'

'We'll go there now.' She was putting on her coat over her windcheater. Underneath that she had a jumper and underneath that two pairs of vests and pants. 'Show me the map and the route.'

He took out the map, spread it on the bed, traced the route for her. She bent over, memorizing the details, then stood up.

'Let's get moving, Philip.'

'Might be better to hire the vehicle later.'

'Then we can't set off now – to the Kellerhorn.'

'Why now? The mist . . .'

'The mist will cover our leaving Sion. No one would dream of us tackling the Kellerhorn route in this weather. And if Brazil – because I'm sure it is Brazil from what you've told me – can fly in by jet later today the action could start pretty soon.'

'You could be right,' he said, getting up and putting on the coat and scarf he'd brought down from his room to go out for a walk.

'I could be wrong. Only one way to find out.'

'What did you slip into your shoulder bag?'

'Easter eggs – in case we meet someone who isn't all that friendly.'

'What about the brandy?'

'Don't drink and drive. I don't need it any more. And I'm sorry I made a fool of myself when I arrived.'

'A natural reaction. What astounds me is the change in you since we came up here.'

'Second wind. I wonder how Tweed and Co. are getting on in Zurich?' she mused as they left the room.

Ignoring Newman's protests, Tweed had left the Schweizerhof in the middle of the night by himself. It had stopped snowing and he looked round the *platz* as he headed for Police Headquarters after a long phone conversation with Beck. Newman had paid a visit to the loo and had not overheard the call.

It was a bitter night but the air freshened him up. He saw a man on a corner standing doing nothing who glanced in his direction. Tweed waved to him. The man, in a reflex action, half-raised his hand to wave back, then lowered it quickly.

'Damn fools,' Tweed said to himself. 'Amateurs.'

Beck had been waiting for him in his room, curtains closed over the windows overlooking the River Limmat. Tweed took off his coat as Beck finished a phone call.

'It worked,' he said as he replaced the receiver. 'My friend Inspector Vincenau moves like lightning. And he had paramilitary troops waiting at Geneva's airport. They wore maintenance overalls as they approached the second jet Brazil uses, the one with his name plastered all over the fuselage. The white jet is standing by at Kloten.'

'It's fortunate you knew the second jet was waiting at Geneva,' Tweed commented. 'Now it's also at Kloten?'

'Yes I think Brazil had that waiting at Geneva as a getaway in case he needed it.'

'And is there any chance of Brazil hearing about what has happened to his second jet?'

'No chance. Vincenau is good at covert operations. The crew of that jet have been arrested and held incommunicado in a secret place.'

'I'd better call Jim Corcoran, Chief of Security at Heathrow, so I can clue him up. May I use your phone?'

Beck pushed one of several phones across his desk to Tweed.

'That's the really safe one . . .'

He watched with an amused smile as Tweed dialled Corcoran's number from memory. As Tweed had hoped, Corcoran was in his office. He was another man who worked through the night. Tweed spoke rapidly.

'You'll have it tucked away out of sight ready for use later?' he ended.

Corcoran assured him he would see to that himself. Tweed put down the phone and Beck used his intercom to summon a man called Joinvin.

'He's very intelligent. With him as your escort no one will see you at Kloten.'

He introduced a tall well-built man who looked as though he would be an asset in a rough-house.

'Joinvin already knows what he has to do. We talked together after your phone call – cryptic as you made it, I understood you.'

'Then what am I waiting for?' Tweed asked, standing up.

'*Bon voyage*,' said Beck.


Three hours later a man called Tweed, wearing horn-rimmed glasses and a muffler which hid most of his face, arrived at Kloten. The police car he travelled in was escorted by outriders and travelled with its horn blaring, its light flashing. No arrival could have been more public.

Escorted by Joinvin, wearing a police uniform, he went straight to the final departure lounge, bypassing Passport Control and Customs. Joinvin sat with him while the other passengers for the first flight to London stared in curiosity. Some VIP, undoubtedly.

Joinvin then escorted him to the entrance to the aircraft when Business Class was called. His ticket had been purchased much earlier by a man in plain clothes. As he had arrived a slim, white-faced man observed the spectacle, then hurried to a phone.

'Tweed is just boarding the flight to London,' he reported to Brazil. 'They're nervous as kittens – he had a police escort. The full works.'

'Thank you.'

In his room at the Baur-en-Ville Brazil sat back and smiled at Luigi and José.

'That's good news. Tweed is on his way back to London. So he's well on his way and out of my hair for good.' He looked up as Eve entered, again without knocking. 'You couldn't sleep?'

'Too much going on. What *is* going on?' she asked saucily as she plonked herself in the chair in front of his desk.

'Tweed has gone. He just boarded the early flight to Heathrow. He's said goodbye to Zurich, to Switzerland.'

'What about the others?' she asked shrewdly. 'Newman, Paula Grey, and Philip Cardon? To say nothing of the two men we've never identified.'

'We're not sure,' José replied to her. 'Our troops at the main station were rounded up by Beck's men. It was a drug bust. Most unfortunate. They took our people away because they found they were armed.'

'Bad luck,' Eve commented without enthusiasm.

'Eve,' Brazil addressed her, 'I am leaving you in

315

charge here while I am away. I'll be coming back to Zurich for a brief visit. Then you can come with me when we leave.'

'Leave for where?'

'You'll find out when I've made up my mind. But I have decided to leave a little later. I want breakfast first.'

'Just who am I in charge of?' she demanded.

'You are aggressive.'

'No, I'm not. But if I'm in charge I like to know who is my staff. Obvious question, I'd have thought,' she continued in her usual forceful manner.

'Karl, Gunnar, and François. I want you to keep an eye on both the Schweizerhof and the Gotthard hotels.'

'When there may be nobody there?'

'I like to cover my bets.'

'Have a nice trip to Xanadu.'

She flounced out of the room, but closed the door carefully and went back to her room.

'Drug bust my foot,' she said aloud behind the closed door.

Lighting a cigarette, she poured herself a large vodka and sat down to think. Then she called Brazil on the internal phone.

'Eve here. What about Igor?'

'It will be coming with me.'

'Just checking.'

Well, that's a bonus point, she decided. Not having to look after a damned dog. She sat thinking again. Philip Cardon, whom she'd spent quite a lot of time with, never entered her mind. So Brazil is coming back to Zurich – that means Bob Newman won't be far behind him.


Philip was driving through the mist in Sion with Paula by his side. He carried a canvas bag with the shoulder strap attached. Paula was navigating, the map on her knees, giving him instructions when to turn.

'Why didn't you go and see Anton Marchat after you arrived?' she queried. 'Archie said he was very important and you have the address.'

'Deliberately gave it a miss. We'll go and try to find him later today – after dark. There are too many motorcyclists floating . . . floating . . .'

'The people of Geneva call them Leather Bombers,' she interjected.

'All right. Too many Leather Bombers on the road. After dark we'll have a better chance of eluding them. We have to protect Marchat as far as we can.'

They left Sion behind, began the tortuous ascent to the Kellerhorn. Suddenly they emerged from the mist, leaving it below them as a white layer with the castlelike building perched on the mist like a strange ship on a sea. Then they really began to climb, the road hardly wide enough for two vehicles to pass safely.

The wheels of their vehicle gripped the ice patches on the road firmly, to Philip's unspoken relief. On his side a sheer abyss dropped into the distant valley. On Paula's side the mountain wall sheered up vertically. She was so close to it she felt hemmed in, but reminded herself it was better than looking down the abyss with no barrier to keep them on this fiendish road.

An added hazard was the way the road kept turning round sheer bends. Philip was constantly expecting to meet something descending the road but so far it had been clear. The gradient was also much steeper. He concentrated all his mind on driving.

Paula, no longer needing to navigate, looked across him and down into the valley far away. The sun had come out, the mist had dissolved, tiny Sion looked like a street map. They were very high up now and still Philip was having to turn the wheel as he negotiated yet another hairpin bend. He was also watching the road

317

surface as the sun had appeared. Snow was melting, exposing the ice below it had masked. He came to a large alcove in the rock wall, turned into it.

'Thank heavens,' Paula said. 'Time for a rest. Why don't I take over the wheel?'

'Not yet. I've got into the swing of it. Let's get out. I feel like one of my rare cigarettes.'

'You can give me one,' she said as they got out of the four-wheel-drive, stretched their legs.

'You don't smoke.'

'Just occasionally. I used to smoke at boarding school just to keep up with the other girls.' She took the cigarette he offered, bent down so he could light it, took a careful puff, spread out her arms. 'What a spectacular view—' She stopped. 'Where are you off to?'

'Just exploring,' he called over his shoulder.

'You've left the engine running.'

'You want a breakdown up here?'

Philip had walked to the back of the large alcove where there was a narrow gash in the rock. Beyond he found a narrow valley snaking down the mountain. The waterfall inside it was frozen solid, the ice gleaming in the sun. At frequent intervals rocks protruded above the ice, the snow on them melting. He pointed upwards.

'There's the summit of the Kellerhorn. And there's the so-called weather station.'

Paula stared in fascination up the ravine. A cluster of one-storey buildings of white concrete huddled together not so far above them. A forest of aerials sat on the flat rooftop of one building, surrounding what looked like a slim conning tower in their midst.

Philip had hauled out a pair of high-powered binoculars given to him by Marler, was studying the buildings, when he suddenly stiffened. He pressed the

318

binoculars closer to his eyes.

'See that conning tower effort?' he said. 'It's elevating and a thick rod of some kind has slid out above it. The rod is flexible, is moving round, pointing at various angles.'

'I see it. What can it be?'

'The rod has become vertical again,' Philip reported. 'Now it's disappearing back down inside the conning tower. If that's a weather station my aunt is a bloater.'

'Didn't know you had a bloater for an aunt,' Paula commented to break the tension.

Philip put the binoculars back in his pocket. He gazed up the ravine.

'You know something. With the right footwear you could climb that ravine and get close to the buildings unseen.'

'I think a guard up there has spotted us.'

'I didn't see anything. Probably your imagination.'

But he slipped back quickly inside the alcove, following Paula. She went back to their transport, climbed into the passenger seat. She said as soon as Philip was behind the wheel: 'I still think a guard saw us.'

'Imagin—'

'If you say imagination I'll clonk you one.'

'Not while I'm driving, you won't.' He grinned. 'We're going higher up. Reach into my pocket on your side – you'll find a camera, a small job. When we get a closer look at that place take pictures. That camera is fast. Take one picture, press the button on top – to take your pic. The mechanism then automatically moves the film along so you can take another in the next second. Use up the whole film.'

'I'll do my best.'

It seemed to Paula that Philip was driving faster. Not dangerously so, but he was now fired up having seen their objective. He swung round blind corners, causing

Paula to hold on to the hand-grip. They climbed and climbed and climbed. No sign of an emotional crisis in Philip now, she was thinking. Tweed did know what he was doing.

She was beginning to wonder when they were going to get to the top when Philip turned round another overhanging outcrop, slowed, drove on to a small plateau, stopped under the cover of a ridge like a tank, hull down. The weather station was less than a quarter of a mile away.

She had the viewfinder of the camera to her eye, was taking shot after shot. Philip had taken out the binoculars again, focused them above the buildings, lifting the glasses slowly until they reached the enormous summit.

'You can see why, as I told you, it's called the Kellerhorn,' Paula said, still taking shots.

'I most certainly can.'

The summit was shaped like a gigantic boar's head. It looked incredibly sinister, coated with a slime of melting ice and snow. What interested Philip was the slanting slope running steeply down from the summit towards the weather station. Enormous boulders and a shale of smaller rocks thrust their sharklike snouts above the snow. The slope looked extremely unstable. He could see the ravine they had observed from the rock alcove lower down continuing up the slope.

'Look at those weird old houses inside the perimeter,' Paula commented. 'They look like some old village.'

Philip focused on the houses. Built of wood long ago, they had all their shutters closed. There were signs of the shingle roofs having been renewed. Most odd, he mused.

'That wire fence round the whole caboodle must be twelve feet high,' he said, examining it through his glasses. 'And it has an alarm wire running along the top

320

with sensors at intervals. You'd think they were guarding Fort Knox.'

'I've run out of film,' Paula informed him. 'Let's hope we haven't run out of time.'

'Not a guard in sight,' he told her.

'That's what worries me.'


They began their descent. The sun had gone in, masked by an army of dark clouds drifting in rapidly from the west. Paula had unzipped her shoulder bag. They were approaching the large rock alcove where they had stopped on the way up.

The bend Philip had to drive round just before they reached it was one of the most savage and hair-raising on the whole mountain road. He saw ice, slowed down to a crawl. Below them Sion, the entire plain, had vanished. He cruised, still crawling, up to the alcove.

'*Look out!*' yelled Paula.

With both hands on the wheel Philip couldn't react. He glanced to his left, saw three Leather Bombers inside the alcove. One held a machine-pistol, had raised it, was taking aim. Paula lobbed the grenade she'd taken out of her shoulder bag. It landed almost at the feet of the three men.

There was a vicious crack. All three men twisted, fell back against the rock wall, lay very still. Philip realized he was sweating. He looked at Paula before getting out.

'You were suspicious.'

'Yes, I was. No guards in sight. And you'd said when we were here earlier it would be possible to climb up that ravine. So I worked out it would be possible to climb *down* the ravine – and this is a perfect place for an ambush.'

'I'll have to get rid of those bodies. They'd be a dead giveaway when they were found. No pun intended.'

'Not funny. Maybe they're still alive . . .'

'Doubt that. Inside that confined alcove – with rock walls – the shrapnel from a grenade would kill.'

'Please make sure.'

'I will.'

He checked the brakes, left Paula, went inside the alcove. He felt the carotids of all three men. No pulse from two of them. The third did have a faint pulse. If he recovered he'd report what had happened. Heaving the first body by its legs, he dragged it behind their vehicle to the edge, peered over. An endless abyss, probably a thousand feet down. He toppled the body over. It spun through the air into space.

He went back for the second body, dealt with it in the same manner. Paula was looking the other way. Then he collected the man who was still breathing, hauled him to the brink, levered him over.

'As I thought,' he lied as he climbed behind the wheel. 'All were dead.'

'Then you did the right thing.'

Not another word was exchanged as they descended the road and eventually entered Sion.

# 34

The Lear executive jet with BRAZIL splashed along the outside of its fuselage was flying over France, would soon cross the sea prior to landing at Heathrow.

Tweed spent most of his time chatting with the pilot and the co-pilot in their cabin. He had found out both men were once fliers with the Swiss Air Force. The radio op. swivelled in his chair to speak to Tweed for the fifth time. He spoke in English as a courtesy to his guest.

'There's a real storm of reports building up. Something weird is happening in Moscow. Rumours that the President has resigned due to ill health. Rumours that a General Marov is bringing armoured divisions into the city. Rumours that the frontiers of Russia have been closed.'

'Pretty much what I expected,' Tweed replied.

'And a personal message from Chief of Police Arthur Beck for you. I didn't understand it first time and asked them to repeat it. He says the rumours are all originating from Zurich.'

'Again what I expected. Thank you.'

The plane was descending rapidly. The pilot turned to Tweed.

'We'll be landing shortly, sir.'

'I'm very grateful to you. You know that this plane and the whole crew are to be placed at my disposal again after you have landed?'

'Yes, sir. You expect to be flying again soon?'

'Very shortly. Now I will return to my seat.'

It was a very satisfied Tweed who sank into the luxurious seat and fastened his seat belt. He would arrive in London three hours ahead of the first scheduled flight.


Beck was furious. He sat in his office, staring at the sheets he'd taken from the teleprinter, giving reports from the international news services. Moscow . . . Moscow . . . Moscow . . . He looked up at Joinvin, who had just entered his office. He waved the reams of sheets.

'We know all this stuff is coming from rumours Brazil is spreading from here – in Zurich. Have you found out where from?'

'No, sir. The detector vans are out trying to trace the source of the radio transmissions but we have a problem.'

'I know we have a problem. Tracking his source.'

'What I meant, sir, was that he appears to be using some kind of vehicles to jam our detector vans.'

'He's also using jamming equipment! Let's face it – the man is a genius at organization. How do we get round that one?'

'We have found one van we know is using jamming apparatus near the lake at the bottom of Bahnhofstrasse. The trouble is we have no authority to search a private vehicle. I have an idea.'

'What is it, then?'

'I'll draw up a list of people who have complained their radios are being interfered with. I'll get names out of the telephone directory.'

'Go ahead. You know, Joinvin, I'm going to think about whether I should promote you.'

'That's all you will do,' Joinvin said good-humouredly. 'Think about it.'

The intercom buzzed, Beck answered it, listened, then pressed the button to shut it off. He looked at Joinvin.

'A brilliant idea of yours. Forget it. The radio transmissions have stopped. That man is playing with me – he's always one step ahead in the game. And now I hear from the security chief at Kloten that the pilot of Brazil's private jet has filed a new flight plan – to leave for Sion later this morning. Always one step ahead of me,' he repeated.

'Not always,' Joinvin reminded him. 'He doesn't know that Tweed has already arrived in London.'


Eve, fully dressed, walked into José's office, her expression livid. She always got on well with José, who looked up, smiled, then frowned.

'What's wrong?'

'I couldn't sleep, so I went for a walk. What happens? I turn down a side-street off Bahnhofstrasse and two young Yanks ask me the way. Then they try to assault me.'

'They didn't . . .'

'No, they didn't. I scraped my heel down the shin of one lout. He yelped, let go. I swung round and kneed the other in the groin. They cleared off damned fast. But I feel I need some protection.'

'Not a gun.' José unlocked a drawer in his desk, took out a canister with a nozzle on top, handed it to her.

'This is hairspray,' she said, reading the printing on the outside. 'If I'd thought I could have got this from a shop.'

'No, you couldn't. And don't press the button. That canister contains Mace gas. The wording is camouflage. It's illegal.'

'Would it kill someone?'

'No. But it would disable them for some while. Keep it in your shoulder bag at all times.'

'Thank you, José. You know I'm being left in charge while you're all away in Sion? I've been wondering, does that include Gustav, who is also staying in Zurich?'

'I wouldn't try giving orders to Gustav. He's an ugly man – and not only to look at.'

'I'll take your advice.' She hesitated. 'I went out for my walk about an hour or so ago. I saw a lot of men who are on Brazil's staff going into a building on Bahnhof-strasse. They were in a hurry. What were they doing at this time of night?'

'I shouldn't tell you.' José himself now hesitated. 'I will, though. They were operating what Brazil called his radio exchange, contacting people all over the world. I don't know why.'

'Sounds bonkers. I'd better get back to bed, try and get some sleep. Thanks again for the canister.'

\*　　\*　　\*

325

Newman and his team were aboard the night express to Geneva. They had boarded the almost empty train separately. Newman sat in the corner of a first-class compartment by himself. He knew Marler was patrolling up and down the corridor at intervals, keeping guard. Newman appeared to be asleep but came awake the moment Marler entered his compartment.

'All's quiet,' he reported. 'What do we do when we get to Cornavin Station?'

'We eat in the buffet – at separate tables. Then we're boarding the Milan express. Only a few stops and we'll arrive at Sion.'

'And when we get there?'

'We check all the hotels until we've found Paula and Philip. I don't like them being on their own in that area. It will be crawling with Brazil's thugs.'

'And after we've found Paula and Philip – assuming we do?' asked Marler.

'We try to locate this ground station which controls the satellite orbiting over our heads. When we have found it – because we will,' Newman said decisively – 'then we destroy the damned thing.'

'There may be a little opposition that will object to that.'

'Then we destroy the opposition.' Newman glanced out of the window. 'In a minute we'll be coming into Cornavin.'


Monica, baggy-eyed, looked up from her desk, astounded as Tweed entered his office.

'This is magic,' she said. 'I had a message from Beck to say you were catching the first early flight out of Zurich. You're three hours early . . .'

'Sometimes a little magic is called for – it catches people on the wrong foot. Present company excluded, I

326

emphasize.' He had taken off his scarf and coat, dropped his bag by his desk. 'Where is Howard?'

'Just back from Downing Street.'

'How many times has he been to the holy of holies?'

'Three times in the past twenty-four hours.'

'Too many visits. He'll just wind up the PM. I'll have to go to perishing Downing Street myself, calm them all down.'

'You've heard about the rumours? They're coming in from all over the world – including Tokyo.'

'Yes.' Tweed was not in a forgiving mood. He looked up from his desk as Howard came in like a whirlwind. 'Have you been wasting your time chatting up the PM?'

Howard, normally immaculately dressed, was a sartorial mess. The jacket of his business suit was crumpled, and the creases in his trousers were still there, but only just. His tie was askew and he'd unbuttoned his collar. Tweed, by comparison, was a fashion plate.

'Thank God you're back . . . Never expected to see you so . . . soon,' Howard almost stuttered. 'You don't know what's happening.'

'Actually, I do.'

'Downing Street is in a frenzy. Washington's gone berserk. Paris is running round in circles . . .'

'Calm down,' said Tweed quietly. 'And do sit down. You are moving round like a tango dancer on cocaine.'

Howard flopped into the largest armchair, arms hanging loose over the arms, staring at Tweed with a glazed look as he went on.

'It's international. It's everywhere. The world has gone mad.'

'So let's not go mad with it,' Tweed said in the same calm voice. 'You're flaked out, exhausted. I'm going to see the PM, put him right about a few things.'

'You'll be careful.'

'No, I won't. I'll be blunt – blunt as the notorious instrument the police talk about when someone's murdered.'

'Oh, dear, you'll add fuel to the flames.'

'Exactly. I'll be taking along a can of petrol with me.'

'How is everyone?' Howard asked in an off-hand tone.

'Thought you'd never ask. They *are* your people. Newman nearly got killed but is all right. Paula and Philip were engaged in a firefight in Geneva. The outcome was six dead bodies – fortunately not theirs among them. The thugs involved in both cases belong to Leopold Brazil.'

'Brazil?' Howard repeated in a dazed voice.

'Yes, Brazil – the individual, not the country. The nice man the White House, Downing Street, and the Elysée hold champagne dinners to entertain. *That* Brazil.'

'You're sure?' Howard bleated.

'No, I'm not sure, I'm certain. I have had it from the horse's mouth. The horse in this case being Brazil. Get that camp bed out in your office, throw some blankets over it, flop there, and go to sleep. Monica will come and tuck you up.'

'That won't be necessary.' Howard forced himself to stand up. 'I'll do as you say. How are things out on the front in Europe?'

'You don't want to know. They are – and will be – taken care of. Bedtime, Howard . . .'

Monica glared at Tweed as soon as they were alone. 'Tuck him up, indeed!'

'I thought that would get you,' Tweed told her mischievously. 'Now get the PM's private secretary on the phone. You speak to him. Tell him I'll be arriving at Downing Street thirty minutes from now to talk to the PM. If there's any protest tell him in that case I won't be coming. Now or ever.'

'That's pretty tough,' she said, reaching for the phone.
'I feel pretty tough.'


In his office in Geneva, where he had earlier returned from Zurich, Bill Franklin picked up the phone. It was Lebrun, his man watching Cornavin Station.

'Yes, what is it?' Franklin enquired amiably.

'The Zurich express came in five minutes ago. One of the passengers who alighted was Robert Newman. He went into the buffet and is eating breakfast. Another intriguing point is three other men off the express came in by themselves at intervals. It's early and there are normally hardly any customers in the buffet at this time. I think they may all be together.'

'What types are the other three men?'

'I wouldn't like to cross swords with any of them,' Lebrun replied. 'And I'm pretty sure they're waiting to board the Milan express, due shortly. In about half an hour.'

'What makes you think that, Lebrun? Rather a wild assumption.'

'Not so wild. I wandered into the buffet and Newman was studying a rail timetable – open at the page with trains for Milan.'

'And he let you see what he was looking at?' Franklin asked sceptically.

'Well, I only paused a moment by his table.'

'A pause which Newman would notice. He deliberately let you see the page he was looking at. I must get moving. Get me two tickets for Milan – one first-class, one second-class. Wait on the platform and hand the tickets to me when I arrive. I'll be boarding the Milan express myself. Better go to the ticket office now . . .'

Franklin sat thinking for a short time just after the call

329

had ended. Milan? He doubted it. He had just discovered Leopold Brazil had a villa in the mountains outside Sion. 'I'd better go and see what's happening in that part of the world,' he said to himself as he got up to collect an already packed case from a cupboard.

Newman didn't give a damn who else boarded the express. He could find out by sending Marler on a patrol along the train once it began moving. So, as his team entered other coaches, he didn't see Bill Franklin, carrying a suitcase and wearing a trenchcoat, climb aboard near the back. But Franklin saw him disappearing inside a coach midway along.

Fifteen seconds before the train left Cornavin another passenger entered a coach at the very rear. Wearing a black beret and glasses with plain lenses, he chose a corner seat, parked his bag on the next seat in the otherwise empty compartment. Archie was unrecognizable. He had even got rid of his half-smoked cigarette stub.

Much earlier, during the night, he had been standing in Zurich Hauptbahnhof when Beck's army of detectives had invaded the station. The detective who checked his identity saw no reason to be suspicious of the mild-mannered little man.

Archie had immediately grasped why the round-up of a number of ugly-looking characters was taking place. He had rushed to his small hotel nearby, used mostly by travelling salesmen, had paid his bill, collected his bag, and returned to the main station. There he had resumed his vigil.

Archie could wait for ever without becoming impatient or tiring. His persistence had been rewarded when eventually he had seen Newman boarding the first express for Geneva. He had then boarded the same train

330

himself and had gone to sleep until shortly before it arrived in Cornavin. Now he was aboard yet another train.

Anton Marchat, he thought as he sat in his corner. I'm sure they are forgetting Marchat. I will go to see him myself when this train reaches Sion . . .

Marler had not yet begun his patrol of the express to check who was on board when Newman, in a compartment by himself, heard the door opening. He slipped his right hand inside his jacket, grasped the Smith & Wesson as he looked up.

'No cause for alarm, Bob.'

Bill Franklin was grinning when he entered the compartment and closed the door. He dumped his bag on a seat and sat opposite Newman. He carefully folded his trenchcoat and placed it on top of the bag.

'Hope you don't object to the intrusion. You're like lightning with a gun.'

Momentarily annoyed that Franklin realized what he had done, Newman recalled his new companion had once been in the army.

'You just never know,' he responded.

'You never know,' Franklin agreed. 'Mind if I light a cigar?'

'Go ahead. I'd have thought you'd have smelt the smoke from the cigarette I've just extinguished.'

'I did. But it's polite to ask,' Franklin said with a smile.

Newman had heard that Franklin played the devil with the ladies. He could understand the reason for his success with his amorous adventures. Franklin had an easy manner, was courteous, smiled a lot.

'How did you know I was on this train?' he asked suddenly.

'Because I have a good team of detectives. I've had one man watching the airport, another down at Anne-masse, a sleepy station on Geneva's southern frontier with France. Just the place where Brazil would bring in his thugs – and he did. Then a third man watching Cornavin. He spotted you.'

'So you decided you'd come along for the ride?' Newman enquired, watching Franklin's reaction closely.

'No. I decided you needed all the back-up you can get. I don't think you know what's waiting for you in the Valais.'

'What is waiting for me?'

'At least forty of Brazil's professional thugs have passed through Geneva, then boarded a train for the east.' He paused as, having trimmed the end of his cigar, Franklin passed a match backwards and forwards, getting it alight to his satisfaction. 'And undoubtedly we missed some of them.'

'So you've come as back-up?'

Franklin heaved his case across to the seat next to Newman. Unlocking it, he lifted the lid, exposing a neatly folded jacket. He lifted the jacket after glancing into the deserted corridor. Nestling on a pair of pyjamas was a Heckler & Koch MP5 9mm sub-machine-gun.

'You don't believe in doing things by halves,' New-man commented as Franklin quickly put back the jacket, closed the case. He took a long puff at his cigar.

'No, I don't believe in doing things by halves. You'll know that little baby has a rate of fire of six hundred and fifty rounds per minute. And I've got plenty of spare mags.'

'I'd call you a pessimist,' Newman said with a smile.

'I'd call myself a realist. We're approaching a major battlefield. You know Brazil has a villa up the Col de Roc, overlooking a glacier? Above Sion.'

'No, I didn't.'

'Had it built to his own design. It's equipped with a high-power radio transmitter. Yes, Bob, that's what is ahead of us. A major battlefield.'

# 35

Tweed returned to Park Crescent two hours after leaving for Downing Street. He walked into his office, took off his coat, put it on a hanger after putting his gloves on his desk. Monica watched him with growing impatience, sure that he was being tantalizing. Then she saw his pensive expression, realized he was thinking. He sat down behind his desk, still with the abstracted look on his face.

'Would you like some coffee?' she ventured.

'Yes, please.' He paused. 'After I've told you what happened.'

'The PM is still at sixes and sevens,' she guessed.

'No, not any more. I talked to him pretty frankly and he listened. By the time I'd finished he'd calmed down. He can even take a decision now.'

'And did he?'

'Yes. He agreed to several suggestions I made. First he's alerted the Rapid Reaction Force to be ready to fly to Europe. Then he phoned the German Chancellor and told him to have the airfields ready to receive it when it lands.'

'*Told* him? Told the German Chancellor?'

'That's what I said. Actually the Chancellor was glad to have someone taking a decision. I also suggested the PM refused any calls from the President at the White House, telling him to inform the President the PM was not available, that his Private Secretary should take the calls.'

'What was the idea of that?'

'To stop Washington spreading their frenzied mood.

The White House is in the greatest panic ever known. All in all I've poured oil on the troubled waters.'

'Not petrol, as you told Howard?'

'That was just to shut him up. How is Reginald coming on with his computer toys?'

'He's still upstairs with his team. They're frantic.'

'They would be. I'll pop upstairs and sort them out. If a pot of coffee was ready when I get back I'd be most grateful . . .'

Tweed strolled up to the next floor. The door to the computer room was open, lights were flashing. He went in to find Reginald, long hair trailing down over his neck, staring fixedly at the master computer. His two assistants seemed equally hypnotized by their equipment.

'Getting anywhere?' Tweed asked.

'I'll say we are.' Reginald's bulging eyes gleamed as he turned to look at Tweed. 'The trouble is we can't cope with the amount of data coming in.'

'Data? The rubbish you're being fed? Nothing major has actually happened so far.'

'You're wrong, sir. Look at the screen. It's reporting extensive troop movements converging on Moscow from all sides.'

'Do the satellites confirm that? They'd see those movements.'

'Well, not yet.'

'Don't you find that puzzling?' Tweed asked gently.

'Modern communications are a complicated business,' said Reginald, sounding pretentious.

'You haven't answered my question.'

'We are getting reports from all over the world . . .'

'I did query whether the satellites confirm these reports.'

'Well, Washington may be sitting on what they're getting from that source.'

'Why should they?' demanded Tweed.

'I've no idea.'

'Then I'll tell you. It's because the satellites have not picked up what those alarming reports are saying. They haven't picked them up because they're not happening. Yet.'

'What does that mean, sir?'

'Keep up the good work. Soon you may really be overwhelmed with shattering news.'

Before Reginald could ask what he meant Tweed left, went back to his office. Monica poured coffee from a large pot, added milk. Tweed sat down, drank a whole cupful at one steady gulp. Monica refilled the cup.

'I'm going to have a nap in this chair,' Tweed said when he had drunk the second cup.

IIe had just closed his eyes when the phone rang. He kept them closed until Monica called out.

'Sorry, I have Beck on the line . . .'

'Hello, Arthur. I arrived here in record time. Your air-crew are superb. They're standing by at Heathrow for when I want to take off again.'

'Good. More news. Brazil has again delayed his flight departure aboard the jet at Kloten. He's playing cat and mouse.'

'What he doesn't know is I'm the cat, he's the mouse. If you call again and I'm not here, speak to Monica. She will know how to contact me. What's the weather like in Zurich?'

'A typical British question. It's snowing, not heavily. Brazil's pilot gave that as the reason why he's changed the flight plan.'

'But he could have taken off?'

'The security chief at Kloten told me he most certainly could have done.'

'Which means Brazil is working to a timetable. Thanks for keeping me in touch. Appreciate it if you'd keep doing so . . .'

'So what are you waiting for?' Monica asked as she put down her phone after listening in.

'Brazil's big bang. The trouble is I'm not sure what form it will take. But we'll know when it happens.'

Tweed closed his eyes again and fell fast asleep after pulling his tie loose and unfastening his collar.


In Zurich Brazil had summoned Craig to his living room. Igor, seated by Brazil's side, stood up and bared its teeth as the visitor entered the room. . . .'

'Sit down, Craig. Is everyone travelling aboard the jet ready to leave?'

'They have been ready for several hours.'

'It's time to go.' Brazil looked at his watch. 'It is a short flight so I should reach the villa in time. I want you to contact the flight controller at Sion airfield to have the runway ready for us to land.'

'The cars are standing by to take us straight to Kloten,' Craig reported smugly.

'I should hope they are.'

'Who will look after Igor aboard the plane?' Craig enquired, eyeing the hound without enthusiasm. 'José?'

'No. You will. He likes resting his forepaws in a lap when he's airborne. Your lap should serve nicely.'

'You said you would reach the villa in time. In time to do what?'

'To send the first signal to the laboratory across the valley.'

'The signal to do what?' Craig rumbled on.

'You'll find out when it happens, won't you?' Brazil smiled broadly. 'Now, off you go, get the others on their way to the airport. And send Eve in to me for a word.'

'She's probably asleep.'

'Wake her up, then.'

*       *       *

Eve was still up, drinking and smoking, when Craig hammered on her door.

'Can't you knock more quietly?' she demanded when she opened the door and saw who was there.

'No. The boss wants to see you. This very second. So make with the feet.'

'You know, Craig, you have the most charming way of expressing yourself.'

Her retort was wasted. Craig was already clumping off down the corridor to tell everyone they were leaving. Eve checked her appearance in the mirror, used a brush to smooth down her jet-black hair behind her neck.

She then walked slowly along the corridor, entered Brazil's room without knocking, closed the door, drifted across to the chair in front of the desk, sat down and crossed her shapely legs. No one was going to hurry her.

'You can certainly move,' Brazil said sarcastically.

'Where is the doggie?'

'Craig will shortly be taking him to the airport. You get on with Robert Newman rather well. Is that right?'

'Yes, I do,' she lied. 'Why? Do you want me to make up to him?'

'Why, I wonder, do men fall for you so easily?'

'Men are propelled by desire for attractive women. It must be my irresistible personality,' she said cynically.

'If you say so.' Brazil checked the time by his watch. 'I must go in a minute.'

'What was the point of asking me about Newman?'

'I was coming to that. I will, in due course, return to Zurich. Some unfinished business I have to attend to. It's just possible Newman will follow me back here. If he's still alive. In that contingency you can practise your black magic arts on him. I would want to know where Tweed was. You could manage that, couldn't you?'

'Shouldn't be impossible. I worked it with those bankers you asked me to get to know.' She leaned forward. 'The ones who were murdered by some un-known creature. After all . . .' She leaned back again. 'I do have Philip Cardon salivating over me.'

'Gustav will stay behind to give you moral support,' Brazil said as he stood up, put on a heavy blue overcoat which had lain folded on a chair beside him. 'He'll be company for you.'

'Company I could do without.'

'He's really quite a nice chap – when you get to know him,' Brazil said with a smile as he picked up a briefcase.

'I have no intention of getting to know him. That man,' she said through her teeth, 'is a creep. Have a quiet trip.'

'I can assure you, it will be anything but quiet.'


'I think Sion looked better in the mist,' Paula said as they walked away from the car park next to the Hôtel Touring where Philip had left their vehicle. 'It could be any small modern town. Oh, Lord, here they come again.'

Two Leather Bombers had appeared on their machines, riding slowly towards them. No one else was about. Philip slipped his hand inside his brown leather jacket and gripped his Walther.

'Keep walking. Don't look at them. We're lovers on holiday.'

He wrapped his left arm round her waist, stopped, kissed her on the cheek. As they started walking again one of the motorcyclists called out something filthy in French.

'Minds like sewers,' Philip commented. 'Just keep walking.'

The motorcyclists had passed them, were continuing down the street towards the station. Paula resisted her impulse to look back.

'I'm hungry,' she said. 'I suppose it's too early for lunch.'

'Not at the restaurant we passed just up the street. So we'll have a leisurely meal. And, if you're very polite to me, I'll start off by buying you that brandy you wanted back at the hotel before we started off up the mountain.'

'That seems a hundred years ago. Yes, sir, I do believe I would appreciate a brandy. Is that polite enough?'

'It will do . . .'

They ordered Tweed's favourite dish, escalope Zurichoise, a substantial dish, and ate two servings. The restaurant was small and tidy with crisp white table-cloths and no one else in the place. Over their meal they tried to work out what to do next.

'We could explore the Col de Roc where Brazil has his villa, on the mountains on the other side of the valley,' Paula suggested.

'We could, but we'd be pushing our luck.'

'What do you mean? I think it's a good idea. Now we've got into the swing of driving up these mountain roads.'

'We would be pushing our luck,' Philip persisted. 'On the map the road up to his villa looks at least as grim as the one up to the Kellerhorn.'

'Any other objections?' she said, piqued.

The trouble was, Philip knew, that when Paula had enjoyed a good meal she was fired up again with energy, with get-up-and-go. He didn't like to throw too much cold water on her courage.

'Not an objection, a worry. Thanks to your swift action we got out of that one alive at the alcove. I'm sure Brazil's villa will be equally well guarded.'

'So we proceed with caution,' she said and smiled.

'All right, I surrender.'

Grinning, he raised both hands high in the air. Paula frowned, leaned over the table.

'You've got at least an equal say in this decision,

339

Philip. I feel I've been rather pushy. What were we going to do if we'd stayed in Sion?'

'Wait until after dark, then go to see Marchat. Did you notice the old part, huddled under that great hulk of a rock with the old building on top?'

'No, I didn't?'

'That's where the old houses are. The original Sion. I saw them. They're built of wood with shutters over the windows and shingle roofs. Just like those houses we saw inside the perimeter running round the fake weather station.'

'You think it really is a fake?' she queried.

'I'm certain of it. You may have security round a weather station, but you don't have thugs armed with machine-pistols to go after intruders to kill them. That is the ground station.'

'We *could* drive up the Col de Roc, then get back in time to go and see Marchat,' she speculated.

'All right. Let's do that. But first I need another cup of coffee.'

Philip didn't say so but he still felt this was a perilous undertaking. And they could find themselves descending a diabolical mountain road after dark. He couldn't rid himself of a premonition that exploring the Col de Roc was going to be a disaster.


'Just going to the loo,' Newman said to Franklin.

He had seen Marler passing their compartment, glancing in and looking away as he continued back to the front of the express. And in less than half an hour they were due to arrive in Sion.

He found Marler sitting in a first-class compartment by himself, smoking a king-size.

'That was Bill Franklin, wasn't it?' Marler asked before Newman could say anything. 'I remember him from when I met him in Tweed's office and didn't give him my name.'

'That was Bill Franklin,' Newman agreed as he sat opposite Marler.

He explained tersely how Franklin had come to be aboard, that he was carrying a Heckler & Koch sub-machine-gun.

'Is he?' Marler remarked. 'With that he could wipe out a whole posse of Leather Bombers with just one burst.'

'Where are Butler and Nield?'

'I have a plan I've worked out for when we get to Sion – so I'll explain it . . .'

He did so and when he'd finished he glanced out of the window, saw an airfield with a runway cleared completely of snow.

'I'd better get back. Give Butler and Nield their orders quickly. You saw the airfield? Good. I must move – we are coming into Sion.'

# 36

The jet without any markings along its fuselage was airborne, had left Zurich behind some time ago. Brazil sat in his comfortable swivel armchair, staring at the illuminated screen above the entrance to the crew cabin.

Clear figures gave the mileage they had come, the mileage still to cover to Sion, the present time, the estimated time of arrival at Sion airfield. He glanced at it frequently and occasionally swivelled round to look at the seat behind him.

Craig sat in it with Igor alongside him, his forepaws resting in Craig's lap. Brazil was amused by Craig's obvious discomfort. The hound saw him looking, made a motion to move towards him, and Brazil lifted a warning finger. Igor subsided.

'One thing worries me,' Brazil told Craig. 'We haven't yet dealt with Anton Marchat. He's a loose end.'

'Not any more. I've made certain arrangements. Anton Marchat won't be in the land of the living much longer.'

'You really are most efficient.'

'I do my job. Including looking after this poodle.'

'I wouldn't advise you to treat him as a poodle.'

'A bang on his nose with the barrel of a gun and you'd see him run like hell, yelping.'

'If you were still alive to hear him yelping. Anyone would think you don't like Igor.'

'I don't.'

Brazil turned away to check the illuminated screen. Behind him Craig grinned to himself. Brazil didn't know everything. Prior to leaving Zurich Craig had phoned The Motorman. Brazil would have been furious had he known what he had done. He mistrusted hired help.

'Craig here,' he had said when he made the call.

'You have another commission for me?' the thin reedy voice had enquired.

'Two targets this time. First, man called Anton Marchat. Marchat,' he had repeated. 'He probably lives in Sion, but I'm not sure.'

'He does live in Sion. Assume the job is done. And the second target?'

'Man called Archie. Don't know his second name. But I hear on my grapevine he's a dangerous nuisance. Can't give you any more info.'

'I don't need any more. I know Archie.'

'You do?' Craig hadn't been able to keep the surprise out of his voice.

'Again, consider it done.'

'You're very reliable.'

342

'I have to maintain my reputation,' the reedy voice had replied smoothly.

'So that's it. I'm in a hurry . . .'

'Not too much in a hurry. As usual, I will expect the normal fee to be paid in cash into my numbered account. You won't forget, will you, Mr Craig? If you did then I have been known to do a job for free – when clients have omitted to pay their debts,' The Motorman concluded.

Aboard the jet, Craig had replayed the conversation in his mind with satisfaction. Except he had remembered he was sweating at The Motorman's last comment.


Keith Kent, expensively dressed, walked into the Zurcher Kredit Bank in Sion. He had travelled on the same train as Newman, had left it at almost the last moment.

As he had done in Zurich, Kent looked along the counter behind the grilles, weighing up the three tellers. One man looked pompous, the type that was easily deflated. Kent walked up to him.

'I have to pay in a certain amount to the main account of Mr Leopold Brazil. Is this the right branch?'

'We never give out information about clients,' the teller informed him smugly.

'No, of course not. I haven't the transfer with me but I can get it in an hour.'

'I see, sir,' the teller replied, not seeing at all.

'Mr Brazil particularly asked me to pay it to his main account. The transaction is urgent.'

'I understand, sir.'

'I don't think you do,' Kent said in his most aggressive manner. 'May I have your name?'

'What do you want that for? Sir,' he added a little late.

'So I can report to Mr Brazil the lack of cooperation I encountered.'

'We always wish to cooperate with clients,' the teller

said, this time his manner showing signs of nervousness.

'But you're not giving me any. Not to worry,' he continued in French. 'I have your description.'

'You put me in a difficult position, sir.'

'You've no idea how difficult it will become. I am talking about a transfer of one million Swiss francs.'

'Into Mr Brazil's account?' The teller was looking very concerned.

'I said into his main account.'

'Yes, of course you did, sir. One million francs, you mentioned, I believe?'

'I did.'

'May I say we will look forward to your arriving again with the transfer?' The teller was smiling.

'It is for the main account. I am fast losing patience.'

Kent began to turn away as though about to leave the bank for the last time. The teller became almost frantic, calling through the grille.

'Sir! Sir! The main account of the individual you named *is* at this bank. Would you like to give me your own name?'

'When I come back. There's a deadline for this deal to be completed.'

Kent walked out of the bank, pulled the collar of his coat up round his neck. Now he had the information he needed.

He was looking for somewhere to eat when Newman appeared, carrying his bag and a canvas satchel over his shoulder.


At Park Crescent the phone rang. Tweed was either asleep or not prepared to be disturbed. Monica answered it.

'Beck here, Monica. Can I speak to Tweed?'

344

'He's not in his office. I'm not sure where he has gone. Can I help?'

'Yes. It's urgent. We're tracking Brazil's jet on its flight to Sion by radar. Tell Tweed Brazil will be landing within fifteen minutes at the outside. It's a difficult approach – too many mountains.'

'Maybe he'll hit one,' Monica said cheerfully.

'You are full of constructive ideas. But I very much fear the devil looks after his own.'

'Then we must be talking about the same person. I'll let Tweed know, as soon as he surfaces.'

The recumbent form in the chair behind his desk opened one eye, winked at her.

'Tweed has surfaced. For a moment, anyway. What was that all about?'

Monica told him, repeating word for word what Beck had said.

'Then it won't be long now,' Tweed said.

He winked at her again, closed his eyes, and fell asleep for the second time.


Because Newman was such a good organizer he had earlier sent Butler to a travel agency while they were still in Zurich to collect all the brochures he could on Sion.

During his brief conference with Marler aboard the express, he had given very detailed orders with the aid of a street plan of Sion and the list of hotels. These Marler had passed on to his subordinates.

So the moment the train stopped at Sion, Marler, Butler, and Nield left it in a hurry, but not in time to see Keith Kent, who could move like the wind, hurtling down the steps and into the town.

Returning to his compartment, Newman had told Franklin he had urgent tasks to complete. Franklin, the one-time soldier, had understood at once.

'Tell you what,' he had said to Newman who was gathering up his luggage, 'why not meet me for a drink this evening? I'm staying at the Hôtel de la Matze. It's just off the Rue de Lausanne.'

'I'll give you a call first,' Newman had replied, prior to leaving the compartment.

Newman had chosen to stay at the Hôtel Élite because it was just off the Avenue de la Gare and instinctively he wanted to be near the station. Butler and Nield were staying in a small hotel nearby while Marler, striking out on his own, had been instructed to stay at the tallest hotel, to get a room on the top floor – facing west so it overlooked the airfield area. His first job was to report back to Newman any sightings of a plane landing. They all knew where the others were staying.

Leaving the express ahead of Franklin, Newman hurried down the steps. Like Franklin, close behind, he failed to see the last passenger alight from the rear of the express. It is doubtful whether he would have recognized the passenger. Archie's disguise was very effective.

'What on earth are you doing in this back of beyond?' asked Newman.

He concealed the fact that he was startled to meet Keith Kent emerging from a side-street onto the Avenue de la Gare.

'You sound a mite aggressive,' Kent replied with a smile.

'You haven't answered my question,' Newman rasped.

'Extracting more information Tweed will value,' said Kent, refusing to be intimidated by Newman's unusual attitude.

'Well, maybe you wouldn't mind letting me in on it?'

'Since we are on the same side – in case you've

forgotten it – I've been checking to make sure where Brazil's main bank account is now. He moves it about, you know. Or,' he added acidly, 'maybe you didn't know.'

'No, I didn't know,' Newman said more quietly.

He had been testing Kent's nerve to see how he stood up to his verbal onslaught. He knew from Tweed that Kent was interested in guns, that he regularly practised on a shooting range. He was a first-rate marksman – not as good as Marler, but no one was. But in the present situation it wasn't impossible he'd find Kent alongside him in a firefight. He decided he wouldn't have anything to worry about.

'Well, you know now.' Kent smiled, adapting to Newman's sudden change of mood. 'And if you're in touch with Tweed you can tell him Brazil's main account is definitely here in Sion. At the Zurcher Kredit Bank. Where are you staying? I don't imagine you're just on a day trip.'

'At the Élite.'

'I know the place. Now, if I find out anything else I can contact you. Good hunting . . .'


What bothered Newman as he walked on up the Avenue de la Gare was his recollection of Tweed's remark made to him at the Schweizerhof.

*I have a strong feeling that we have already met, and know, The Motorman.*

Now he found Keith Kent and Bill Franklin had both turned up in Sion. He found it difficult to imagine either in the role of professional assassin. What motive could either have?

Then he remembered that Bill Franklin spent a fortune on keeping his string of expensive lady friends happy. And Kent had extravagant tastes. For a money

347

tracer it was odd how money slipped through his hands like water. He heard a vehicle coming down the road towards the station, looked up.

Philip was behind the wheel and beside him Paula was waving madly. The vehicle pulled over to the kerb and Paula, jumping out, ran towards him.

# 37

The Lear jet was losing height rapidly. It was a brilliant sunny day now and from his window Brazil looked down at his ground station below the Kellerhorn. He smiled with satisfaction. So much research, so many months to obtain the capital by any means to build it. Now he was about to succeed.

Some time before leaving Zurich, he had phoned Ivan Marov in Moscow, had confirmed the vital timetable they would both work to. It was fortunate that Marov spoke perfect English, albeit with an American accent. Marov had once been an unnoticed attaché at the Soviet Embassy in Washington.

Brazil turned round in his chair. Craig had at long last managed to attach the harness to Igor, prior to landing. Igor did not like the harness and only sharp commands from Brazil had enabled Craig to complete his unwanted task.

'Excellent!' he said to Craig. 'We'll make a good dog handler out of you yet.'

'Not with this animal,' Craig grumbled.

Swivelling his chair further round, Brazil was amused by the fat Luigi, who ate too much pasta. On take-off from Kloten he'd had trouble fastening his belt into the last hole, unlike the white-faced slim Marco, who had closed the belt and sat quite comfortably.

'We are coming in to land, sir,' the pilot's voice informed him over the tannoy.

Brazil swivelled his seat round again, so he could look out of the window. From that height he could just see the long white block which was his villa, and the glacier below it on the other side of the valley.

He checked his watch, trusting it more than the time shown on the illuminated panel. Yes, he would have time to spare before sending the first signal to the ground station. Probably well over an hour – even allowing for the drive up the diabolical road into the mountains.

He glanced across at José, who occupied a seat on the other side of the central aisle. The smooth-skinned man was fast asleep. Brazil's expression became grim – he was recalling his treachery, the recording he had listened to supplied by Gustav, the recording which had proved beyond any doubt that José had been informing on him. Well, he had worked out how to deal with that problem before they reached the villa.

From the high window in his hotel Marler watched the jet landing through high-powered glasses. His binoculars were so good he saw Brazil with his dog, descending the step-ladder, followed by three other men.

A limousine with tinted windows was waiting close to where the aircraft stopped. He saw José run to the car to bring it to Brazil, get in behind the wheel. He waited a moment longer before reporting to Newman at the Hôtel Élite. Five minutes later, after trying to start the limo, José got out, spread his hands in a gesture of frustration. Men in overalls appeared, began to fuss with the engine. Marler made his call.

'Black Beaver has landed. There seems to be some delay in leaving. The limo won't start. Mechanics are looking at the engine.'

'That gives you extra time then. Get into your four-wheel-drive and wait across the Rhône at the agreed point.'

'On my way.'


There had been furious activity after Newman had met Paula and Philip in the Avenue de la Gare. He had asked them where they had obtained the vehicle. Climbing aboard, he had stopped on the way to the Élite to get the phone number of the vehicle display room. Immediately on arrival at the Élite he had phoned Marler, given him the number, told him to phone up the company to ask them to send him a four-wheel-drive with chains on the wheels and he'd pay in cash if it arrived in fifteen minutes.

The vehicle had arrived at Marler's hotel in ten minutes. He had paid over the money, adding a generous tip, then confirmed to Newman that it had arrived.

In the meantime Newman had taken Philip and Paula up to his suite, had listened for ten minutes without once interrupting while they told him of their exploits when they had visited the ground station on the Kellerhorn. He watched both of them as they took turns putting him in the picture. Philip insisted Paula explained what had happened when they were nearly killed at the rock alcove on the way down. While they talked, he occasionally glanced at the map Paula had spread out over the bed.

'I'm truly staggered,' he said when they had finished, 'staggered at what you have achieved. I thought that would be our great problem – locating the ground station – and you've done it while I was on my way here.'

'Couldn't just hang around and get bored,' said Paula, being very British and glancing at her fingernails.

'You look very fit,' Newman said, gazing at her.

350

'It was good exercise. Exciting at times, but I don't waste time meditating on that bit.'

'So what do we do next?' Philip asked.

'I'm sure Brazil, when he lands, will drive up to that villa of his. It sounds like his control point. I'm amazed you traced that.'

'Well,' Philip pointed out, 'it is really all down to that waitress in the station restaurant where I called in for a cup of coffee.'

'Yes,' said Newman, 'but you talked to her and – even more important – you let her talk to you. Now, when Butler and Nield arrive, I will outline the master plan for tomorrow. At least,' he grinned ruefully, 'I hope it will turn out to be a master plan.'

'Why don't we attack the ground station today?' suggested Paula.

'Because,' Newman explained, 'having intruded today the enemy will be on the alert. Tomorrow morning they will be more relaxed. Then we hit them with all we've got.'

'What is Marler doing?' Philip asked.

'He's going to follow Brazil's limo – when they get it going – up to his villa. Marler is a man who can do a lot of damage.'

'Shouldn't he have back-up?' Paula objected.

'No. He functions much more effectively on his own. By the by, Bill Franklin was on the express which brought me here. Called in on me in my compartment.'

'He's good company,' Paula remarked.

'Also,' Newman continued, 'Keith Kent is in town. I bumped into him just before you arrived. Interesting, isn't it?'

'If we're going to be in Sion this evening,' Philip said in a determined voice, 'Paula and I can visit the elusive Anton Marchat. After dark.'

'Good idea,' Newman agreed.

351

'What did you mean when you said interesting?' Paula enquired. 'After you'd mentioned that Kent and Bill Franklin are here?'

'Well, it just occurred to me that when poor Ben, the barman at the Black Bear in Wareham, was murdered, both Franklin and Kent were in the area. And from the way Ben died we know it was the work of The Motorman.'


Eve, feeling at a loose end in her room at the Baur-en-Ville, decided she would go along to see Gustav. It was time she got sorted out whether or not she was in charge of the whole staff who had remained behind.

Reaching a corner, she heard a door close. Peering round she saw Gustav, dressed far more smartly than was normal for him, walking furtively away from her until he disappeared round the corner leading to the stairs.

'I wonder?' she said to herself. She knew Gustav had a liking for the strange ladies you could encounter on the streets in certain parts of Zurich. She tried the door handle. He'd left it unlocked. In a hurry to get on with it, she thought contemptuously.

Opening the door she was met with a strong stench of cheap hair oil. That confirmed her suspicions. So he wouldn't be back for some time. She looked round the untidy room, was about to leave when she saw a bunch of keys almost merging with a cushion on a couch.

'He's forgotten his keys!'

This was too good an opportunity to miss. She picked up the keys, checked to make sure his car key wasn't among them. No car key. Nothing to bring him back unexpectedly.

She walked over to the steel filing cabinet which, she had noticed earlier, he always kept locked. In no time she found the master key which unlocked every drawer. The top drawer was full of files which held papers concerning accounts, bills.

She opened the second drawer. This drawer held files with their contents marked on tabs attached to each file. She riffled through them, stopped at one file labelled *Scientists*.

Something echoed in her memory. An article in the *Herald Tribune*. Just a short piece tucked away on an inside page. Headlined *Missing Scientists Mystery*. She began to study the sheets inside the fat file. Each was devoted to one scientist. Gave a lot of personal data, the kind of data she had mugged up before getting to know one of the bankers Brazil had told her to go after.

### ED REYNOLDS

**Age:** 45.
**Marital status:** Wife, named Samantha.
**Children:** None
**Weakness:** Samantha an alcoholic

**Nationality:** American.
**Salary:** $400,000.
**Address (home)** . . .
**Expertise:** sabotage communications.

Sabotage?

The word stopped Eve. And earning that kind of money he had to be tops. She got out the notebook she always carried in her shoulder bag, scribbled down the wording about Reynolds.

She then checked other sheets. *Irina Krivitsky*. Her speciality was laser control of satellites, whatever that might mean. She scribbled down more details. As she examined more sheets she noted down several other names, none of which meant anything to her.

'You'd better get the hell out of here,' she told herself. 'You've got enough and Gustav *might* come back early.'

She was careful to leave the files as she found them. Then she locked the cabinet, put the bunch of keys where she had found them. As she opened the door she heard footsteps approaching. She froze with terror. If she closed the door the sound might be heard. A waiter, carrying a tray of food, walked past, never glanced at the partly open door. She went back to her room.

Locking the door, she opened a secret compartment in her shoulder bag, took out a folded newspaper cutting going brown. Pouring herself a vodka, she lit a cigarette, sprawled on the couch, read again the newspaper cutting she had rescued from Brazil's wastepaper basket in his Berne office. She had overheard what he had said and had slipped into the office after he had left it. The cutting had been screwed up before being tossed into the basket. The text under the small headline was brief.

> Strange rumours are circulating that top scientists are abandoning their jobs with private outfits. For bigger pay they are joining some international organization located abroad. Among those mentioned are the brilliant Ed Reynolds, Irina Krivitsky (from Russia) . . .

Several other names were listed, all of them with sheets in the file Eve had examined. She carefully folded the cutting, put it back in the secret pocket.

'Come back to Zurich, Mr Bob Newman,' she said aloud.


After they had repaired the limousine at the airfield Brazil surprised José.

'I'll drive. I just feel like some action after being cooped up in that plane.'

'Are you sure, sir?'

'Put Igor in the back, then get into the front passenger seat.'

'I feel I'm not doing my job, sir.'

'Just do as I tell you. Get on with it.' Brazil checked his

watch again. 'We'll arrive at the villa in good time in spite of the delay, so I won't be hurtling up that mountain road, if that's what's making you nervous.'

'I'm not nervous, sir.'

José was telling the truth. Brazil was a superb driver. Once, while in America, he had competed in a racing car on the West Coast. He had won, being proclaimed Champion of the Year.

'Igor will be quite happy on his own in the back,' Brazil continued as he drove away from the airfield. 'He likes looking out of the window. Incidentally, I think it is time we considered giving you more money. We will discuss it after we have got to the villa . . .'

Brazil was driving up a steep road which reproduced many of the features Philip and Paula had encountered during their journey to the Kellerhorn. On Brazil's side a rock wall sheered up vertically hundreds of feet above them. On José's side an ever-deepening abyss fell away and the drop was not guarded by a barrier.

The road turned and twisted as it climbed ever higher and its surface was covered with hard-packed snow. Brazil observed this with a sense of some relief – he knew that under the snow there would be a sheet of ice.

'There's a helicopter,' José remarked. 'It's not one of the Swiss weather planes.'

'No, it isn't, José. You probably saw it with another one waiting on the airfield. That machine has Marco aboard. He will arrive to make sure everything is ready for me at the villa before we get there.'

'You didn't tell me,' José replied.

'I don't tell you everything,' said Brazil and chuckled.

'Now it's hovering. I wonder why?'

'Obviously he is checking our progress up the mountain.'

*   *   *

355

Aboard the helicopter Marco, sitting next to the pilot, was not interested in Brazil's progress. What had caught his attention was a four-wheel-drive proceeding up the mountain some distance behind Brazil. In the vehicle Marler also saw the chopper hovering and knew the reason why.

'Well,' he said aloud, 'I've been spotted. That means a reception committee will be waiting for me. I think I can handle that.'

As soon as the helicopter disappeared he slowed down, braked beyond a bend. He unzipped the canvas hold-all nestling on the seat beside him, took out several objects, slipped them into each of the pockets of his fur-lined, thigh-length coat. Then he continued his arduous drive up the mountain, constantly turning the wheel to take another bend.


'José,' Brazil said as they reached a great height, 'I think we are being followed.'

It was a lie. Brazil had no idea that Marler was coming up behind him. José peered back, shook his head.

'I think you are wrong. I have been keeping a close eye on my wing mirror and I have seen nothing.'

'Call it instinct,' Brazil said cheerfully. 'You know the turn-off we shall soon come to – the one taking us up on to a plateau?'

'I remember it well. It is a good viewing point.'

'For a certain distance, anyway. I think we will drive off up the turn-off. We have the time. Then you can check to see if I am wrong. Am I usually wrong?' he enquired breezily.

'No, you are nearly always right.'

'Not sure I like the phrase "nearly always", but I will overlook it.'

José glanced sideways at his chief. Brazil seemed to be

356

in an exceptionally good humour. He decided it must be because soon they would be at the villa where something – he had no idea what it might be – was going to happen.

They reached the turn-off, little more than a wide gash in the rock wall, and Brazil swung off the mountain road, easing the large car up a steep track with inches to spare on either side. At the top they emerged on to a flat, arid, rock-strewn plateau, layered with snow. Brazil drove across the plateau, did a U-turn about fifty yards from where the ravine he had driven up ended. He looked at José.

'Now, go and stand on the overhang and look back as far as you can down the road. Watch it for a few minutes until I call you back. If you see another vehicle you raise your right hand and run to the beginning of the ravine. I will pick you up there. Then we drive down almost to the mountain road and wait. A perfect ambush point. There is a machine-pistol on the floor at the back under the travelling rug.'

'I take the weapon with me,' José suggested. 'Then I can kill the people in the car.'

'No, you can't. If they reach the overhang they will be hidden from you. Just do as I say, José.'

Brazil waited until José was away from the car before he gave Igor a one-word command. The wolfhound jumped over into the passenger seat previously occupied by José. It began to get excited as Brazil opened a compartment, took out a black glove, pulled it over his right hand.

He had had Igor trained, when younger, at a special school for dogs in Germany. He had told the master of the school that it was a game he wanted to play – then had given him details. He had stayed, putting on the black glove to activate Igor – papier-mâché dummies the size of men had been used.

José had reached the brink of the outcrop or overhang

which shielded the portion of the road below him. He stared for a moment down into the endless precipice falling well over a thousand feet, then switched his attention to the section of the road he could see.

Inside the car Brazil pointed at José with one finger of his gloved hand, leaned over to open the passenger door. In his mind he recalled the recording Gustav had played back to him of José's treacherous phone call. An informant, a traitor . . .

Igor left the car. It bounded forward at increasing speed, its paws making no sound on the snow. As it came close to José, still standing with his back to the car, Igor leapt high into the air, thudded into the exposed back, then dropped flat onto the plateau, as trained to do when it hit a target.

José, perched on the brink, lost his balance, raising his arms as he fell forward, plunging down into space, missing the mountain road by feet, his body cartwheeling as his yell of terror echoed into eternity. Then the silence of the Valais returned; an ominous silence.

# 38

Igor sat beside his master in the front passenger seat for the remainder of the journey up to the villa. He knew he had performed his 'trick' well.

Brazil drove up the final steep section, came out onto a large plateau. In the near distance, beyond a large concrete blockhouse which guarded the approaches, the white villa sat near the edge of the plateau. Immediately below it lay the chilling glacier, partially melting due to the sun shining on it with even feeble warmth.

'Why wasn't there anyone in the guardhouse?' Brazil wondered aloud. 'They need shaking up here.'

The chopper which had brought Marco rested on its helipad inside the twelve-foot-high perimeter fence of wire mesh. The protective fence was quite close to the villa. On the flat roof of the building was a tangle of aerial masts.

Pulling up, after passing through the gate which Marco had opened, Brazil left the limo, followed by Igor. He ran up the steps to the long terrace which fronted the villa. In the clear fresh mountain air he felt in the peak of fitness. Marco opened the heavy front door backed by steel.

'Marco, where the hell is everyone? There was no one in the guardhouse.'

'I found there was only the cook-housekeeper Elvira here when I arrived. The guards misunderstood the message you sent them while we were airborne.'

'Misunderstood! I said they were to send a section of the guards over to the laboratory to reinforce it.'

'I know, sir,' Marco agreed in a placatory tone, 'but the message must have been garbled. They thought you ordered *all* the guards to go to the Kellerhorn.'

'Their bloody commonsense should have told them I would never send such a message. Does that mean you are the only one here – except for Elvira?'

'Yes, sir, I'm afraid it does.'

'You know,' Brazil commented, looking back, 'we should have had that fence erected further away from the villa. It can't be helped.'

'There is a small problem,' Marco informed him as he followed his chief into a vast hall with a marble floor. 'You had better know about it now.'

'Well, get on with it. I have to go to the transmitter to send the first signal in the next thirty minutes. No, in less time,' he said, checking his watch. 'The satellite will be in orbit over Germany.'

'You were followed up the mountain,' Marco said quickly, expecting an outburst.

'You are sure?' Brazil asked quietly.

'Yes. A four-wheel-drive with one man inside it.'

'One man? Heavens, Marco, that should be no problem for you.'

'Oh, it won't be,' Marco said confidently. 'But I thought it best you should know. You may hear noise from outside.'

'Just get rid of him. Make sure he never drives back down the mountain again. There are plenty of places to hide a body easily. The glacier, for example.'

'I had already thought of that.'

'I must go to the transmitter . . .'

He paused as a short stocky woman, very fat, with a swarthy face, came into the entrance hall. She bowed.

'Good to see you back, sir. What would you like for your meal?'

'I must go to the transmitter!'

He had walked briskly to one of several doors leading off the hall, was taking out his keys, selecting the two which opened the double-locked heavy door, again backed by steel, when Marco followed him.

'What is it now?' snapped Brazil.

'Do you mind if Elvira gives the helicopter pilot his meal before you eat?'

'She can stuff him to the gills.'

Unlocking the door, he walked into a huge room with a large picture window of armoured glass. From the window he saw the distant Kellerhorn summit – below it, the buildings from which Luigi would send the first signal to the satellite. He could also see the huddle of old houses which accommodated the scientists and their wives or girl friends.

'The first signal will throw the world into panic,' he said to himself. 'But that will be nothing compared to

360

what happens when the second signal is sent, probably tomorrow or the day after.'

Brazil had never felt more confident in his life as he sat in the padded secretarial chair in front of the transmitter, put on his headphones, took off his watch so he could time it perfectly, his hands hovering over the keys.

Leaving the airfield with José, he had seen in his rear-view mirror fat Luigi climbing aboard the other helicopter, on his way to the Kellerhorn. With Luigi in charge the system would operate perfectly. Once Luigi had received his signal he would operate the mobile conning tower to track the satellite, would lock on to it with the flexible directional mast, then press the button.

As the second hand on his watch reached the correct position he began tapping out the signal. All hell was about to break loose.

'What did Professor Grogarty tell you when you phoned him?' asked Monica.

Tweed smiled grimly. He had woken up earlier, had gone to the bathroom, taken a shower, and changed into clean clothes. When he had come back he had asked Monica to see if she could contact Grogarty.

'He's been studying those photographs again – the ones you sent by courier a second time. The photos taken secretly in French Guiana just before the satellite was launched, when its innards were exposed.'

'He's been brooding about them, worrying over them when he's thought some more about them?'

'You hit the nail on the head,' said Tweed. 'He's totally convinced that it's a highly sophisticated system designed to sabotage global communications. He hasn't worked out yet completely how it could be done. But he insists that somewhere there is a ground station controlling the whole system.'

361

'If only Newman would phone us,' Monica said wistfully.

'He will at the right time. What's that . . . ?'

Returning from the bathroom, he had left the office door open because the room was stuffy. Suddenly a terrible screeching sound filled the office. Worse than that, brilliant lights, almost blinding, were flashing. The phenomenon, Tweed realized, was coming from the upper floor and down the stairs. Monica had her hands over her ears, an agonized expression on her face.

Tweed jumped up, ran to Paula's desk where he knew she kept several polythene bags containing earplugs. She used them when she was close to a large helicopter landing. Grabbing one of the bags, Tweed ripped it open, saw Paula's smoked glasses, grabbed them, too.

He rushed to Monica's desk, slipped a pair of the dark glasses over her eyes. When she opened them he pointed to the earplugs, gesturing to his own ears. She was inserting them as Tweed inserted a pair in his own ears. He snatched his own pair of smoked glasses from a drawer and put them on as he ran onto the landing outside. Looking down the stairs he saw Howard, obviously just woken up, stumbling into the hall.

'Howard!' he roared. 'Get back into your office, close the door and stay there. Get a bloody move on . . .'

Shocked by the violence of the orders, Howard obeyed, disappeared into his office, slammed the door shut.

'George!' Tweed shouted at the top of his voice to the ex-soldier who guarded the front door. 'Run into the waiting room. Stay there with the door closed until I come down.'

George, looking dazed, staggered into the waiting room, shut the door.

Tweed took a deep breath, adjusted his earplugs. The fiendish shrieking, very high decibels, was reverberating inside his head. He forced himself to run up the stairs. The door to the communications room was open. Once again they had been working late. The emphasis was on *had*.

Appalled, Tweed entered the large room. The computer screens had gone mad. No longer green, they were flashing at immense velocity, a variety of incredibly brilliant colours, blindingly bright. The colours seemed to recede for a fraction of a second, and then lurch out of the screens again.

The screeching sound emitted from the screens varied in intensity, a deafening blast which he could hear clearly despite his earplugs. But what appalled him most was the state of the three men who had worked there. Reginald was flopped back in his chair, his head hanging over the rest. Tweed checked his pulse. Nothing.

He compelled himself to fight the sense of disorientation which was in danger of overcoming him. The other two men lay sprawled on the floor beside their chairs. When he checked their pulses he found nothing.

He glanced round the room, saw the main cable. Taking a grave risk, he grabbed hold of it, hauled it out of its socket. The screens died quickly, fading away into blanks. The diabolical noise, rising and falling, rising and falling, also faded. Tweed pulled out his earplugs, was struck by the heavy silence, took off his smoked glasses. Leaving the room he ran downstairs, opened the door to his office.

Monica, looking very shaken, had just taken out one earplug. She removed her dark glasses when she saw Tweed was without his.

'What happened?' she croaked.

'I imagine the telephone is out of action.'

Tweed lifted the receiver, was surprised to hear the normal dialling tone. He handed the receiver to her.

'Call an ambulance urgently. Paramedics vital. Three men unconscious, may be dead.'

He left his office as Monica began dialling madly. He had little hope that even paramedics could do anything, but in medicine you never knew. He dashed downstairs to the ground floor, opened the door to the waiting room.

'What was that, sir?' George asked. 'Start of World War Three?'

'Not as bad as that. You can go back to your desk.'

He ran to Howard's room, opened the door. His chief was staring out of the window. He turned round with a bemused expression. Shock.

'What's happening?' he whispered.

'Brazil has started. That's just the first phase. We have to stop him before he launches the second one. You look flaked out. Go home to bed. I'm taking charge . . .'

He left before Howard could reply but he sensed he would not be protesting. Running back upstairs, he opened the door to the room where the night duty staff worked. Fortunately, there were no computers here or any of the junk which went with them. Four men looked up at him as though emerging from a dream. The fact that their door had been closed had saved them from a dreadful experience.

'What was that, sir?' the senior member asked. 'I opened the door and then slammed it shut.'

'Damned good job you did. You're all right, then – all of you?'

'Yes, sir.'

'Then carry on with what you were doing before it started. It won't happen again. I've immobilized the equipment in the computer room. *Don't* go down there.'

On his way back to his office, running down more stairs, Tweed called down to the guard.

'George, paramedics will arrive at any moment. Show them up yourself to the Computer Room, then go back to your post. Tell them where I am.'

He went back into his office, closing the door. Monica was on the phone. She gestured madly to his phone.

'Paramedics are coming. I've got a chap at the MoD on the line. Manders. He's scared out of his wits.'

'Hello, Manders. Tweed speaking.'

'There's been a catastrophe. All our computers have gone down. The operators are dead. There were violent flashing lights and—'

'I know what there was,' Tweed interrupted. 'We've had the same thing here. I know what it is.'

'You do!'

'Yes.' Tweed was emphatic. 'So leave it to me.'

'GCHQ is out of action. There are more bodies there. A member of the staff phoned me from outside the building.'

'I said I know what it is. I repeat, leave it to me. I have to go. Goodbye.'

GCHQ. That was the key communications station at Cheltenham. Its staff listened in to signals, conversations on telephones all over the world. Even the Americans respected it.

'I've forgotten something.'

Tweed jumped up, ran to the door, opened it in time to see below a team of paramedics coming up with George leading them. He stopped the first paramedic.

'One thing you should know. There's a live cable on the floor. So watch it.'

'Thank you, sir.' The paramedic called back over his shoulder as his team hurtled up the stairs, disappeared inside the computer room.

Tweed returned to his office, closed the door. He looked at Monica.

'Better get Cord Dillon at Langley on the phone if you can reach him.'

Tweed knew the Deputy Director of the CIA worked all hours, was seldom away from his desk. Monica was reaching for the phone when it began ringing. She listened, told the caller, 'He is here,' and stared at Tweed.

'Cord Dillon – calling you.'

'Hello, Cord, just about to contact you,' Tweed managed to say.

'Tweed, total panic in Washington. The White House is going completely crazy. All my computers have been sabotaged – a lot of dead men in this building,' Dillon added calmly.

'We've been subjected to the same attack. It's Brazil. Leopold Brazil. I warned you not to trust him. This is phase one of a global operation which hinges on Rogue One.'

'Phase one, you said. You mean you anticipate a phase two soon?' Dillon enquired in the same deadpan voice.

'I don't anticipate it, Cord. I *expect* it. Don't worry. I know what is happening. My team are in Europe hunting his key apparatus.'

'Tell them to kill the bastard.'

'I think they may have the same idea. Everything is under control.'

'The Pentagon is immobilized. Plenty of corpses there. I have to go see the President. You haven't met this one. His predecessor admired you. So what do I tell him? Tweed says the situation is under control? Don't worry? He'll say who the four-letter word is Tweed?'

'Then put in a *good* word for me,' Tweed suggested amiably.

'I suppose I could. I owe you favours. Keep calling me.'

Tweed suggested a cup of coffee would be welcome as he put down the phone. Monica hurried to the percolator in the corner. He drank two cups straight off. Then the phone rang again.

Monica answered it, then an ecstatic expression

appeared on her face as though she was hearing from a long-lost lover. She could hardly get the words out as she called across to Tweed.

'Bob Newman is on the line . . .'


'Good to hear from you, Bob,' Tweed said. 'Where are you calling from?'

'From a call box in the street. Place called Sion, in the Valais. We've located the ground station – or rather, Paula and Philip, who arrived earlier, tracked it down. They've seen some action.'

'Are they both all right?'

'In the pink of condition. Paula is sizzling. I'll give you the details.'

Tweed listened. More than any man he had ever met Newman could compress a complex situation into as few words as possible. He presumed it was his training and experience as a foreign correspondent.

'So,' Newman concluded, 'the earliest we can launch an assault on the ground station is tomorrow. That will be done. If you want to contact me I'm at the Hotel Élite. Telephone number . . .'

'Could you leave someone there I could talk to in your absence?'

'No.' Newman's tone was hard. 'I'll need the whole team for the job we have to do.'

'Understood.' Tweed took a deep breath. 'Bob, it is essential that ground station *is* destroyed, even if it means taking heavy casualties.'

'Message understood . . .'


Monica, who had heard, was staring in horror as Tweed put down the phone. She bit her lip, then came out with her comment.

'I've never in all my experience with you heard you send an order like that.'

'What do you think we're playing at – a game of Scrabble?' Tweed rasped.

'Sorry.'

'Then get me the PM on the phone. No, I'll get him myself.'

He brushed aside the private secretary who answered the call, who tried to extract from him why he wanted to see the PM.

'I said I wanted to speak to the PM. Put him on the line now or your job is at stake.'

'I beg your pardon, sir.'

'I said your job is at stake,' Tweed growled.

'I'll only be a minute.'

In less than a minute the Prime Minister was on the line.

'Tweed here, PM . . . Yes, I know what has happened. I shall be at Downing Street in fifteen minutes from now. I will expect to see you the moment I arrive.'

He put the phone down before there was any reply. Getting up from behind his desk, he put on his coat.

'Shall I get someone to drive you there?' Monica asked.

'I'm perfectly capable of driving myself there. And I'll be quicker.'


Tweed returned two hours later, entering his office with a brisk step. He hung up his coat, sat behind his desk.

'Would you like some more coffee?' Monica asked tentatively.

'Monica, I would love some more coffee. I think the situation calls for two cups, please.'

'How did you get on with the PM?' she asked while she was pouring it.

'What's happened has shaken him to the core, rattled his cage. As I thought, he was in a mood to listen to me without interruption or argument. This is very good coffee. Thank you.'

'He took a decision?'

'Between the two of us I took the decisions for him – at risk of my sounding dictatorial. The Rapid Reaction Force is being despatched to strategic airfields in Germany. The first flights take off this evening.'

'The German Chancellor stuck to his guns, then.'

'Not at first,' Tweed said grimly. 'After my last call at Downing Street he'd consulted his cabinet in Bonn. The weak willies had expressed concern. Wanted to consult NATO. I told the PM he must call Bonn again.'

'What happened?'

'While the PM made the call I listened in on another extension. I practically stood over the PM, dictating his conversation by scribbling notes on a pad and pushing them under his nose. Key communications in Germany have been wrecked, and there are more bodies. I think that factor persuaded the Chancellor. He agreed to receive the Rapid Reaction Force – even went so far as to thank the PM for his cooperation. When I left Downing Street the PM looked exhausted.'

'I'm not surprised – with you standing over him,' Monica commented tartly.

'Now, try and get Newman on the phone at that number he gave me.'

While Monica was trying to get through Tweed sat with his hands clasped in his lap. Then, restless, he got up and poured himself a third cup of coffee from the percolator. He had drunk half the cup when Monica signalled to him.

'Bob?' He paused. 'Operator, this is a very bad line.' He waited – for the hotel phone operator either to reply or for the sound of the click of a switch. He heard nothing. 'We are alone,' he went on. 'This call is just to let you know I shall be flying to Sion airfield soon in a jet. By courtesy of Mr Brazil – although he doesn't know I've borrowed one of his jets. The one with *Brazil* flashed all over the outside of the fuselage.'

'I can't recommend that. This is a danger zone,' Newman warned.

'Did I ask for your recommendation? Do I have to remind you who is in charge of this operation? I'm only telling you so you don't shoot up a jet with Brazil's name on it.'

'I'll try to avoid that happening,' said Newman, who had recovered his good humour.

Tweed had hardly put down the phone before he made a new request to Monica.

'Please call Jim Corcoran, security chief at Heathrow. Tell him to warn the aircrew of the jet that I will be flying to Sion. Tell Jim that I'll give him one hour's notice before I want the machine airborne – with me inside it.'

'He won't like it. That doesn't give him much time.'

'Tell him. By now he'll have heard the news of Brazil's strike at world communications. That will make him pull out all the stops.'

'Anything else?' Monica enquired. 'Before I make this call?'

'Yes, in case I forget. Later, phone Arthur Beck in Zurich and tell him what I'm doing. But only after I am airborne, on my way.'

'I don't think he'll like that either.'

'I'm not in the business of being popular. I'm in the business of destroying Brazil.'

# 39

Marler, following Brazil's limo up the mountain, braked as he reached the large plateau, saw the fence, the villa, its roof festooned with aerials, the empty limo parked at the foot of a flight of steps. He was exposed with nowhere to hide and he had no idea how many guards Brazil might have at his disposal.

He saw a narrow track descending below the edge of the plateau, released the brake, continued down the track – out of sight of the villa. He drove on down the track, stopped suddenly. The track ended – at a sheer rim dropping into the glacier.

I should have brought my Armalite rifle, he thought.

He got out, approached the rim cautiously. The view down into the glacier just below was one of the most spectacular sights he had ever seen. The long sea of sheer ice glittered in the sunlight, refracting various colours.

He frowned, blinked, closed his eyes, opened them again. Yes, he had been right – the glacier was on the move. Very slowly, like some incredible animal stalking its prey. Crevasses, which looked bottomless, were appearing as the ice broke apart. It reminded him of a graveyard for dinosaurs – because the glacier was as ancient as the prehistoric beasts which no longer roamed the earth.

There was something sinister, doom-laden, about its almost imperceptible, implacable movement. He found it hypnotic, jerked his eyes away from this phenomenon of the might of nature. With his canvas satchel over his shoulder, he followed the edge of the rim which climbed upwards. To his right was a gradual snowbound slope, slanting down from the top of the plateau. He had to find some way of approaching the villa unseen. He had already made up his mind he must destroy the aerials on top of the villa, the key, he suspected, to Brazil's communication with the outside world. There would be no telephone inside the place – even Swiss engineers would balk at laying phone lines up the mountain and radio telephones could be intercepted. He stopped suddenly. A figure had appeared.

Marler was close to the first sign of vegetation he had seen. A fossilized tree, bare of all foliage, twisted and gnarled, its thick trunk bent over, a few branches extended towards the sky as though in supplication. He moved in front of the trunk, looked up.

Marco, the sunlight on his face, wore dark glasses, his slim body swathed in a fur coat. Marler stared. Something twitched at the back of his mind. The Reeperbahn, the notorious district in Hamburg. He had strolled inside it once at night. Outside a club he had seen the picture of a knife-thrower. He had paid the entrance fee, had joined the audience inside.

The knife-thrower was entertaining the audience by throwing knives at figures of men painted on sheets. Each knife had dived into the chest of the figures – and the figures he was throwing them at appeared without warning and from all directions. The knife-thrower was Marco, the man who now stood looking down at him.

The white face grinned, a deathlike grin. Marco opened his coat, revealed a belt round his waist holding at least a dozen long wide-bladed knives. He held up his hands, cupped them over his mouth, shouted in French.

'You should not have come, my friend. Say your prayers.'

He had a knife in his hand in a second, raised his hand above his head, hurtled it through the ice-cold air. Marler, still in front of the tree trunk, ducked. He heard a swish, glanced at the tree trunk. The knife had landed, was twanging just where his chest had been.

Marler recognized Marco had the tactical advantage – he had the high ground. Something would have to be done about that. He was too far away for a certain shot with a Walther. Marler slipped behind the tree trunk, was no longer an easy target.

As he had hoped, Marco advanced down the slope, coming closer, moving sideways so he could see behind the tree trunk. Still not close enough for a Walther. He had to encourage Marco to use up his collection of knives.

He peered quickly round the tree, dodged back instantly. A second very close swish. The knife was embedded in the edge of the tree trunk, where the side of Marler's head had been. Marler calculated Marco would expect him to peer round the other side of the tree. He peered round the same side as he had before.

Poised on the slope, Marco had to change the direction of his throw. The third knife thudded into the side of the trunk Marler had peered round. Too close for comfort. Then silence. Marco was trying a new tactic, Marler felt sure. He felt inside his canvas satchel, brought out what his fingers had grasped. He had risked taking off his glove. Marco was wearing gloves on both hands.

Marler ran out into the open along the rim. He had been right. Marco had run silently down the slope so he could target Marler behind the tree. Caught off balance by his enemy's sudden move, Marco, close to the rim, raised his hand, holding another knife. Marler threw the stun grenade. It landed at Marco's feet.

The knife was never thrown. Marco flung both hands up, dropped the knife, staggered forward. He seemed to pause at the edge of the rim, then stumbled forward. Marler watched his body spinning as it fell toward the glacier. It was not a long drop and Marco, still vaguely conscious, tried to clamber upright on the ice. He lost balance for the second time. Marler continued watching

373

as the knife-thrower vanished, sliding down inside a crevasse. The ice began to close over it.

Looking up as he hurried up the slope, Marler saw that the villa had been in view during the last deadly duel. It couldn't be helped. He must move quickly.

Inside the villa Brazil had observed Marco's attempt to wipe out the intruder, had seen Marco's grim end as he disappeared down the crevasse. He hurried to the door of his transmitter room, opened the door, called out.

'Elvira, we have an intruder. Marco is dead. The intruder is approaching the villa. Deal with him.'

'I am not leaving the villa. Your meal is ready.'

'You were trained to use a machine-pistol,' Brazil raged.

'You said Marco is dead. The man who can kill Marco is good. I am not leaving the villa,' the squat woman said obstinately. 'Your meal is ready.'

'Then put the wretched thing on the stove and keep it warm,' Brazil shouted at her.

He'd have to get Luigi to fly back some of the guards from the Kellerhorn. He had a helicopter pilot, a local hired for his knowledge of the area, not one of his own men. He hurried to the transmitter room, shut the door, composing the message he would send in his head.

'Marco is dead,' Elvira repeated like a litany as she waddled back to her kitchen.

Taking the risk that more guards would appear, Marler ran up the slope, paused. No one in sight anywhere. Most odd. He ran again until he was within a few feet of the perimeter fence.

He extracted something else from his satchel, something protected with great care. All the way up the

374

mountain he had worried that he might encounter a rocky patch which would shake the vehicle. The drive up had been smooth all the way. He would be very relieved to get rid of what he was carrying in his gloved hand.

He stopped for a moment, estimating the distance. They hadn't built the fence far enough away from the villa. Holding his right arm high up, behind his shoulder, he hurled the stick of dynamite.

It sailed through the air, landed exactly where he had aimed, exploded with a roar amid the network of aerials. The masts were shattered, fragments flying up into the air, larger pieces toppling over on top of each other. Where they had stood on top of the flat roof there was now a scrap heap of tortured, twisted, destroyed metal. Marler turned and ran back to his four-wheel-drive.

Sitting in front of the transmitter inside the villa, Brazil shuddered under the impact of the explosion. Plaster from the ceiling showered down into the room, but the roof held firm. It had been bult of reinforced concrete to withstand the huge weight of winter's snow and ice.

Compressing his lips, Brazil, wearing the head-phones, attempted to tap out the message. Nothing. The transmitter was dead. He now had no means of commu-nicating with Luigi. Cursing, he went to the kitchen, which also served as a dining room.

The table was laid and the moment he appeared Elvira carried a steaming dish of pasta and mince meat to the table in front of where he sat. She glared at him. Brazil sat down, looking at the pilot who was reading a magazine in a corner.

'Have you plenty of fuel?' he asked.

'Well tanked up,' the pilot replied. 'It was only a short flight here.'

'Then, when I have eaten, you could fly me across to the buildings on the Kellerhorn?'

'Easily. It would be safer if we landed there before it is dark.'

'Eat!' Elvira commanded. 'The stomach must be fed. I heard a bang,' she said placidly.

'Never mind about the bang.'

'Marco is dead,' she said.

'For God's sake don't say that again,' Brazil shouted, slamming down his cutlery.

Marler drove back down the mountain road in a happier frame of mind than when he had ascended it. He had been only too glad to get rid of the dynamite. And it had done the job. Which meant Brazil could not summon more of his thugs to meet him, coming up as he drove down.

He was still puzzled by the lack of more guards, but Marler never wasted time or energy on mysteries he couldn't solve. Now he was concentrating on reaching Sion before night fell, although at the moment the valley way below the abyss was aglow in the dusk.

With a sigh of relief he reached the bottom, drove on into Sion. He parked his vehicle, walked the rest of the way to the Hôtel Élite to report to Newman on the day's work.

'Excellent news,' Newman commented in his room. Marler had reported while Philip and Paula also listened.

'Mind you,' Marler warned, 'I'm sure Brazil is now on the Kellerhorn. I had just reached the valley when I heard – then saw – a helicopter flying from the direction of that villa towards the Kellerhorn. There was a chopper on a helipad outside the villa when I arrived.'

'So we assume Brazil has now taken personal control of the ground station. Ready to activate something far more terrible. Let's pray he's inside the place when we go in and attack tomorrow.'

'It's been pretty terrible so far,' Paula interjected. 'I've been listening to the radio. All normal BBC programmes on the World Service have been suspended. They're continually broadcasting more news of smashed communications systems all over the world. To say nothing of the people who have been killed. Even, in a few cases, businessmen working from their homes with all their computer equipment linked to the information superhighway.'

'Plus,' Philip added, 'the most alarming rumours from Moscow. That the city is ringed with advancing troops – crack divisions. And a General Ivan Marov is supposed to have issued a proclamation closing the frontiers of Russia from Vladivostok on the Pacific to Belarus in the west. The President, it's alleged, is ill, has been taken to a clinic.'

'Terror tactics to unnerve the West,' Newman commented. 'But really it's developed into a duel between two men – Tweed versus Brazil.'

'You have a plan for destroying the ground station?' Marler enquired. 'If so, I ought to know the details.'

'We do have a plan,' Newman assured him, 'a plan largely devised from something Philip observed when he was on the Kellerhorn with Paula. They worked out the plan between them. I have approved it. Give you the details after Philip and Paula have left.'

'Bob,' Paula said emphatically, 'when did *you* last get some sleep?'

'Can't remember.'

'I thought not. As soon as we leave you get some kip. You can tell Marler the plan when you wake up. You'll be fresher. Marler can stay on guard while you're comatose which – from the look of you – you will be the moment your head hits the pillow.'

'Where are Butler and Nield?' Marler asked.

'Prowling the streets,' Newman replied. 'Both wearing

377

black leather outfits and helmets like the Leather Bombers, and riding Fireblades. They're checking for signs of the opposition. Butler is keeping an eye on that airfield.'

'We could shoot them,' Marler objected.

'We thought of that. Both Harry and Pete have red crosses painted on the fronts and backs of their helmets.'

'And where are Paula and Philip off to?' persisted Marler, who always liked to be in the complete picture.

Paula had taken out her .32 Browning, was checking its action. Philip had just slipped the mag out of his Walther, examined the weapon, then rammed the mag back inside the butt before returning the gun to his hip holster.

'They're on their way to try and find a man called Anton Marchat,' Newman told him.

'Last seen at Devastoke Cottage in Dorset,' Marler recalled.

'When you find him,' Newman went on, 'ask him if he knows anything about the Kellerhorn, about the ground station.'

'Do our best,' said Philip as he got up and left with Paula. 'We're walking there.'


The streets of Sion were deserted and silent after dark. Philip, who had studied the street plan, guided them in the right direction. Paula realized they were heading for the enormous hunk of rock with an ancient building on its summit which dominated the town.

'How are you getting on with Eve, Philip?' Paula asked. 'Or would you sooner not talk about it? You haven't seen her for awhile.'

'I've decided she's no good for me. She's a consummate liar. I've detected that, even when I've been glad to be with her. One part of my brain seems to function in

378

spite of the grief for Jean. I know now my feelings for Eve were an infatuation, a dangerous one.'

'So you're going to ditch her?'

'One way of putting it.' Philip laughed without humour. 'I think women are more realistic than men about women. More ruthless in their assessment, too. If they've got brains, and you're fully equipped with them.'

'I didn't put that very nicely.' She paused. 'Philip, we are being followed.'

'I know.' They rounded a corner. 'Quick! Get into that doorway. Keep perfectly still. Don't say a thing . . .'

As they huddled into the alcove-like porch Philip took out his Walther. Paula already had her Browning in her hand. They waited, listening for the sound of approaching footsteps.

Paula found the atmosphere eerie. The side-street was as black as coal tar. The nearest street lamp was a long way away. The silence was oppressive, like a heavy blanket pressing down on her. They went on waiting, two figures like waxworks, neither moving a muscle.

When five minutes had passed Philip told Paula in a whisper to stay where she was. He walked quietly out into the street, peered round the corner. No one. Nothing. Not a sound. He went back to the doorway.

'I don't think it was our imagination, but whoever it was he's gone. So let's get moving. It could be a relevation – talking to the highly elusive Mr Marchat.'

# 40

'Well,' Philip remarked, as they neared the great rock, 'we should certainly recognize Marchat.'

'He looks a most unusual character,' Paula agreed.

They had both studied their photos of Anton Marchat

379

before Marler had arrived in Newman's hotel room. His full face was hairless, very smooth skinned. The face was roundish, the eyes were the most compelling feature. They stared out of the photo from under heavy lids, as though hiding secrets. A gentle face but without the hint of a smile, and a note of determination about the chin. The hair had been smoothed down so it appeared as though it had been painted on his skull.

'What's this?' whispered Paula, grasping Philip's arm.

It was a place which encouraged whispering, as they huddled under the massive rock which sheered above them. As he had at frequent intervals, Philip suddenly looked back, plunged his hand inside the satchel looped over his shoulder.

'Don't be startled,' he hissed.

Turning round, he hurled the object in his hand at the place where he had seen the stooped shadow. The stun grenade landed, the shadow vanished behind a wall. The grenade exploded. The weird silence was broken by the sound of its hideous crack. Philip stood quite still, the Walther now in his hand.

'Have you gone mad?' Paula whispered. 'You could kill a pedestrian.'

'I definitely saw the shadow of a man following us. He won't be so keen to follow us now. Don't forget that Newman believes The Motorman is in Sion. We don't want to lead him to Marchat.'

'I suppose you know what you're doing.'

'I do know. We're close to the street where Marchat is living . . .'

Paula stared ahead, her eyes now well accustomed to the dark since clouds had obscured the moon when they had started out. A small colony of ancient houses had come into view and she realized what old Sion had once been like.

Crouched under the sheer rock face towering above

them the old houses stood almost shoulder to shoulder, were built of wood, two storeys high with sloping shingle roofs. One house was even perched on a mass of rock with a wooden staircase leading up to it. The windows all had shutters which were closed. Here and there was a gleam of light where shutters met, but some of the old houses were empty, Paula felt sure. They were a world – a century – away from modern Sion.

'Which one?' Paula whispered.

'They have numbers.'

Philip shone a pencil torch briefly on a square of wood with a number, just visible, carved into the square.

'Number 14 is where Marchat lives. It must be that one standing back between two other houses.'

His pencil torch flashed on and off quickly.

'This is it. Take a deep breath. Say a little prayer. We're a long way from Devastoke Cottage.'

Paula's heart sank when she saw there were no gleams of light showing between the shutters. Philip lifted the wooden knocker, shaped like the head of some animal, knocked quietly several times, waited.

They seemed to wait for ever and Paula, looking up, could have sworn the huge rock outcrop above them was leaning slowly further out. Then there was the sound of a key grinding in a lock and the heavy wooden door opened about a foot. A chain with huge links was still holding the door so no one could enter. A woman's voice spoke in French.

'Who is it?'

'We have come all the way from Dorset in England to see Mr Marchat,' said Paula, believing she had a better chance of persuading another woman to open the door at night.

'You must have the wrong address. There is no one here with that name.'

'I am Paula Grey. I have a friend with me, Mr Philip

Cardon. We are both English. My friend saw Sterndale Manor burning with the old General and his son, Richard, inside it. Your husband escaped death only because he was at a public house in Wareham, having a drink.'

There was a pause. They couldn't see the woman because there appeared to be no light on in the place. Paula felt sure there was someone else close to the woman.

'This means nothing to me,' the woman eventually said.

Oh, Lord, Paula thought. Did I make a mistake assuming she is his wife? She ploughed on.

'The man responsible for setting fire to the manor was Leopold Brazil. He has his own house near Sterndale Manor. It is called Grenville Grange.' More silence. Paula was becoming desperate. 'We have come to warn Mr Marchat that the man who killed Partridge, thinking he was murdering Mr Marchat, is in Sion. He is called The Motorman.'

'Let them in, Karin,' a man's voice called out.

Paula puffed out her lips with silent relief as Karin removed the huge chain, opened the door, told them to come in. They walked into the dark slowly, checking with their feet for invisible steps, but there were none. The door was closed, a light came on, a lantern suspended from a chain in the middle of the small room. Karin locked the door, refastened the chain.


Philip blinked in the light. In a rocking-chair sat a small man, his face the image of the photo they had studied. He wore a green jacket and heavy dark brown trousers and his clean white shirt was open, revealing a strong neck. The lids were half-closed over the eyes as he gazed at each of them, then they opened wide. His voice was soft.

382

'Please sit down. Those two chairs are comfortable. Karin, bring our guests some wine, please. The wines of the Valais are very fine,' he told Paula.

'You will want to see proof of our identity,' Philip said, taking out his SIS folder.

Marchat waved the folder aside. He smiled, a slow smile.

'I heard every word you said. Your information is more convincing than any identity card – those things can so easily be forged. Years ago, I earned good money forging them myself.'

Philip would have waited but Paula plunged in so he looked round the room. Everything was made of wood. A table laid for breakfast. Karin was a methodical housewife. The chairs, carved and stable-looking, were made of wood. The floor, covered here and there with rugs, designed in tasteful colours, was made of wooden planks. He felt he had been transported back to the beginning of the century. But the room was cosy – a pleasant warmth glowed from an old stove in the centre of the room with a round metal pipe rising vertically and disappearing through a hole in the wooden ceiling.

'You won't have heard, but there has been a disaster all over the world—' Paula began.

'Excuse my interrupting, but I have heard.' Marchat indicated an old radio, made of wood, of the type popular in the nineteen-thirties. 'A communications blackout. That is Brazil?'

'That is Brazil's work,' Paula agreed. 'But there is far worse to come – unless we can destroy the ground station he has built on the Kellerhorn. You know about what he calls a weather station?'

'I have seen it. But first I drink to your health.' He lifted an old-fashioned wineglass. Paula raised hers along with Philip and Karin who, having served the drinks, sat close to her husband. 'Karin is my wife of many years,'

Marchat said, putting down his glass. 'I met General Sterndale by chance, he said I looked a good worker and offered me the job at his manor. He paid me very well in cash. It will help us during our old age. And that weather station is something far more sinister. He has great scientists from all over the world working for him. He pays them a fortune.'

'They are there voluntarily?' Philip asked, continuing to speak French.

'Oh, yes. They make more money in one month than they could make in a year in the countries he has brought them from. He was clever. He said he would arrange luxurious housing for their wives or girl friends to keep them happy. Inside the fence built round the main buildings was an abandoned village . . .'

'Abandoned?' queried Paula.

'Oh, yes. Up in the mountains there are a number of such places. The young people do not wish to endure such a hard life. They leave the Valais and go off to well-paid jobs in Montreux and Geneva. The Valais is dying.'

'Sorry, I interrupted you,' Paula said.

'Yes, he had the Italian architects who built the complex convert those apparently unused houses into small palaces. Occasionally the wives are taken with their men to a dinner in a private room at one of the big hotels on Lake Geneva.'

'What worries us,' Philip intervened, 'is how to destroy the fake weather station, which is where Brazil is using his system to annihilate world communications. When Paula and I were up there this morning I noticed the slope above the buildings looked unstable.'

'It is very unstable. One day it will slide down when it is disturbed. That will be the end of Brazil's evil plan. The Italian architects he employed told him it was perfectly safe. They wanted the job of designing the place. He got them in the end.'

384

'How do you mean?' asked Paula.

'The project is completed, Brazil puts them in an air-conditioned bus to take them to the railway station. He hands out bottles of excellent wine. The bus starts off. Halfway down the brakes fail, it goes over a precipice. No one can talk about what they have built.'

'Can I ask how you know all this?' queried Philip.

'Because I lived here then. Just after the so-called accident to the bus I met General Sterndale and went to England. Earlier I used to walk up the mountain, taking a pack on my back with sleeping bag and food.'

'You *walked* up!'

Paula was astounded. She couldn't prevent herself glancing at Marchat's stocky legs, bulging against his trousers.

'I took my time. I made friends with one of the workmen, a man from Slovenia who spoke French. He told me what was going on. I went up dressed like one of the workmen so the guards would not notice me. So many workmen.'

'I think we've taken up enough of your time,' Paula said. 'The information you have given us is invaluable.'

'Use it to wreck that man,' Marchat growled.

'Thank you for the wine.' Paula had turned to Karin who, slim and calm, had listened. 'It really was very good.'

'I made it myself,' Karin admitted and flushed with pleasure.

Marchat reached out a gnarled hand, grasped his wife by the wrist affectionately, squeezed it.

'One thing before we go,' Philip warned as he stood up. 'Under no circumstances let any stranger into this house – whatever yarn he spins you. Just keep the door shut.' He deliberately held Marchat's gaze. 'We know The Motorman is in town . . .'

\*     \*     \*

385

Newman listened to their report of the visit to Anton and Karin Marchat when they had returned to his room at the Élite.

'They sound a nice couple,' he said when they had finished. 'And, without realizing it, Marchat has confirmed our plan will work. So, let the morning come quickly.'

'Bob,' Philip said earnestly, leaning forward in his chair, 'I think we should give them a guard. Butler – or Nield – would be ideal.'

'I can't do that. Reluctantly,' Newman replied firmly. 'We will be heavily outnumbered when we attack. Every man – and woman – will be needed. Sorry, but that's the way it is. The top priority is the destruction of that ground station.'

'I'm nervous about their safety,' Philip persisted.

'And I agree with him,' Paula chimed in.

'Then you'll both have to control your nerves,' Newman told them grimly. 'This is a time when hard decisions have to be taken. I've just taken one.'

He stopped, jumped up at the sound of a peculiar tattoo on the door. Even though he recognized it he had his Smith & Wesson in his hand as he unlocked the door, opened it a crack, then wide. Butler and Nield walked in, holding motorcycle helmets, clad from head to foot in black leather. Paula noticed the red crosses painted on their helmets.

'Coffee?' Newman offered as he locked the door. 'It's fresh, delivered for Paula and Philip not ten minutes ago.'

'Black and strong as sin for me,' said Butler. 'And we didn't locate any sin on the streets. No Leather Bombers.'

'And no ladies of the night, unfortunately,' said Nield humorously.

'Shame,' Paula chaffed him.

Newman, still looking serious, waited until Butler and Nield had drunk their coffee and Paula had refilled their cups. Both men were beginning to look fresher after a few minutes in the warmly heated room.

'When you've drunk your coffee – and don't hurry – do you think you could face another patrol of Sion? This time on your feet, checking all the bars and drinking places, including hotels.'

'Just what I was hoping for,' Nield joked, 'a walk out there in a temperature way below zero. And the exercise will be so welcome.'

'What are we looking for?' asked the terser Butler.

'Bill Franklin and Keith Kent. They're somewhere here in Sion. I'd like to pinpoint where they are. Don't approach either of them, just give their locations back to me over a phone. One name, one place, then get off the line.'

'We'd better get going,' said the sturdy Butler.

'What I've always found so endearing,' Nield remarked drily, 'is Harry's enthusiasm. Oh, well. If we have to freeze, then freeze we will.'

'Be back here in one hour,' Newman ordered as they went to the door and he followed them. 'You need sleep for tomorrow . . .'

'I don't understand what you hope to achieve by that,' Paula said after the two men had left the room.

'If they get lucky and locate one man, or very lucky and locate both, I'll call Beck in Zurich. I can ask him if he would contact the local police chief and request surveillance by plain-clothes detectives on both men.' He looked at Paula. 'More than that I cannot do.'

'But how can you expect them to recognize either Franklin or Kent?' Paula demanded.

'You must be tired. They're pros – Butler and Nield. I gave them two names. Take a hotel. They'll go in with some story cooked up about looking for two friends with those names. If one of the targets is in the bar they'll ask to have him pointed out, then say they have to go to the

387

loo, sneak out, and call me. That's just one angle I thought up on the spur I'd use if I was searching for them.'

'I must be tired,' Paula agreed.

Newman put on the radio, ordered more coffee, and some sandwiches from room service. He sat listening to the flood of reports while he drank and ate, all reports about a breakdown in communications in some other part of the world.

Philip and Paula, seated on a couch, chatted quietly with each other. Precisely one hour later Butler and Nield returned.

'How did it go?' Newman asked.

'It didn't,' said Nield. 'I don't think there's a bar in Sion we haven't visited, plus a number of hotels. No sign of Franklin, no sign of Kent.'

'You did your best,' said Newman. 'Take off that gear, make yourselves comfortable when you come back. I'll order some food and more coffee for you.'

'I think I'm going to bed,' said Paula, standing up as the two men left. 'I'm dog-tired. See you in the morning.'

She went back to her room, forced herself to have a shower, flopped into bed, switched off the light, and turned over. She was depressed by the fact Butler and Nield had failed to track down either man. She was thinking about the Marchats and her anxiety grew. If only Tweed was here, was her last thought before she fell fast asleep.

# 41

Tweed checked his watch, allowed for Swiss time. The paramedics had gone, taking away their sad cargo. The chief of the team had come in to see Tweed briefly.

'Sorry, sir. No good news. All three men in the computer room are dead.'

'I thought they were,' Tweed said quietly.

'Can't understand what happened to them. The autopsy will tell us.'

'I can tell you. Shock. Brought on by unbearable pressure of sight and sound. Their systems couldn't take it. You haven't heard the news on the world bulletins?'

'Been too busy to listen to any news.'

'You'll hear about it. I won't delay you. Thank you for coming so quickly.'

He made his urgent request to Monica as soon as they were alone.

'Try and get Newman on the phone. Keep your fingers crossed that he's still at the Élite.'

'Bob's on the line,' Monica called out triumphantly a few minutes later.

'Tweed here. I'll phrase this carefully,' he said, knowing the call was passing through the hotel switchboard. 'You recall what you and Philip were practising with when you were last down at Send?'

'Yes.'

'When is zero hour for the party?'

'At dawn tomorrow morning. At least, that's when we move off.'

'I'm bringing one with me in the jet. With plenty of what you feed into it.'

'That present would be just perfect for the party,' Newman said regretfully. 'But you'll arrive too late.'

'No, I won't. Have a vehicle waiting at that airfield.'

'You'll be too late,' Newman insisted.

'Not if I fly there overnight.'

'You can't do that,' Newman protested. 'It's only a small airfield. Only daylight landings are safe.'

'So I'll inform Beck. He will make arrangements. He'll have to.'

389

'I have to advise you not to attempt this madness,' Newman said with great force.

'I have to remind you who is in charge. I am. So kindly have transport ready to pick up the present. You can do that, I presume?'

'I could . . .'

'So you *will*. Beck will inform you of my ETA. Get a good night's sleep.'

He went off the line before Newman could protest. Monica was clasping her hands in her lap as she spoke.

'He didn't like the idea of a night landing at Sion airfield, did he?'

'Newman is sometimes so cautious,' Tweed replied blandly.

'And rightly so,' she snapped. 'What is your idea of the ETA at Sion?'

'I'd like to take off from Heathrow in that jet waiting for me at about 3 a.m. That should get me to Sion about 4.30 a.m. or 5.30 local time.'

'It will be as black as the hole of Calcutta,' Monica shouted at him in despair.

'You've forgotten something. Swiss pilots will fly me there. They know their own airspace better than any pilots in the world. And the moonlight will help.'

'It may not. The moon is often obscured by clouds.'

'It won't be. I am lucky. Now you have a lot to do.' He counted off items on his fingers. 'First, call Jim Corcoran at Heathrow, tell him when I wish to fly out to Sion. Ask him to alert the aircrew. The present for Newman is downstairs, just brought up from Send on my orders. It is in a jeep, carefully packaged, and George is guarding it along with the men who brought it up. Have it sent to Heathrow so it can be put aboard the jet. It is to be handled only by the men who brought it up from Send.'

'Not an atom bomb, I hope,' said Monica, half-joking, half-fearful.

'Of course not. Although when used it may well have a similar effect. Check that the aircrew agree they can take off at 3 a.m. Warn Corcoran that a delicate cargo has to be put aboard, that it is on the way, ask him to warn the crew that it – the cargo – is perfectly safe, that it is weapons which have *not* been armed.'

'Is that all?'

'By no means. Get Corcoran to phone you the moment the jet is airborne, then phone Beck. Tell him I'm aboard, that I will be landing at the agreed ETA at Sion. Ask him to warn the airfield to be ready to receive the jet when the pilot contacts the control tower. Above all, do not phone Beck until I am in the air, beyond recall.'

'Beck will blow a gasket.'

'He may, but he'll do all he can.'

'That sounds ominous.'

'Nothing is certain in this world. We are all, at some time, poised on the edge of a precipice.'


Leaving Park Crescent, Tweed drove himself through the night to Professor Grogarty's quarters in Harley Street. He had, earlier, phoned Grogarty to see if it would be convenient for him to call on him. Grogarty's response had been typical.

'Of course. Where do you think that I would be at this hour? Asleep? Surely you know by now I – like you – do my best work when the rest of the world sleeps . . .'

Grogarty answered Tweed's ringing of the bell himself and once again his *pince-nez* was askew. Oh, Lord, thought Tweed, I'll spend my time trying to decide which eye to focus on.

'Have a brandy,' Grogarty said jovially as he escorted his guest to a comfortable armchair. 'Yes, I know you rarely drink, but just a small one. I hate drinking on my own.'

'If you insist.'

'I do, sir!'

Tweed glanced round the large, so well-furnished room while Grogarty poured the drinks. On an antique sideboard he saw a strange microscope, very squat and with a series of lenses. Grogarty caught his glance.

'Yes, that's what I examined those photos from French Guiana with. I designed it myself. Most of my equipment I have knocked up myself – can't get what I need from manufacturers. They tell me what I want is theoretically impossible.'

'Which spurs you on – to prove they're wrong.'

'Exactly. Your health, sir. Now what can I do for you this time?'

'Speaking of time, I won't take up much of yours. I'm due to fly off somewhere at 3 a.m.'

'You're always flying off somewhere. At 3 a.m.? Didn't know there were flights at that hour.'

'I invented one.'

'You would.'

Grogarty, a tall man, was standing with stooped shoulders. Tweed stared at him strangely, so strangely that his host reacted.

'Got a pimple on my nose?'

'Sorry, I just had an idea. Forget it. Now . . .'

Tweed described concisely – but vividly – what he had experienced in the computer room at Park Crescent. He ended by telling his host that the three operators inside the room were dead.

'This happened, but I wanted to check with you. Does it make sense?'

'Most certainly.' Grogarty had settled himself in another armchair facing Tweed. 'Nowadays we are cursed with TV pictures – and *sound* – transmitted from satellites orbiting the earth. Scientists have become the devil's disciples. They don't care what happens so long as

392

they can make their names designing some infernal contraption. Mobile phones – so we no longer have privacy, personal computers which can be operated from the home, et cetera, et cetera. But what is the result of all this so-called scientific advance? The world is being brought so close together everyone has become neighbours. Pressures are increased on the human mind – which can only take so much. I am a scientist but I know the world would be a safer place if most of the top scientists were shot.'

'Coming from you, that is an original thought,' Tweed remarked.

'A thought I suspect you have already had. The core of the danger is this – scientists are so intent on making a name for themselves in their chosen field that they never give a moment's thought beforehand about the *consequences* of what they plan to invent. They are amoral.'

'A profound thought.'

'Also, many think they are kings of the earth. They will mould the future. I have an old-fashioned idea that it is governments who are expected to guide us out of danger.'

'You would advocate controlling science?' Tweed suggested.

'I have done, sir! Many times. At secret seminars which receive no publicity. I said earlier all the world has become neighbours. Where, in private life, does serious trouble so often start? With your neighbour – over the garden fence. Now the bloody boffins are creating a world where all the nations will be at each other's throats. I suspect the man behind what you described as happening at Park Crescent – and all over the planet – is bent on wiping out modern science. Especially in communications, which bring nations too close to each other. I drink to him.'

Grogarty raised his glass, swallowed more brandy, smiled at his guest.

'You don't look shocked.'

'I'm not.'

'So, as I have explained – only briefly – what is happening is perfectly possible, given the murderous advance of science. I use the word carefully. Mentally, they are murdering our civilization, reducing us to the servants of infernal machines. I also believe you are set on countering this terrible menace.'

'I am doing what I can,' said Tweed, standing up to go.

'Then it will be done.'


Brazil had felt relieved when the helicopter landed him inside the perimeter fence surrounding the complex on the Kellerhorn. He immediately held a meeting with Luigi in his subordinate's ornately furnished office. Weird tapestries and old posters decorated the walls. The chairs arranged round a circular table of solid glass were stark, modern, uncomfortable.

Craig had come into the room, was wriggling his bulk trying to find an easy position. He gave up, leaned forward, and rested his thick elbows on the glass.

'Congratulations to you, Luigi,' was Brazil's first remark. 'You did a splendid job.' He looked at Craig. 'You have heard the news?'

'Had my ear glued to the radio. Chaos everywhere. Just what we hoped for. What's next?'

'I will personally send the second signal tomorrow, the one which will totally smash the West's morale. That will enable other events elsewhere to take place. Then we evacuate this establishment – after destroying the equipment.'

'What about those pesky scientists and their grouching women?' Craig wanted to know.

'That is your job. After the signal is sent you will cut

off the air-conditioning system to the houses they live and work in.'

'Cut it off?' Craig raised a thick eyebrow. 'You had those old cabins sealed off so not a bit of outside air could get in. Cut off the air-conditioning and they're dead in thirty minutes.'

'That,' Brazil said quietly, 'is the idea. To coin a cliché, dead men tell no tales.'

'True,' Craig agreed. 'Just tell me tomorrow when to do it.'

'Scientists are the curse of humanity,' Brazil ruminated aloud. 'They rush us ever faster into a future I do not wish to contemplate. With Ed Reynolds leading the team I have organized the destruction of the worldwide communications system they created. They were happy to do this – for money, and to prove to themselves it could be done. We have the élite of the world's scientists inside what was a deserted village. Eliminate them and we put science back many years.' He smiled grimly. 'You could say I am a benefactor of humanity – although that is only part of a much greater global plan.'

'Where is José?' asked Luigi.

'I left him at the villa. Someone had to be there as well as Elvira. That's a detail you can leave to me.'

'We pack up our personal belongings ready to depart?' Luigi questioned.

'Do that. Luigi, you take the team to Milan. Once you reach Italy everyone scatters to their homes – or hotels. Individually. Use several expresses to leave in small numbers. That way you don't draw attention to yourselves.'

'And what about me?' Craig demanded.

'You take an express to Geneva. Stay at a top hotel for a few days. Relax – you've been under great pressure. After a week return to Grenville Grange where I will be waiting for you. Dorset will be a relief after all these mountains.'

395

'You can say that again,' Craig said with feeling.

'I have no intention of repeating myself.' Brazil smiled drily. 'I will be flying back to Zurich to clear up my office, destroy all my papers.'

'What about Gustav?' asked Luigi. 'And Eve?'

'I left them behind in Zurich. I will give them instructions when I reach the city.'

'Sounds as though that's about it,' Craig commented. 'A funny thing happened earlier today. Three of our men disappeared. Last seen going down a ravine. Don't know why.'

'Perhaps they fell over a precipice,' said Brazil.

# 42

Tweed was airborne, the jet carrying him and the cargo now passing over France. He sat relaxed in his seat, recalling the last-minute conversation he'd had when Cord Dillon of the CIA had phoned him before he left Park Crescent.

'That suspect submarine you asked us to track – the one you thought sent a signal to a mansion in Dorset – it has arrived at Murmansk, the only ice-free Russian port in the West at the moment.'

'So it was a Russian sub,' Tweed had replied.

'It sure was. Latest type of silent nuclear-powered vessel. The kind that worries us. Moves like a torpedo.'

'Where did you track it from?' Tweed had asked.

'From our air base near Keflavik in Iceland. Thinking it wasn't observed, it sailed for long distances on the surface,' Dillon had reported. 'So we have pictures of it.'

'When you said it sent a signal to the Dorset mansion on the coast,' Tweed had corrected, 'it received signals and, I think, simply acknowledged them. Philip Cardon, one of my best men, happened to be on the clifftop when he saw a light flashing from Grenville Grange. That's the mansion which is owned by Brazil. He must have had one of his men waiting inside to contact the sub at an agreed time.'

'Brazil again,' Dillon had said grimly.

'Yes. And your tracking the sub is important. It gives us a direct link between Brazil and General Marov. I've heard Marov now controls the whole military machine.'

'General?' Dillon had queried.

'Yes. He's kept that fact quiet. Thanks for calling – have to go now.' Tweed had ended the conversation.

Aboard the jet Tweed once again marvelled at the element chance played in life. It had been pure chance that Philip should have been on the clifftop with Eve Warner when the signal flashes had been exchanged. Philip had told Tweed, emphasizing he could have been imagining the incident. Privately, Tweed had dismissed Philip's doubts, remembering other times when Philip had been right.

As the jet flew on through the moonlit night Tweed turned his thoughts to the situation in Sion. He tried to put himself into Brazil's shoes, inside his head. He had an idea which might be the key to the coming assault, but was unsure whether to intrude on Newman's territory.

'We'll be landing soon, sir.'

Tweed jerked himself into the present, realized the co-pilot was standing beside him. He thanked him.

'One thing,' the co-pilot went on, 'to get on the right path for landing we'll pass pretty close to the peaks of the Bernese Oberland. Don't worry about what you'll see out of the window.'

'Should have brought my camera,' Tweed joked.

Less than a minute later the co-pilot returned, handed Tweed a small camera with a flash. He showed Tweed how it worked. Tweed listened patiently, although he was familiar with the model. The co-pilot walked briskly back to the crew cabin.

The jet began to slant, to descend in a curve. Outside the window Tweed looked down on savage snowbound peaks, which appeared to be within inches of the fuselage. One jagged summit loomed towards him like a gigantic knife. He raised the camera, took several shots.

Then the floor of the Valais came into view, rushed up to meet them as the pilot was forced to descend at a steep angle. They not only had the moonlight, they also had a flare path glowing to show them the way in. Tweed was reminded of old films he'd seen on the TV of wartime in the 1940s. This was the moment when he tensed. The moment before the wheels safely touched the ground. He peered out as far as he could along the window. Almost down. No sign of a runway.

The Swiss pilot landed the jet so smoothly the wheels seemed to kiss the concrete. The moment it had stopped the exit door was opened and Tweed was escorted to the mobile staircase which had been run up to the machine. Newman stood waiting for him, hands on his hips.

'Isn't there somewhere we can hide this jet so there's no risk of Brazil seeing it?' Tweed asked as Newman took him into a canteen.

'Stop trying to run the show.' Newman clapped his hand on the shoulder of the man he was so glad to see. 'We've thought of that. Nield and Butler are already on board, bringing out the cargo of weaponry. *And*, before you ask, we do have transport to take it away from the airfield at once.'

'Good,' said Tweed as he paced up and down the well-heated canteen to stretch his legs.

'And,' Newman went on with a grin, 'the jet will then be parked inside a small hangar, the doors will be closed and locked. All thought of – and arranged – by Beck who is in constant touch with the airfield controller. Now, sit down and drink your coffee.'

'Don't you have to leave?'

'*And*, there you go again. It will be dark for a couple of hours yet. The coffee here is good, isn't it?'

'Almost as good as Monica's,' replied Tweed, who had sat at a table with Newman. 'Very welcome, too. How is Paula?'

'Raving at me when last I saw her. She wanted to come and meet you. I practically had to sock her to make her stay in bed. She needs the sleep. She's OK.'

'And Philip and the others?'

'Everyone is OK. Including Marler, who has never slept so much in my experience. But he did have a tiring day. Do not ask me why.'

'Bob' – Tweed paused, his manner suddenly brisk, in full control – 'I have one idea I'd like to put to you. Before I do, I emphasize you are in command of this operation. If you don't like the idea, which is only a suggestion, throw it into the wastepaper basket.'

'Go ahead.'

'I tried to think myself into Brazil's position, bearing in mind what has happened. I think he'll be on cloud nine. Almost ecstatic about what he's achieved. I am sure he has something much worse planned in the very near future. Maybe today. Bob, *I don't think he'll anticipate an attack on the ground station* in his present mood.'

'What an intriguing observation,' Newman said thoughtfully.

'That being so,' Tweed continued, 'his army of thugs won't have been put on the alert. So what we need is one thing – a five-minute massive onslaught out of the blue. Then run.'

'My God, I think you've hit the nail on the head.'

'It's only a suggestion,' Tweed warned.

'It's one I like. Like a lot.'

Newman stood up, put on his coat and a glove on his left hand. He shook Tweed's with his right hand.

'It was worth your coming for that one idea alone. I must get back and finalize the battle plan. You'll wait here? Good. There's a small bedroom with loo and washbasin beyond that door. The staff, when I told them you were coming, have been cleaning it up. It looked OK to me before they started. See you . . .'


Paula was woken by a nightmare. The Motorman, a faceless hunchback, had been strangling Karin Marchat, his huge hands squeezing her throat. Behind him Paula hammered at his skull with the butt of her Browning. It seemed to have no effect. Karin was gurgling horribly. Using all her strength Paula brought the gun down on the back of the creature's head, time and time and time again. Then she woke up.

'Why the hell didn't I shoot him,' she said aloud.

'What was that?'

Newman was gently shaking her awake. He put on the bedside light, after warning her what he was doing. She stared at him, gave a gasp of relief.

'Don't bother about me. I just had a nightmare.'

'Good job I woke you, then.'

'You didn't wake me,' she snapped. 'I woke myself up.' She sat up in bed, pulled on her dressing gown. 'Is it time to go already?'

'No, and I apologize for disturbing your sleep. There's been a change of plan. I have to tell everyone. Won't be time later – we have to start so early. I've had to wake up everyone. And you didn't lock your door.'

'Sorry. I was so tired. In your room?'

'Would five minutes from now be too quick?'

'Not if you push off now . . .'

Paula could dress very quickly. After slopping cold water on her face, she put on leggings, both sweaters over two layers of underclothes, and her short, fur-lined coat, grabbed her shoulder bag with the Browning inside, and went to Newman's room. When he opened the door and she walked in she saw everyone had arrived.

'I came to you last,' Newman explained, 'to give you a bit more sleep.'

She looked round the room. Butler and Nield, fully dressed, sat in armchairs. Marler had adopted his usual stance, standing against a wall, smoking a king-size.

'Haven't seen you in ages,' she said, looking at Marler.

'I've been sleeping the sleep of the just.'

'Tell me how to do it sometime.' She sat down. 'Where is Philip?'

'I woke him first,' Newman told her. 'He's gone to pay a quick visit to the Marchats. He has to ask them something important which occurred to me.'

'I'll go with him,' she said, jumping up.

'Sit down!' Newman ordered. 'He left a while ago. He'll be back soon.'

'I don't like it,' she told Newman abruptly. 'He could lead The Motorman to them.'

'You have that little faith in Philip?' Newman asked ironically.

'Sorry, I'm only half-awake. I'll be *compos mentis* in a minute.' She saw his expression. 'All right, fire away. I'll take in whatever it is you've replanned.'

Newman explained the technique of the new plan. Paula listened carefully. When he had finished she asked her question.

'What's this new weapon?'

'Harry,' Newman said, turning to Butler, 'show Paula the weapon Tweed has brought us.'

'Tweed is here?' Paula almost yelled, then lowered her voice. 'Well, where is he, Bob?'

'Waiting at the airfield. Then he's there to take any calls that come in from Beck.'

'I'd like to see this weapon which sounds so important to the new plan. I agree your plan is brilliant.'

'Not my plan,' Newman informed her. 'Tweed thought up the whole thing while flying here in the jet. Harry, show her.'

Butler went behind a couch, picked up something, emerged with a rocket launcher, hand-held, pressed into his shoulder. Paula gazed at the large muzzle Harry was aiming at her point-blank. She thought it looked like a miniature cannon.

'Don't worry,' Harry called out to her, 'it isn't loaded.'

'Thank heavens for small mercies,' she said and smiled.

'And this is what it's loaded with, what it fires a fair distance.'

He dived behind the couch, laid the launcher on the floor, came up holding a sinister-looking shell.

'Makes quite a bang,' Harry went on. 'Newman will be the one who uses it. The rest of us are protection. Tweed brought spare shells.'

'One should do the trick,' Newman said. 'If it doesn't we're all in trouble.'

'I think it will work,' Paula said, ever the optimist.

There was a rapping tattoo on the door. Newman unlocked it, peered out, let in Philip, who took off his fur-lined coat as he entered. The room was now very warm.

'It's still not snowing,' he reported. 'It's cold enough to freeze the whatnots off a brass monkey but the moon casts a good light.'

'How did you get on?' Newman demanded anxiously.

'Because they recognized my voice they were going to let me in but I told them to keep the chain on the door. They were both still up, fully dressed. I suppose what Paula and I told them gave them a lot to talk about.'

'Get to the point,' Newman snapped.

'It's OK. Anton told me there are no villagers left on the Kellerhorn. A few years back there was a landslide and even the old villagers ran for it and never went back. The youngsters have gone looking for the bright lights, as Anton explained.'

'I don't quite get it,' Paula said.

'Bob was worried,' Philip explained. 'Worried that if there were still occupied villages on the mountain there could be casualties. Innocent Swiss.'

Newman decided: 'I'll explain the new plan to Philip. Lucky we got that jeep.'

'Where on earth did you get a jeep from at this hour?' enquired Paula.

'Butler and Nield – much earlier – leaned against the bell of the garage which supplied the two four-wheel-drives. The owner lives over the shop,' Newman told her. 'He wasn't pleased, I gather – until Nield showed him a fistful of Swiss banknotes. Then he could have bought the shop's whole stock. That gives us three vehicles. One is really a spare – in case a vehicle is put out of action.'

'I'm not going back to bed,' Paula decided, 'now I'm up and dressed I'm staying that way. I'd get very little extra sleep before dawn – if any.' She took off her coat.

'I'll stay up with you,' volunteered Philip, 'after Bob has finished with me. We've still got food and I can go down and persuade the night clerk to make coffee – by showing him my Walther, if necessary.'

'You *are* joking,' said Paula. 'Of course you are.'

'I'm staying up, too,' said Marler. 'Anyone fancy a game of poker? Provided we play for big money . . .'

# 43

*A five-minute assault.* Paula found the words echoing in her mind as the convoy moved off at dawn. Again a heavy mist had descended over Sion as had been the case when Philip and Paula had first arrived in the town. Its clamminess cloyed at their faces, it deadened all sound. They seemed to move out of a ghost town.

Philip and Paula, in a four-wheel-drive, led the way at the beginning. Newman had agreed it was sensible since they knew the route. Behind them followed Butler and Nield, each clad in black leather and helmets and riding a Fireblade. They would move to the head of the convoy when the beginning of the road up the mountain was reached.

'We need a distraction if they see us coming,' Newman had decided. 'If we're spotted too early the sight of what will appear to be a couple of Leather Bombers will confuse the opposition.'

Behind the motorcycles Newman drove the jeep with the rocket launcher and spare shells beside him. He had chosen the jeep because it would be easy to leap out of.

Bringing up the rear Marler sat alone in the second four-wheel-drive. Like Philip, Butler, and Nield he carried a canvas satchel with a shoulder-strap. They drove with their headlights dimmed and met no other traffic and not a single soul on the streets.

With Philip behind the wheel, they soon left Sion behind and paused as the beginning of the mountain road came into view. Butler and Nield rode into the vanguard and Newman followed behind them.

'There would be a mist,' Philip commented.

'Just what we need to cover our departure,' Paula assured him.

'You're not driving,' he reminded her.

'I'll take over the wheel anytime,' she retorted.

'I'll hang in here for awhile.'

They emerged suddenly above the white layer of heavy mist and Paula was surprised how high they had climbed already. Above them was an azure sky, cloud-free. She looked back and thought the huge rock near the Marchats' house, appearing to float, was like a Japanese painting.

'We're making good progress,' Philip said as he swung round yet another hideous bend. 'And the snow is hard so we can move faster.'

'Newman is going like the wind. The trouble is he has Butler and Nield ahead of him. Put those two on motorcycles and they jolly near break the sound barrier.'

She was surprised, had a funny feeling, when unexpectedly they passed the rock alcove where they had fought off a three-man ambush. Don't think about it, she told herself. Concentrate on what lies ahead.

Behind them, Marler was whistling a tune to himself. He had waited at the bottom while Newman took the lead in his jeep, with only the motorcycles ahead. He was impressed with the way Newman was negotiating the bends, bearing in mind that he hadn't had the experience he had built up driving to the villa the day before.

Butler and Nield, finding the surface hard, were storming up the mountain with Newman not far in their wake. They had to hit the ground station before the guards woke up. They were banking on the sheer mountain wall muffling the sound of their headlong approach.

'Boy,' Philip exclaimed, 'are they moving!'

'So are we,' responded Paula.

She had stopped gazing down into the abyss. She

wanted her nerve steady as a rock – steady as the rock wall they were skimming past – when the inevitable battle began. She took out her Browning, checked the action.

'That's the second time you've done that,' Philip joked.

'It gives me something to do.'

'I know. The sooner we're there and get on with it the better as far as I'm concerned.'

'Me, too. I'm worried about Bob.'

'Why?' asked Philip with a note of surprise. 'He can look after himself.'

'I realize that, but when they see what he's aiming they'll make him their main target – the enemy will.'

'Which is why we've all been fanned out in the plan – just so we can back him up. He showed us, remember? Using salt and pepper cellars to represent who was who.'

'Looked all right – on a tablecloth. But it's theory.'

'It will go according to plan,' Philip insisted.

'Famous last words.'

'Be optimistic, like me,' Philip told her.

'You can't see your expression. You look as grim as one of those mountains.'

'I'm concentrating on my driving. Which is rather a sound idea, don't you think? Under the circumstances?'

Philip had just swung round another hair-raising curve in the road, which now rose very steeply. He was deliberately keeping her talking, to take her mind off what lay ahead of them. At times he provoked an argument while they came closer to the plateau where the ground station was located.

'You're driving very well, Philip,' she said.

'Famous last words!' he joked.

'We're nearly there, aren't we?'

'Very close now. Better check the action of your Browning again,' he needled her.

'I know why you said that. But if we are very close then I think I'll take your mocking advice.'

She extracted the Browning from her shoulder bag, held it in her lap, the muzzle pointed away from Philip, tension building up inside her as the great boar's head of the Kellerhorn came into view.


Inside the main building of the ground station it was Brazil who first had an inclination of what was heading straight for them. He slept little, liked to advertise his boundless energy.

'I'm always up first – before the world has woken up,' he had told many people. 'That is how I steal a march on the rest of the world. While others slumber I work.'

It was still a couple of hours before he planned to send the second, major signal. He had had his breakfast alone and was staring out of the large window of armoured glass which overlooked the approaches to the heights. The large room was his HQ, his living and sleeping quarters. A door leading off it led to an even larger room which controlled the mobile conning tower perched above it, the sophisticated laser system which contacted the satellite.

He had been working, so it was well after dawn when he pulled back the curtains, stared in disbelief at the convoy of vehicles below him. He was confused for a few vital minutes by what he thought were two Leather Bombers on motorcycles, then he raised the alarm. Why the hell hadn't he posted heavy guards round the perimeter during the night? He cursed his omission. Pressing a button on his intercom he shouted down it.

'Craig! We're under attack . . .'

*     *     *

Rounding the last corner, Butler and Nield rode up towards the ground station, keeping well apart to provide a smaller target, looking for guards. Newman drove the jeep into the middle of the space between them, continued a long way forward.

'He's going too close,' said Paula.

'He's determined the first shell lands in the right place,' Philip told her.

As ordered by Newman earlier, he swung the four-wheel-drive in a U-turn, so it faced the way they had come, ready for a swift retreat. Marler brought his own vehicle close to them, also performed a U-turn, left the engine running when he had braked. Philip also left his engine running before diving out of the vehicle after Paula.

She was already running over the hard-packed snow, holding her Browning in both hands, ready for instant firing. She raised her automatic as guards appeared near the gates to the compound, flung them open, came running out. Men clad in black leather who, like Butler and Nield, looked sinister silhouetted against the white snow.

Above them, way beyond the ground station, loomed the huge summit of the Kellerhorn – while below it descended the long snowbound slope with rocks protruding at frequent intervals, a slope which ran down to the rear of the ground station.

Marler had brought his Armalite rifle this time. He stood in the open, well to the left of Newman and close to Nield, the weapon tucked into his shoulder. A Leather Bomber, holding a machine-pistol, was running down to get within range. Marler saw him in the crosshairs, pulled the trigger, and saw his target sprawl forward, lie still. It was the first shot. It provoked a fusillade from the advancing guards, now pouring through the open gates, drawing closer to Newman.

Butler and Nield, plunging their hands inside their canvas satchels, brought out grenades, hurled them into the nearest guards. They threw more and more grenades. The guards fell like ninepins, not close enough for their weapons to reach the attackers. Not yet.

Craig rushed out of the gate, ducking and weaving, gripping a machine-pistol. His target was Newman, still standing like a statue, taking very careful aim at a point on the slope, midway between the Kellerhorn summit and the ground station. Craig somehow missed all the bullets flying over the snow, came within range. He raised the machine-pistol.

'Newman, no time to say your prayers. You're going down. For ever . . .'

Despite the fusillade Newman heard his voice, filled with venom, clearly. The thought flashed across Newman's mind that Craig was recalling the time when he had bested Craig during the fight in the Black Bear, way back in Wareham.

Everyone seemed occupied, holding back the tide of oncoming guards. Craig's large face split into a grin of hate. His finger tightened on the trigger.

More shots rang out in a brief silence as men reloaded. Shot after shot. Craig staggered, a look of sheer disbelief on his face. He stumbled forward close to Newman. More bullets hit him. Dropping the machine-pistol, he lifted both hands, sprawled forward. More bullets entered his prone form.

Marler glanced towards Newman, saw Paula, Browning held steady in both hands, emptying the eight-shot automatic into Craig. No particular expression on her face. She slipped in a fresh magazine, looked for another target.

Rocket launcher pressed into his shoulder, Newman pulled the trigger. The shell *whooshed* into the air, in a high arc. It landed exactly where he had hoped.

Detonated on the unstable slope Marchat had referred to. A ton of snow and rocks soared into the air. Then came a sound which muffled all the shooting, a dreadful rumbling like the fall of a gigantic waterfall. The whole slope began to move.

'*Evacuate!*' Newman shouted at the top of his voice.

Paula suddenly noticed the rotor blades of the chopper on the helipad inside the perimeter were moving, whirling faster and faster. Brazil ran out of the building, climbed aboard the machine beside the pilot. The blades became a whirling blur, the machine lifted off.

'Brazil's getting away,' she screamed to Newman.

'*Evacuate!*' Newman roared again.

They rushed to the four-wheel-drives. Philip, running, threw a grenade under the jeep. It exploded, the petrol tank blew, the jeep burst into flames. No point in leaving something the guards could follow them in. Butler and Nield had earlier thrown their motorcycles over sideways, had used the barrel of a gun to smash a vital part.

Newman climbed in behind the wheel of a four-wheel-drive. Paula came behind him, noticed Butler was stumbling, helped him climb into the back and joined him. Newman drove off.

Marler had taken over the wheel of the second vehicle. Philip leapt in beside him while Nield jumped into the back. They followed Newman who was already driving like a madman to the road leading down the mountain.

A menacing rumble like thunder made Paula look back. She was awestruck as she gazed at the spectacle. The whole mountain below the peak was collapsing, a tidal wave of snow and rocks thundering down, smashing through the fence surrounding the ground station, overwhelming the buildings, smashing the wooden edifices housing the scientists. She had no way of knowing Craig had earlier shut off the air-conditioning system.

The ground station vanished, the wooden houses crumbled, disappeared, the tidal wave of rocks and snow rushed down the mountain with gathering speed. Newman caught a glimpse of what was happening in his rear-view mirror and his expression became grim.

'We've done it!' shouted Paula.

'Now we have to survive,' Newman warned.

*You can't out-race an avalanche.*

The words of his advanced instructor when he was once skiing at St Moritz came back to Newman. They did not make him feel any better as he reached the road and began the frightening descent. He knew he couldn't go as fast going down as he had coming up. He'd observed that the avalanche had divided into two great rivers of flooding rock and snow. The major river was veering away from the road. It was the second, smaller river – still an awesome killer – which worried him. It was heading straight for the cliff edge and at some point would roar over the mountain road.

Marler was close behind him as he swung round the bends again, keeping up as fast a pace as he dared. In his vehicle Newman was aware Paula was talking to Butler, her mouth close to his ear, and then she began unfastening his black leather jacket. It was only then he realized Butler was wounded.

He forced himself to resist the impulse to move faster. He couldn't call back, ask Paula how badly Butler was hurt. The implacable roar of the descending avalanche was deafening. At a bend he slowed for a few seconds, glanced back. Paula had taken out her first-aid kit from her shoulder bag.

'Just keep going,' he said to himself. 'Maybe pray a little.'

Paula had opened Butler's jacket, which had a tear in it where a bullet had penetrated. His shirt underneath was bloodstained. She had a tricky job – to cut away a

411

portion of the shirt with the vehicle rocking from side to side. She managed it, was surprised – and relieved – to find he wore only one woollen vest, very bloodstained. She told him to keep as still as he could, then carefully cut away a portion of the vest. The bullet could be seen, embedded in his flesh.

'This will hurt,' she warned him, mouth close to his ear. 'I have to guard against infection. Now . . .' She treated the wound. Butler remained quite still.

'Does it hurt?' she asked.

'Only when I laugh.'

God, she thought, he's tough, is our Mr Harry Butler. She applied dressings and a bandage, then tucked his clothes back in position. Looking up, she shuddered.

Newman's hands instinctively tightened on the wheel. Ahead was a huge overhang of rock, way above them but curving over the narrow ledge the road ran along. Pouring across the overhang was an endless cascade of huge rocks, snow and shale. At the moment it was carried by its momentum straight into the precipice on one side of the road.

Was it his imagination, Newman wondered? The overhang seemed to be slowly bending under the strain of the second river crashing over it. The cascade was about fifty yards below Newman on a rare straight stretch. He saw patches of ice appearing under the snow covering the road. Once again he resisted an almost overpowering impulse to speed up dangerously. His eyes never left the overhang as he drove closer and closer.

The deafening rumble rose to a crescendo. Paula felt relieved about one thing only. She had dealt with Butler's wound. It would have been impossible for him to hear a word she said now. She sat transfixed, gazing at the on-coming cascade as larger rocks – boulders – toppled from the overhang. Butler nudged her.

She glanced at him. He was grinning, gave her a

thumb's-up sign. She forced herself to smile, squeezed his arm, then stared ahead again. Remembering that Marler, behind him, had to pass under the cascade, Newman took a chance, pressed his foot gently on the accelerator. He felt the vehicle begin to skid towards the abyss, went with it, turned the wheel slowly. Inches from the drop the vehicle responded, returned to the ledge. Now he was passing under the cascade. The sound hammered at their eardrums. Then they were past it.

Paula looked back quickly. She saw Marler's face and he had never looked so grim. He nodded at her, passing under the cascade, smiled at her. As she continued looking back she saw the overhang give way, a vast chunk of rock falling on to the ledge, followed by a stream of rocks, snow and shale piling up over the immense rock now blocking the road. She sighed with relief and sagged against the back of the seat. The horrific noise was fading. Butler leaned towards her.

'Bit close that, wasn't it?'

To his right Newman saw the helicopter escaping with Brazil on board descending towards the airfield outside Sion. He wondered what Tweed was doing, how he would react.

# 44

Tweed endured one of the most agonizing experiences of his career. Standing outside the canteen in the bitter cold, he had witnessed the cataclysmic events high up on the Kellerhorn through a pair of field glasses.

If only I could have been up there with them, was his recurring thought.

He had not been able to pick out individual figures, but he had seen the enormous collapse of the mountain as it turned into a rolling avalanche. He guessed that Newman's rocket launcher had triggered this off. He felt thankful he had brought the weapon, but fearful for the survival of his team.

His vigil had been interrupted by phone calls from Beck.

'How is it going, Tweed?'

'The ground station has been destroyed. A huge avalanche.'

'A natural one, of course,' Beck had replied quickly. 'We do get them at this time of the year. There have been a number of small ones in the Valais already.'

'This is a monster.'

'I understand. Tweed, Brazil's pilot has filed a flight plan by radio, a flight plan for the jet to take off soon for Zurich.'

'I'd better let him go.'

'Please do,' Beck had urged. 'We shall track his movements nonstop . . .'

That had been the third call. Tweed had rushed outside with his glasses again. Even without his glasses he could see an immense cloud of dust rising above the Kellerhorn. Then he saw the helicopter. He decided to stay under cover when it landed. Brazil was escaping, leaving behind his own men to face the music. Some music, Tweed thought, then he caught sight of vehicles moving down the mountain road.

Fearfully, he focused his binoculars on the two four-wheel-drive vehicles. He thought he could see Newman driving the first one and Marler behind the wheel of the one close behind. Then, appalled, he saw the avalanche cascading over the precipice, the two vehicles approaching it.

He held the glasses very steady, glued to his eyes. He was counting how many people were in the vehicles. Six. He heaved a sigh of relief. He thought he saw Paula in the rear of the first vehicle. Then his relief turned to chronic anxiety. They were close to the hideous cascade.

He had an almost irresistible desire to stop watching, but continued to stare through the lenses. He saw them pass under the cascade, then saw the overhang collapse, realized that had that happened seconds earlier it would have hurled both vehicles over the precipice.

'Christ,' he said aloud.

Few people had heard Tweed swear. No one had heard him use sacrilegious language.

He lowered the glasses. His arms and wrists were aching with the tension. The helicopter was coming closer. His team was safe now. They'd make it the rest of the way down the mountain. Time to get under cover. He went into the canteen where a nice Swiss girl was on duty.

'I could do with a cup of coffee,' he said. 'Very strong. Please.'

'You look exhausted,' she said in French, the language he had used. 'Shall I put a drop of cognac in the coffee?'

'Yes, I think you'd better. Then I'll go and sit in the room set aside for me. A helicopter is landing. You don't know I'm here.'

'But you are not here,' she said, and gave him a lovely smile as she handed him the cup and saucer.


Inside the room, he locked the door, sagged onto a couch, sipped at the drink. He rarely touched alcohol but he found its warmth comforting as it settled in his stomach. He got up, closed the curtains over the window, so no one could see inside, sagged again on the couch.

He heard the helicopter landing a few minutes later. It's a good job I haven't a gun, he was thinking. I'd go out and shoot the swine.

He sipped more of his coffee and cognac, wondered

415

why now he was so warm. He was still wearing his overcoat. He took it off, sat down again. Outside he could hear the whine of a jet's engines starting up. Brazil doesn't waste much time, he mused. I suppose that's why he's got where he has. Well, he won't stay on top of his pinnacle much longer if I have anything to do with it. The phone in the room rang. He snatched up the receiver to stop the noise.

'Tweed?' Beck again.

'Speaking. The chopper with Brazil on board has landed. I can hear his jet starting up.'

'Radar will track him all the way to Zurich. I'll have men at Kloten to follow him wherever he goes in this city.'

'Are you going to arrest him?'

'For what? I have no evidence.'

'Of course. Just wanted to check.'

'I'm really phoning to say Inspector Leon Vincenau will be arriving shortly on an express from Geneva. He's of medium height, and fat. He'll show you identification. I've instructed him to give you full cooperation. He thinks he travelled with one of your team recently from Geneva on the early morning express.'

'That would be Philip Cardon.'

'Keep in touch. Thank you for all you're doing . . .'

Tweed put down the phone, surprised that Beck had thanked him. Then it struck Tweed that Beck regarded Brazil as an enemy – but because of Beck's official position he could never have attempted what Newman's team had achieved.

Hearing the jet's engines building up power, Tweed risked pulling the curtains aside slightly, peered through the crack. The white jet stood at the end of the tarmac, ready for take-off. Igor the wolfhound was leaping delightedly up the staircase, vanished inside, followed by Brazil.

There was a pause, presumably while Brazil settled himself in, then the mobile staircase was removed. The engines climbed into a powerful nonstop roar, the jet sped ever faster down the runway, lifted off, headed upwards into the clear blue sky.

Tweed watched it as it flew towards the mountain peaks at what seemed a dangerously low altitude. He went on watching – in the vague hope the machine would smash into one of the fearsome jagged peaks. It cleared them, flew out of sight.

'Well, at least I know where you're going to, my friend.'

Tweed later heard the two four-wheel-drives approaching, went out to meet them. A small portly man wearing a dark business suit hurried up to him.

'Mr Tweed? I am Inspector Leon Vincenau from Geneva. I have been instructed by my chief, Arthur Beck, to give you every assistance.'

'Thank you. Excuse me, my team has arrived.'

Paula dived out of the back of her vehicle, ran across to Tweed, and flung her arms round him. He hugged her.

'Am I glad to see you!' she said, standing back. 'Harry Butler has a bullet in his thigh. I treated it, dressed it as best I could . . .'

'Pardon me.' It was Vincenau who had heard what she had said. 'You have a wounded man? With the bullet in him? Then he must be rushed to hospital in Sion. I will make all the arrangements. I must use a phone.'

'Take me to Harry.' Tweed stared. 'Look, he's trying to get out by himself.'

Paula ran to the vehicle Harry was laboriously clambering out of. Newman, who had left the vehicle after telling him to stay where he was, also swung round, running back. Paula got there first, with Tweed and Newman close behind her.

417

'You damned fool,' Paula admonished him.

'Always have been, always will be,' Butler said with a grin.

Tweed took one arm, Paula the other as they helped him towards the canteen. Butler kept telling them all this was unnecessary but they ignored him. When they had him settled on a couch in a private room, he grimaced, then looked at them.

'All this stupid fuss. Anyone would think I'd been shot.'

Vincenau put down the phone, told Tweed an ambulance was on the way. Paula said she would go with him. Tweed called Beck, told him what had happened. Beck asked to speak to Vincenau when they had finished talking.

'I'll get the name of the hospital he's being taken to in Sion. I'll call the chief administrator, tell him if Butler is fit to board the jet after treatment I'll have an ambulance standing by at Kloten to rush him to a clinic here. Put Leon on, if you would . . .'

As they waited for the ambulance Tweed studied the faces of the people in his team. They all showed signs of strain – except for Marler who stood leaning against one of the walls, smoking a king-size. Marler was indestructible. Butler, he saw thankfully, had fallen asleep.

'What's the next move?' asked Newman, his face drawn with fatigue.

'We stay here, give you all a rest,' Tweed said firmly.

'Brazil's got away . . .'

'I know. Forget about him. For the moment. Beck will be tracking him. At the present Brazil is on his way back to Zurich.'

'Can he arrest him?'

'No. I asked Beck that same question. No evidence.'

'No evidence!' Newman repeated.

Sagged in a chair, he recalled what he had seen on the

418

battlefield in the mountains. Bodies lying all over the snow, all looking very dead. Some crumpled in pathetic attitudes as though only asleep. Certainly they were thugs, men who lived by the gun, but they lay there, doubtless for ever, because of a man called Brazil, who was probably now drinking coffee in a comfortable chair aboard his luxurious jet. Reliving the horror, Newman felt sick in his stomach, but nothing showed in his face. It was all part of the job.

The ambulance arrived, took a still protesting Butler with Paula accompanying him to the hospital in Sion. By then Newman had drunk several cups of strong coffee, was feeling more like a human being.

He proceeded to give Tweed a concise report of everything that had happened. Tweed listened, watching Newman for signs of returning fatigue. At one stage he deliberately turned to Nield to ask him to enlarge on a point. Nield immediately caught on that Tweed thought Newman had talked enough and completed the story. He used his little finger to smooth down his neat moustache when he had finished.

'So the ground station is totally destroyed?' Tweed asked.

'A complete write-off,' said Marler, entering the conversation for the first time. 'Flattened under so many tons of rock I don't think the Swiss will ever bother to try and unearth it.'

'And the cabins the scientists occupied?'

'Another write-off. For the same reason.'

'That doesn't disturb you? The thought of all those high-flying scientists perishing with their wives?'

'Not really,' Marler responded. 'After all, they created the system which caused world chaos – and knew what they were doing. And, I'm sure, were being paid huge fortunes to work for Brazil. World could be a quieter place without them.'

'An interesting point of view,' Tweed mused.

'I'm glad we're staying on in Sion,' Newman said, standing up and putting his coat on.

'Where are you off to?' Tweed snapped.

'To the Hôtel Élite to get some sleep. It was your suggestion. I need to be fresh for tonight. I think now we should all stay at the Élite. They'll have a decent room for you, Tweed. And you're looking a bit flaked out, if you don't mind my saying so.'

'I do mind!' Tweed reared up. 'I've just been sitting on my backside while everyone else was up on the Kellerhorn.'

'Worrying yourself sick as you watched through those binoculars I see beside you. And, talking of sleep – when did you last get some?'

A blank look came on Tweed's face. He realized he could not remember the answer to that question.

'I thought so,' said Newman, reading his expression. 'I recommend a meal for you as soon as we get back – if you can face one. Then straight to bed for you, Mr Tweed.'

'And I had a strange idea I was in charge of this outfit,' Tweed said ruefully.

'We all dwell under our illusions,' commented Marler, poker-faced.

'Anyone else care to comment on the state of my health?' Tweed enquired, looking round.

'Yes,' said Philip, who had sat quietly so far, not saying anything. 'You look terrible.'

'You're taking after Paula,' Tweed replied.

'I'm leaving for the Élite now,' Newman said with a return of his normal vigour. 'I'll take Philip and Pete Nield with me. Marler can bring you later when you've rested here a bit longer. You do look terrible!'

420

'Bob!' Tweed called out as Philip, putting on his coat opened the door, disappeared. Newman paused at the open door. 'Why did you say earlier,' Tweed went on, 'that you needed to be fresh for tonight?'

'Because The Motorman is in Sion. I want to kill him before he kills someone else . . .'

Tweed blinked, trying to keep his eyes open. He stood up, hurried to the open door.

'Bob,' he shouted. 'I know who The Motorman is.'

His words were lost as Philip, behind the wheel, started the engine of the four-wheel-drive and Newman dived into the seat beside him.

# 45

Darkness had fallen on Sion when Philip, wakened by his alarm, compelled himself to get up, stumbled across to the bathroom, turned on the cold water tap, and sluiced his face, hands, and arms. It seemed very quiet in his room as he dressed quickly for bitter weather. He still hated silence when he was alone – it brought back memories of Jean.

He decided it wasn't worth putting on the radio, which had become his friend. He left his room, went downstairs and out into the Siberian night. He was going to visit the Marchats – he felt it was the least he could do, to tell them what had happened. After all, the information they had given him had helped the success of the operation on the Kellerhorn.

The night seemed even colder than it had been when with Paula he had visited the Marchats. Frequently, he stopped suddenly, looking back down a dark tunnel of a street, anxious in case he led The Motorman to two more possible victims. He heard nothing, saw nothing. The heavy silence of a windless night pressed down on him. The moon was obscured by clouds.

His feet made no sound on the hard rocklike snow as he finally turned the corner leading to the colony of old houses. In his hand he held his Walther, a precaution he had taken the moment he left the Élite he had moved to.

Again no lights showed in the ancient house where the Marchats lived, set back from the houses on either side. No light shed even a gleam from the closed shutters. Taking one last look behind him, standing close to another house's wall, he walked up to the heavy front door. Stopped.

The door was open a few inches. No chain across it. By now Philip's eyes had become well accustomed to seeing in the dark. The cold had penetrated his coat earlier, but now he was chilled to the bone. Chilled with dread.

He eased the door open inch by inch in case it creaked. It didn't. Karin Marchat kept the hinges well oiled. He stepped inside, a torch in his left hand, listened, listened for the breathing of another human being. Not another sound, except his own suppressed breathing.

Crouching down, to make a smaller target, he switched on the torch. The beam shone on Anton Marchat, lying at the foot of his favourite rocking-chair, his neck twisted at a grotesque angle, his eyes staring into eternity. Philip, who hardly ever used foul language, swore foully to himself. He advanced into the room.

The door to what he presumed was the kitchen was open. Again no light. He approached it cautiously, saw nothing he would bump into, switched off his torch which made him a perfect target. Reaching the open door, he listened again for another man's breathing. Heard nothing.

He stood to one side of the open door, switched on his torch. It nearly jumped in his hand. Karin was lying with

422

the upper half of her body sprawled over the working surface, her head inside the enamel sink full of water, her head twisted in a weird way beneath the water, which gave the angle of her neck an even more grotesque appearance.

As if he had witnessed the murder, Philip saw what had happened. Karin had run screaming into the kitchen, followed by The Motorman who had dealt with Anton. Her screaming had annoyed him, so he had turned on both taps, filling the sink swiftly, then he had forced her head under the water to shut her up. She was probably half-drowning when his hands had done their devilish work, breaking her neck. Water was slopped all over the tiled floor.

Philip left the house of death, ran back to the Élite to tell Newman.


Newman had woken out of a deep sleep, had washed, dressed, combed his hair, when the phone rang.

'Yes, who is it?'

'You can recognize my voice, I am sure.'

Archie's. Soft and calm as usual. Little more than a whisper.

'Yes, I can.'

'I am going up the huge rock which rises up behind Marchat's house. There is only one pathway. The beginning is behind his house. The Motorman is out. I am going to lead him up to the top. This time you can get him – the pathway is the only way back . . .'

'Archie!' In his desperation Newman let out the name. The phone had gone dead.

He was reaching for his overcoat when someone rapped on his door. Despite his anxiety to leave at once Newman had the Smith & Wesson in his hand when he unlocked the door, opened it a few inches, then flung it wide open. Philip, ashen faced, walked in, closed the door.

'I've just come back from the Marchats' home. I was going to tell them what had happened, to thank them for their help.'

'I've got to leave—'

'I found both Anton and Karin murdered, their necks broken. Karin had been half-drowned in a sink full of water before he broke her neck . . .'

'I've had a call from Archie.' Newman was putting on his coat, picking up his gloves. 'He's going up that hunk of rock behind their house. The Motorman is still there. Archie is using himself as bait. I'm off . . .'

'I'll come with you.'


They ran through the night. They ran, keeping pace with each other like racers in a marathon approaching the finishing post. Again the streets were deserted, but this was the middle of the night. It was not snowing and the ground was still paved with hard-packed snow, so there was no ice to trip them up. And the moon was shining brilliantly.

The looming mass of the great rock came into view. Philip took the lead, knowing the way to the Marchats' home. He went behind the house, explored swiftly, found the start of a steep, narrow path protected on one side by a drystone wall. They paused to catch their breath and Newman put out his hand.

'Philip, you wait here. If The Motorman gets me he has to come back down this way. Then you kill him.'

'I'd sooner come with you . . .'

'Who's in command of this team?' snapped Newman. 'That was an order.'

Philip gritted his teeth, watched Newman start to climb, moving swiftly and silently, the Smith & Wesson in his hand. He watched him until he disappeared round a bend higher up, then he stepped back into the shadows thrown by the houses, slipped his Walther out of his holster.

Because he couldn't see – or hear – what was happening, Philip couldn't keep still. His eyes never left the path as he paced a few steps one way, then another. He almost disobeyed Newman and followed him up, but all his training had drilled into him that you took orders from the head man in a team.

Newman, thankful only that the moonlight showed him the footpath, which here and there had patches of ice and sharp stones protruding above the snow, continued his ascent. To his right a panoramic view was opening up of the snowbound rooftops of Sion which, at that hour, looked like a dead city. He glanced at it only once and then concentrated on reaching the top, thinking of poor little Archie at the mercy of a professional killing machine.

At the summit, some distance above where Newman ran, Archie pulled up the collar of his coat against the freezing cold. He was standing in the shadow of the Chapel, an ancient building which looked like a ruin by the light of the moon. Left-handed, he adjusted the cigarette stub in the corner of his mouth. It gave him a certain comfort.

He was at the top of the path and in front of him, a few feet away, there was a break in the outer drystone wall where it had crumbled. He wriggled his toes inside his shoes to try and bring back the circulation.

Out of the shadows behind him a waiting shadow emerged silently. The first Archie knew of his presence was when a powerful arm was wrapped round his neck. He sagged back against the figure.

'You've talked too much,' a reedy voice said in English. 'Now you'll never talk again.'

Archie's left hand clawed out the small automatic in

his pocket, quickly pressed the muzzle against the lower part of the strangling arm, just below the elbow. He pulled the trigger. The arm relaxed, there was a groan of pain, the arm fell away from him. He took two steps forward carefully, near the gap in the wall, swung round.

He held the automatic in both hands now, aimed at the stomach of the figure which had straightened up. They stood looking at each other for a few tense moments.

'You can't shoot me again,' said Bill Franklin in his normal voice.

'I can empty the magazine into your stomach without a second thought,' Archie said. 'Now, turn your back to me or I'll pull the trigger again.'

On Franklin's face disbelief and fear were mingled. He turned round, stood with his back to Archie.

'Now step backward a few paces so we are not so close,' said Archie, moving to one side.

Franklin was moving backwards, as ordered, forcing himself to move his right arm, flexing the fingers of his right hand, waiting for the chance to throw himself at Archie, to knock the automatic to one side.

At that moment Newman appeared at the top of the path in a rush. He stopped, stunned as he gazed at the scene unfolding, remaining perfectly still so as not to distract Archie. He had never felt so taken aback in his life.

'I told you to take several paces,' Archie ordered. 'I'm about to press the trigger nonstop if you don't do what I told you to do.'

There was something in the quiet tone of Archie's voice which scared Franklin. He noticed that the automatic levelled at his stomach was steady, showed no sign of even a quiver. Newman gazed in fascination as Franklin obeyed the order.

His second step took him through the gap into space over the precipice below. He yelled, fell, grabbed with both hands at the edge of the path, his fingers clawing at,

426

holding on to two small rocks protruding above the snow.

'Help me!' he screamed. 'For God's sake have pity.'

'It depends on whether you tell the truth,' said Archie. 'First, you are The Motorman?'

'Yes! Craig paid me a lot of money.'

'To kill, among other victims,' Archie continued, 'the bartender, Ben, at Bowling Green in Wareham?'

'Yes! Yes!' Franklin yelled desperately.

'And Rico Sava in Geneva was another victim?'

'Yes! I can't hold on much longer . . .'

'And Anton and Karin Marchat here in Sion,' Archie went on remorselessly.

'Yes! Yes! Yes . . .'

Franklin's right hand slipped off the rock. He held on with his left hand, sweat pouring down his face, freezing into small beads of ice almost at once. His right hand reappeared, clutched again at the rock.

'Time to go,' said Archie.

'You can't leave me here!' screamed Franklin. 'I can't hold on much longer.'

'Those people you killed horribly were my friends,' Archie told him.

He started to walk back down the path and Newman followed him. They descended in silence for some time. Newman could not think of anything to say – he was still stunned by what had happened. Of all people – Archie.

'He'll have dropped by now,' Newman said as they arrived at the bottom of the path.

Philip was standing on the far side of the road in the moonlight, staring up. They joined him, looking up to the summit. A tiny figure was still hanging there, suspended over the almost sheer precipice, which had occasional outcrops of huge boulders. No one spoke after Newman had told Philip: 'It's The Motorman up there. Guess who he is. It's Bill Franklin . . .'

427

He had just spoken when the hanging figure began its fall. Franklin plunged down, struck an outcrop with a force which made Newman wince, was bounced off and then turned as he completed his fall, landing on the snow a hundred yards from where they stood with an unpleasant crunching sound.

'Why didn't you finish him off up there?' Newman asked.

'I'm not a sadist,' Archie replied, 'far from it. But he made many people suffer, the friends and relatives of all those people he murdered, I believe in crime *and* punishment.'

# 46

'How on earth did you know The Motorman was Bill Franklin?' Newman asked Tweed. 'I *thought* I heard you call out as I rushed away from the airfield.'

It was late the next day and Newman was driving Tweed to the airfield with Butler and Paula in the back. Butler had insisted on being discharged from the hospital in Sion, overriding the doctor.

'A chance incident,' Tweed explained. 'I was with Professor Grogarty, a tall well-built man, in Harley Street. He was stooped over and suddenly straightened up. It struck me that Keith Kent is of medium height – as Grogarty looked when he stooped. But when Grogarty straightened up he was the height of Bill Franklin. We know The Motorman, whenever described, stooped. It was his way of disguising that he was tall. Simple.'

'Simple,' Paula called out, 'but you noticed it, unlike so many people would have done – and drew the right conclusion. I'm still flabbergasted that it should have been Bill. He seemed such a nice chap.'

'Which is what people say after the event about a lot of killers,' Tweed reminded her.

The rest of the day had been full of frenetic activity. Butler had had the bullet removed from his thigh at the hospital. The doctor had said it was just a deep flesh wound, that he had been lucky. Butler had spun him a yarn about how he was checking his Walther, not realizing it was loaded, and had shot himself. Paula had explained Arthur Beck, Chief of Federal Police, was a friend and this had satisfied the doctor. Plus the fact that Beck had arranged for an ambulance to meet the jet when they arrived in Zurich.

Tweed had been on the line from the Hôtel Élite, where he had moved to, calling Beck. Which was how they knew Brazil was still at the Baur-en-Ville in Bahnhofstrasse. Tweed was determined to arrive in the city before Brazil left it.

All Sion was talking about the avalanche on the Kellerhorn.

Prior to Tweed leaving the airfield, he had witnessed a second avalanche roaring down from the summit. The second tidal wave of rocks and shale had buried the bodies of Brazil's men. Searching the mountain through his field glasses, he had seen no sign of any of the casualties. He doubted that they would ever be discovered.

'No need for that ambulance when we get to Zurich,' Butler called out. 'I feel fighting fit.'

'You will go in the ambulance,' Paula told him sternly. 'I'll be coming with you. We're not going to risk any infection setting in. So pipe down.'

'You're bossy,' Butler grumbled.

'I know I am,' replied Paula, and laughed.

Close behind them Marler drove the other vehicle with Philip beside him and Nield in the back. They all carried satchels, containing the remains of their armoury.

429

On the way down the mountain the previous day, Newman had stopped briefly when they were passing a narrow setback in the mountain. Carrying the rocket launcher, he had eased his way inside the crevice, had found a deep hole in the ground. He had dropped the launcher down it and when he never heard it hit bottom he knew he had chosen the right place.

It was still daylight when they reached the airfield. Tweed had warned the controller they were coming, had asked him to alert the aircrew. Paula looped her arm inside Butler's to help him up the mobile staircase. His only comment had been amiable.

'And I never thought you cared . . .'

The jet took off minutes after they were all aboard, climbed steeply and headed for the mountains. Paula, by a window seat, looked down on the Kellerhorn, thinking she never wished to see it again. Then it was dark. Tweed called back to the others.

'Beck knows we're coming. He'll have two unmarked cars to take us to the Schweizerhof. We'll be in time for dinner.'


After landing in Zurich in his white jet, Brazil had been driven to a bank in Bahnhofstrasse. To his fury he found the bank had just closed. Inside were the proceeds he had obtained by secretly selling some of the bearer bonds in his possession. The considerable sum of cash they had been converted into was his nest egg.

Fuming to himself, he had ordered his driver to take him back to the Baur-en-Ville. It meant staying overnight in the Swiss city. Not a prospect he desired – his one desire was to return to Dorset, to get out of Switzerland quickly.

When he walked into the lounge Eve was sitting in a chair, reading a fashion magazine. She was wearing an expensive white two-piece suit which she had just bought.

'Have a good trip?' she called out.

Brazil walked straight past her, as though unaware of her existence. He disappeared inside a lift. She dropped the magazine.

'Rude devil,' she muttered. 'You can get stuffed.'

To get over her annoyance she lit a fresh cigarette from the one she had been smoking, stood up, and strolled into the bar. Perching on a stool, she ordered a large vodka, downed it, ordered another. She made eye contact with several men who gazed at her with interest. She held their gaze just long enough to make them think she was intrigued, then tossed her head and looked away.

She spent several hours in the bar, drinking more vodka, but still remaining as sober as the proverbial judge. Then she decided she would have a long walk. Newman was on her mind. Now Brazil had returned she felt sure Newman and Tweed would reappear. Newman was her target. She had never given a thought to Philip since Brazil had left for Sion.

It piqued her that, because of the cold, she had to put on the overcoat she had carried into the bar. She would have liked to flaunt her new outfit along Bahnhofstrasse, watching men lick their lips at the sight of her.

She walked in the direction of Bahnhofplatz and the Hotel Schweizerhof. Entering the lobby, she marched up to the concierge, her manner supremely confident.

'I have an appointment with Mr Robert Newman when he arrives,' she lied.

'He's expected any moment.'

The concierge stopped speaking, wondering if he had committed an indiscretion. He was standing in for the permanent concierge and had not yet sorted out who was who. The very attractive woman with the imperious

431

attitude had given him the impression she was staying at the hotel, which had been Eve's intention.

You can fool men any time, she thought as she descended the steps into the Bistro leading off the lobby.

This further confirmed to the concierge that she was a guest and he felt better. He would not have felt so relieved had he seen Eve leave the Bistro immediately by the second door on to the street.

She descended by an escalator into Shopville, the shopping centre under the *platz*. Ignoring the shops – she preferred Bahnhofstrasse where the prices were sky-high – she rode up an escalator on the far side which took her into the main station. She then stood at the top of the steps a few feet inside the station. From here she could see any arrivals at the Schweizerhof.

She had been so concentrating on the pleasant feel of the new suit under her coat it never occurred to her that she might have been followed from the Baur-en-Ville. Across the *platz*, standing in a doorway, Gustav patiently waited, never taking his eyes off Eve.


Tweed and Newman, carrying their cases, with Philip behind them, left the unmarked police car which had brought them from Kloten Airport. They disappeared inside the Schweizerhof. Still wary, Tweed had arranged for Marler and Nield to stay at the Gotthard nearby.

Arriving at the airport, priority had been given to Butler, who, with Paula in attendance, had been taken off the jet first, put inside a waiting ambulance, rushed to a hospital where a waiting staff and doctor had examined him at once.

The doctor, expecting far worse, had been surprised. He had treated Butler, replaced the bandages. Then he had a word with Paula in the corridor outside the private room where Butler was kicking up merry hell.

'No sign of infection, Miss Grey, the doctor at Sion did a good job. He's very rebellious. What would happen if I let him go now?'

'I'd take him to a hotel, make him go to bed and rest.'

'Really what he now needs is a good night's sleep.'

'I'll see he gets that,' Paula had replied with determination.

'Mr Beck has supplied an unmarked police car to take him from here when I give the go-ahead. Mr Butler doesn't like anything medical. I think you should take him to a hotel.'

Which is how Eve, who had walked halfway across the *platz* and was standing on a pedestrian platform, came to see a car pull up outside the hotel, a tough-looking man get out, while Paula firmly held one arm.

Paula happened to glance across the *platz*, saw Eve staring. Their eyes met for a brief moment. Paula's expression was blank but Eve's was full of venom. She disliked Paula and sneered to herself. So that's her boy friend, she thought, and she hangs onto his arm like a leech.

Accompanying Butler inside, Paula told the concierge he had had a fall so could she take him up to his room at once? She would bring his passport down shortly and deal with the registration. The concierge agreed without hesitation, gave her the number and key of a good room on the first floor.

Paula was troubled as she took Butler to his room and waited in the bathroom while he got undressed and into the pyjamas he had unpacked from the case she had carried. It was the unexpected sight of Eve which worried her and made her think furiously. Should she tell Philip? In spite of what he had said earlier she knew some women had only to crook their little finger and the men came running.

After he was settled in bed and had given Paula his

passport, Butler promptly fell fast asleep. She phoned the concierge, obtained the number of her own room and an assurance that the housekeeper would be waiting outside her room with the key.

She unpacked very quickly, went down to the concierge, completed the registrations, went back up to Tweed's room. The three of them were sitting in armchairs – Tweed, Philip, and Newman. Taking a deep breath, she turned to Philip as she sat down thankfully, crossing her legs.

'Philip, I saw Eve floating about in the *platz*.'

'Let her float – to kingdom come as far as I'm concerned. Don't want to see that woman again. Ever.'

'Curious she should be near this hotel,' said the ever-suspicious Tweed.

'I suppose she's staying with Brazil,' Paula remarked.

'He's welcome to her,' said Philip. 'They make a pretty pair.'


Eve crossed the *platz* to outside the Schweizerhof, weighing up whether to go in and ask for Newman. No, best to phone him, bearing in mind what she was going to demand.

She hurried back to the phone box in Bahnhofstrasse she had used before. Opening a small notebook, she checked the number of the Schweizerhof and called it, asking for Mr Robert Newman.

There was a pause. Newman was on his way back to his own room and heard the phone ringing as he entered. Locking the door, he ran to the phone.

'Yes, who is it?'

'Bob, it's Eve. I've missed you.'

'All right. What are you after?'

'Don't be like that. We could make music together.'

'Discordant music.'

434

'You're not being at all nice to me.'

'Get to the point.'

'I will.' Her voice hardened. 'How would you like the scoop of your career? Something so sensational you would hit the headlines all over the world.'

'Go on, if you must.'

'I can give you the real story of Leopold Brazil. And I have evidence to back it up. How he seduced twenty of the world's top scientists to work for him.'

'Did he?' Newman enquired in a bored voice.

'You listen to me,' she snarled. 'I had notes taken from his secret files giving all the intimate details about those missing scientists. Later, I was able to photograph the sheets from those files. Ed Reynolds, Irina Krivitsky, and others. Are you listening?'

'Vaguely.'

'I want one hundred thousand pounds for the information.'

'You don't want much, do you?'

'You can syndicate your exposé. You'll make another fortune. I'm offering it to you cheap for one hundred thousand pounds. Other people would pay one helluva sight more.'

'Go to other people.'

'You'd make the most terrific job of it. I've read some of your stuff. And on top of the hundred thousand I'd want five per cent of the total profits.'

'You're making my mouth water,' he said cynically.

'When you ponder it you'll come round to my way of thinking. I'm at the Baur-en-Ville. Give your name as Cross when you phone me.'

'Mr Double-Cross?'

Newman put down the phone. He had a reaction of complete revulsion.

# 47

Eve flounced out of the phone box, hurried back to the Baur-en-Ville. She was going to the bar. She needed a large vodka.

Gustav had watched her from inside a shop front across the street. As soon as she was hidden by an approaching tram he ran across to the phone box. A grim-looking woman had her hand reached out for the door of the phone box. He brushed her aside, ignored her abuse, pretended to look up a number.

As soon as she had gone he detached the miniature listening and recording device he had hidden, pulling hard at the suckers which held it in place. Gustav had hoped that if she made another call she would use the phone box he had seen her use before.

He wasted no time getting back to his office in the hotel. Once inside, he locked the door, extracted the cassette, placed it in the machine which played it back, listened with growing excitement. He had never liked Eve.

He was walking along the corridor to Brazil's room when his chief came up behind him. Gustav dropped back as Eve came out of her room. She had freshened herself up and was on her way to the bar.

'Where is José?' she asked.

'José decided to stay behind,' Brazil told her cheerfully. 'I think he's gone home.'

'I'll be in the bar if you want me,' she said.

'Where else?' replied Brazil, even more cheerfully.

He was unlocking his door when Gustav came up behind him, said he'd like a private word.

'Is it important?' asked Brazil.

'I think you should judge that for yourself.'

'Oh, all right. You'd better come in. But not for long.'

Brazil sat behind his desk, hoping Gustav would soon go away. He wanted to listen to the latest radio reports – particularly if anything had slipped through about the situation in Moscow.

'I want to play you a tape,' Gustav said.

Brazil frowned, nodded his head, sat back while Gustav inserted the tape in the machine on his desk, pressed the play button. Nothing changed in his expression as he heard what was on the tape. Brazil had iron self-control. When the tape ran out Gustav looked at his boss expectantly.

'I had seen her go into that phone box before,' he explained. 'So, thinking she might use it again, I attached one of my recorders inside the box. The same recorder which I put under José's desk.'

'Leave the tape with me.'

'You don't want me to . . .'

'I want you to go and get on with your work.'

He waited until Gustav had left, got up, locked the door and returned to his desk. Gustav had rewound the tape before leaving. Brazil pressed the play button and listened again.

. . . the scoop of your career . . .

I can give you the real story of Leopold Brazil . . .

. . . I was able to photograph the sheets from those files . . .

. . . one hundred thousand pounds for the information . . .

When the tape was finished Brazil rewound it, extracted the cassette, slipped it into his pocket. He sat down again behind his desk, his expression grim.

I trusted her, he thought. I paid her a huge salary, but even that wasn't enough. More treachery among my own

437

ranks. Greed is her driving force. Loyalty to no one except her hideous self.

Brazil spent a long time gazing at the opposite wall, replaying in his mind what he had heard on the tape. He pulled himself together with a jerk, switched on the radio.

Now he would never be able to send the second signal – which would have obliterated *all* world communications. But he had done enough to give Marov the opportunity to seize full control. Russia was now again a major power, a menace which would wake up the West.


Newman had sat in his own room for awhile. He was writing down in his swift hand the gist of his conversation with Eve Warner. Then he had a good wash, brushed his hair, and went along to Tweed's room.

Tweed was listening to the World Service as more and more reports came through. Paula sat in a chair close to Philip as they also listened. Tweed switched off the radio when Newman was let in by Philip.

'Brazil has achieved a lot of his plan,' he told Newman. 'It's strange, but I still find myself agreeing with the blackguard's ideas. I'm sure Brazil planned to send a second signal – probably to do it himself as he was at the ground station – but you stopped him by destroying the ground station. Which is a blessing.'

'Why?' asked Newman.

'One of our agents flew out of Russia before Marov shut down the frontiers. He tried to call me from Frankfurt and talked to Monica when I wasn't available. There have been rumours of Russian troops massing on the border separating Russia from Ukraine. I'm sure Marov – with the aid of the considerable Russian population there – planned to occupy Ukraine. Then we would have faced a huge world crisis.'

'Because Ukraine has a long border with Poland,' Newman suggested.

'Exactly,' agreed Tweed. 'The Russian Army would have loomed over Western Europe. People forget they still have most of the immense armoury of weapons they built up during the Cold War. And it's quite definite that a proclamation has been issued, making all the previously private shops state concerns. Bread rationing has been brought back. The Russian people may not enjoy queuing up but they'll know there is bread to be bought at controlled prices daily.'

'That's Communism,' Newman objected.

'No, it isn't. Marov is being very clever. He's using the bits of Communism which guaranteed food supplies – but the proclamation was issued in the name of All The Russias. The ailing President signed it, but Marov has countersigned it. So we know who is now in charge.'

'Their economy is still in ruins,' Newman objected again.

'Not really. It was when Gorbachev dabbled with a capitalistic economy – and the Mafia took over. It's also been announced the state is taking over all the factories – including those making armaments. With the borders shut down tightly the economy will stabilize.' He changed the subject. 'You took a long time having a bath.'

Newman glanced at Philip, then told them about his long phone conversation with Eve. Philip exploded.

'There you are! She's shown her true face. She'll do anything to grab hold of money.'

'I think she'll try and get back to me,' Newman commented. 'If she does I'll listen again and say nothing.'

'While you were enjoying yourself,' Tweed said with wry humour, 'I had a call from Monica. Howard is spinning round in circles again. I got a taxi over to Beck's HQ. I needed a safe phone to call the PM.'

'What happened?' asked Paula eagerly.

'Howard had disturbed the PM. Of course. I quietened him down, suggested he immediately created a second Rapid Reaction Force, despatched it to Germany. Then brought back conscription. And made the announcement in the House of Commons *before* he informed Washington. I said Britain would appreciate some strong leadership. That got him.'

'And what about Brazil?' asked Philip.

'Oh, we're going to finish him off, one way or another.'

# 48

Gustav came out of his room at the Baur-en-Ville and ran into Eve, just returning from a long session in the bar. His ugly face twisted into what he imagined was a grin, but only succeeded in being a sneering grimace.

'The boss isn't too pleased with you,' he said.

'Oh, really? That's funny. I thought it was the other way round. That he wasn't at all pleased with you. How do you know about me? I think you're lying.'

She waited. Having provoked him she wanted him to give her more information. It was a tactic she often used. Gustav grimaced again.

'A little birdie told me.'

'And what was the name of the little birdie?'

'Wouldn't you like to know? I have to go out now.'

The air simmered with hostility between them. Eve was determined to make him talk.

'I see you're all dressed up for another trip out on the town. Looking for another woman who's cheap enough to accommodate you?'

'I'm going out to keep an eye on the Schweizerhof,' he

spat out, enraged. 'The boss thinks maybe Tweed and his lickspittles are back in town.'

'And you haven't caught on to what he really wants?' she snapped, her mind moving like lightning, bent on revenging this insulting creep. She lowered her voice. 'He wants you to kill Tweed. Think of the great fat bonus he'd give you if you could pull that off.'

Gustav, who was an expert in street fighting – better still in a gun battle – was rather thick, as she had correctly assumed. He stared at her.

'You think that's what he really wants?'

'Of course it is, you stupid man.' She was still seething with anger although careful not to show it. 'He often gives instructions in a suggestive way – assuming you'll have the brains to catch on to what he's telling you to do.'

'I see.'

Gustav unlocked the door to his room, went inside as Eve peered through the open door. Taking a 7.65mm Luger out of a drawer he had unlocked, he slipped it into his deep coat pocket, came out, locked the door. He leered at her.

'You don't think I can do it, do you?'

'Damned sure you can't,' she replied, egging him on.

As she watched him disappearing round a corner she began to think maybe she had gone too far. Running back to her own room, she put on a cashmere coat, locked her door, and ran along the corridor before he vanished into the street.

She knew that, in the heat of her rage, she had calculated that Tweed would be well guarded, that if Gustav did attempt to assassinate Tweed he would be shot down. Now she was trying to work out how to prevent any risk of that happening. Brazil had told her how much he admired Tweed, even though he was leader of the opposition.

She reached the lobby, ran out into the street, was just in time to see Gustav's black-garbed figure hurrying up Bahnhofstrasse. She followed him.

'I promised the PM I would call him back about now,' said Tweed, checking his watch in his bedroom. 'That means a brisk walk over to Beck's HQ to use a safe phone.'

'Take a taxi as you did before,' Newman suggested. 'It is dark outside and Brazil will have it in for you.'

'I'm sure he won't. We got on well together, which is the irony of the situation. Besides, I fancy a breath of fresh air.'

'Then we're coming with you,' said Paula, putting on her coat and slipping the strap of her bag over her shoulder.

'I agree,' said Newman breezily. 'I fancy a breath of ice-cold air myself.'

They descended in the lift. The three of them, with Tweed between his two companions, headed for the exit, walked down the steps after the automatic doors had opened, went out into the night where light traffic sped past the hotel.

Gustav, in his black overcoat, had plodded purposefully up the street. It never occurred to his limited intelligence to question what Eve had told him. Or why a woman he had ignored or sneered at should do him a favour.

He was concentrating on what lay ahead. After he had shot Tweed he would run down into Shopville, across the underground plaza, and up into the main station. There he would slip into a cubicle in a public lavatory, wipe his fingerprints carefully off the gun, then stroll along to the River Limmat where he would pause

442

on the bridge, hands on the parapet, and drop the gun into the water with a gloved hand.

Gustav was one of those killers who worried the police most. They appeared out of nowhere, shot their targets, disappeared by a pre-planned escape route. They were rarely caught. Gustav had killed his first victim when he was eighteen, had shot the man in London's Soho, had then vanished. An older man had trained him, had showed him how to file the serial number off a gun, had emphasized he must know the area where the killing would take place.

'If the police pick you up after you've got rid of the gun you say nothing,' his trainer had hammered into him. 'If, after hours under the bright lights, you get really thirsty, you say you will talk if they give you a drink. Swallow the whole glassful, then say "Thank you," and nothing else. Except if they persist, then you say "I did talk. I said thank you . . ." '

Behind him Eve was hurrying to catch up with him. But she couldn't work out what to say to him. Her fear was that he might be angry enough to use the gun on her. She was in one of her periodic moods of uncertainty. She had set in motion something she didn't know how to stop.

Gustav reached the corner of the *platz* nearest the Hotel Schweizerhof after crossing the street. He paused where he could see the exit, studied the traffic. Not much of it at this hour, only the occasional juggernaut trundling round past the station, half-circling the *platz* and then continuing over the bridge which spanned the Limmat.

His right hand was in the pocket of his coat, gripping the butt of the Luger. He couldn't miss at this range if he was lucky enough for Tweed to come out of the hotel. Gustav was patient, could wait a long time for his target to appear.

443

What he didn't know was that there was another man across the street who was even more patient.

As they stepped on to the pavement outside the Schweizerhof, Newman, Tweed, and Paula paused, adjusting to the bitter cold. From where Gustav stood, Paula was shielding Tweed. He waited.

A juggernaut with a tired driver at the wheel trundled round the *platz* past the station. He had driven for too many hours, over the permitted limit. Newman, Tweed, and Paula began walking towards police HQ. Gustav raised his Luger, aimed point-blank at Tweed. Three shots rang out, so swiftly they almost sounded like one.

Gustav staggered, three bullets in his back, stumbled off the kerb in front of the juggernaut. Too late, the driver applied his air-brakes. His huge truck rolled over the body lying in the road, crushing Gustav's skull and the rest of his body.

'Keep moving,' Newman said quickly. 'Across the street.'

Marler, the automatic he had fired back inside a pocket, met them, joined them as they continued towards Beck's HQ. Tweed said nothing until they turned down a side-street. They heard the distant wail of the sirens of an approaching patrol car near the *platz*.

'Thank you, Marler,' Tweed said quietly. 'How did you know?'

'Thought I'd better take up guard duty outside your hotel. Noticed this chap just standing, stamping his feet as though feeling the cold, but he still stayed there. Decided to keep an eye on him.'

'And you said Brazil admired you,' Newman snorted.

'I saw Eve near this end of Bahnhofstrasse,' Paula said. 'She hoofed it pretty quick when she saw what had happened. I wouldn't put it past that hellcat to have set this up.'


Eve's mind was racing as she hurried back to the Baur-en-Ville. She was in a bad jam and knew it. She had to be the first to inform Brazil of what had happened. She was making up a story in her head as she entered the Baur-en-Ville, got into a lift, hurried to her room.

Once inside she poured herself a stiff vodka, lit a cigarette while she thought. To give herself extra confidence she changed her coat, putting on a long trenchcoat with wide lapels. Earlier, because of its length, it had flapped against her as a wind blew up Bahnhof-strasse from the lake. She stubbed out the cigarette, took a deep breath, went along to Brazil's room, and, this time, knocked on the door.

'Come in.'

Brazil, behind his desk, smiled broadly when he saw who it was. He made his comment as she shut the door and came towards him.

'I like that trenchcoat. You look very smart, my dear.'

'My latest purchase. There's something bad I have to tell you about.'

'First, take off your coat. It's warm in here. Then sit down, make yourself comfortable. I expect you could do with a drink.'

'That would be very pleasant.'

She waited while he poured two vodkas, a large one for her. Going back to the chair behind his desk, he raised his glass, smiled again.

'Cheers! Now, compose yourself and tell me what this is all about.'

'Gustav is dead,' she burst out. 'It's awful. He tried to shoot Tweed, but someone else shot Gustav first. It was ghastly. Gustav fell under a passing juggernaut.'

'So probably,' Brazil said after sipping his drink, 'the police won't easily identify him. In any case, as you know, members of my staff never carry any identification when on a job. I wonder why he tried to kill Tweed?'

'When he went out he was drunk. I passed him in the corridor and smelt it on his breath. I was worried as to what he was up to, so I put on this coat and followed him up Bahnhofstrasse.'

'You say Gustav was drunk?'

'Pretty high, I'd have said. Not reeling. He walked up the street quite steadily. Then when Tweed comes out of the hotel with Newman and Paula Grey he tries to shoot Tweed.'

'Fortunate that it sounds as though Tweed had someone posted outside the hotel, someone armed. I've dismissed François and the other guard I left behind, paid them well. So that just leaves you and me to depart tomorrow.'

'Where?' Eve asked, eyeing him over the rim of her glass.

'Dorset. Grenville Grange. There's one more banker I want you to soften up for me.'

'There aren't any big banks – or top men, anyway – in that sleepy county.'

'Oh yes, there is one. Who lives there in his country farmhouse at the weekends. Separated from his wife, so he'll be interested in some feminine company.'

'Not the bedroom,' she warned.

'Of course not. Have I ever asked you to go that far? They're more pliant when they go on hoping. We'll fly there in the jet, land at Bournemouth International, and I've already arranged for a car to be waiting for us.'

'Sounds as though you've thought of everything.'

'Believe me, I have. Now let's go downstairs and have

a long, leisurely dinner.' He smiled again. 'I could do with some pleasant company myself. You can pack your case tomorrow. I have to call in at a bank.'

# 49

Before Paula and Newman had entered Police HQ, Tweed had warned them not to say anything about the attack on himself.

'It could make life difficult for Beck – he would have to investigate the circumstances of the shooting of the gunman, whoever sent him. That would involve you, Marler. I don't want anything to delay our departure from Zurich when Brazil leaves – which I'm sure he will soon.'

Marler had volunteered to stay outside on guard.

'We can't tell how desperate Brazil is. He may have just changed his mind about you, Tweed. I know this is police headquarters, but four men armed with machine-pistols could rush the place and get inside.'

'Don't freeze to death,' Tweed told him. 'We'll be as quick as we can be.'

Beck jumped up from his desk to greet them warmly. He told the officer who had brought them up to order coffee and cakes for everyone.

'The pastries will be from Sprüngli,' he said when the officer had left the room.

'I'll make a pig of myself,' Paula told him.

'That's why I ordered them,' he replied with a smile. 'Now, I have news. Brazil is playing tricks, I'm sure. Is out to confuse us.'

'What tricks this time?' Tweed enquired.

'The pilot of his jet waiting at Kloten has filed three flight plans provisionally. One for take-off at 11 a.m.

One for 1 p.m. The third for 3 p.m. All being provisional.'

'That's to confuse me,' Tweed said. 'For what destinations?'

'All for the same destination. Bournemouth International Airport.'

'So he's returning to where it all started. Grenville Grange in Dorset. Interesting. We're going after him.'

'I guessed you would,' Beck said with a wry smile. 'You never give up. By the way, after you'd landed in Brazil's plane in an obscure area, I asked the controller to keep the jet under wraps – out of sight in the same area. To have the machine fully refuelled and maintained. A Swiss aircrew will be ready to take off the moment you wish to. It will probably be the same crew which flew you from Sion. They are spending the night getting some sleep.'

A uniformed policewoman had brought in a tray with coffee and pastries. Paula lunged for an exotic concoction with a lot of chocolate and whipped cream.

'Scrumptious,' she announced. 'What a generous plateful. I'm going to have another.'

'That's what they're there for – to be consumed,' said Beck, amused.

'What I'd like to do,' said Tweed, 'is for all of us to be aboard our jet by 10 a.m. Then we're ready to take off soon after Brazil has left – whichever flight plan he uses.'

'It shall be done,' said Beck. 'In which case I'll have two unmarked police cars pick you up from the Schweizerhof at 8.45 a.m. In case Brazil chooses the 11 a.m. flight, you'll be safely aboard the other jet.'

'Your service and organization are truly remarkable,' Tweed commented. 'Thank you for all your help.'

'You'll let me know eventually what has happened to Mr Brazil, please. Heaven knows he's succeeded in turning the world upside-down. Having heard of the decisions in London, the Swiss Army has been put on partial mobilization.'

While Tweed called the PM, Beck picked up napkins, wrapped them round another of the pastries Paula had liked, presented it to her with a little bow.

'I will send you some Sprüngli chocolates, a really big box. For a brave lady.'

'Thank you. You're always so kind to me.'

He hugged her, they left, found Marler chatting up the very attractive policewoman who had served their coffee and cakes.

'Sorry, said Tweed, tapping him on the shoulder, 'but duty calls.'

Marler reacted instantly, walking into the night ahead of them, pausing to glance round the paved space in front of the building, then gesturing for them to follow.

'Tomorrow should see some interesting developments,' Tweed remarked as they made their way back to the Schweizerhof.

'We've had enough interesting developments for today,' Newman rapped back.


Throughout their long dinner, Eve had conversed with Brazil with one part of her mind. Another part was trying to work out how she could contact Newman before they left Zurich. She was convinced Newman was playing hard to get.

The fact that Gustav had been crushed to a pulp under the juggernaut had gone out of her thoughts. It never occurred to her that she was responsible for his grisly death.

To her concealed annoyance, Brazil stretched out the dinner until well after midnight. When he accompanied her upstairs he opened the door to his suite, showed her the wolfhound lying fast asleep on a couch protected with a cloth.

'I fed it before we went down to dinner,' he remarked.

Eve didn't care tuppence whether Igor was fed or not. She said good night and went to her own room. Closing the door, locking it, she lit a fresh cigarette from the one she was smoking, poured herself a large vodka, began to get undressed.

Psychologically, it was too late to ring Newman now. So in the morning while Brazil went to the bank she would call the Schweizerhof again. The phone rang. She ran to it, sure it was Newman calling her back. Instead, it was Brazil.

'Make sure you're up and ready for breakfast by eight in the morning. We'll have breakfast together.'

'Got it.'

She slammed down the phone. She'd been hoping for a good night's sleep. She decided she couldn't be bothered getting undressed any further. Tossing an unwanted pillow on the floor, she stubbed out her cigarette, got into bed, switched off the light, and fell fast asleep. Conscience had never kept Eve Warner awake.


The following morning she joined Brazil for breakfast. He ordered a full English, strung out the meal while Eve tried to hide her impatience. Brazil was in a good mood, kept chattering away to her, ordering more coffee.

She smoked cigarette after cigarette, hiding her impatience, wondering when the hell he was going to push off to the bank. It was getting on for nine o'clock when he eventually rose from the table, warned her to be ready for instant departure when he returned.

'How long will you be?' she asked casually.

450

'How long is a piece of string?' he replied amiably.

'Well, how long is it?' she persisted.

'You'll know when I get back and knock on your door, won't you?'

Fuming, she went back to her room, leaving the door ajar a few inches. When she heard him locking his door she waited a few seconds, peered out, was just in time to see him disappearing round the corner, the same corner Gustav had disappeared round on his last fateful walk. It was a thought which never crossed her mind.

She had decided she'd have to risk phoning Newman from her room. Brazil might return sooner than she expected. Walking up Bahnhofstrasse to the phone booth could land her in a difficult situation. She dialled the Schweizerhof from memory.

'Please put me through to Mr Robert Newman. He's expecting me to call.'

'I'm afraid he's checked out.'

'Put me on to the concierge, then.'

'Concierge speaking.'

'I understand Mr Robert Newman has checked out. Is that true?'

'Yes, indeed, madame.'

'Something has happened he must know about. Where has he gone to?'

'I have no idea, madame.'

'Has he caught a plane, a train, or left by car?'

'I really have no idea.'

'But he knew I was going to call. He must have left a forwarding address. Check your records.'

'He has left no forwarding address.' The concierge's tone was becoming brittle. 'I cannot help you.'

'You're useless!' she shouted at him, and broke the connection.

She packed in a rage, stuffing expensive clothes into her suitcase, ramming in the folds which protruded over

451

the edges. The laundry could sort out the creases. They'd better make a perfect job of it or they'd hear from her.

'Damn and blast you, Bob Newman,' she muttered. 'Well, the price has just gone up to a hundred and fifty thousand pounds.'

The only items she took care with were the sheets she had later photocopied from the files in Gustav's cabinet. These she folded neatly, tucking them into a flap after taking out the canister of Mace gas José had given her. She put the Mace back last, zipped up her shoulder bag. It contained a fortune – with those sheets inside it.

After locking the case she sat down, crossed her legs, tapping one foot as she glanced at another fashion magazine, deciding what she would buy next. She never looked at the prices.

Aboard the jet at Kloten, Tweed sat patiently, reading a paperback. He had brought a collection from Shopville. Newman sat opposite him across the aisle, reading the latest reports.

Marov had sealed up Russia tight. No ships were allowed to leave the two ice-free ports – Murmansk in the west, Vladivostok on the Pacific coast. A new organization of secret police, called MOVAK, was patrolling the streets of Moscow and other major cities, rounding up the Mafia. Parliament had been dissolved, 'pending new elections'. No date was given for when they would be held.

Behind him Butler, in the most comfortable seat, normally occupied by Brazil when aboard, was fast asleep. Pete Nield, keeping an eye on him, was also reading a newspaper. Paula, seated in front of Tweed, was immersed in her own paperback. She had one more in reserve in her lap. Paula read swiftly. Across the aisle from her sat Philip. She glanced over, saw him gazing into space, put down her book, and went over to perch by him.

'Thinking of Eve? Or shouldn't I ask?' she said quietly.

'Lord, no! I mean I don't mind your asking,' he said hastily. 'I was thinking of Jean. The only other time I've passed through the Valais was when the two of us were returning from a holiday in Verona. Had a marvellous time. Jean loved Verona – so old. We explored the amphitheatre, which is in perfect condition. Then we had a day trip to Venice – Jean thought a day there was long enough, magical though it is. I agreed with her. We returned aboard an express from Milan. It was dusk when we passed through the Valais, so we didn't see much of it. We were moving on to spend the last few days in Geneva. Had kir royales at Les Armures. A wonderful evening – although I don't expect you to recall it with any pleasure after what we experienced there.'

'A pleasant memory.'

'Yes.'

Philip gulped, turned his face away, said he had to go to the loo.

Marler appeared from the crew cabin. Restless as ever, he had been strolling up and down the aisle, smoking a king-size, spending time chatting with the aircrew. He continued his slow patrol up and down the aisle, went back into the crew cabin.

He returned quickly, stopped by Tweed's seat.

'The pilot has just told me Brazil has arrived with a woman. They've boarded their jet. Expected to take off at 11 a.m. Destination still Bournemouth International.'

'How time has passed.'

Tweed glanced at his watch, surprised to see it was close to eleven in the morning. He closed his book, saw that Newman had heard what Marler had said.

'Here we go,' said Newman. 'The last phase, I suspect, of a long saga.'

'Let's wait until we're sure the control tower can let us take off soon after Brazil,' Tweed warned. 'This is a busy airport these days, even in March.'

'I agree,' said Newman. 'It's going to be tricky. We have to land at Bournemouth International soon after he has left for Grenville Grange – but not too soon after.'

'In fact,' Paula pointed out, 'this jet has to land when Brazil is far enough away *not* to see it landing with his name splashed along the fuselage.'

'You're right,' said Newman. 'It's going to be a nerve-racker.'

# 50

In the absence of José, Brazil held Igor's leash as the wolfhound bounded up the steps and inside the Lear jet. Igor loved flying. Sitting in his favourite seat, the dog peered out of the window as Brazil tied the leash to the arm of the seat.

He went back for his case and met Eve, wearing the trenchcoat, and carrying her own suitcase. She dumped the case, went and sat in the seat behind Brazil's swivel chair. The moment he occupied it the outer door was closed, the mobile staircase removed. The whine of the engines, already warming up, climbed to a roar. Brazil swung round in his seat to face her, checked his watch.

'Splendid! We're taking off exactly at eleven o'clock.'

'Great. You got your money from the bank?'

'Who said it was money?' He tapped the smaller executive case on his lap. 'Important documents,' he lied.

He was carrying one million Swiss francs in high-denomination banknotes, the proceeds from the bearer bonds he had sold.

I don't believe you, she thought as she lit a cigarette,

puffed a smoke-ring into the air. She stuck her finger through it. The steward appeared.

'I'll have a large vodka,' she called out.

'Bit early, isn't it?' suggested Brazil.

'It's never too early.'

The jet, tearing down the runway, became airborne, left behind the stands of fir trees surrounding that part of the airport, soared up through clouds, emerged above them into brilliant sunlight.

'One of these days,' Eve said, 'you'll have trouble with Igor. You're not supposed to take him into Britain like you do. Igor should spend six months in quarantine.'

'Oh, I'll put him inside his special crate before we land. The top compartment is stacked with boxes of Swiss chocolates in case it is ever opened by customs, which it won't be. They know who I am at Bournemouth International, that I'm a friend of the Prime Minister.'

'Where the hell's my vodka? You ought to change that steward, get someone who knows how to do his job.'

She had just spoken when the steward appeared with a large glass, the equivalent of three normal vodkas. Eve brightened up as he pulled out a tray, set down the glass inside a deep aperture.

'At least you remembered I wanted a large one,' she said ungraciously.

'Another is available as soon as Madame requires it.'

The steward knew her tastes. He couldn't understand how she could consume so much hard liquor and leave the aircraft sober. He gave her a smile, which she ignored. Never coddle the staff was her motto – if you did they became familiar with their betters.

She had folded her trenchcoat carefully because she was always fond of her latest purchase. Striding down Bahnhofstrasse after she'd bought it, hands in her pockets, she had felt like a general commanding his troops.

'When we land a car will be waiting for us,' Brazil informed her. 'We'll drive straight to Grenville Grange.'

'I hope you've alerted servants to clean up the place before we get there,' she responded.

'I did put in a phone call. Let's hope they got the date right.'

'Well, if they haven't, I'm not doing it. I wasn't hired to do menial work.'

'It would be a waste of your talents in other directions,' Brazil said, smiling.

'Is that a compliment?' she asked, eyeing him warily over her glass.

She had already drunk three-quarters of the contents, was thinking it was time the steward reappeared.

'Of course.' Brazil smiled even more broadly. 'A genuine compliment to a unique lady.'

'Steward!' she yelled, having emptied her glass while Brazil was speaking. 'A repeat performance. In record time.'

The steward managed a smile as he took away her glass. He was wondering whether he ought to look for another job if Brazil persisted in travelling with this woman.

'Look, there's the Bernese Oberland,' Brazil said, pointing. 'As spectacular a sight as you can find in the world, including America – where they think they have the biggest and the best of everything.'

Eve didn't bother to look at the distant range of massive, jagged peaks, covered in snow and glinting in the sunlight. Brazil gazed at the Jungfrau, thought it impressive, but no more so than the Kellerhorn. Then he put all thoughts of the Valais out of his mind as the jet sped on, heading for France.

\* \* \*

The airport controller had radioed to the pilot of Tweed's jet, as requested to by Beck. The pilot left his cabin, stopped by Tweed.

'I'm sorry, sir, but it will be at least half an hour before we can take off. Scheduled flights have got in our way. The other jet took off on time at 1100 hours.'

'Can't be helped,' Tweed said amiably. 'I understand. The controller has his priorities.'

'That means,' Newman called out after the pilot closed his cabin door, 'that we'll have the devil of a job catching up Brazil until long after he reaches Grenville Grange.'

'Not necessarily,' said Philip, again sitting opposite Paula. 'I have an idea.'

'Tell me,' Paula coaxed him.

'Not yet. Let's see how things turn out when we arrive.'

Paula took out the cream pastry Beck had given her, which she had kept in the fridge overnight. She began to munch it, using the extra napkins Beck had thoughtfully supplied to keep crumbs off her suit.

'You'll get fat as a piglet,' Philip joshed her.

'No, I won't. I can eat as much as I like and my weight remains constant. You're just jealous because you haven't got one.'

'My mouth is watering,' he admitted.

She selected a crust with plenty of cream, got up, told him to open his mouth, and popped it inside.

'That was good,' he said when he'd finished it. 'Thank you. In my book you are a generous lady.'

Philip then took out from his case a map of Dorset. It intrigued Paula that he was studying it. She called out as he folded it up, put it away.

'I'd have thought you knew Dorset like the back of your hand by now.'

'Just checking something.'

'Connected with your mysterious plan?' she pressed.
'Maybe . . .'


'England, beautiful England,' said Brazil, peering out of the window.

The jet was coming in to land at Bournemouth International. Eve was more concerned with putting on her trenchcoat when she should have been sitting with her seat-belt fastened. The plane was descending at a gentle angle so she wasn't bothered.

'I hope the chauffeur is waiting with the limo,' she called out.

'Joseph is off colour, won't be there.'

'Then we have a different chauffeur.'

'Yes.' He swung round in his seat. 'You're looking at him.'

'You mean you're driving?' she asked with a note of disbelief.

'Maybe I should remind you I passed my Advanced Motoring Test.'

'I could drive,' she said. 'I'm a good driver.'

'Maybe later. I'm taking the wheel to begin with. It's a pretty short drive via Corfe, anyway.'

'The roads will be flooded. I looked out of the window. They must have had more rain. The countryside is a lake.'

'We're landing,' he said, swivelling round to face the crew cabin.

The pilot landed the jet smoothly, cruised along the runway, stopped. They waited. A green light came on over the entrance to the crew cabin. Eve got up, buttoned her trenchcoat, but couldn't be bothered with the last few.

Carrying her case, she alighted down the steps first, her coat flapping all over the place. Brazil called for a porter to take his two cases. Earlier he had lifted Igor in mid-flight and lowered the dog into the bottom compartment of the crate, well padded with blankets, with airholes cunningly disguised. The huge dog had been quite at ease, trusting his master, knowing he had to keep perfectly quiet until released.

Brazil had then replaced the second compartment holding several large boxes of Sprüngli chocolates. Finally, he had attached the lid, held in place by four large screws. All this had been completed when the jet was within fifteen minutes of landing. The steward had been told to stay in the crew cabin while Brazil discussed something highly confidential with Eve, who had sat watching her boss do all the work.

Now, with the jet on the ground, Brazil showed his fitness and strength by carrying the crate off the plane to the waiting stretch limousine himself. The customs officials had joked with him.

'More sweetmeats for your lady friends, sir?'

'That's the trouble with having so many,' Brazil had joked back.

Fifteen minutes later, driving by a devious route into the open countryside, which skirted Bournemouth, he had backed the car into a quiet field in the sunlight blazing out of a clear blue sky. A gusty wind was blowing as he released a sleepy Igor from the crate and resumed driving.

He hit his first snag when he arrived at the car ferry which crossed the entrance to Poole Harbour. FERRY OUT OF USE UNTIL THURSDAY, a large notice proclaimed. He climbed out of the limo, swearing.

'What's the trouble?' he asked a workman in yellow oilskins.

'A freighter comin' in grazed the ferry as it was crossin' the exit. It's berthed on the Shell Bay side over there while they works on it . . .'

Brazil returned to the limo, was sitting behind the wheel when the workman approached him.

'Where you goin' to?'

'Corfe,' Brazil answered through the window he had lowered.

'Only way there is by Wareham. And you'll run into more trouble. Roadworks. Lights, single-line traffic, the lot. Take for ever,' the workman said with satisfaction.

'Thank you for the warning. Why do these people love to give you bad news?' he snapped as he drove off, heading for distant Wareham.

'Because the lower orders love to take a smack at someone driving a decent car,' she commented. 'I'd like a drink. Can't we stop at that hotel over there?'

'No, we can't. We'll just keep going,' he snapped.

'No need to be such a boor.'

'Don't ever talk to me again like that,' he replied in a calm voice.

They drove off round Poole Harbour. Brazil noticed what looked like storm clouds coming in from the west. The wind also was rising.

At Kloten Airport the Controller was as good as his word. The jet was given permission to take off. Inwardly, Tweed sighed with relief. Waiting until the machine levelled above the clouds, he went back to have a word with Butler and Nield.

By now the steward had served coffee and sandwiches on Coalport china he had found in a cupboard. Mr Brazil does well for himself, thought Tweed as he reached the seat where Butler, now fully awake, had devoured his plate of sandwiches, was asking for a second helping.

'Harry, I've been in touch with the Controller based at

Bournemouth International. There'll be a car there waiting for you.'

'Not another ambulance!' Harry bridled.

'I did say a car,' Tweed reminded him. 'A car to take
you with Nield to a rest home. You stay there two days
and then Pete drives you to London. You have had a
bullet in you.'

'Which is no longer there. The doctor in Zurich said I
should take gentle exercise as soon as possible.'

'Fine. Go for a walk along the front.'

'I might drive Pete to London,' Butler said aggressively.

'I'm giving you an order. Pete drives you back.'

Having sorted that out, Tweed returned to his seat
and his meal. Newman, who had heard his conversation
with Butler and Nield, walked along the aisle, bent over
Tweed, keeping his voice down.

'Without Butler and Nield we'll be short of manpower, just supposing Brazil has another gang of thugs at
Grenville Grange.'

'We'll cope. We have done before,' Tweed told him
firmly. 'Go back and finish your meal. We don't know
when we'll eat next.'

Marler, who had been passing with a plate in his
hands, waited until Newman had returned to his seat. He
also kept his voice down when he spoke to Tweed. He
was carrying a satchel over his shoulder.

'I don't think we need worry, whatever's waiting for
us. Bypassing Passport Control and Immigration, we
have kept what's left of our armoury, which is quite a
lot.'

'Just keep it under cover when we land,' Tweed
warned.

Paula was gazing out of the window, fascinated by
the sight of the grim but magnificent Bernese Oberland.
Tweed tapped her on the shoulder, told her to eat while

461

she could. From now on he was taking over control as they approached the climax of their long trek from Dorset to the Valais.

# 51

Landing at Bournemouth International, still in brilliant sunlight, Tweed supervised the transfer of a protesting Butler to a waiting car. He had a driver, so Nield sat in the back. As it vanished in the direction of Poole, Marler pointed to two four-wheel-drive vehicles parked nearby.

'That's what I ordered, as you suggested,' he told Tweed. 'I'll deal with the paperwork, then we can get cracking.'

While he was doing this Tweed had a word with the Controller, referring to his friend Jim Corcoran, Chief of Security at Heathrow. He was told that Brazil had left with a lady in a large limo three-quarters of an hour earlier. He went back and told Newman and Philip while Paula listened.

'He's got a head start on us,' Newman said grimly.

'The hazards of chance,' Tweed replied.

They drove from the airport with Philip behind the wheel of the vehicle carrying Tweed and Paula. Marler drove behind them with Newman by his side, his case in the back.

They drove a more direct route to the car ferry than the one taken by Brazil, were confronted with the same depressing notice informing them the ferry was out of commission. Tweed pursed his lips, then took his next decision.

'We'll have to go via Wareham, it's a long roundabout route, but there's nothing else for it.'

'Take you hours to get there,' the same workman who

had spoken to Brazil informed them. A minute before he had explained with glee what had happened to the ferry.

'This is no good,' said Philip. 'I know what we must do.'

Gesturing for Marler to follow, he backed away from the ferry point, drove along a road which ran parallel to the large harbour. Frequently Paula saw forests of masts swaying gently between trees. They were sitting together in the back and Tweed called out: 'Philip, maybe you'd let me in on what you propose.'

'When I was up on Lyman's Tout with Eve, the night of the fire, I noticed an old jetty at the foot of a nearby cove. There was a footpath leading down to it. If we hire a boat that's the quickest way to get to the area.'

'By boat?' Tweed was horrified.

'Take these,' Paula whispered. 'Two Dramamines for sea sickness. You've taken them before. And I've got a small canister of water – Tupperware – in my shoulder bag. Now don't argue. Just swallow them.'

Reluctantly, Tweed did as he was told, swallowing all the water to get the two tablets down. He hated the sea, as Paula knew.

'Are you sure it's going to get us there quicker by boat?' he demanded.

'Absolutely certain.' Philip had the bit between his teeth. 'That's what I was checking on the map aboard the jet. I have plenty of money and I also have a certificate for handling any kind of craft. I used to sail a lot before I met Jean. Hardly more than a kid, I was.'

He turned off the main road down a side road with a sign, TO MARINA. When they arrived Tweed saw the masts swaying. He turned to Paula.

'Looks as though the sea is rough.'

'Just a gentle swell,' Philip assured him.

'I seem to have heard those words before,' Tweed said without any enthusiasm.

'The Dramamines will have worked by the time we're aboard,' Paula whispered.

Philip had been joined by Newman and Marler. He argued with them forcefully, convinced them he knew what he was doing. Marler also knew about handling boats so it was arranged he would back up Philip if necessary. The next thing they discussed was the choice of the craft available.

Tweed wandered with Paula out onto the marina. Even inside the harbour there was Philip's so-called 'gentle swell'. Tweed began talking to take his mind off the coming ordeal.

'Brazil is a strange man. I suppose we're all a weird mix, but he has changed the course of the world and his name will never appear in any history book. I'm sure he knows this.'

'Then why has he done it?' Paula wanted to know.

'Not for personal glory, that's certain.'

'Yet he seemed to love being on close terms with the occupants of Downing Street, the White House, the Elysée, and so on.'

'I think he was just using his powerful personality to weigh up what sort of people were running the world – and was appalled by the lack of ability he found in high circles.'

'But he's such a ruthless man,' she persisted.

'If you set out to change the balance of world power you have to be ruthless, I'd say. He's a unique mixture of statesman and villain. The unusual aspect of his character is he must be completely lacking in vanity. And, unlike most of the men at the top, his view is global.'

'I get the impression he doesn't like modern communications.'

'I'm sure he doesn't. Neither do I. The way to a truly catastrophic explosion is to bring everyone on the planet on top of each other. People sit in front of their TV and think they're getting the news. All they're getting is sensational horrific pictures, often of something which doesn't have any effect on the way the world is moving. Important news is ignored if it doesn't produce lurid pictures. TV so-called news is entertainment – if that's the right word for the horrors they love to show us.'

'And we don't like mobile phones. At least, I don't,' said Paula.

'Carting one of those about means you never have time to think. The knowledge that anyone can contact you even when you're out for a walk is disturbing. Brazil was so right about scientists – they never consider the possible conequences of what they're inventing.'

They both turned round as they heard someone running up behind them. It was Marler.

'We've found a beaut. It's costing a mint to hire but it will get us there fast.'

'I'm looking forward to this,' Tweed said ironically.


Paula glanced at Tweed with anxiety as they arrived at where the chosen vessel was berthed. A gangplank with rails was in position. It was a huge power cruiser and had a high, closed-in bridge. Philip was already inside, behind the controls. Newman was unfastening a rope round a bollard, waiting to cast off.

'Has the Dramamine started to work?' whispered Paula.

'It has.'

'There's a very luxurious-looking cabin. I think you will be comfortable there.'

'Well, I'm not going below decks. First, it's closer to the water. Second, I want to see what's happening. I'm going onto the bridge.'

'If you feel like that,' Paula replied dubiously.

'I do!'

Tweed walked across the gangplank with a firm step. He never grasped the rails although the gangplank was swaying with the swell. Newman called out to Paula, handed her a pair of powerful field glasses he'd dug out of his satchel.

'One for you, one for Tweed.'

Philip had started up the engines. He slid aside a window, poked his head out, shouted down.

'All aboard that's going aboard. Look lively down there.'

'He's in his element,' Paula commented as she caught up with Tweed.

Marler and Newman cast off at bow and stern, rushed across the gangplank, hauled it on board. Tweed reached the bridge as Philip began to manoeuvre the cruiser into the main channel. He stared round in surprise at the size of the bridge, at the array of controls, at the chart obtained from the boat hirer on the chart table.

'It's like the control panel of a Boeing 747,' he said quietly to Paula.

'Don't worry. It won't become airborne.'

Below them Marler and Newman were coiling up their ropes. They passed Brownsea Island, a low hulk masked by trees, looking more like Devil's Island than a pleasure resort. Then they were coming up to the exit. Tweed stood grasping a rail, guessing what was coming when they hit the open sea.

They cruised past the impotent car ferry at a few knots. Paula could see where some other very large vessel had collided with its hull, leaving a brutal graze which men were working on. They emerged into the open and the swell increased in magnitude as Philip opened up the engines and they roared across giant waves. Taking one hand off the wheel briefly, Philip pointed shoreward.

'That's Studland Bay.'

'I know,' said Tweed, who was studying the chart. 'In summer on that Shell Bay beach it's near-naked bodies lying shoulder to shoulder. Sardine sunbathing. And look at it now.'

A strand of sandy beach was deserted, behind it was a ridge covered with miserable gorse, wind-blown and grey. One word summed up the whole stretch of this coast. Desolation.

'Old Harry Rocks coming up,' called out Philip. 'We're making good progress.'

The strange large stacks of chalk cliff, standing isolated from each other, projected into the sea and had a prehistoric appearance. Behind them, like a wave, a far larger wave than those which they were swooping up and down over, rose the Purbeck Hills. Almost bereft of trees, they had a grim look and no sign of habitation anywhere.

'Well, Eve and I drove over those hills,' Philip recalled. 'What a bloody waste of time.'

Paula noticed there wasn't a hint of nostalgia in his tone. He had spoken in a quite matter-of-fact way. Well clear of the coast, they were passing the chalk stacks. They roared on, past distant Swanage and its long bay. Smoke rose drearily from several chimneys, was blown helter-skelter in all directions the moment it emerged. Paula peered out of the window Philip had now closed.

Marler and Newman were sheltering on the starboard. On the port side spume and sea water splashed over on to the deck. Philip pointed to a cape.

'That's Durlston Head. We're getting there. Once we pass that it's only St Alban's Head. Then we're there.'

When she had peered down to starboard Paula had seen that Marler had his Armalite slung over his shoulder along with his satchel. She began to feel tense. Glancing at Tweed she could see no sign of nerves in his expression.

'Brazil,' he said, 'must pay for the people who died –

for Ben, the barman at the Black Bear Inn, Partridge, an innocent bystander, mistaken for Marchat at Devastoke Cottage, Rico Sava, arms dealer in Geneva, General Sterndale, and his son. To say nothing of the bankers who were murdered. Eve Warner was a willing accomplice. She shut her eyes to what was happening. And Karin and Anton Marchat. Yes, Brazil must pay his dues.'

# Epilogue

Driving towards Corfe, Brazil was held up for a long time by roadworks. He thought he had never driven along a stretch of road with so many traffic lights controlling single-file traffic. The light was always red when he came to it.

Eve, in a bad temper because she had been moved to the back of the limo, was grouching constantly, which didn't help Brazil to keep his temper. Her main grudge was that Igor was sitting in the front passenger seat alongside its master.

'I don't see why I should be stuck in the back just to give a dog the best seat,' she grumbled on.

'Igor likes to see what is coming, to look at the view,' Brazil replied, waiting for a green light.

'Damn all for him to see,' she grouched.

'You never notice scenery,' he reminded her. 'I know what's eating you – the lack of a drink.'

'I could do with a vodka,' she admitted. 'We should carry a bottle in the car.'

'Then we're stopped by a young eager beaver policeman, he sees the bottle, and we waste time while I'm breathalysed.'

'You don't drink and drive,' she nagged on.

'They don't know that until they've tested me.'

'I haven't seen one policeman in the Purbecks.' She leaned forward to emphasize what she was saying. 'And I drove all over these sodden hills with Philip Cardon.'

'Have a good time with him?' Brazil enquired.

'So-so. He's just another man. Keep your eyes open,' she said suddenly. 'The light's changed.'

Brazil was wondering how she had charmed all those bankers as he drove on. The threatening storm clouds had passed over without dropping any rain. Again it was brilliant sunshine. Brazil thought the Purbecks had a quiet beauty all their own. He had been wise to buy Grenville Grange. He came up to another traffic light, which turned amber, then red. He braked.

'You could have got through the amber if you'd rammed your foot down,' Eve ranted on. 'Why not hand over the wheel to me? Then we might get there.'

'I prefer to get there alive,' he said with an edge to his voice.

'I'll have you know I'm a damned good driver,' she replied, leaning forward again.

'Good for you.'

She lit a fresh cigarette, leaving her previous stub in the ashtray, still smoking. Brazil glanced back, told her to put it out properly. She stabbed viciously with a lipstick holder she took from her shoulder bag. In her impatience she almost pulled out the canister of Mace gas.

Sitting back, she went on smoking, tipped ash on the edge of the tray so it fell onto the previously flawlessly clean floor. Someone else can clean that up, she said to herself. The light changed to green.

'Don't miss this one,' she hissed.

He waited until he'd passed the roadworks before he stopped the car. He turned round and looked at her, his voice cold.

'If you don't shut up I'll have to consider terminating your contract.'

'Go ahead. See if I care.'

He drove on, reached the beginning of Corfe, drove through the old village, turned up the steep hill to Kingston. On the way up he couldn't avoid a large watersplash. Water cascaded up, covering the windscreen briefly, running down the windows on Eve's side of the car. He glanced in the rear-view mirror. She was grinning wickedly.

'Drive up the middle of the road and you can avoid that happening,' she said, assuming a bored tone.

'With a blind bend ahead of me and maybe another vehicle speeding down?'

'There's very little traffic on this road. I remember when I was driving with Philip. He, at least, dodged all the watersplashes,' she goaded.

'Good for him.'

A heavy silence descended inside the limo as he drove through Kingston, then later approached the drive leading to Grenville Grange. Even in the sunshine the old pile had a forbidding look. As they slowly came closer Eve leaned forward.

'I don't see any lights. And all the shutters are closed. I thought you said you'd arranged for staff to have the place ready for us.'

'Maybe they got the date wrong.'

'In that case, let's have dinner together at the Priory in Wareham.' Her tone was suddenly pleasant, coaxing. 'The food there is very good, very good indeed.'

'And the bar isn't bad either, I assume?'

'You know they have a good bar. You told me you'd had dinner there several times. Let's turn round and head straight for the Priory.'

'We'll check the situation here first.'

'Bet there's no one at home.'

'We'll find out, won't we?'

\*　　\*　　\*

The power cruiser had left St Alban's Head behind, was several miles out to sea from the coast, when Philip spotted the steep-sided ridge which was Lyman's Tout. Through his powerful field glasses Tweed could see something Philip, concentrating on steering the cruiser, couldn't.

Perched like a gigantic guardhouse at the summit of the slope running down away from it, was Grenville Grange. Paula was also using her glasses to scan the mansion. She dropped her glasses, looped round her neck like Tweed's.

'That's funny, I can't see any lights. The place looks closed for the season.'

'It's rather early for lights,' Tweed mused.

'From what I can see it's the sort of place where they need the lights on all the time. Even the shutters appear closed.'

'Wait till we get nearer.'

Philip was having to exert all his efforts to control the cruiser. A powerful current was running athwart the direction towards the cliffs he wanted to take. He felt confident that he could guide the cruiser to the old jetty he had seen, but he was bothered by the power of the current. Unless the jetty was protected by a nearby cape it could be a tricky business bringing the boat alongside the jetty so they could disembark.

Like a good skipper, he kept his worries to himself. Newman appeared, holding his field glasses.

'I've spotted the jetty you're aiming for. Luckily there's a huge rock projecting out just to the west of it. The sea looks reasonably quiet there.'

'We'll make it,' Philip said and concentrated on steering.

'The headlights of a car, a limo, have appeared,' Paula said as she stared again through her glasses. 'It's coming round the side of the house very slowly. Can't yet see who is driving – or who else, if anyone, is inside. Can we

471

speed up a bit? Or shouldn't I make suggestions like that?'

'The lady can have extra speed,' Philip assured her. 'Just a little more. Here goes . . .'


'They haven't even opened the gates,' Eve exploded as they arrived at the entrance to Grenville Grange.

Brazil didn't reply. Taking out his computer card-key, he leaned over to the box attached to a pillar, inserted the card, withdrew it. The electronically operated gates swung slowly open.

'That must mean the blasted servants aren't here,' she snapped.

'Not necessarily. They may have closed the gates after going inside as a security precaution. The shutters at the front are often kept closed, if you remember.'

'Looks like a morgue to me.'

'We'll take a look round the back. They may be preparing a meal.'

'Why no guards, then?'

'Oh, that's simple. I had every guard despatched to Europe. We'll have to hire some more.'

As he answered her Brazil was driving slowly up the drive. Coming to where the drive forked, he took the left-hand track, drove on round the side of the mansion. The sea came into view and the wind hit the car. Leaning forward, Brazil continued on to the end of the track where it petered out and the slope towards the cliff edge began. Here, because the ground was so arid, embedded with rocks, the surface was hard. He stopped the limo.

'What the hell have we come this way for?' Eve demanded.

'You see that large power cruiser out at sea? It's coming this way – and there's an old jetty with a footpath leading up from it on the other side of Lyman's Tout. We need to find out who is on board.' He reached down by his side, grasped a pair of binoculars, handed them to her over his shoulder. 'Take these, go to the edge of the cliff so you are closer, check if you recognize anyone.'

'These aren't the high-powered pair.'

'They'll do. I've lost the others,' he lied.

'Oh, all right. I suppose I have to work even to get that dinner at the Priory. There's no one in the house . . .'

Brazil sat in the limo perched at the top of the slope as she walked away, her trenchcoat flapping round her like a cloak. The words of the cassette Gustav had played back to him were echoing in his mind. She would have sold him out to Newman for a hundred thousand. And he didn't for a moment believe that Gustav had decided on his own to try and kill Tweed. Someone had put the idea into his head – had probably relayed a fictitious order from himself. He knew who that someone had to be.

Eve reached the edge of the cliff, glanced down, backed away with a shudder several paces. She pressed the binoculars to her eyes. Couldn't make out who was on board the incoming power cruiser.

'Damned fool,' she muttered. 'I told him they were the wrong glasses. Now I'll have to wait until the thing gets much closer.'

Inside the car Brazil unlocked a compartment, took out the black glove, slipped it over his right hand. Igor began to get excited. Brazil pointed his index finger at Eve.

Leaning over, he opened the passenger door. Igor bounded out, began loping towards Eve who had her back to him. Brazil folded his arms, watched, waited with no expression on his face.

Igor, unlike the time when it had toppled José over the brink, was not running over the snow which had muffled the sound of its fast-moving paws. Here the ground was hard and its paws hammered down on the surface, no longer muffled.

Eve, with her acute hearing, realized what was happening. At the last moment she dropped the glasses, dropped her body flat on the ground, cushioning her fall with her gloved hands. Her chin was protruding over the abyss.

Igor had already taken off, leaping up to crash into her back before he dropped to the ground. Instead, there was nothing to stop its flying leap and it continued on into space, then began falling with nothing to stop it until it reached the rocks and the sea far below.

Eve stood up, her expression ugly. She composed herself before she turned round, began to march steadily back up towards the car. One hand opened her shoulder bag as she studied the position of the limo perched at the beginning of the downward slope.

Brazil reached across to open the passenger door he had closed. He started speaking as soon as she reached the car.

'Get in. That's the last wolfhound I have anything to do with.'

'You bastard!'

Her face was twisted in manic rage as she spoke and aimed the canister full in his face, pressed the button. Mace gas enveloped Brazil. He let out a choking cry, both hands over his eyes as he endured agonizing pain, unable to see anything.

Eve slammed the passenger door shut, ran round the car, opened the driver's door, reached in to the automatic controls, moved the gear lever from 'park' to 'drive', released the brake, slammed the door closed. Shoving the canister back inside her shoulder bag, she leaned against the side of the limo, used both hands to push it with all her strength. It began to move downwards. She grinned sadistically. Inside, Brazil was using one hand to fumble for the door handle, couldn't find it. Eve felt herself moving with the car.

She glanced down, saw with horror the wind had blown a large flap of her trenchcoat inside the car, so when she had closed the door it had trapped the flap inside. The limo's momentum began increasing, unbalancing her. She crashed down on to her shoulder, still dragged along beside the car. Desperately she extended her left arm, clutched at the trenchcoat on the outside of the door, trying to rip it free with her hand. But the cloth was strong, remained fixed inside the door.

Her body, keelhauled along the hard ground, was partially protected by her clothing, but her shoulder bag was caught underneath her and the canister dug into her body. The limo was picking up speed now, she glanced ahead, saw the cliff edge rushing towards her.

The car hit something as the front wheels went over the brink. A large long rock, shaped like a huge log, had trapped the chassis midway and began to act as a fulcrum, stopping the limo. Eve was perched over the edge from her waist. The car began to see-saw over the rock fulcrum. She was staring down the three hundred foot precipice, down its sheer face to the huge rocks like fangs at the base of the cliff. A huge wave crashed against the cliff, briefly submerging the rocks. The wind blew spume and spray high up the cliff, into her face.


'What's happening on that cliff?' Philip asked. 'I can vaguely see a car hanging over the edge.'

'I think it could be Brazil's car,' Tweed replied carefully.

'But don't you see—' Paula began.

She was stopped saying anything else by a nudge in the ribs from Tweed. He shook his head, nodded towards Philip's back.

Through their glasses they had seen it all. Tweed was able to make out the terror on Eve's face as she gazed down into eternity. He felt it better Philip did not know the details.

The power cruiser was still some distance from the cliff-top and Philip was struggling to fight the current, his whole attention concentrated on steering the vessel.

Tweed and Paula, along with Newman and Marler on the starboard deck, continued gazing through their binoculars at the horror on the cliff.


The limo continued to see-saw slowly. The front wheels would be lifted into the air while Eve tore away with her left hand at the trenchcoat, hoping her body weight, uplifted with the car, would pull the cloth free. At the summit of the see-saw she glanced down, saw the ground at the edge of the precipice below her, knew that if she could get free she had a chance of falling on to *terra firma*. Then the front wheels would begin to descend and, once more, half her body was poised over the edge.

Inside the car Brazil, who had taken the brunt of the Mace gas in his left eye, could see, mistily, the sea rolling in, realized the car was half over the brink. His clawing hand found the handle, grasped it, tried to open the door. But the cloth caught in the door had jammed it. He hardly knew what he was doing as the car continued its diabolical see-sawing motion.

Eve's body was jolted. She knew something had happened. Something fateful. The limo was slipping forward off its fulcrum, sliding over the rock which had held it there for so long. There was a sudden lurch and her mind blanked out.

The car slid forward, paused as the rear wheels met the fulcrum. With the major weight of the car now poised over the cliff the rear wheels were hauled forward. Eve had a glimpse of the precipice again, of the sea rushing up to meet her. She became unconscious.

The car, with its second passenger attached to its side, plunged down, sheering past the black wall of the precipice, gaining more and more momentum. It hit the biggest of the fanged rocks on the tip just as a monster wave broke over the rock, exploding water halfway up the cliff. When it receded the car had vanished. The tide was going out, the savage sea had claimed another portion of its prey.

'Philip, take us back to Poole Harbour,' Tweed said after he had lowered his binoculars.

'The car went down, didn't it?' Philip asked.

'Yes, it did.'

'Who was inside it? What happened?'

'Brazil was inside it,' Tweed said quickly. 'I think his brakes failed him at just the wrong moment, as brakes sometimes do. Paula, come with me. Time we had a word with Newman and Marler . . .'

He ran down the steps leading to the deck, this time holding onto the rail. The vessel was pitching and tossing as Philip began to change course, and the wind was blowing like a banshee. Tweed spoke when he had Paula, Newman, and Marler together inside the luxurious cabin.

'You all saw what happened. Philip, not using glasses, only saw the car go. I told him Brazil was inside it. After we've landed I'm going to tell him Eve was *inside* the car, sitting next to Brazil. I know he no longer has any emotions about Eve, but I think he'd find what really happened very upsetting. So, all of you, keep your stories straight. Understood?'

They told him they did understand. Tweed suggested they might as well stay in the huge cabin until they docked. Paula said she thought it was a good idea, but she was going back on the bridge to keep Philip company. When she had gone Tweed switched on a radio to the World Service.

'*It has just been reported,*' the announcer said, '*that General Marov has called for a summit conference of the great powers to be held in Vienna. The President of the United States has agreed to attend, as have the Prime Minister, the Chancellor of Germany, and the President of France. It is understood that the ailing President of Russia has handed over plenipotentiary powers to General Marov to negotiate. That is the end of the announcement.*'

Tweed switched off the radio. He smiled without humour.

'In short, that means first that Marov has established Russia again as a major force in the world. Second that Marov is the man who controls the new, sealed-off Russia. We may be busy in future.'

'What happened to Archie?' Tweed asked Marler just after they had re-entered Poole Harbour and were close to disembarking.

'Oh, Archie,' Marler drawled. 'When he'd seen the end of The Motorman he just vanished, the way he always does. He'll be in touch with me sooner or later.'

'And Keith Kent will be sending me a big bill,' Tweed ruminated.

'Kent did call me at the Élite,' Newman remarked. 'I told him there wasn't anything else he could do. He promised to send you his account. Feel that bump? We've landed . . .'

They waited by their transport until Philip returned after dealing with the formalities of handing back the power cruiser. Paula took him to one side as the others climbed into their vehicles.

'Philip, you're not going back to that empty house on your own, are you?'

'Why not?' He gave her a warm smile. 'That's my home.'